MICHIGAN ROLL

Selected by *The New York Times* as one of the Top Books of the Year!

"ONE OF THE TEN TOP CRIME NOVELS OF THE YEAR . . . ORIGINAL . . . brutal . . . nightmarish adventures . . . Kakonis—a sharp new gambler in the literary crap game—he just takes the pot."
—*The New York Times Book Review*

"FINELY KNIT . . . One also sees a folk hero in the making: the mercurial Timothy Waverly. . . . This is no cheap dimestore thriller. It is, rather, real-crime literature, with TERRIFIC PACING and characters who are more than one-dimensional."
—*Detroit News*

"QUITE SIMPLY, THE BEST CRIME NOVEL I HAVE READ THIS YEAR . . . A KNOCKOUT NOVEL!"
—Eugene Izzi, acclaimed author of *The Take*

"*Gripping and marvelously entertaining!*"
—*New York Newsday*

"A wonderful read—it's smart, tight and mean. Chilling and very funny—a damned good novel."
—T. Jefferson Parker, bestselling author of *Laguna Heat* and *Little Saigon*

MICHIGAN ROLL

TOM KAKONIS

ST. MARTIN'S PRESS/NEW YORK

MICHIGAN ROLL

Copyright © 1988 by Tom Kakonis.

Cover photograph by Marc X. Witz

Library of Congress Catalog Card Number: 88-15859

ISBN: 0-312-91684-1   Can. ISBN: 0-312-91686-8

Printed in the United States of America

St. Martin's Press hardcover edition published 1988
First St. Martin's Press mass market edition/September 1989

10 9 8 7 6 5 4 3 2 1

Note to the Reader

For Daniel, Tom, and Judith. Also for Lou Gorfain, who makes things happen.

In the glossary of his *New Complete Guide to Gambling*, John Scarne defines a Michigan Bankroll as "a large bankroll consisting mostly of dollar bills with a bill of large denomination on the outside." Put another way, it is something other than what it seems.

ONE

EVERY QUACK AT THE TABLE WAS FRIED BUT one, and since that was the same one had been shorting the pot all night, Waverly had to fear for the quality of health care in the republic. The game was low ball, five card. Three were already down. The five-and-dime cheater, Sven Fish by name, was doing the dealing. A urologist. He slapped out cards like they were OR tools: jack, forceps, eight, ten, scalpel, sponge, king. Waverly drew a six, dealer a deuce. Everybody folded but the two of them. Fish adjusted his best sandbagging face and checked. Waverly bet six bills.

Why not? It was the agreed-upon last hand, and though he had long since got well, it held every promise of further renewing his fiscal vigor (to keep the figures apt, given this company). The count was, if not favorable, at least neutral, and anyway by now he knew his man, Dr. Fish.

The urologist pushed in his chips—no shaving them now, too many attentive witnesses—and peeled off the last cards. At the sight of his queen, an exasperated wheeze escaped him. Waverly's card was a five. Three, five, six, and eight showing. Very powerful-looking hand. And a very big king downstairs. He let the corner of his mouth

1

drift upward slightly, barest wraith of a smile. "Six more," he said.

Fish studied him. He had one of those skull-like Scandinavian faces, all knobs and hollows, eyes deeply socketed and teeth prominent. He was a young man but the wintry bearing of his vocation had already settled over him. "Well now," he said, "and what would a professional have hiding down there." It was phrased not as a question but a thoughtful, voiced musing. This was an unimpressed doctor of medicine.

"Six to see," Waverly said.

Fish hesitated a moment longer, long enough to give him away, and then with a precise flourish flipped over his cards and yawned elaborately. Probably calculating the number of dicks he'd have to restore to working order, get himself even this trip. Waverly gathered in the pot. "Would you gentlemen care to cash me in?" he said, doing the riverboat gambler number for them.

They would, but not without a certain amount of grouching, and not all of it good-humored either. A long way from when he had been over five dimes down. Then it was all rollicking good fun, whoop and shout time, drinks and cigars all around, fraternity days revisited. So much rackety bluster, so many words. Till he started climbing out of that hole, and then the decibel level in the room dipped in inverse proportion to his steady measured ascent.

They were conventioners, these physicians, midwesterners, off on a wicked five-day Florida fling: booze, high-priced night ladies, serious cards, general riot; along with, he supposed, an occasional seminar or two on new directions in duodenal-ulcer treatment, or some such, thrown in for the sake of appearances. And he was just another part of the entertainment. The risk factor; emissary of chance. They were playing for themselves first, of course, but they were gunning after him too, close second. Particularly Dr. Sven Fish, who seemed bent on establishing the ultimate primacy of the medical mind. They had come at him in platoons, play a few hours and send in the relief, grind him down. Or so they saw it. Shrewd thinkers, M.D.'s. Uncommonly easy to dislike, if you thought about it. Which after close to thirty-six hours of play, Waverly was not much inclined to do.

Fish asked if he was coming back tomorrow night.

"You'll want to speak with my associate about that," Waverly said. He had already pocketed the plunder and was moving toward the door.

"Oh? He makes your appointments for you, does he?"

Waverly turned and faced him. "He does. But as you see, I still make house calls. And I don't have to filch from the patient's coin purse on my way out."

Fish lifted a brow and displayed some teeth. It was his faintly amused expression, well-practiced and flawlessly executed. "Card player's cryptic wit?"

Their hostility rode the funnels of blue smoke in the air. A bleary-eyed onlooker stepped in and clapped Waverly on the shoulder, forcedly jovial. "Oh, we're going to lure you back here. We've got another shot coming."

"We'll see," Waverly said.

He waited for the privacy of the elevator to massage his achy neck and shoulders. Give them nothing. The Sheraton lobby was all but empty, its organic gaudiness the more melancholy for the high tinkly laughter of a few afterhours losers here and there, still on the desperate hustle. Briskly as his sluggish circulation would allow, he walked to the desk and called for his car. The clerk, a youth with an abundance of straw-colored hair and Florida cool, snapped a finger and sent somebody running. "You have a profitable evening?" he asked. He knew who Waverly was and he put the question around a distant, in-on-the-action smirk.

"Passable," Waverly said, and laid a twenty on the counter

and left it at that. He had had enough of seamless chatter and he was not in a humor to critique his luck with a clerk. Let him do his own speculating.

He stood waiting outside the entrance. The night was thick with soggy heat, the prickly feel of the wrap of a dank woolen blanket. No different from any other night this time of year, but somehow less tolerable than usual. The car arrived with the air turned up on max, good for a healthy toke to the jockey, but the synthetic chill did little to revive him and he drove directly to the condominium he called home, and there he slept.

The next morning he stepped out the door and felt the fierce August sun pressing into his eyeballs like a pair of determined thumbs. Inside of thirty seconds little rivulets of sweat formed on his back and stomach and sides, and headed south. At his feet the parking lot tar was already turning gluey. Who needs this? he asked himself rhetorically; life's too fucking short, who needs this? Answer was nobody, least of all him, so he got in his car and drove over to North Lake, searching out a travel agency. He knew of none, had no reason to, and it was his habit never to clutter his head with unnecessary information. In three years down here he had traveled no farther than Miami south, Tampa west, and Orlando north, and always under his own steam, popping the big Bro-Ham Roy-Al´ (as Bennie liked to call it) into cruise and letting it sling him along smooth as a baby's ass (also Bennie's image).

First likely looking place, he pulled in.

I want to go somewhere cool, he told the girl hunched over the keys of a computer, gazing at the screen as though awaiting the appearance of a mystic vision. She turned up a tanned pretty face framed in a swag of cotton-candy hair, electric smile, perfect teeth, blank eyes. Pretty Florida face.

"Cancún is big this year," she said brightly, oiling out the words the way they did here. "Or maybe you'd like a Carnival Cruise. I been on one myself. They're a rip."

Waverly started over. "No. Temperature cool. Climate cool."

Two vertical puzzle lines stitched her brow a second, loosened. "Oh. Like that you mean. Okay, how about Montreal? Or one of those Alaska cruises?"

"No cities. And no ships."

She tapped the sides of a fine straight nose, gave it some thought. "You could go to Yellowstone. Or that one in Montana, I think it is. Forget its name."

"Glacier."

"That's the one. Glacier National Park."

"No."

So she sat back in her swivel chair, arched six-gun breasts, and turned up helpless palms, leaving it to him. She maintained the smile, but her eyes sought out the ceiling.

"Michigan," he heard himself saying, wonderstruck he could get out the word. Tried it again. "Maybe Michigan." Not so bad.

"Michigan's cool, I guess. This time of year. Myself, I never been there. Where you want to go in Michigan? Detroit?"

"Come on. Pay attention."

"What else *is* there in Michigan?"

Well, he might have told her, for openers there's Jackson, world's largest walled prison. And then there's Ypsi, short for Ypsilanti, home of the Center, short for Center for Forensic Psychiatry, kindly name for asylum for the criminally insane. Neither was cool in August, he could have told her, either sense of the word, hers or his. What he said was, "Up north somewhere. Traverse City, say."

The pretty face went utterly vacant.

"Can you get me a flight to Grand Rapids?"

"Michigan?"

"That's the one."

"Today?"

"Today."

"Lemme check."

Back home he started to pour a glass of milk, changed his mind, and popped a can of beer instead. It was vacation, right? He was on holiday, right? Had it coming? Right—even if the clock on the kitchen wall did read 10 A.M. It was a couple of hours yet till his flight, plenty of time, but with one nagging bit of business remaining. He stared at the phone awhile, finished the beer, got another. It tasted strange this early in the day. Not bad, but not so good either. Which was the problem, it appeared, with a stiff and inflexible discipline. Which was what Bennie kept advising him: Loosen up, grab yourself some of the good times.

Eventually he dialed.

"Bennie? Waverly."

"Hey, Timothy. How they slappin'?"

"All aces."

"'s what we wanta hear. And what's by you?"

"Oh, nothing much." He could do this little ritual dance, good as the next man, when he had to.

"Watch the game last night? Jets got creamed. Cost me a bagful. You have anything down?"

"I was working, remember?" As if he'd ever forget. Dropped a bagful—what a wad of poormouth shit.

"So how'd that one go?"

"We did okay, nothing sensational. Six K and some decimal points, to be exact."

"Not what you'd expect, your pill-pushers," he said, sounding not so cheered. "But better'n a stick in the eye, right?"

"That about says it all."

"So. See you at the Crazy Horse?"

"Yeah, well, that's what I'm calling about. Look, I'm thinking of taking some time off. Getting away. Not long, week, ten days." There was silence on the other end, so he added quickly, "Before I leave I'll put your share in the mail."

"Check's in the mail, huh."

"Come on, Bennie."

"What's this gettin' away caca. You're *in* funland. People take time off, they come *here*."

"Not in August."

"In August. Florida's like pussy. Anytime's the best time. Besides, they want you back out there tonight, the quacks. You must of scored some hit with 'em. And next week's the contractors. Remember them last year, down in Boca? Nice piece gabardine, huh."

"You can get Angelo."

"Angelo. Sure I can get Angelo, but Angelo's a Greek. He gets emotional when he plays."

"Give him a Valium."

Now there was a considerable pause, and waiting it out Waverly could picture him sitting there sunk a good yard deep in his cream-colored puffball couch. Cigar going in a crystal ashtray on the marble-and-glass-top coffee table. Probably a hooker gussying up in the bath, and Bennie sitting there silk pajamas on, plump pink face freshly shaven, reeking of Old Spice. A few limp hairs combed up from the base of his skull and splayed out over the scalp in great oiled swirls that resembled nothing so much as an astronomical photo of spiral nebulae receding across a distant galaxy. Bennie S. (for Saul: "Owe me money, call me Saul; otherwise it's Bennie.") Epstein: agent, greeter, booker, matchmaker, more accurately pimp, at thirty-percent drag. Sole proprietor, Bennie's Key Line Services, Inc. Inc gives it class, he said. Bennie. Many ways a turd, but basically a decent one. Without Bennie and his bankroll and connections, where would he be? Nowhere was where.

"You got your mind made up, sounds."

"A few days is all."

"Okay. Where you bound?" There was a shrug in the voice, a show of remote interest. To wind things down.

This was the part he was leery of. "North," he said, noncommittal. "Find some shade."

"North?" The interest picking back up, wary. "Where abouts, north?"

"Michigan," he said, slurring it over, and he started to say it's all right, but Bennie broke in—"Hey, Timothy. Jesus fuck, man, I thought you had your head right by now. All this time."

Very deliberately Waverly said, "There's no problem, Bennie. It's the only place I know cool."

"You want cool, turn up the air. Jesus f-word Christ. Michigan. Now you're gonna tell me Traverse City, right? Shake up the ex and her old man? Tumble 'em a little? Run a-fuckin'-muck?"

"No such notion."

"Why Michigan then? Don't say cool again."

"Okay," Waverly sighed. "I've got a kid up there, remember? Maybe I'll look in on him, see how he's doing. Introduce myself."

"So you got a kid, so what? Think you're flyin' solo, that way? Prob'ly a dozen or better little B. Epsteins jackin' around various parts of this great nation ours. You don't see me doin' no memory lane tours. You know why that is?"

"Safe bet, you're going to tell me."

"Why is because ol' Satch got it right, no percentage, lookin' back. What's it been for you, ten, fifteen years?"

"Closer to ten."

"Ten," he repeated, heavy finality. "Go near him now, you'll come on like a short eyes in a raincoat. Anyway, he ain't your kid no more. You go up there, they'll book you a one-way direct, Five Block, which as you remember ain't exactly your Breakers."

"I hear you, Bennie. I haven't forgotten."

"Timothy," he said, adopting a sober dialectic tone, the irresistible force of logic and sweet reason, "listen up a minute, what I'm tellin' you. We got a good thing goin' here or no?"

"The former of the two."

"Huh?"

"Yes. A good thing."

"Heavy on that *good*, my friend. Think about it. You got yourself a nice place there. Cabinet full of booze, freezer full of steak. Big new car. Some rubles stashed away in the bank, few there in the wallet, too. Tail any time you need it, near as a call to your accommodatin' Key Line Services. You with me so far?"

"Not lost yet, Bennie."

"Okay. Let's look back. When you come down here, you didn't have your basic diddly. Am I right?"

"That's fair to say."

"Also maybe it's fair—you correct me now, I'm wrong—say old uncle Bennie had just a little something to do with all this prosperity we're discussin'."

Waverly took a moment to reply. It was inarguable, everything he was hearing, but it was, equally, a violation of the unspoken rules of their peculiar alliance. Yet the very fact Bennie was willing to breach that protocol was a measure of the urgency of his not totally self-serving concern. Waverly didn't know whether to feel gratitude or annoyance. He felt both. "Look," he said, "you know what I owe you, Bennie. And not just as stakehorse. You need to hear the words?"

"Thanks ain't what I'm after here. Good sense is. You and me, we go back. Also we could be goin' forward, you stay straight. That little talk we had, while back?

Goin' partners? Expandin'? That wasn't just blowin' smoke, y'know."

"I know that," Waverly said, and then, looking to lighten things, he added, "How about if I promise to behave."

A defeated sigh rode through the line. "You're goin' anyway. Well, I done my best."

The way he said it Waverly could see the globe head shaking side to side and the liver lips curling. Dismayed at life's manifold folly but reconciled, more or less.

"You gonna pay Chop a visit, you're up there?" Bennie asked.

"I don't know."

"Old Chopper. Where's he at, these days?"

"Jacktown, last I heard. But he was fishing for a vacation in Ypsi. Might be there by now."

"T.C., Jackson, Ypsi—you're gonna be all over that fine state, you decide to stop by. Listen, I got advice for you. Free for nothing. Don't change careers mid-life. Stay out of the travel business. A tour guide, you ain't gonna make."

"No kidding. No money in that?"

"Ahh, go have a nice day, fuckhead. You get over to Jacktown, send me a postcard."

"You keep watching for it."

"Hey, Timothy. Stay out of trouble, f'Chris' sake."

Three hours later he was settled in a window seat, puffing a cigarette, about his fortieth already and the day not half gone, but sipping a sensible ginger ale. Contradictory habits, the irrational and the soundly, calculatedly pragmatic balled in one, and the farther north he got the more they scrambled. Scrambled—that was right on the mark. What was he doing here anyway? Thirty thousand feet in the air, flashing four hundred miles an hour in the direction of ruin and grief. Dead on course. And for what? Bennie's memory lane jaunt? Come on, quit lying to yourself. A glimpse of a twelve-year-old? Kid probably didn't know he even existed, and if he did, would be overcome with shame. Some preposterous demented notion of a payback on the ex? It took Bennie the beat of a second to get to that one. Shrewd man. There was, in fact, no rational reason for this trip and, knowing himself, maybe a hundred or more real and serious risks. Three years' worth of order and system and plan and, yes, even a kind of serenity, empty as it might be; and all of it riding on a perverse whim. Yet here he was, and they weren't likely to turn the plane around for him now.

A shag of dusky cloud streaked on by. The citizen on his left made persistent conversation: "You from West Palm? Sure hot back there. Where you headed?" Looked like somebody who'd belong to the Elks. Waverly picked up the flight magazine but it didn't help, and in time the citizen got to it.

"What business you in?"

For a moment he considered getting out his card and handing it over. Card read:

Timothy Waverly, M.A.
Applied Probabilities Analyst

It was a little joke. Then he glanced at the matchbook in his hand (he didn't own a lighter because he sincerely intended to quit some day soon). On the cover it showed a happy-looking guy in a suit and tie, big house and car in the background. The legend said, *Make Big Money Selling Mason Shoes*. "I'm in the shoe line," he said, palming the book. "Mason Shoes." And he turned to the window and put his head on his shoulder and promptly fell asleep.

In a fashionable western suburb of Chicago, at the uncivilized hour of nine o'clock that same morning, the maid, Drucilla, had hammered on her door and insisted she wake up and take the call.

"Go away," said Holly Clemmons.

"It's Mistah Clay," Drucilla bawled. "He say get you up, he gots to talk."

God, she despised that, that black-mammy routine. Give her a circus tent for an apron and a red-checkered bandana, have her do some eyeball rolling, and you've got *Gone With the Wind* north. Already she had the hoarse squawk down. Drucilla needed new material, and before suddenly. "All right," Holly said. "All . . . right. Tell him I'll be on in a minute."

"Yessum. But you best hurry. He callin' long distance from Mish-gan."

Pork-barrel bitch. Probably been into the liquor cabinet already, with Daddy out of town and no one else in the house. Holly got out of bed, stretched her long limbs lazily, wandered into the bathroom, examined herself in the full-length mirror and was not entirely displeased with what she saw. She came back and plugged in the phone and sank into a dressing chair and said, "It's nine-o-fucking-clock, Clay. A.M."

"Ten up here, luv. Shine time."

"Huh! Tell that to your Auntie Drucilla."

"That's quick, sis, very quick. But very wrong. Drucilla loves us, even you."

"Jesus, what am I doing, talking ethics at nine in the morning. And with a thinker like you. What do you want, advance on your allowance? Daddy's not here."

"No daddy? What a shame. I'll have to rush out and hurl myself in front of the first speeding truck."

He was putting the customary deliberate melody in his voice, but she thought she detected something unusual too, a discordance around the edges. Not quite breathless—he was much too cool-conscious for that; more like the trace of a flutter. "Ha ha," she said.

"Ohh, big sis is brittle this morning. What's the matter, humor decamp in the night?"

"Tell me what it is you want or I'm going to hang up. And spare me the 'sis'."

"All right, luv. Just chill out a bit. It's nothing much, nothing you can't handle. Actually, I come with remarkable news."

"Can't wait."

"Well, truth of it is, it's a bit complicated. Too much to go into over the phone, long-distance rates being what they are."

Whenever he used his 'truth of it is,' it was time to check your cash, right down to the coins in your purse. "I swoon with anticipation," she said.

"Knew it! That means you've got to get right up here to Traverse City. Without delay. Immediately. Have Drucilla pack you a bag and climb into that breakaway machine of yours, and you'll be locked in my brotherly embrace—or its equivalent—by nightfall."

Holly made an elaborate sniffing sound into the phone. "That's fucking poetic, Clay. I was so hoping you'd ask. Afraid I'm going to have to pass, though. It happens I've got an audition today. And another engagement tonight."

"No kidding. A real audition. You going to play Juliet? Or a nun? A nun, I'll bet."

"It's a commercial," she said, putting as much haughty distance into it as she could.

There was a moment of silence, and when he spoke again his voice was flat, as earnest a note as he was capable of striking. "Look, I'm in, well, what Father would call a little scrape. Nothing serious, more like a misunderstanding. I could use some help. Will you come?"

"God damn it, why should I? I've got a life too, you might try and remember. Independent of yours. You ever consider anyone but number one?"

"I know you do," he said, purring in the studied way he did so well. "I know that. But it could be better if you'd scoot on up here. Your life, I'm talking about. Mine, too. Both of ours."

"Better." She was acutely conscious of the familiar quicksand feel of this conversation, sinking down fast. "Sure. Like all your other 'little scrapes' have made it better."

"This one could be different," he said, remarkably close to pleading now. "I need your help."

"Goddamit, I should have guessed. Should never have picked up the goddam phone. Goddamit, goddamit, god-*dam*it. Traverse City. I don't even know where it *is*."

"Just follow the map. You can be here in six, seven hours."

Holly had been studying herself in the vanity mirror as she spoke. Now she felt she looked a mess, though one of your better messes. Soundly defeated, resigned, she said, "More like ten. What's your address?"

"No!" he said sharply, barking it, not at all cool.

"What?"

"I mean, no, I've, uh, moved out of that dump. Don't go there. What you do when you get here is check into a hotel. There's one downtown, Park Place. It'll do. Then you call this number I'm going to give you. Got a pen?"

She found one. "What is all this?" she asked after he enunciated each digit slowly, precisely, like he was talking to a retard, and made her say them back. "Clay?"

"Don't ask. When you get here, call that number. Say, eight o'clock. You can make it by then. Guy named Rusty will answer. Rusty Barker. My roomie. Ex, to be more exact. He'll have something for you, news, instructions, whatever. You taking this down?"

"But I *am* asking. Where are you?"

"Don't. Everything's cool. I'm moving around. When

you get here I'll explain. Show some faith. And, hey, I'm in your debt. I'll owe you one."

"Are you all right?" Try as she might, it was impossible to keep the genuine concern out of her voice.

His, in contrast, was returned to its habitual jaunty bounce. "Doing just fine, sis. And listen, here's the best part. There's reward money in it for you. Heaps and stacks. Kind would make your old Daddy proud. Enough, maybe, to spring you free from his smothering arms."

Holly thought about that, but only for a moment. "So who needs money?" she said archly. "Certainly not me. Or you, even."

"Money's like tail. Never enough. But who knows that better than you, huh? See you soon."

She put down the phone and went to the stairs and called, "Drucilla, get up here. And bring two bags." Catching another glimpse of herself in a mirror at the end of the hall, she said, "Make that three."

Ten hours later, a somewhat less than affable Holly Clemmons waited in a room on the fourth floor of the Park Place Hotel, Traverse City, Michigan. It was another hour yet till mystery phone call time, so she showered and changed and made herself gorgeous, for something to do. Later she might go downstairs, have a drink, unwind, but for the remaining five minutes she fidgeted. At eight o'clock she dialed the number.

"I want to speak to a Rusty Barker," she said imperiously.

"This is him."

Earlier that day, at about the same time Waverly was boarding a plane for Michigan and Holly Clemmons was behind the wheel of her Porsche, bound for the same destination, Gaylon Ledbetter had driven the fifteen miles up the Leelanau Peninsula from Traverse City and was seated now in the plush living room of the beach house Mr. Dietz either owned or rented, he wasn't sure which. He was listening attentively or at least putting on the face that said he was, but Christafuckinmighty, it took Dietz a month and a half to spit out anything he had to say. Never could talk at you straight, man-to-man; always had to go the long way around, like he was playing some circle-jerk game with you. They were drinking ice tea, the only thing offered. Himself, he would have taken a whiskey straight up.

". . . so I said to myself, Well, maybe I should get away," Dietz was saying, or trying to say. "Take some time. Off. Maybe do some fishing."

"Yeah, there's an idea. Chicago's gotta be mighty hot, this time of year." They were talking about the fucking weather? Now he was nodding like he had to give that one some deep thought.

"Except the problem is, Gaylon, I don't know anything about fishing."

What's he expect me to do? Start diggin' worms? Gaylon said, "You could hire somebody. An Indian. I hear some of them Indians, they'll guarantee you a catch."

Dietz lifted one eyebrow, to show astonishment. "Isn't that remarkable. They can do that. That's like guaranteeing the sun will shine. Or it won't rain."

Gaylon didn't know it for a fact, but he figured him and Dietz were about the same age, downside of fifty. You could never tell it though, looking at him. Sonbitch sprawled one leg up on a couch about forty foot long and all one piece too, not even sections; got out all in white, white docksiders, socks, shorts, belt, polo shirt. White hair too, none of it missing. Fucker looked like a snowbank, sitting there. Must go an easy six-four, big shoulders, no fat on him, not even a giveaway half-moon sagging under the belt. Gaylon was five-seven with his lifts on, weighed 240. Day to day he wore slacks and sport shirts with wide, pointy collars, both in pastels or checks, northern Michigan style. But for this meet he'd put on a suit, figured it looked more professional. It was a summer one, but the old pits were dripping anyway. Dietz, he looked cool.

"You should have brought a bathing suit, Gaylon. Got comfortable."

Cocksucker reads minds, too. "Well, I sort of thought maybe you'd want to talk some business." Might as well get down to it.

"Bus-in-ess," Dietz said, stringing it out like it was new to him, Jap word or something. Behind the couch and through some French doors was a wide deck full of rose-colored rattan furniture. And just beyond that, pissing distance, was Grand Traverse Bay. Looked like some god-dam calendar picture with the sun glinting off the blue water and the white sailboats scooting right along. Gaylon loved money, right down to the change in his pockets, but he didn't like rich people, especially the Dietz kind, who was no better than he was, never mind the big beach house and the white getup. He'd heard a story once about Dietz, from the old days, how Dietz killed a guy with just his fists, nothing else. Hung him from a rafter in the cellar of a South Side warehouse and beat on him till the blood came out every hole: mouth, nose, ears, asshole, even the pisser, he'd heard. Punched him out dead. Thing of it was, the guy wasn't your ordinary welcher or snitch, was a Blackstone Ranger, they said. Said even the boogies were scared to fuck with Dietz. Looking at him now, slit of a mouth and eyes like a couple of stones underwater, Gaylon thought, Yeah, maybe something to that story. He decided not to say anything yet.

"How long has it been now since this boy got into the wind on us?"

"Couple days, is all. We're on top of it."

"You know, Gaylon. The business we're in, you and

me, it's what they call a high-overhead enterprise. There's going to be waste. Losses. Some pilfering, time to time. Have to expect that. Tolerate it. Say, you want some more, umm ... umm ... ah. ..." He was staring at Gaylon's empty glass like he'd forgot what was in it.

"Tea?"

"Yes. Tea."

"Don't mind," Gaylon said and immediately wondered why. Already he had to take a leak, and his shorts were creeping up behind, and his hemorrhoids itching. He wished he was biting down on the cigar that ordinarily protruded from his mouth like a smoldering cannon, but there wasn't an ashtray in sight. Sissy didn't smoke, either.

Dietz turned half in the direction of the kitchen. "Oona." No response. He said it again, a little louder, what he probably figured was a shout but what anybody else would call a regular tone of voice. Most of the time he spoke so soft you had to bend in to hear.

Some slope girl in a halter top and denim miniskirt, kind with buttons in the middle run right up to the beaver, came padding in and filled their glasses from a lead-crystal pitcher. Brown skin, mouth painted red like a target, black ponytail dusting her apple ass. She looked about fifteen. Last piece of candy in the box.

"Oh, thank you, Oona," Dietz said, like she'd just handed over the queen's jewels. Slope did a quick bob, aimed her titties at him, and disappeared. Gaylon considered asking Dietz if it ran sideways, make the old joke, but then, remembering the warehouse story, he thought better of it. Anyway, Dietz was back doing his president of General Motors number.

"Still, we've got to be conscious of inventory control, we want to keep a profit margin that's, well, reasonable. You see that, don't you? Gaylon?"

"What you said, that's the whole ticket, right there."

"Good. Glad we're communicating. For a change. Let

me tell you about a book I was reading a while back. *Management by Exception*. It told how, in a business, any business, you had to account for all the exceptions that can arise in your plan. That is, you had to make certain they didn't, these exceptions I mean, well, disturb your plan. Upset it. Keep you from arriving at your original goals. It's a useful book, Gaylon. You ought to read it."

"Yeah, I'll have to get hold of that one," Gaylon said, thinking how the last book he read, last winter when a blizzard socked everybody in couple days, was a dog-eared suck-and-fuck he got off Shadow. "What'd you say its name was?"

"What we've got here sounds to me like a pretty big exception," Dietz said, not having any trouble getting *them* words straight out, looking him right in the eye, hard. Boogies were right to be scared. Circle-jerk time was over.

"I can 'preciate what you're sayin'. But you got no cause to worry, Mr. Dietz. We're gonna get it all back, goods or money, one or the other. An' you can take that to the bank." Gaylon had rehearsed that speech before he came, and he hoped it sounded as tough now as it did when he was saying it into the mirror back home.

"Those are words I'm hearing, Gaylon. Can't take words to the bank."

Gaylon wouldn't give a shit if he'd quit saying his name all the time. What kind of a name was Gaylon anyway; made him sound like a fucking fairy. He wished it was something stand-up, like Jack or Vince. Bart would be good, too.

"You know, Gaylon, those were high-quality goods. Cut three times, they'd go for, oh, four, four twenty-five. On the street. More up here, nice little resort community, your better class of people. What I mean is, the arithmetic, it's faulty. Thousand or two skim, well, that's human nature. You and I aren't going to change that. That's part of the overhead. I was speaking about. But the number five, all those zeros behind it. Close to it. That range anyway. That could make a man weep, Gaylon, lose that."

Thousand or two skim—what a fucking hoot. This is the same guy could squeeze shit out of a stone. "We ain't going to lose it, Mr. Dietz. I guarantee you."

"Like the fish?"

"Huh?"

"You said they guaranteed fish."

Gaylon squeaked out a laugh sounded even to him like a duck quacking. He wished to Christ he was someplace else.

"Let's be sure we understand each other, Gaylon. I put you in charge of this territory. That makes you accountable, any substantial losses, and I think we're talking substantial here. Also I think you know what accountable means, our kind of business. Are we still communicating, Gaylon?"

Gaylon nodded dismally. After that laugh of his, he didn't trust himself to speak.

"I'm going to be up here a few days. I'll be waiting to hear when you've recovered our goods."

"Mr. Dietz, you'll be the first."

Dietz walked him out to the car, moving about as fast as he talked. "Who did you say this boy is, again?" he asked, almost a conversational tone.

"Name's Clemmons. Clay Clemmons. Don't think you'd know of 'im."

"He work for us before?"

"Uh unh. Just this summer I took 'im on. Thing of it was, he's a sensational diver. Drop a dime in the middle of the bay, he'd bring it right up for you. One time, right after a delivery, this big squall comes up, blows the marker buoy away. I tell you, I figured we could kiss that merchandise goodbye for sure. This kid, he takes a boat out in just your general area, the drop, flips over the side,

and half an hour, forty-five minutes tops, he comes bob-bin' up wavin' the bag. He's about the best we got. Had."
Now Gaylon had the uncomfortable feeling of talking too much. Apologizing more than was maybe needed. It was hard to stop, but he did.

"He local?"

"No, from the city. Suburbs, actual'. Oak Brook, I think I heard."

Dietz shook his head sadly. "Comes from a good fam-ily, I suppose."

Yeah, the prick come from a good family. Had it all, looks, build on 'im like a Mr. Fuckin' America, money, clothes, cars. Up to his ears in gash, for certain. Not enough for the little rat's ass; had to get into the goddam *under*world. Then even that ain't enough, had to go into business for himself. Jesus, it was a crazy world. Who could figure? "We'll tag 'im," he said.

"Who've you got assigned?"

"Hawkins and Skaggs," Gaylon said, and when Dietz just looked dumb, he added, "They're the best, both of 'em. They done lots nice work for us here." He meant it, too; he'd put them up against anybody Dietz could bring up from Chicago.

"Let's hope they're reliable," he said, all the chummi-ness gone out of his voice. "For your sake."

"They're on it right now. I could maybe have some-thing for you tomorrow. I'm thinkin' Monday, latest."

"Make it soon, Gaylon."

"Be in touch," he said and slipped the car into gear but stalled it somehow—Fleetwood Caddie, too—and had to grin weakly at Dietz standing there with a lizard smile, and start it up again and stutter away.

Messers. Hawkins and Skaggs, Gilbert and Willis by Christian name, respectively, but better known as Gleep and Shadow, also respectively, were indeed on it, though at that moment it would have been difficult to tell. They were slouched on a bench in the shade near Traverse City's waterfront park, licking double-dip ice cream cones—raspberry marble—and appraising the snatch on the beach. Shadow wore rust-colored slacks and a pale-blue sport shirt with flame patterns rising through it. His partner, an inordinately large man, was dressed all in black, a hulking *memento mori*, come to call. On Grandview Drive behind them, the midday traffic barreled on by. Delighted shrieks rose from the kiddie train chugging around the zoo.

"Lookit that," Shadow said, nodding in the direction of a teenage wonder, bronzed, sun-streaked hair, ascending like a sea nymph from the waters of the bay. A breath-choker if he ever saw one. "Y'know, I'd crawl over a mile of broken glass just to kiss the dick a the last dude that fucked her."

"Legs too skinny," said Gleep. His red slab of a tongue slid over the top dip, took it right out.

"Yeah, that may be. But they do go all the way up to her ass."

"I like 'em more meat."

"That's good too, meat on 'em. But y'know, sometimes you need little variety." Shadow was trying to think when was the last time he got the old knob polished, outside of a hooker. He couldn't remember. That bitch out there, she'd look through him like he was invisible. His face and neck were still splotched with the purple volcano scars of a faded acne. He had blue-black eyes, very dark, set in a field of livid pink, nose with a hook in it, fish lips, and scarcely any chin, which gave the lower half of his face a pared-off look. Hair was oily and lank. Not a handsome man. Also he was thin as a blade. Any angle you saw him from was a profile, which was one reason he got the name Shadow. The other reason, the one made him proud, was he was the fastest man with a shank in

Stateville Prison, bar none. Put a tool in his hand and he moved with liquid grace, come at you out of nowhere, light or dark, day or night, didn't matter which, unzippered you in a fingersnap, quicker than cat shit, and was out of there, gone, bye-bye, e-*vap*-o-rated, *dis*-solved. One of the eleven years he was in (armed robbery, two counts, and assault with a deadly weapon, one; what they missed were the six rapes, four solo and two gang; seventeen UDAA's; about three dozen B and E's, give or take a couple; and thirteen other armed robberies—all before he was legal voting age), the *Tribune* did a feature on conditions at Joliet, an "Oh my, isn't it just too awful to *con*template!" piece. Said there were fifty-two reported nonfatal stabbings the past twelve months. Shadow could have claimed credit for eight of them. Man had a right to be proud, record like that.

"Absolutely," Gleep said.

"We was born twenty years too soon, you and me," Shadow mused philosophically. "All that tender young stuff out there. And they're givin' it away. Bangin' before they're even bleedin' now'days. We was kids, you was lucky to get an inside feel. Come off a dry hump and it was like—hey, lookit me, I won me the goddam lottery! Ain't nothin' fair, you know that, Gleep?"

The way Gleep saw it, his partner spent way too much time thinking about pussy. Probably had all his life, probably pulling the pud when it was still a needledick. Which was also probably why he got all them pimples on his face. Must of been a real mess, back then, real pizza face. Now take himself. He liked a piece of ass same as the next man, but he could only think about it so long and if he couldn't get the job done, why then he'd go bowling or shoot some pool. Right now, he was getting sick of talking about it. He didn't feel like arguing, though, so he said, "Co-rect. Absolutely."

Jesus, some conversationalist, Shadow thought. Comes

from being a breed; Indian half of him. No manners, either. Look at him, mouth wrapped over the top of the sugar cone trying to suck the last of the ice cream out, making slurping sounds like some goddam starved hound. They got along okay, though, two of them. Gleep had more muscle than you'd ever need and he watched out for your back, and that last especially was a bigger talent than talk, long run. Down on the beach some young studs were moving in on the broads, ragging them, making them squeal. "Know what I'd like to do, Gleep, right about now?"

"What's that?" Gleep asked. He bet he already knew.

"I'd like to just stroll on over there, across that sand, an' open up one of them wiseass schoolboys, just for display purposes, y'understand. An' then I'd like to fuck the livin' shit outta every last twat on the beach."

Gleep thought about that a minute. "Me too," he said finally.

They were killing time, best way they knew how. Earlier that morning they had been to the apartment complex where Clemmons and his buddy had a place. Nice one too, three floors, U-shaped with a pool in the middle and tennis courts behind it, looked like a motel. Too nice for a couple shitheads like that. They were in a ground-level apartment, but naturally nobody was home. No surprises there. Shadow and Gleep walked down to the manager's place and pounded on the door. The manager, a squat little fellow with an English accent and bad teeth and breath, told them no, he didn't know anything. Shadow asked him to let them in the apartment, but he said he couldn't do that without proper authorization, so Shadow looked at Gleep and turned up his hands like he was in despair and said, "I wonder what we're going to do now. Mr. Clemmons, he really wanted us to bring him his tennis racket."

The manager looked at Gleep too, sideways. "I wish I could help you," he said.

"Oh, I betcha you can," Gleep said. "This one time."

"See, this fella here," Shadow said, wagging a thumb at Gleep, having some fun with it, "he's Mr. Clemmons's cousin. He come all the way down from the UP just to play tennis. It's a family thing. They get together every summer 'bout this time, see who's got the best game. Improved the most."

"You say you're . . . related?" the manager asked, grinning a little to let them know he was in on the joke, showing off the jack-o'-lantern teeth. "You?" He addressed Gleep directly. "And Mr. Clemmons?" But the Indian—and he was sure as bloody hell an Indian, black hair stiff as broom straw and skin the color of mahogany, color that never came from sunshine—didn't return the smile.

"Cousins. Like he said. Our mothers' sides."

"How it is," Shadow said, "you'd be doing us a real favor."

The manager stared at Gleep a moment. Man looked like a docked dreadnought, standing there looming over him. Or, from his angle, more like a pillar, wide square hips and shoulders, untapered, solid. Hands so big they were just this side of freakish. Mongol face broody and dolorous, like a devil weary of sin. "Well, I suppose it can't do any harm, this once," he said, putting lots of lilting Britisher music in it. "But I'm afraid I must be there while you're inside. Rules."

"Oh, we want you to come along," Shadow said to him. "And hey, we really appreciate, y'know, you being so helpful and all."

The apartment had a galley kitchen, sunken living room with glass sliders that opened onto a tiled patio that led out to the pool, where already the meat of the day paraded around in skimpy bathing suits, frying itself in the sun, and two bedrooms, each with its own bath. Shadow imagined all the ass gone down, those two rooms, all of it willing, free, and it made him mad.

He and Gleep split up and turned the place down. They didn't expect to find anything, but it never hurt to grope around a little. That was part of doing the job thorough. The clothes were out of the closets and every dresser they yanked open was empty.

All the while they were going through it, the manager stood with his back pressed against the door, sickly grin still parting his face. A recognition of his own immediate and very real peril overtook him suddenly. His legs felt numb. "Now you fellows realize I've got to take responsibility for—this," he said as Shadow was flinging cushions off the couch, checking down the sides. From one of the bedrooms they both could hear a sound very much like a mattress ripping. "Letting you in here this way."

"Yeah, we figured that one out. And say, listen, Mr. Clemmons, he's going to thank you, you did."

"What I mean is, you see, this is a furnished apartment. All these furnishings are the, uh, property of the management company. My employers."

"No kidding," Shadow said genially. Furnished apartment and the dumb fucks didn't even take the teevee. "Boy, they sure do get these places up nice. Bet you got a waiting list clear out to the bay." He was in the process of tearing the fabric from the underside of an upended ottoman. He didn't bother to look up.

"Perhaps if you could leave me your names . . ."

Now he looked up. He made a vinegary face and snapped a finger, like it just occurred to him. "Y'know, that's right, come to think of it. We never actual' introduced ourselves, did we? Your name is?"

"Lloyd-Granger," the manager said. "It's two names.

With a hyphen. English. I'm from England. Originally. Bristol."

He sounded to Shadow like a goddam engine running down. "Now ain't that a coincidence. See, I got two names, too. Mine's Ashley-Jones. Got one of them hyphens in it, too. So's my friend in there, Mr. Clemmons's cousin. He's Winston Little Feather. Except he don't have no hyphen." He put a cupped hand to one side of his mouth, winked, whispered, "No real class."

"Oh, come on now. What is all this anyway?"

"No, honest. I'm not shittin' you."

"Look, you came for a tennis racket and there it is, over by that diving gear." He pointed at a tank and mask and fins lying in a corner of the room. Sure enough, there was the racket. "I think you'd best take it and leave now," he said, no-nonsense tone, kind he probably used to warn a tenant to hold down the noise. No-more-crap tone. But the grin had collapsed and the spine stiffened, thrusting out the round belly so it looked like a bass drum. One hand gripped the doorknob, ready to turn it and open up and usher them out. Or get the fuck out of there himself fast, more likely.

Shadow wasn't worried. This distance he'd be all over him before he could give it the first twist. Find out if that drum was hollow inside. "By George," he said, "I think you've found it." He went over and picked up the racket and twanged its strings, like he was playing a harp. A smile always looked dippy on Shadow, kind of lips he had, so he didn't use it very often, but this time he worked up a nice big sunburst and called, "Mr. Little Feather, could you step in here a minute?"

Gleep just sort of materialized in the room. Another good thing about Gleep, he moved quick for a guy his size.

"I believe Mr. Ashley-Lloyd here located the tennis racket."

"That's real good," Gleep said. "I was wonderin' where it got to."

"You didn't come across no other rackets back there, did you?"

"Uh unh."

"Then this one's got to be it. Ain't that the way it looks, Mr. Ashley?"

"It's Lloyd-Granger. But yes, yes. That seems to be the racket, all right." He had removed his hand from the knob and clasped it with the other, letting them both hang loose down over his nuts, like he was hiding them.

"Oh, you got to excuse me. I just can't never remember names, especially two of 'em. How about I call you Mr. Hyphen? That be okay?"

"That would be fine, too," the manager said. He looked as if he needed a shot of Maalox. Gas-X tablet, at the least.

Shadow and Gleep went up the two living room steps and stood close beside him, one on either side. With the rim of the racket, Shadow tapped the palm of his hand, gently. "Since you been so good as to help out, Mr. Hyphen, maybe you could do us one more favor. If it ain't too much trouble, 'course."

"No trouble."

"See, what Mr. Little Feather and me was wonderin' was, could you maybe tell us where these boys went to. So's we can find 'em and get the game going today."

"No idea," the manager said. "I've not—I've not seen them for . . . several days. Around the pool, I mean. Or elsewhere."

Jesus, Shadow thought, fucker's going to piss his pants yet. Good thing he's got his hands down there. Catch some of it before it leaks all over the floor. Wouldn't that be something, see him standing there with a handful of wee wee. Shadow rubbed his chin pensively, feeling the spiky pits under his fingertips. "Well, that's okay," he said agreeably, "you can't keep track of everybody. But maybe, you think about it, you could tell us where they hang out, where their friends are, things like that."

"Think hard now," Gleep rumbled. They had worked together long enough they had this nice sense of timing.

"But how would I—I don't—well, wait, there's a young lady, spends a good bit of time here. I've seen her with them. At the pool."

Shadow stuck a finger right up by his eyes. "See! See there, Mr. Hyphen! See how much you remember, you think on it. Now, I bet you're going to remember some more about her. Name, where she lives, what she looks like." He glanced over at Gleep. "What do you bet, Mr. Little Feather?"

"Dime."

"You're on. Dime it is." He turned back to the manager, whose face wore the look of a spooked cat.

"Please, I have work to do, I—"

"There's a dime ridin' here, Mr. Hyphen."

"She works at Shimmers, the Holiday Inn. I only know that because I heard her say it once. Out by the pool. She said she had to leave for work. She always left around four. To go to work, I imagine."

"Catch her name?"

"Ladonna, they called her. I've no idea her last name. She's young, early twenties, blond hair, shapely figure. And I honestly—do—not—know—another—thing about her."

"Mr. Hyphen," Shadow said, laying a comradely arm on the manager's shoulder, "you just made me a dime. You been real good to us. That right, Mr. Little Feather?"

"Absolutely," Gleep said. "Neighborly."

"You can go now, you want," Shadow said. He did not, however, disengage the arm.

"Yes, thank you. Thank you very much."

"We're leavin' now, too. We're parked right across the

street. Light-green Chevy over there. Caprice. Got them classy furry dice hangin' on the rearview. Y'know, you could go down to your place and peek out the window shades when we drive away, take the license and call the cops. You could do that." The manager was shaking his head no, emphatically, but Shadow ignored him. "They'd for sure pick us up, small town like this, haul us into the station house for in-tear-oh-*gay*-shun. Just like on the television. But what could we tell 'em? Tell 'em we come lookin' for our friend Mr. Clemmons's tennis racket, like he asked, this one I got right here in my hand. Being as how nobody can find Mr. Clemmons, there don't seem no way they could check that out. We'd have to tell 'em you let us into the apartment even though the company says that's against the rules. Said, 'That's okay, fellas, let's go see can we find it.' Three of us come in and see the place is real messy. Untidy, you might say. But that's kids now'days, no respect for the other guy, his property. Full of the bejeezus. Everything's going to shit, whole world. So anyways, we looks around and finds the tennis racket and we leave. Peaceful. Police say you say we was nasty to you, made threats. We say, 'Gee, Mr. Officer, that just ain't so. We was real mannerly. And the man, he did let us in.' Officer looks at us real mean, way them policemen can do, says, 'Okay this time. But I'm tellin' you boys, I don't want to hear nothin' more about you botherin' that fine gentleman out there. I do, I'm going to run you in.' We say, 'Thanks a million, sir. But it's just a misunder-standing is all. Fella's an Englishman, tea-sucker. He don't talk American, can't tell when somebody's just funnin' him.' And then we leaves. We stop in over at Kelly's, have a beer maybe, Mr. Little Feather and me. And then we come out here to look you up again on our way outta town. You follow what I'm sayin' to you?"

The manager bobbed his head affirmatively, said nothing. He seemed to have gotten down behind terrified eyes.

"One other thing, Mr. Hyphen. You got to do something about your breath. It'd stop a bull dead in its tracks."

It was not quite noon when they left. They stopped at a cafe for chili dogs and slaw and fries, and then they drove downtown and parked. They considered having the beer Shadow had mentioned, debated it awhile, then settled on ice cream. Beer early in the day made Gleep sleepy, and they had work to do yet. They strolled down Front Street, bought the cones, and took them over to the park. It was a pretty day, nice fresh breeze coming in off the bay. And there they were, killing time. Waiting till four o'clock. To talk to Ladonna.

It was a quarter to four when the plane touched down at the Grand Rapids airport, Kent County International, as they called it now. Waverly didn't recognize the place, it had changed that much. But then it had been a dozen or more years since he had been there last; no reason it shouldn't change. He waited twenty minutes for his bag, smoking a cigarette and ashing on the carpet since there were no trays close to the luggage turntable. The woman standing beside him batted the air in front of her and edged away, mumbling something about common courtesy. Soon the bags came thumping off the belt. His was among the last. He lugged it over to the nearest car-rental booth and the lady there asked him what kind of vehicle he preferred—that's what she said. He said it didn't matter, something reliable. And comfortable. Foreign or domestic? Jesus, it was a complicated world, away from the card table. "Give me a Mazda," he said, and watched the disapproving frown etch her face. Welcome to Michigan.

He drove out of the lot, which looked about four times the size he remembered, and down a boulevard full of

TOM KAKONIS

splashing fountains to the first light, turned there and drove to Twenty-eighth Street. It surprised him some, recalling streets and directions as well as he did. The light was red, so he had sixty seconds to change his mind: turn right to Jackson; left, and he was on the road to Traverse City. The green came on and still he hesitated, trying to resolve in an instant why he was here. The car behind him laid on the horn, and he hung left. After all, he reasoned, it had been March since he had heard from Chop and the message encoded in the rambling, opaque letter seemed to imply he was working to swing a transfer to Ypsi. He could picture Chop doing his psycho number. Very convincing performance. So he was probably at the Center by now anyway. On the way back, Waverly promised himself, he would stop by, whichever place.

Still, he felt just a twinge of guilt, so when he came on a large bookstore, new to him, he pulled over. Chop had long since mastered Latin and was well into Greek, so Sanskrit had to be next. Half for a joke he'd buy him a Sanskrit grammar if he could find one.

A few people browsed around: intense males who managed the difficult physiological feat of combining soft and skinny in the same package, wearing jackets with patches at the elbows, some with beards, all with glasses; horsey looking females with broad hips and incipient mustaches; a couple of kids that looked like they were on the high school debate team, or belonged to the Chess Club. Waverly remembered the types, all of them. Inside the counter box, two languid clerks were talking about organic unity. Piped-in Mozart tranquilized the air.

"Sanskrit?" the clerk said, holding the sneer back from his lips but with his voice letting it fly. "No, I'm afraid we have nothing in *that*."

"I assumed as much," Waverly said. He was, just for the hell of it, testing his own verbal rhythms. "Thought

I'd inquire all the same." Not all the silky arrogance it could have, but not bad, a little ragged.

"We do, however, have a rather extensive language section. Quite adequate for most persons. Perhaps you'd be interested in something a bit less . . . exotic." The clerk favored his organic-unity associate with a sidelong smirk.

It was hard for Waverly to imagine he had ever been like that, but he had to admit, in fairness, he probably had. About a thousand years ago. "No, it's the Sanskrit I'm after."

"Sorry," the clerk said. "You may have a problem turning it up. Here in Grand Rapids."

"In Lansing, possibly," said his limpid friend. Waverly suspected he was not the organic half of the team.

"I'll try there."

On the way down Twenty-eighth Street, he toyed with the notion of swinging the Mazda around and heading back to the Belt Line, over to Woodcliff Avenue by Calvin College and past the two-story colonial house with the well-tended lawn with the white birch in front and weeping willow out back, house where he had grown up. But to what end? Gawk at the place? Pull into the drive and step right up to the door and knock boldly, invite himself in, say, "I used to live here, when I was young"? Ask the dumbfounded owners, almost certainly another college professor and his frumpy wife and placid kids, for the nostalgia tour? Conjure up half a lifetime's memories in this peculiar warp of time? Listen for the echoes of the vanished voices off the walls and ceilings? Uncover the secret of what happened, what went wrong? It was Freud who said the man not interested in his past is a scoundrel. Something like that.

He kept on driving. Better scoundrel than fool or, worse, lunatic. At the Highway 131 exchange, he turned north. Inside of three hours he would be in Traverse City.

* * *

At four o'clock that afternoon, Shadow and Gleep were parked in the Holiday Inn lot, engaged in thoughtful discussion. Their topic: flatulence.

"You ever see a fart lit?" Shadow inquired of his partner. "Y'know, a match right up by the ass, catch the breeze."

Gleep, picking his teeth with a thumbnail, had to contemplate a moment before he replied, "No, can't say I have."

"Me either. Now, I seen it tried plenty times, and I know there's guys swear you'll get a pop that way, like a little explosion. Least turn the flame blue. But I never seen it done, myself."

"There was a guy in the joint, black dude, could fart like a musical instrument. Trombone, or one of them big ones you get inside of, wrap around your neck, horn part's at the top."

"That's a tuba you're thinking of."

"Okay, whatever. Anyway, you'd name a tune and this fella, he'd blast out the first line or so. Sound just like it every time."

Shadow looked at him skeptically. "You making that up?"

"Listen, I'm tellin' you. I was there. Heard it. Smelled it, too. Helluva stink. He could do Frank Sinatra real good. 'Strangers in The Night' was something to hear. Come Christmas he'd do a nice 'O, Holy Night,' too. Guess night songs was his speciality."

Shadow snorted. "Take a spade, learn to do something like that."

The reason they had settled on this subject was that Gleep's gastrointestinal tract was convulsing under the weight of the three chili dogs he had eaten at lunch, and in the narrow confines of the car—windows down notwithstanding—the odor was particularly noxious.

"I think beer farts are your worst one," Gleep opined.

"You ever get a beakful of popcorn ones? They got to be right in there. 'Course your chili doggers, they ain't so hot, either."

The little jab didn't seem to bother Gleep, who was deeply interested in the matter. "Know how they'll say, for a joke, guy's so deaf he can't hear himself fart? Y'ever think about that? Think about that. You been in a situation where you're out in, like, public, or company's around, and you got one rollin' off the line you just can't hold 'er back. What do you do? What you do is, you squeeze it out silent, right? Well, now take your deafie. How's he going to know—for sure, I mean—his is silent or a boomer? Huh? Answer me that one."

Even for Shadow the metaphysics of the question were too baffling. He looked over at Gleep and shook his head slowly. "I got to think about that."

There was, however, no time to consider it, for at that moment he saw a girl hurrying across the lot, blond hair and butt both swinging, doing the strut of the broad who knows without a doubt she sits on top of the world's greatest persuader. She was got up in the uniform of a Shimmers cocktail waitress, scanty Roman slave-girl outfit that barely covered her crotch, lots of creamy flesh showing everywhere. "Betcha that's the one," he said, nudging Gleep. They waited till she was even with the car and then stepped out and stood in her way.

"Beg pardon, Miss," Shadow said amiably. "We got a little problem here and was hopin' maybe you could help us out."

Up close this way he could see she was no early twenties, like Lloyd-Hyphen said. Probably never got his eyes no higher'n her jugs, which had a nice rubbery bounce to them when she walked and which didn't look so bad just hanging still either, real handfuls. Pushing closer to thirty, was Shadow's guess. Some creases starting to show under the paint, especially up around the big saucer eyes with the blue grease all over the lids, which eyes moved over him now like he was a bug needed squashing. What he'd like to do, he wasn't working, was wrestle her right down to the ground and lay a blade across that tender throat and put the old wang to her. Make them eyes roll back in their sockets.

"I'm late for work," she said, that tone of voice they get says stay in your own dishwashing league, creep. "Why don't you ask somebody at the desk inside."

She made as though to step around them. Neither one moved. Shadow knew at once he was going to enjoy this.

"Oh, this won't take only a minute your valuable time, Miss. Name's Ladonna, am I right?"

She lifted one brow, looked wary but not a bit afraid. "How would you know?"

"Lucky guess. See, thing is we was informed you was friends with a couple young fellas we're lookin' to get in touch with. Mr. Clemmons and Mr. Barker, that's their names. We're friendsa theirs too, and we figured maybe you'd be able to help us locate them."

She gazed at him steadily. "Friends of yours? Rusty and Clay? Okay. Sure. And last night I won the Miss America pageant. Didn't you hear?"

"No, you got the wrong idea," Shadow said, drawling it out, still loose and friendly. "Y'see, this gentleman here"—pointing at Gleep—"owes them money, and he's real strict about payin' his debts back. It's kind of like his good name is at stake. That right?" he asked Gleep.

"Right, absolutely."

"So you can understand why we need to get hold of them."

All the while he was talking, Ladonna made a tapping sound on the parking lot tar with her spike-heeled sandal. When he was finished she said, "Are you and Frankenstein there going to let me by, or do I have to start screaming for security? I give great scream."

"Boy, I'll bet them security guards are real mean," Shadow said as he stooped down and lifted his pant leg and removed a double-edged, polished steel knife from a sheath fixed by Velcro to his bony calf. He held it in front of him, pointing upward, twirled it lightly, letting it catch the sunlight. "You ever see a tittie nipple lopped off?" he asked Gleep.

"No, that's one I ain't seen. Yet."

"Something to see."

Ladonna stared, droopy-mouthed, at the twirling blade. She took two short steps backward. Her eyes darted furiously, left to right. There was no one else in the lot. Shadow gave her a nice wide grin. Second one today. It was a day for smiling.

"I bet, you think about it, you're going to remember *some*thing could help us out, Miss Ladonna. Like maybe you seen these boys someplace last couple days. Heard from 'em. Know where they're at. Think a minute."

"Think hard now," Gleep said. He really liked delivering that line.

"I heard them say they were going to meet some guy. From Saginaw. Colored guy. No name. Out at the airport, I think it was. Yesterday, or the day before. I can't remember which."

It came spilling out a gasping stuttered torrent, and Shadow turned to Gleep and said, "Ain't the human brain something? Amazin' organ. Regular warehouse, you get inside it." To Ladonna he said, "That's real good, you remember all that. But y'see, we already had a talk with the man from Saginaw. Turned out he couldn't be much help, which is why we're inquirin' from you." He brushed his underlip with the knife tip, pensively, as though lost in thought. "Where 'bouts you live, Ladonna?"

"With my folks."

"Your folks? Grown-up lady like yourself? That ain't so convenient, is it? What do you do when nookey time rolls around?"

"I've got a kid."

"Ain't that nice!" Shadow said. "Being a mother." He laid the flat of the blade on her bare shoulder, watched her wince. She looked about to faint. "Still, there's got to be times when, y'know, you're going to get the old itch, going to want to do the old dance with no steps, right? Why, I bet you and them boys made lots of san'wiches, three of you. Maybe you can think where that was. Little love nest you got somewhere? Friend's place? Try hard."

"There's an apartment," she said, naming the street and number. "It's in the basement."

"And the boys, they're over there?"

"They were this morning when I left. But that was early. Listen, that's all I know. You got to believe. I don't know what they're up to. They just asked could they stay a couple nights. We're friends is all. Can I go to work now?"

"Oh, sure. You go right on in, so's you won't be late."

She looked back and forth between them, took one tentative step out to her left.

"An' we believe you, too," Shadow said. " 'Course, if there's any problem, like we got the wrong address or we get there and find out the boys just left, got a phone call tellin' 'em we're on our way over, something like that, say, well, then we'll be back to see you, maybe tonight after closing. Or tomorrow night. Anyways sometime soon. This gentleman and me, we make a good san'wich, too."

"We're the best," Gleep said, adding some reinforcement. "Absolutely."

Ten minutes later they stood at the foot of some rickety

stairs behind an ancient crumbling stucco house. At their knock, the door opened just a crack, just enough for half a male face, top half, eyes and forehead, to peer out at them. Just enough. Shadow was right; this was sure as shit his day for smiling. "Hi, Rusty," he said, "how's she goin'?"

Inside of an hour they had everything out of him they were going to get. Even Gleep, who did all the muscle, was tired, complained his knuckles were getting sore. "Kid ain't soft like some you do," he said.

Rusty Barker lay in a heap in a corner, his hands bound behind him with heavy tape, spitting blood around the gag in his mouth. He had told them as much of Clay's scheme as he knew himself. Told how they had secured the goods in the watertight bag, same as always, up off Northport harbor, forty feet down. Said how Clay—it was Clay's idea right from the start, not his—had set up a sale with the Saginaw man; how they ducked out of the delivery to Mr. Ledbetter that night, hid out here. But when yesterday they went to connect with the Saginaw man, he didn't show, and Clay figured something was definitely wrong.

We know all that already, assface, Shadow told him, signaling Gleep to lay another lick on him, step it up a little. Who you think it was met your Saginaw spook? And what do you 'spose that fine gentleman of color is up to now?

After a while, not very long, Rusty told them he and Clay got into an argument this morning. Rusty wanted out was all. Just out. All he wanted was to give Mr. Ledbetter back his goods and go home to Cadillac and then down to Ferris State for football camp. As it was, he was late reporting in.

Because he was straying from the subject, Gleep covered his mouth with one enormous hand, stifle the scream some, and brought the other fist down on him like a hammer, broke his nose. That got him back on track.

Clay was pissed but agreed finally he could get out. Said he'd take care of the goods himself, some Chicago connection, get some help from his sister, he said. Said he'd leave the apartment, didn't know for sure where he'd be. All he wanted Rusty to do was take this call he'd set up with his sister for that night. Eight o'clock. Tell her to sit tight for now, somehow they'd connect tomorrow night. Just tell her that, was all. He didn't know where Clay went or if he had the goods with him or if they were stashed someplace or where the sister was staying —he didn't know. Swore to God he didn't know.

Another half hour and they believed him.

They were getting close now and Shadow felt real good. It was good to get down to business, earn their pay, for Christ sake, instead of all the jackin' around, fartin' around. Smiley conversations. Man could get sick of that, he took any pride in his work. They turned the place down anyway, just to be sure, but there was nothing there. Kid was so lollyhole-drippin' scared, he had to be telling the truth. Look at him over there, whimpering like a spanked baby. Big fuckin' football hero. Jesus, it was disgusting.

All they could do is wait. Bitch Ladonna had some vodka in a cupboard, nothing else, so they fixed themselves a couple vodka-sevens. Cunt drink, but what are you going to do. Gleep flipped through the pages of a *Cosmopolitan* he found. Shadow sat up at the kitchen table just marking time. Rusty, slumped in the corner, his whole body aching in a way it never had before, like no football game he'd ever played, tried to remember some prayers he learned at a Bible camp he attended the summer he was thirteen.

Eight o'clock arrived and the phone rang. Shadow picked it up, and a female voice demanded to speak with Rusty Barker. "This is him," he said.

"All right. I'm Clay's sister. It's my understanding that you're supposed to have something to tell me."

Shadow had thought about what he would say, tried to construct a scenario but had finally given it up, figuring he'd have to wing it. Now he was put off by the smartass voice coming down the wire. "Well, I haven't got much. Clay, he's okay but he's been out all day. You heard from him yet?"

"Would I be calling you if I had?"

Way she said *you* sounded like she'd rather be saying *garbage* or *turd*. He was going to like talking faceup to this one, time came. "He said he'd be calling soon, tomorrow probably. He thought you and me should meet so I could let you know what's going down, this end."

"That's not quite what he told me. He said you would have information for me. Tonight."

"Yeah, well, some things come up sudden and his plans got changed."

"You *are* Rusty Barker?"

"Oh yeah," Shadow said quickly. This was no dummy. He was going to have to be careful not to spook her. "Me and Clay roomed together all summer. Where you stayin', by the way?"

"I don't see that's any concern of yours. Look. I've been driving all day and I'm tired and in no good mood for riddles and games. Do you have anything for me or not? If it's not, I'm hanging up."

Shadow had to think rapidly now. She could be at any of a hundred spots, and under any name. Take a week to find her, if they were lucky. Worse than that, he had no idea how much she knew or didn't know, how far she was in it. Sounded like not far, but he could be wrong. Also sounded like nobody you could crowd in the daylight, not like no Ladonna or Mr. Hyphen. That part he knew he got right. He could read a voice. He was walking a wire, this one. Blow it now and they were in the deep shit, asshole-deep. Nothing to do but take a calculated risk. He put the smile back on his face, hoping it would maybe help out on his voice. "Why don't we do it this way, Miss Clemmons. I'm not going to be at this place anymore. After we hang up you won't be able to get me, this number. Clay said we should set up a meet for tomorrow night. Meantime, I'll look around, see if I can find him. I do, I'll just have him show up where it is we decide. How's that sound?"

In the short pause that followed, Shadow gnawed at a thumbnail. Hoped to Christ he'd swung it.

"Has anything happened to him?"

"No, he's doin' real good."

"You're sure about that."

"Oh yeah. But you know Clay. Been a little mix-up here, need to get it squared away. So it'd be real helpful, we could both of us find him."

Another silence, longer. Felt as though his skin were crawling. Finally she said, "You're not going to be at this number?"

"No, I got to scat out of here tonight."

"And you are Clay's roommate?"

"I'm the one. All summer long, me and your brother."

"All right. Where are we going to meet?"

With difficulty, Shadow held in a long, expiring sigh. "How about we say up at the Indian's casino. Peshawbestown. You know where that is?"

"No, but I imagine I can find it. When?"

"Let's say around one. In the morning, that is. That'll give me the whole day, if I need it, see what I can turn up. There's a parking lot, left-hand side you're facing the casino. I'll be over at the far end, away from the road. Be in a green Chevy, Caprice."

"Do we have a password?"

"Huh?"

"Never mind."

"I'm lookin'—" Shadow started to say, but he was talking to the dial tone. He finished anyway. "Real forward to meetin' with you, Miss Clemmons."

It had been a productive day. Maybe not your drumroll and bugles success all around, but the kind of day a man feels like he got something to show for it. They had one last bit of business to attend to and then they could pack it in. Shadow nodded at Gleep, who went over and yanked Rusty to his feet and dragged him up by the sink. Kid's eyes were glazed, like he was in shock. Gleep had to support him, keep him standing.

"Mr. Ledbetter tells me you're a football star," Shadow said. "Earned lots of letters. That right?"

Rusty moved his head up and down.

"Says you play tight end. Got to have good hands for that position, I bet. Let's have a look at 'em, can we, Gleep?"

Gleep stood behind Rusty, holding him by the armpits. He shoved him against the counter and undid the tape. Then he forced Rusty's hands around in front, where Shadow could see.

"Yeah, them was good hands, all right," Shadow said, and he looked at Gleep and then at the sink; and in that instant Rusty understood what was about to happen, though he still couldn't believe it as he saw his right hand going down the drain, wrist-deep, and under the gag he started to make little animal screeches but nothing much came out, and when Shadow flipped the disposal switch and the blood and bone chips came spurting out of the sink, the screeches turned to squawks and then to gurgling sounds and Rusty sank to his knees, one arm still draped over the rim of the sink.

Driving away, Shadow said, "Going to be awhile before he plays any stink finger with that hand."

"Absolutely."

Shadow said nothing for a minute. Then, "Gleep, you do me a favor?"

"What's that?"

"Quit sayin' 'absolutely'?"

Gleep, who was behind the wheel, kept his eyes on the road. "Sure," he said mildly. "When you quit talkin' about pussy."

Holly Clemmons was pretty, but not in any Florida way. Her hair was so richly black, it seemed to absorb all the light around her, swallow it right up, an antipodal halo, and her eyes were black too, which was how she came by the name a select group of friends called her: Midnight. In contrast, her skin was white as bone dust, wafer-thin, almost translucent, but with a luminous glow, as though there were a bulb beneath it. Good skin. Face was narrow with nice sharp angles and planes, same as the body, nothing rounded anywhere, no backside and scarcely any breasts, all fine even lines. A model's body, long and elegant. It sent out extraordinary signals. She looked smashing there, all five-ten of her in ass-grabber jeans and filmy summer blouse, top two buttons undone, perched on a stool in the Park Place Lounge, and she knew it.

Down at the other end of the bar sat two couples, older folks, prosperous and well-fed. The men were talking louder than necessary, making what they thought were hilarious jokes and peeking her way. Their ladies scowled. She was used to that sort of thing, ignored it. They were chattering about some play, so when the bartender, a swishy kid, came over to check on her drink, she asked where the play was.

"Right here in the hotel. Right upstairs." He seemed astonished she wouldn't know. "Are you staying with us?"

She told him yes.

"Then you've probably got complimentary tickets. If you're on a package. Want me to check?"

One thing about being Holly Midnight Clemmons, people were always volunteering to do things for you. She was used to that, too. She said that's all right, she'd look into it later, but one of the old boys, eavesdropping, boomed at her, "Better catch it. It's about the only nightlife we got in Traverse City."

She gave him her demure look and said nothing. Not to be putoff, he turned heavily in his seat, facing her, sucking in his belly and working up a Rotarian smile. "*Plaza Suite*. Star-ring, ta dum, Hugh O'Brian. Mr. Wyatt Earp himself," saying it mock wide-eyed, like she was supposed to be impressed he wasn't impressed.

"Simon can be funny," she said, since he was clearly hanging on a response. "Sometimes."

"Oh, it's a pretty fair play," he said, wise critic now, "some laughs." Then, remembering he had the wife along, he said without looking at her, "Right, Wanda?"

"It's a riot," Wanda said and stood up and made for the john, tugging a dress full of gold sunburst patterns down over her chunky rump.

The husband gave a "What did *I* do?" shrug. Plunged on. "You just visiting our little community? Vacation?"

He had Richard Nixon cheeks, and a broad bald highway fringed with white shrubs spanned the top of his skull. From where she sat, it looked damp. "Vacation," said Holly Clemmons sweetly.

"Where you from?"

"Oak Brook," she said, and when he just kept staring, she added, for explanation's sake, "It's near Chicago. A suburb."

"Oh. Well, you're going to find it's not exactly your Loop up here. But then it's not downtown Detroit, either." Voice rich with sly small-town savvy.

"I expect I'll find plenty to do," she said, batted her

lashes once just to keep in practice, and looked off into some middle distance.

He couldn't leave it alone, though. "You like water sports, this is paradise."

What do you say to that? There was already enough to unscramble, so she wasn't wild to feed the fantasies of some horny old fart. Wasn't exactly tired yet; still too wired for that to set in. She had intended to leave it all for tomorrow—nothing to be done till then anyway. But since he wouldn't quit and since she had to pick up directions sooner or later, she said, "I understand you have gambling."

"Whoa, Ernie, hear that? Little lady's a card player." Ernie, who had been gaping at her all this time, merely snorted and licked his lips. He looked decidedly uncomfortable, Ernie, his wife glowering at him. The other one, worldly rascal, said, "Well, it's no Vegas, but you're right on. We got ourselves a casino. Right here in Traverse City. Haw haw."

He was, she guessed, cackling at the "right here in River City" echo. Probably saw that one too, in the theater upstairs. And *right on*? He said that? Jesus. Next would come *groovy*. How much easier just to ask at the desk. Too late now. To the wit, she said, "Here in town?"

Apart from the five of them (including the absent Wanda in the count), the lounge was empty, and the young bartender had been standing there taking it all in, head swiveling back and forth on his delicate neck like a spectator at a tennis match. Now he saw a chance to leap in and he seized it. "No, it's in Peshawbestown. About twenty miles north of here. Leelanau side. Just past Suttons Bay."

Like all those names were supposed to mean something to her.

The man looked annoyed, upstaged by a fag. "Indians run it. It's on their reservation. All perfectly legal. Been open, oh, how long now, Ern?"

"Five, six years," Ernie mumbled, still gawking. "Don't know for sure."

"You can take Highway 22," the bartender said.

"Couple blocks from here."

"They have poker tables and dice and twenty-one, I think. I've never been there. Can't gamble on my salary. But it should tell about it in the brochure in your room."

Such a rush of intelligence. She offered each of them a honeyed smile and caught the man glaring at the kid. Didn't matter, though, because Wanda was back saying she was all worn-out and wanted to go. Ernie's wife seconded it smartly. Over his shoulder, on the way out, Mr. Groovy (no doubt figuring why not, going to catch hell from Wanda anyway) got in a parting line. "Watch out those redskins don't lift all your vacation money off you. Burn your little wagon."

With them mercifully gone she ordered another drink. One more, gentle, to ease down. Monosyllables cut off the bartender effectively, so he washed a few glasses and then vanished somewhere. Might as well; she held down the only seat in the house. She could see out into the lobby and it was deserted, too. Her watch said ten forty-five. Friday night, some town. What did the old geek call it—paradise? Trust Clay to turn any paradise, even this bogus, bib-overalls one, inside out and upside down. Damn him anyway, getting her up here. Coming here himself, in the first place. If he had to ferret out trouble everywhere he went—and God knows he had a positive genius for that—and had to drag her into it, as he invariably did, supremely confident she would always be there, and she always was—well, then, he might at least have picked a diverting setting.

Soon she was going to have to think what to do, and while she didn't mind thinking, in the abstract, she didn't like puzzles, wasn't any good at them. Details, choices, decisions—other people always worked those things out for her. Tonight she wasn't going to muddle her head with any of it. Tomorrow was time enough. She got a cigarette, Carlton Ultra-Long, 120 mm. She didn't much like smoking but she liked the look of it in her hand, feel of it. Let her shrink wrestle with that one.

Ten-fifty. Under normal circumstances—if there were such a thing as normal, in her life—she'd be right now sitting in some quaint new place Erik had discovered, ethnic most likely, exotic food and drink, swarthy unctuous waiters, soulful folk music drifting through a dimly lit room. Of course that would also mean he would have to be there too, Erik, part-time drama coach, would-be playwright, anatomizing in microscopic detail all the nuances of his latest "effort," as he liked to call it. Unproduced, naturally. He wasn't much in any other department either, so maybe that part of it was small sacrifice. But he did have some local contacts, got her that audition, bagged now and irretrievably lost, even if it was a commercial for a suburban cycle dealer: pretty girl, scantily clad, draped languorously over a background Honda, sleek and erotic-looking as the machine. Schlock or not, she would have been perfect for it. And if breaking out on her own was ever to be anything more than a wistful dream, there had to be a starting gate somewhere. It made her peevish, thinking about it, all of it.

About eleven, a man came in and took a seat down where the happy couples had been. He didn't look around at all, didn't seem bewildered or irritated there was no one to wait on him, just sat there patiently with his hands clasped, gazing at them. She wondered if he was saying grace.

Ordinarily Holly Clemmons didn't pay much attention to men; no need, since they were always crowding her. But this one—and he had a perfect opening—didn't utter a word, didn't glance at her once, acted as if she weren't there. That she noticed. He was lean, which was good, but not particularly tall and not what you'd call healthy-looking. Kind of an indoors pallor, like a librarian or a bookkeeper. Nice jawline, though. Hard chin with a cleft in it. Three distinct vertical creases, two on either side of the slightly bent nose and a deep one between the brows. Must be a worrier, she thought. Eyes looked weary. Lots of gray in the otherwise nondescript brown hair. Not a handsome face but tolerably interesting. For up here. Something to be said for that even, these days. He had on a tan jacket and conservative tie, no gaudy pink sport shirts like Ernie and company, which was a relief. She judged him late thirties, forty maybe. All this was taken in from a single imperial sweep. She was accomplished that way.

She waited for the look or the start-up remark. Neither came and it made her just a trifle vexed. Oh well, he was probably gay, here to hustle the bartender, who at that moment happened to appear, gushing apologies. She finished her drink and slid off the stool, sashayed down the narrow aisle and right on by, putting a little coil in her hips just for the drill. At the door she heard him say, "I don't know, maybe a ginger ale."

It was not long after he had arrived in Traverse City that Waverly discovered there was nothing really for him to do. He had asked for and secured a double room on the second floor, new wing, of the Park Place Hotel, even though the desk clerk, seeing only one of him, said singles were cheaper and they had some left. I'm from Montana, he told her, I need plenty of space. But you wrote Florida in the registry, she reminded him, a little skeptical now; Palm Beach Gardens it says right here. Sure did. Both places, he said, extemporizing, Montana in the summer, winters down in the sunshine. And he gave her such a wide innocent smile she just had to shake her head, amused and tolerant. He was a consummate liar but when that failed, he could be charming, too; it was what you learned. Never hurt to keep in practice.

But now, ten o'clock that night, he sat alone in his spacious double room, two full-sized beds, bath with a heat lamp on the ceiling, dressing area with mirror and sink, television screen staring back at him, some abominable art on the walls. Unpacked and wondering what to do, now the impulse that had seized and brought him here was played through and done. He was more stiff than tired. He got up and pulled back the sliding glass door and stepped out onto his deck. Deck came complete with wire chairs and table, kind made for sitting at in a robe or smoking jacket sipping a drink and passing easy judgment on the goods and ills of this woeful old world. In a parking lot across the street, a gang of rowdy kids milled about, scuffling, shouting obscenities at the passing traffic. Generally whooping it up. Otherwise the streets were all but deserted. Out over the bay the Michigan sky looked vast and deep. A bleakness such as he hadn't felt for years washed over him. Bennie was right, he had no business here. Anyway it was cool, almost nippy; about that at least he hadn't been wrong.

He went back inside, pulled the drape, stripped to his shorts, and dropped to the floor and did seventy-five pushups. Then, remembering William James on habit, the meticulously rolled ball of twine undone by a single lapse, he flipped over on his back and did three hundred situps, huffing mightily on the last fifty or so. From Chop, who did a thousand of each daily, he had learned the James dictum, discovered it worked for just about everything. Except cigarettes. There it failed him. He'd have to put his mind to it one of these days, after this holiday maybe.

He came out of the shower wide awake and restless.

He stretched out naked on one of the beds. There was, of course, a phone directory on the nightstand, and after looking at it awhile, he picked it up and found the F's and ran a finger down the columns till he came to Foss, Arthur-Annetta, and yanked it away as if he'd touched a live coal. Foss, Annetta. Anymore he could barely resurrect an image of her, this woman who, so many years gone, had once been his wife, mother to his lost son, and who had set him on the unlikely rutted path his life had taken. And she beckoned him now, quite unknown to herself, toward yet another ruinous crossing. If her image escaped him, with a small effort he could trace every dark convolution of her faithless wicked heart. Arthur's as well.

The son they had taken, those two, was little more than a blur, but for one crystal memory out of that stormy time. A carnival, a carousel the boy was enamored of. He had taken him there, this silent nervous child, bewildered by the sudden domestic upheaval, spirited him away actually, in defiance of court order. Now, in the memory, he counted out the last bills in his wallet and stood holding this sober miniature horseman who clung to a pole thrust like a spear through the spine of a grinning mount that rose and fell in fluid time to the tinsel music. And watching him riding continuously, gravely, his childish features pinched into an expression compounded of wonder and woe, as though out of some instinctive wisdom he somehow understood the metronomic rhythms of the carousel and the music were finally powerless to shield him from pain—watching him that way Waverly was struck by the closeness he felt existed between them, father and son, in such baffling proportions. And remembering it now, a prodigious sorrow swept through him.

So they were still here, the Fosses. And now he was too; and what's to be done? Nothing, was the answer, for all the boundless grief and fury rising in him; about some things there was nothing could be done. Even if it ought to be. There were some paybacks life stubbornly refused to accommodate.

He should never have come. He should be in the Gardens right now, revving up for the quacks tonight and the contractors next week.

This way lies madness, Waverly told himself, expert as ever at internal dialogue. He set aside the directory and replaced it with an entertainment-leisure guide, turning the pages idly. He skimmed over the paean to Traverse City: sophisticated little community grown up on the shores of magnificent Grand Traverse Bay; pop. fifty thousand or thereabouts (if you counted all the friendly citizens up and down the arms of either flanking peninsula, and they did); superior hostelries in abundance, more than enough to satisfy every taste and budget; elegant dining; sparkling nightlife; water wonderland; sportsman's paradise; jewel in the crown of Michigan's fabled north country. That's how it read. Chamber of Commerce rhapsody.

Nothing captured his attention till he came across an advertisement for something called the Leelanau Sands. Casino gambling, it announced: craps, poker, blackjack, pull tabs. Gambling? In Michigan? News to him. Had to be a catch, play for prizes probably, one with the biggest pile of chips at the end of the night wins a Polaroid camera or dinner for two at the B and K Lounge, all the whoppers you can eat. Not his style.

It was almost eleven and he could tell he was a long way from sleep. Television didn't interest him. All those laughing sorrowing figures flickering across a screen. Behind his very own eyes he could run reels a thousand times more imaginative and diverting. That was another thing he had learned.

He put on fresh clothes and went downstairs to The Parlor, what the guide described as a "fun-filled 1890s-style pub." It was done in bordello hues, blacks and blood reds. Painting of a fat nude on one wall, high wicker stools, subdued lights, silence. Which maybe accounted for the fact that nobody was there, not even the help. Well, not quite. At the opposite end of the bar sat a most outstanding brunette, absolutely the blackest hair he had ever seen cascading over her shoulders and down her back, angular, tall, with a narrow Modigliani face that contrived to look at once bored and exotic. Singular face. Like that singer Cher when she was young, only good-looking. And all by herself, it appeared.

He felt her glance sliding over him but he didn't look up. Why bother? Probably a hooker, if they had them up here, or if not, a hooker on holiday, same as he. The wood-grained bar reminded him curiously of those cutaway diagrams of the trunks of Redwood trees, the age rings keyed to long-ago events in history: Christ's birth, fall of Rome, Charlemagne, the Reformation—right on up to the day before yesterday. In time the bartender came scurrying in saying oh, I'm so sorry, you should have shouted out or something. He had the same vocal inflections as some of the lesser trade that floated around Jackson. Moved the same way too, like he held a dime pinched in his ass. As soon as he appeared, the other half of the evening's crowd got off her stool and left. The barest hint of an elegant fragrance lingered in the air after she swept on by. Waverly ordered a ginger ale and, for something to do, questioned the bartender about the Leelanau Sands.

"Isn't that odd," he said. "Lady just left was asking about it, too. That makes two of you, in one night."

It was approaching 2 A.M. this late-August Friday night, now Saturday morning. Most of the bars were already shuttered; those still open were winding down. The FlapJack Shack was filling with spillover drinkers, the grill crackling and spitting under their burger—eggs—short-stack orders. Teenagers still cruised Front and State Streets downtown, poised at the lights in juiced suicide machines and jacked-up rear-end rods, rubber-squealers, that looked curiously like predatory buzzards about to swoop. In an alley behind the NBD bank, a fistfight was underway. A few lights were visible yet out on the arms of the bay, holes in the night. The residential streets were mostly dark. Traverse City was tucking itself in after another long and profitable summer's day.

A few miles north of town, in a room of the splendid beach house overlooking the bay, Gunter Dietz lay on his back on a silk-sheeted bed. A gentle lake-scented breeze drifted through the open windows, and down between his outspread thighs, Oona's head bobbed furiously. Yet for all the tingly sensations, Dietz's mind was still focused on the missing goods and he was still seething, thinking about that fuckup Ledbetter's bungling and about some junior asshole had the balls to try and stiff *him*. They wanted stiff, he was just the man to show them how it was.

Gaylon, alone in his bed, slept soundly, relatively speaking. Shadow's news had cheered him. Enough at least, he could crap out without some goddam pill to take him down, just a hot sitzbath, couple belts, and a good cigar. The way things were going he'd maybe have it all wrapped up by Sunday, Monday, and Dietz could go home and everybody could settle down to normal business.

Gleep sat by himself at a corner table in a tavern outside of town. Since there was nothing they could do till late tomorrow, he was quietly getting himself soaked. For the most part he thought about nothing at all, though occasionally an image of the forests and rivers and lakes up by Ishpeming, where he spent his boyhood, danced behind his eyes and then was gone.

Shadow lay astride an Indian whore he'd hired for the

night, bucking and heaving. She was spread-eagled under him, arms and legs tied with packing string to the four corners of the bed. Because his face was buried in her oily hair, he was unable to see the absent expression on her brown face.

In the basement apartment Rusty Barker lay unconscious on the linoleum floor by the sink. A little blood still leaked from his shattered hand, but not much. Periodically through the night the phone had rung, but naturally he heard nothing.

In her room at the Park Place Hotel, Holly Clemmons had finally fallen into a slumber of the sort that comes after a long, agitated, exasperating day. Since the television came without any remote, it was still on. The late late show was playing. It was a horror feature.

In another room two floors down and one wing over, Waverly sat at a table, clad in pajamas, unaccountably insomniac, dealing rapid-fire blackjack hands and testing himself with the count. He had only a single deck, so of course it wasn't representative; nevertheless, he was curious to see how much he remembered of the point-count system, how quick he was. It had been a long time since he had played any blackjack. Three years, in fact, when directly after his release he drifted into Atlantic City and scored consistently till every casino in town hung out an Unwelcome sign and he had to head south, sign on with Bennie.

From the bartender he had learned the Indian casino was real, legitimate; money changed hands, though how much, what kinds of limits were imposed, that the kid didn't know. Waverly figured he should stay with the blackjack —if indeed he decided to go at all. About an hour at a casino-run poker table, all those eager amateurs, and he'd be getting first the sour looks and then the tap on the shoulder and the pointed invitation to leave. Blackjack, it might be a diversion, keep his timing keen—and that could go flabby in a week. Keep him out of mischief. If he decided to go.

The object of all these persons' intense interest (Rusty's, by virtue of his present condition, and Waverly's, for the moment, excepted), Matthew Clay Clemmons, was at that same time comfortably sprawled on a hide-a-bed sofa in the basement of a cut-rate furniture store three miles south of town, the kind of store that merchandises its wares by way of garish signs proclaiming: OVERSTOCK SALE! EVERYTHING MUST GO! WAREHOUSE PRICES! He was munching on a prepackaged deli sandwich and sipping a Pepsi Light, a bit irked that the stupid little cunt had forgotten the Doritos.

All the same, he had to be grateful she had bailed him out. Thanked the smiling gods that one day early in the summer he had picked her up at the beach and it turned out her old man ran this sleaze emporium, so he got her to snitch the key and that night he humped her on a La-Z-Boy. She wasn't much, but there had been a few other times, when there was nothing better to do. Uncharacteristically, he had never mentioned her to Rusty or anyone else. The girl was only thirteen, no sense in buying ridicule. Or any trouble.

This morning, after the dispute with his Jello-spined partner, he called and she came to get him on her motor scooter. A motor scooter! But he couldn't run the risk of showing his fire-engine red Trans Am around town, or anywhere else this side of this goddam state, came to that. Not with those two Cro-Magnons Ledbetter for certain had on the prowl by now. What else could have happened to the suntan from Saginaw? So they rode out into some woods, to what she called her "secret place," and he had to do her, off and on, all afternoon till discount city closed, which was not until ten. No way could he get back to Rusty by eight o'clock with instructions for Midnight. Even if he'd had the slightest fucking idea what those instructions might be. But the girl did get him into the basement and found a safe spot he could duck into during the day if he had to, some dank storage room that looked and smelled like a dungeon. But then she had to hang around, couldn't get enough of him, which in his experience with women was not particularly unusual but which was annoying this particular time, all the things he had on his mind, the overdue phone call, some kind of plan, everything else. Finally he talked her into going home—after dropping off the food, which of course she had to fuck up, forgetting the corn chips.

And now he had to regroup. Beat or not, he had to think of a next move.

Five times after she left, he'd phoned the apartment and nobody answered. Which meant one of two things. Either that cocksucker Rusty had taken off the minute the scooter turned the first corner. Or—and this he didn't like to contemplate much—they had got to him. And if they got to him, they either did or did not know about Midnight. If they didn't (so went his logic), there was nothing to sweat over, though it occurred to him he should have thought to tell her to sign in under another name, but Jesus, who can think of everything? And if they did . . . He didn't want to follow that one too far. Maybe he should call the Park Place, alert her, leave a message or something. But that could be risky too, if—

Ifs, fucking *ifs*. Everything had turned up a fucking tangle. From the start, all he'd wanted was to hit on one big score, a score of his own making, conceived and crafted and carried through himself. For once in his life. He didn't want to see anybody hurt, certainly not Midnight; if there was anyone in this world he cared about, she had to be the one. Or not even Rusty, who was, all right, stupid and a coward but basically a harmless shithead. But he could feel this desperate need to show them all—Midnight, the old man, everybody. Show them there was more to Matthew Clay Clemmons than they'd ever understood, some shrewdness they'd missed before, some . . . substance. Depth. Was that too much to ask? Look where it got him, that simple worthy ambition. Bargain-Basement Heaven. He was going to have to uncover some new moves, somehow. How, he wasn't sure.

For just the flash of a moment, he wished he hadn't begun all this. But then he reached down and patted the bag of goods under the sofa. Still secure, as was he. For now anyway. Probably Rusty was home in Cadillac right now, in bed, with all the lights on and his head under the sheets. And almost for sure Midnight was okay. And he felt really worn-out, punished by the snarled-up events of the past couple days. He needed sleep. Tomorrow he'd think things through, unrattled fashion, when his head was clear. Come up with something. Every problem is a challenge, his father liked to say, and for every puzzle there is a solution. Tomorrow he would find it. Tonight, he could have used those Doritos.

TWO

AT SEVEN THE NEXT MORNING WAVERLY came firing out of a dreamless sleep, confused at first and a little shaken by the unfamiliar surroundings. He had to lie there awhile, reconstructing where he was. Then he got out of bed and slipped on bathing trunks and found his way down to the enclosed pool, big transparent dome over it, let the slanted rays of the gathering sunshine in. He swam forty laps, nice easy crawl, watching the trace of his shadow stroking effortlessly beneath him, then did twenty more in a lunging, driving butterfly breaststroke, and then just floated around getting his wind back, cooling down. There was a compact exercise area off the pool, so he went in and did some sets on the Universal machine.

When he got back to the room, he felt good. Somewhat righteous, he understood, but good, animal good, like he inhabited his body again, almost the way he felt years ago coming off a long afternoon's session in a college pool. Under the pitiless yellow light of the bathroom mirror, he checked himself out. Not so bad, he concluded; for thirty-six, not so bad. True, the hair that dusted his chest was an anachronous pure white and his stomach was not the ledge of stone it once had been, but many of the ridges were still intact, and along the sides, where most everyone else had pudgy handles, he still had hollows. So it could be worse.

He took breakfast in the hotel's dining room and then he went downtown, strolled its three-block main street, both sides, peered incuriously in the windows of a few souvenir and geegaw shops, many of which were still closed, stood reading in a magazine-paperback store that went under the name Little Professor, read till a clerk sidled over and began elaborately dusting the shelves around him. She asked finally if she could help him find anything, and he replied no, thank you, accepting the nudge graciously, and stepped back out onto the street and looked at his watch and discovered it was barely half past nine. And there he was, Mr. Health and Harmony, standing in the lenient northern sunshine, squinting not at all, breathing the clear moist air—remarkable air, the kind you couldn't see. And without a goddamn thing to do.

A block down was a little outdoor patio-cafe, so he went there and got a table and drank coffee and smoked cigarettes. Watched the streets come slowly alive with the morning tourist parade. Watched through the store windows shopkeepers scurrying about like urgent rats in cluttered cages. It occurred to him to wonder if he sat there long enough if the Fosses, Arthur and Annetta, would pass by. And—as long as he was wondering—would they have the boy with them, and if they did, would he even recognize him? After a decade? Gone unseen from age two to twelve? Not a prayer. Probably couldn't even pick the contented couple out of a crowd anymore, all those years. Almost certainly just as well. Arthur, he dimly remembered, had hair fine as gossamer, and Annetta, he seemed to recall, leaned toward the plump even when she was young; athletic or not, she had the seed of obesity in her. So by now maybe he was bald and she was fat, and if such was the case, then maybe some of life's smaller conflicts turned out all right after all.

He recognized that none of this was doing him any good, these memories and dismal spite-freighted conjectures. After an hour or so, he wandered back to the hotel and found his room was not yet made up. He tracked down a snappish maid who said she'd get to it quick as she could, the hotel was full of guests, and then he went down to the lobby, plopped in a leather chair, and sat gazing glumly at nothing much at all.

Nothing, that is, till he saw the elegant young woman from the bar last night come out of the dining room and stop at the desk to ask the clerk something, he couldn't hear what. He could, however, catch the assured intonations in her voice, the cool imperative of rank. Seen in the daylight this way, she looked even more regal. Same astonishing black hair and marmoreal skin, same angular body, very tall, but with a soft confluence to it he had missed before, a blending fusion of joints and limbs. She was dressed in casual skirt and blouse that appeared almost weightless, like lightly tinted air. Because his experience of women was at best limited, and most of that bitter, Waverly took perhaps less than ordinary male notice of them; but this one, he decided, would excite the dullest imagination, and kindled even his. She looked the way he imagined the first breeze would look rising off a heat-scorched plain. He decided also she was probably not a hooker; more likely a fine young lady of means, urban, accustomed to deference and attention, come to the north country to take in the quaint sights. Evidently she was staying at the hotel. And if there was a husband or companion in the picture, he was, twice running now, nowhere to be seen. She turned away from the desk and walked right by his chair. He looked directly into her eyes, but she favored him with not so much as a glance and, moving with a studied sinuous roll, all the bearings lubricated, disappeared down a corridor.

So much for that overture, if in fact that is what it was.

Most of the afternoon he dozed, waking from a sleep this time riddled with furious dreams punctuated by disjointed, off-center images of shrieking children, misdealt card hands, females blurry and indistinct but all of them sporting taunting smiles, some blood trickling out of god knows where, rooms without doors or windows and with walls of damp sponge. It was four o'clock. He was sweating. He reached for the entertainment guide and leafed through it to the Leelanau Sands blurb. Open Saturdays at noon, and from the conversation last night, he knew already how to get there. All right. So be it. He showered again and dressed, putting on jacket and tie because it was familiar, that's what he wore, fashionable up here or not. Since morning he had eaten nothing, but that was all right, too; his sharpest concentration came off an empty stomach. He went directly to the lot and pointed the Mazda north on Highway 22.

All the scenery was lost on him, for on the drive he played a series of hands in his head, first running by the basic strategy, then picking things up with a simple aces-fives count, then finally settling into a serious numerical count, precise values assigned each card and a cumulative total ticking off independently in a remote but accessible room of his mind. Numbers, card faces, totals—all of them laser-flashing across the screen he held in sharp and steady focus behind eyes that displayed all the serenity of a saint, while inside was gathering the turbulent inexplicable heat he never failed to experience going into a game, any game, even a dalliance like this one would necessarily be. Anymore it had nothing to do with money; that much he knew. Somehow it was linked with notions of order, imposed patterns, the jamming of static. Anything beyond that was mystery, and as with all therapies that succeeded, it was best left unexplored.

He arrived none too soon, almost missed it since there was only a small road sign announcing Peshawbestown, no neon whatsoever, and in spite of the suffix, nothing even vaguely resembling a town. There were two parking lots, and the one handiest to the four frame structures was already full; no choice but to pull into the farther one. A head-'em-up, move-'em-out traffic director, all business, pointed him to the casino with a nonverbal toss of the head. He was, Waverly noticed, not an Indian and his job was to arrange cars, but he had nonetheless the canny arrogant look that infects everyone associated, however distantly, with the mechanical churning of money, the hustle. The casino sat at the peak of a gentle rise and was distinguished not at all from the cedarwood bingo parlor, which resembled a town hall, the souvenir shop, or the administration building. These distinctions he learned by eavesdropping on the couple ahead of him in the line that inched toward the entrance.

Once inside, he saw it was a casino only by the loosest definition of the term. There was none of the customary Mask of the Red Death decor: crimson walls, scarlet ceilings, carpets of blood. Rather, the interior had the appearance of a church basement or VFW club (beige walls empty of ornament, floor fans pumping the thick air) rented out and rigged up by the Kiwanians for an evening's charitable fund-raiser, Las Vegas Nite, fun for everyone. And the patrons were a match for the place. Waiting to be processed for a seat at one of the half-dozen tables visible from the door, or a place at the single craps table along one wall (the poker, he overheard, was conducted somewhere in the back), they had the guileless expressions of peppy partygoers, utterly free of the poison discontent, adrenaline-clogged impatience, desperation, superior ennui, numb expectancy that uniformly and by turns stamps the faces of gaming addicts. They were here for an evening's entertainment, nothing more; copartners in the frolic, quite unencumbered by runaway dreams.

There seemed to be an even mix of Anglos and Indians

running the operation, though there was no doubt who was in charge: cocktail waitresses and many of the dealers, white; pit bosses, cashiers, and security muscle, red. All of them, regardless of race, had The Look down: remote, layered in ice, inward turning eyes of the connoisseur sampling a slightly acid wine. Yet there was something ersatz about all of them too, like amateur actors straining after conceptions of difficult parts, and something not quite easeful about any of them either, like short men consciously persuading themselves confidence will make them tall.

Eventually he made it to the head of the line and handed over his ten-dollar admission fee to a hefty Indian lady behind a counter, and got for it one of the last remaining seats at a table. It was squarely in the middle of the semicircle, facing the dealer dead-on, three players on either side of him. Not your most desirable spot. He did a quick scan of the chip stacks around him, most of them tidy little pillars of ones and fives, a few twenty-fives scattered here and there. Recreational play, no hurt feelings. He bought an innocuous couple-hundred worth, and to the dealer's denominations query replied pleasantly, you decide, an assortment. "Changing two hundred," she called to no one in particular, the wall maybe, and from behind her came the smart bass echo, "Change 'em."

Down the chute went the bills, and the game rolled on.

After a dozen shoes of basic strategy only, half of Waverly's pile was gone. Which was okay; it quieted any dealer doubts and established him among the company of the other marks, most of whom played as if it was their intention to erase their collective guilt over the treatment of the Indian nations, hitting some stiff hands wildly, incomprehensibly standing on others that stared down a dealer ten, splitting fives and even tens, generally egging fate on. Mugging victims, handing over the loot. Come to town fully clothed and leave in a barrel.

He bought another two-hundred worth and began a simple count, tracking the aces and fives. It was easy because the first dealer, a slender, brown-skinned girl, was not at all quick. Her eyes, partially hidden behind tinted glasses, were keen enough, but it was as though she had not yet mastered the electric connection, eye to arm to hand and nothing in between, nothing conscious, just reflex recording of numbers and symbols and trans-mittal thereof down the nerve channels: bets down—hit?—no?—stand?—double down?—split 'em?—bust—scoop it in—dole it out—hand a minute—bring home the wampum—baby needs new moccasins. When the deck was ace-rich, he put down a few bets for her, and by the time they spelled her, it amounted to a nice little toke. She turned away with a murmured "Thanks for the bets, sir," and just the barest hint of a smile.

The next dealer, also an Indian girl, chubby pretty face, was a little better but not much, and inside of another hour he was getting well, almost even. A near miracle in light of the death-wish play going on around him, either side, and his steady circumspect betting. The wide vari-ances, unwelcome attention-grabbers, he was saving for later. It was nine o'clock. He'd been at it almost three hours and could have used a break. Unfortunately, breaks were not a part of the system here. It was a players' room only, no thumb-up-the-ass gawkers or kibitzers, no prof-itless milling around, no catching the second wind. Leave your chips and you could take a leak or a stretch; be gone too long and you could go sample the night air. Plenty of fodder still waiting in line. Sit 'em up, dazzle 'em, grind 'em into a stuporous daze, spit 'em out. Crisp in-dustrial hum. Welcome to the chopping block.

So he deferred the break. It was okay; like an experienced typist, eight hours at the keys, he had learned how to sit—slight forward tilt, spine cocked, neck and shoulders loose—and he had sat far, far longer than this. He ordered his first drink of the evening, tomato juice. Players and dealers came and went. Cards slapped across the felt. His columns of chips rose and fell. Exercise.

Ten o'clock. Warmups were over. He got up and went into the john, relieved himself, washed his hands with all the controlled attention of a surgeon scrubbing down, splashed cool water in his face, dried, tensed the muscles in his back and shoulders tight as a coiled wire, then let them sag utterly, drain right away. And then he adjusted his tie and walked back out onto the floor and resumed his seat and began seriously to count.

By midnight there was roughly three thousand dollars in chips stacked beside his elbow. And a pit boss hovering behind the dealer, trying to appear nonchalant, running a thoughtful finger back and forth the length of his Valentino mustache. One of two things was coming next: the exit invitation or, if they had one, the introduction of a mechanic dealer, a cooler.

When she arrived she was an unlikely looking bundle: Caucasian, young, skinny, uncommonly homely, dishwater hair and sour pucker lips her best features. The girl who never got asked to the prom. But she had the mechanic's transfixed gaze, global vision, robot hands. And she had the moves, all of them: the steaming deal and magic retrieval, cards down, cards vanished in a dizzying blurr, whole shoes winging by, burn card a little higher each time, jamming the count, rounds without transitions, blink and it was history, you lose, sorry. Inside of thirty minutes she had recovered from him half the house's rightful store.

Waverly sat out a few hands, smoked a cigarette, studied her rhythm. She was chilling him, this ice maiden, but she was a challenge, too. He figured he had another half hour's focus left in him. The shoe was down and she was shuffling at a speed that defied reason, physics. He took a series of quick shallow breaths and plunged back in, tunneling in on the cards and nothing more, blotting out the narrow surrounding world like some mystic in a self-induced trance locked onto a vision of light.

They seesawed. He'd begin to come around, she'd bring him back down again. It was a standoff and he knew it. She was as good as he was, maybe better. He wondered where they ever found her and if they knew what they had, a wallflower exacting revenge for a lifetime of snubs. Abruptly, he dropped the count, just let go all the numbers and tallies dancing in his head, let them ooze on out. The ends of his nerves felt fried. Blackjack, played tough, was maybe not his best game. He placed one more bet, one for him, one for her. They both lost. He rose and gathered up his chips, leaving her four of the twenty-five color. "Thank you, sir," she said sweetly. "Have a nice night."

He said he already had.

"Nice weekend, then," she said and, unwilling to let it go, "Come back and see us."

The pit boss, poor man's Geronimo, who had never left the table and who, if he didn't stop fingering that little pussy-tickler was going to rub it away, ruin his love life forever, said nothing.

Waverly's chips totaled eleven hundred and some change. Deduct the stake and he was seven bills to the good. After about as many hours' work. Better at those wages to have a citizen's honest job. Buy you a little fishing tackle, Bennie would say, ever the optimist; every buck ahead's the one what didn't get away. He tried to remember he was on vacation, and he knew he was supposed to be hungry. He stepped out into the clear moonlit night and headed down the slope to his car.

* * *

Shadow and Gleep got to the casino a little after eleven. Since Gleep was well-known there, they got right in, no heels-cooling lines for them. A place was made for Shadow at the craps table, and in half an hour he was down four hundred, which didn't improve his humor any (he was still whipped from the workout he'd given the squaw, and a hangover still lingered) and which especially was not promoted by the asshole standing next to him, looked like a spic, whooping, pounding the rim of the table, beating his fucking chest and bawling "Aw-right!" every time he won (which was often) and hollering such can-dyass poop as "Drop shee-it, pick up luck!" every time he had the dice in his hands. Finally Shadow turned to him and said, "Hey, how about holdin' it down, rest of us ain't in the woods over there, y'know." Fucker just looked at him, said, "This is America," and kept on yelling, and there was nothing Shadow could do, couldn't crowd him there, all those people, so he left. He went over and joined Gleep, who was standing by the snack bar talking to a security guard almost as big as he was.

"How'd you do?" Gleep asked him.

"Ahh, they picked my pocket. Four bills. Hadn't been for that greaser there, I'd of done okay, concentrated. They ought to put muzzles on shitbirds like that."

"Too bad," Gleep said, though he didn't really much care, didn't gamble himself. To change the subject, he told him, "Elmo says they got a counter in the place."

"No shit. Where?"

"Dude in the coat and tie. Over there." He nodded in the direction of a table opposite them.

"Looks like a pussy," Shadow observed. "They going to walk him?"

"Nah, Elmo says they gonna send in Dolores first."

"She the white one? Ugly?"

"That's the one."

"She'll trim off his nuts and hand 'em to him. You ever seen her deal?"

"No. But I heard."

"We had time, I'd like to watch. But we better get down to the car, case she shows up early. I'm going to take along couple beers, see if I can get my fuckin' head well. You want one?"

"Oh, I guess. Shouldn't be much to this tonight."

Their car was the last in the file and it was parked facing outward, so they could watch the road. While they waited, Shadow deliberated aloud on the vagaries of fate.

"Y'know, Gleep, it's really crazy the way things shake down sometimes, y'think about it. Weird almost. Man can be sittin' on top of things, got all his shit in order, mindin' his own store, and then out of nowhere comes something gonna zap him. Cave him right in."

"Whata you mean?" Gleep said, slurping the beer. He drank with both his lips cupped around the neck of the bottle, like it was a dick he was sucking, Shadow thought, and when he swallowed, his Adam's apple bobbled in his throat, big as a goiter.

"What I mean is not some*body* does him, somebody else, but some *thing*. Like it's inside him. Take this fella I knew in Joliet. He was always chewin' toothpicks, always had a wet one hangin' out the side of his mouth. Did it he said so's he wouldn't smoke. He carried boxes of them the way you and me carry packs of weeds. Okay. One day we're hangin' out in the yard, not doin' much, just generally fuckin' the dog, and a bunch of boogies decide to run a train on a punk. We gets in a circle to watch and this fella I'm tellin' you about, he's chewin' his pick, naturally, and he gets so excited just eyeballin' the action, he swallows it and chokes to death, right on the spot. Went out lungs clean as a baby, but just as dead. Y'see what I mean?"

"I thought maybe you was goin' to tell me it was the

Dutch Elm disease got 'im," Gleep said, grinning widely at his own droll wit.

Shadow was not amused. "You got to be a comedian now, I'm tryin' to explain something serious to you here?"

Gleep figured his partner was still pissing inside over the four hundred, thinking if he didn't like the dice and gash so much, maybe he'd have something to show for himself, nice car, say, Caddie like Ledbetter drove, and maybe a house even or some money in the bank. Gleep, he was saving all he could stash away and when he got enough he was going to turn in his resignation and head back on up to the UP, get himself a cabin in the woods, hunt and trap some, fish. Away from everybody. Ice fishing in the winter; there was nothing could beat that.

Shadow, meanwhile, pursued the topic. "Give you another one. I was in this bar one time, forget where, Gary, I think it was, and there's this guy walks in, young guy, build on him, says he can beat anybody at pool and he can drink more'n anybody in the house, and faster. Nobody pays him no mind, figures he's just another shit-dribbler, so he buys a pint and takes it over to the pool table where everybody can see, and he disappears it. Full pint. One good gulp. You know what happens?"

"Crashed, I 'spose."

"Better'n that. He picks up a cue, squares off on a double bank shot, calls the pocket, and makes the sucker. And then he falls on his face on the table. Fucker is *dead*. How about *that*?"

Gleep shrugged. "Well, he made the shot. Must of died happy."

Shadow laid his forehead in the palm of a hand. "You ain't gettin' my point."

"Oh yeah, I think I do," Gleep said mildly. "Listen to this one. When I was a kid, all's we had was them outdoor crappers. That's all everybody had. We was used to 'em, but they could be real bears too, come winter. Squat too low and you was likely to be there till spring thaw, your ass froze right to the hole. So anyway, long about when I was fifteen, we got the indoor kind and we're all thinkin' we're livin' in shit. Which is not some kind of joke I'm makin' here, once you hear the rest of the story. Across the road there's these people got their granny livin' with 'em, and she's maybe ninety or better and she's not gonna change she says, her age. Old four-holer's good enough for her. So they keep it for granny. 'Course it starts gettin' rickety, nobody ever uses it except her, and nobody ever moves it either, so the pit starts fillin' up. One day she goes out there to drop a load and the whole thing just collapses right out from under her. Granny, she dies. Drowned in shit."

"Jesus, Gleep," Shadow said with some heat, remembering his own grandmother who raised him after both his parents split, till she died when he was ten and he went into foster homes till he broke out on his own, "that's a disgusting fucking story to tell. That ain't true."

"Listen, I was there. They had to fish her out with logging hooks. She was that deep. It was some stink too, I can tell you. I'm talkin' big-time, downtown stink."

Shadow didn't want to take it any further. Fortunately, it was just then a sleek Porsche came tooling up the highway, slowed and turned into the lot, creeping their way. "What you bet this is the lady we're lookin' to see?" he said.

"Bet you're right."

What Waverly heard first was a whimpering, then some sounds of scuffling, and then an unmistakable cry of pain. Female cry. He walked to the end of the line of cars and saw two men, their backs to him, standing over a woman sunk to her knees. Every instinct told him to stay out of it, turn around and get in the Mazda and speed away, tend to his own affairs; and he would have too but for the lemon shaft of moonlight slanting across the woman's face, marking her as the same woman from the hotel. And he saw that she saw him. "Help me," she said simply, a simple direct claim on his service.

One of the men, smaller of the two, whirled about and faced him, taking his measure. The other, the size of a Sasquatch, only half-turned, keeping an eye on the woman. Both of their features were shrouded in the dark.

"This here's just a little lovers' spat," the facing one explained to him in the same sneering, snake-rattle ugly voice he had heard a thousand times in Jackson. "Nothin' for you to worry yourself about. You keep truckin' right along and everything'll be fine."

Waverly looked from one to the other. Right now they stood close together, but he suspected they would be savvy enough to put some distance between them once it was clear he wasn't leaving. He held the car keys in his hand, and he slipped a finger inside the ring and fit each key around a knuckle, ragged edges pointing out. "Why don't you let the lady up," he said amiably, phrasing it more as a reasonable suggestion than a demand or threat.

The smaller one took a step to the left and then another one toward him. "Well, it was me, that's what I'd do. But the way I see it, man ain't got no right nosin' in, a couple's arguin'. Might even be—" He broke off and leaned in closer, squinting hard. "Hey, Gleep," he called over his shoulder, "it's the counter."

"Don't say." He didn't move but he turned slightly, for a better look.

"Yeah, same fella." To Waverly he said, "That's a real gift you got there. You make any money tonight?"

"Not much. Cigarette money."

"Shame. Listen, let me give you worda advice. Countin' cards, that's a kind of dumb idea here, gets the Indians all riled, and this fella here, he's an Indian. An even dumber one is what you're doin' right now, which looks sorta like a citizen's arrest. You wasn't thinkin' about something like that, was you?"

"No, nothing like that," Waverly said. "But I think you should let the lady up."

Shadow shook his head sadly. "Y'know, for a guy can keep track all them cards in his head, you ain't really too smart. Now, I already give you one opinion. Next one you get's comin' from an undertaker. You follow what I'm sayin'?"

"I think I understand," Waverly said, and at just that moment the woman tried to get to her feet and the Sasquatch, sensing it, leaned over and swung the back of his hand across her face, casually, as though he were swatting a pesky hound. This time her cry came bubbling through a mouthful of blood. The smaller one bent down and tugged at his pant leg. Waverly had seen that movement before, many times. He drew back his right leg, football punter fashion, and kicked him squarely in the face, hard as he could, full follow-through, everything behind it. And then in one smooth motion, he reached down and scooped up a handful of parking lot gravel and flung it in the eyes of the charging Sasquatch, but not quite in time because an off-center blow, heavy as a swung bat, caught him in the clavicle with the jarring force of an explosion, staggering him. Through a shimmery glaze, Waverly could see him clawing at his eyes, and he knew he had maybe a shaved second, no more. He hurled himself laterally into him, punching upward, driving the keys into the lump of Adam's apple, grinding them. The arms that clamped him at the chest, pressing out what breath remained, began to sag, and Waverly fell away and watched him slump to the ground, gagging. He spun around and brought a foot into the kidneys of the other one, who was still down and who screamed sharply, curled himself into a tight fetal ball.

"Smarts a little, doesn't it," Waverly said, and he kicked him again.

He got the woman by the arm and yanked her up. "Come on," he said, gasping after air. "Hurry."

She had a hand at her mouth, dabbing the blood. She seemed astonished to find it there. She stooped down and recovered her purse, brushed the dirt from her clothes with a dazed meticulousness. "Is it over?" she asked, and he said, "For right now. Come on."

He sprinted her down the row of cars to the Mazda, but at the door she balked. "My car. I've got a car."

"Forget the goddam car. Come *on!*"

"How did you do that, anyway?" she was asking him, leaning back in a chair in his room, feet propped on one of the beds, a damp towel at her puffy lip. "How did you handle those two cretins? Alone like that." Her slacks were dirt-streaked and there was a rent in the sleeve of her blouse, but she was calm now, though on the drive in, squealing curves and barreling straightaways, fast as the Mazda would peddle, she had dissolved in a frantic hysteria, laughing and sobbing at once, sometimes babbling without much coherence.

"It's not like the movies," Waverly said. "Never is."

He was himself sitting up at the table, shirt undone, examining a bruise that extended from his upper chest out to his shoulder, seemed to be spreading visibly, like an accelerating cancer, a mix of purples and yellows not at all unlovely. And he was remembering, as he responded to her question, Chop's dictum for survival in Jackson: Play dirty. In everything. Another one for Chop.

"Are you some kind of boxer? One of those karate types?"

"Boxer? No, ma'am. Concerned citizen, sees a civic duty, does it."

"I've seen you before."

Waverly looked up from the fascinating bruise. Her eyes were narrowed on him, black as the edges of the sky on the other side of the drape, unflinching, cautious, skeptical. "Sure you have," he said. "Part of the furnishings, like the pop machine the end of the hall."

"Who are you? What's your part in all this? How is it you just happen along, rescue the damsel in distress? And where's Clay?"

He didn't like the lofty assumptive note, and he didn't like the staccato rhythm of the questions. He said coldly, "Lady, I don't know who *you* are, never mind anybody who'd call himself Clay."

So she told him. Told him everything, or just about everything: who she was, where she came from, why she was there, what she knew. Because, she said, not so much helplessly or gratefully as exasperatedly, there was no one else to tell, and, a little softer, because he had been kind.

It was more than he wanted to hear. He sensed that women like this came equipped with the full baggage line of trouble, and of all the things he needed in his managed life, trouble was not among them. "You'd better talk to the police," was his best advice.

"I can't *do* that," she said, clearly vexed at his thick-wittedness. "Can't you understand? I don't know what kind of trouble he's in. And Daddy's told me never to go to the police till every other option's exhausted."

Daddy, she had let him know, was a corporate attorney, megabucks man, shrewd dealer. Daddy knew best. And Daddy could be no help because he had given up on Clay, washed his hands of him. Kicked him out, actually. And besides, Daddy was out of town.

"Ordinary circumstances, I'd say your daddy was right. But that little scuffle tonight, that wasn't ordinary. If I were you, I'd bring in the experts."

"I'm going to find Clay first," she insisted, adamant. "I've got no choice. There's nobody else to help him. Only me."

"Yes, well, all the best. I'm guessing, though—purely a guess, you understand—your brother's done something more than get a pom-pom girl in a family way this time."

"Half-brother," she corrected him. "We had different mothers."

The relevance of this seemed murky. "Okay," he said, "half then. But whole trouble. Hundred percent."

She reached for a wallet in her purse, flipped it open, and handed it to him. "Here's his picture."

The color snapshot revealed a young man in swim trunks standing at a boat dock, hip cocked, arms folded across a wedge-shaped torso cut with ripply muscle, great swatch of yellow hair dangling rakishly in his eyes, chiseled features breaking in a smile that reached his ears, pure narcissistic joy, kind of smile that displays an innocent wonderment over why you wouldn't share that joy, even if you could never participate in it. To Waverly he looked like any of a thousand machine-stamped Florida surfers, or like one of those exquisite male catalog models who seemed perfectly at ease in their bikini briefs, fondling symbolic rifles or bows and arrows and grinning at empty space. "Handsome lad," he said, returning the wallet. It was noncommittal, a thing to say.

"He's a bodybuilder," she said. "Last year he won second place, Mr. Illinois. Best-arms trophy, too."

"There's an achievement."

Her face darkened a little. "If you knew him," she said coolly, "the way I do, you'd understand that behind all the showy muscle and devil-may-care there's a decent kid. Basically. And a rather weak and frightened one at that."

"Miss Clemmons, what is it you want from me?"

"I want you to help me," she said. Same simple injunction as when she was helpless on her knees in the casino lot, same straight-on presumption, manifest obligation out there, universally acknowledged and particularized now in him. It put him off, that haughty presumption, but even less did he care for the sinking feel of what was going on here. Yet gazing at her, as he was, he had to admit she was the most unusual-looking woman (not beautiful, exactly; unusual was right) he had ever seen; hypnotic looks, they seemed apart somehow from her manner and voice and what it was she had to say, independent of them all, full of sustained promise, rainbow visions.

Waverly dropped the gaze to his own upturned palms. "You don't know what you're asking," he said. "Or who I am."

"That's so. But I saw what you did tonight. Back there. And I see you now. I'll pay you if you like."

"There's more than money going here," he said, mostly to the carpet and to himself.

"You'll help, then?"

He nodded. "But only for a start. Get you started. Then you'd better call your daddy, like it or not. Take your instructions from him."

"Where *do* we start?"

He wasn't much taken by her ready use of the plural, but he let it go. "By getting you checked out of this hotel and into someplace else. Under a different name. Before those two choirboys come knocking at the door. Next time we're not going to walk away with just a fat lip and a purple shoulder." We. Jesus, now he was doing it.

"Tonight?"

"Right now."

"But where would I go? At this hour."

"We'll find a place."

Unlike him, she had not gotten to her feet. She made a slow, lazy, appraising survey of the room. "What's wrong with here?"

"Here?"

"Here," she said, looking now directly into his eyes, steady and composed, on top of things, the way some women know for a certainty they are, moving through elements they controlled. "Nobody knows who you are. And," she added, unblinking, "there's two beds."

Waverly had a sudden spontaneous vision of his orderly world, so painstakingly assembled out of a slender balance of lockstep routine and governed risk, each indispensable to his renewed life, all of it crumbling like the burned-out ashes of an abandoned fire. "Here it is," he said.

Gaylon Ledbetter, at this same hour, felt much of the same dismay as Waverly did, probably more, though of a somewhat different order. He was pacing the living room of his home, doing aloud the "Why me, O Lord?" number he had been doing lately in private, more times than a few. His audience, Shadow and Gleep, sat in facing chairs, nursing their considerable hurts. "Wormfood," Shadow kept muttering. "He don't know it but that's what that asswipe counter is. Wormfood." Gleep massaged his raked and bleeding throat, occasionally mumbling thickly something unintelligible.

Gaylon, however, was interested in neither recriminations nor vows of revenge. He couldn't believe all this was happening, and happening to him. First his wife, ten years his junior, picks up and runs off, and with the goddam *post*man, for Christ sake, ten years at least her own junior. That was six weeks ago, just about the time he was starting to get accepted a little, getting some invites to chin-and-grins at some of the fancy places over in Grand Traverse Resort, washing down the chow with brandy out of glasses big as flower vases, chewing his cigar and talking sideways about markets and investments, all that substantial shit, choosing his language careful, leaving out the "fucks" and "ain'ts" and trying not to drop his g's, letting on he was a retired business-man, importer, better than well-off and still liked to keep a hand in, maybe good for a little seed money, something come along looked right. One of them people, little guy always wore an outfit like a ship captain, talked with a lisp but drove a boat about the size of a barge, was even hinting maybe he'd put him up for a country club mem-bership. Wouldn't that of been something: Gaylon Led-better, Cicero, Illinois, swinging a golf club and hollering out "fore" or whatever the fuck it was they yelled. Took three years up here to get that far. Where he'd always wanted to be in life, secretly. Then that cunt Mardella flies the coop, cleans out the accounts before she does, leaves him with a wallet running on empty and a big house in the woods that won't sell and a mortgage to pay. So it came to if he *had* to make good with Dietz, he couldn't come close.

There was another thing, Dietz and the sweet arrange-ment they'd worked out. Talk about your God's-fool luck. After all those years on the dime-ante hustle, Dietz, who he barely knew, approaches *him* and spells out this scam—project, Dietz calls it—where they send in the goods by sailboat, sort of like sportsmen coming up the lake, drop them in the bay at night, mark the spot with buoys, and bring in the minimum-wage divers next morn-ing, recover the stuff. It was genius. Gaylon, he was in charge of distribution, a district manager, like; and it was Dietz's plan to branch out slow, work on down the state till they started moving in on spade country, Detroit, come at them from their blind side. Shake loose some real money then. Jesus, it was a sweet arrangement, every-thing he'd ever wanted. Get to be part of the community, was what Dietz said, act like a regular businessman, meet some citizens, join the Rotary, coach a Little League team, give to charities. It was such a sweet arrangement.

Till all this.

"I want to know what the fuck went wrong," he demanded.

"It was like we just told you," Shadow said. An ice bag covered his split face, all but the hole in the middle, from which he smoked furiously.

"So tell me again. I want to hear how a broad and some wimp off the street beats the shit out of the two terrors of the northland. And then I want to hear what's your next move."

"Like I said, he just caught us is all. What else can I tell you? How the fuck was we to know he had his jujitsu license?"

" 'Cuz that's your business to know. That's what you *do*."

"No," Gleep said thoughtfully, "that wasn't no jujitsu. Dude fights like that, he learned same way we did." There was a distant croak to his voice, as though it rose from an empty well overgrown with moss and brambles.

"Let me start over," Gaylon said. "I ain't got a whole lot of interest in a postmatch round table. What I want to know is where the bitch is and how you're going to find her so's we can get to her brother and get back our goods."

Neither of them had anything to recommend.

"Well?"

Finally it was Shadow said, tiredly, for he was blurry with fatigue and his whole body was a wash of throbbing aches, "Gaylon, all's we can do is check out the hotels. We get to that tomorrow. And watch her car, up at the casino. It's a Porsche; somebody's going to come after it."

"Who's watchin' it right now?"

"We got somebody. Fella Gleep knows up there. Indian."

All this while, Gaylon had never stopped pounding the rug. Now he did. "That's your plan?" he asked.

"That's what we got," Shadow said.

"So let me total this up, see I got it right. So you got an Indian watchin' the car. And tomorrow, after church, you two are going to cruise every hotel and motel in town and up both sides of the bay, askin' "—here he did a sissified imitation of a fuddled tourist, lost his way— " 'Oh, can you help us please, we're lookin' for this lady name of Clemmons, least that's what we think is her name, maybe it's something else, and she drives this fancy Porsche car but it ain't here right now, you understand, and she's got this brother, he's a thief, and he's maybe with her but more'n likely not. You got a lady like that here, could you ask her to come down to the lobby, couple fellas here want to talk to her? No rush, tell her; after she's done shittin' and showerin'.' Meantime, nobody's lookin' for the kid, who's maybe in Zanzibar by now, all we know. And nobody's got the slightest pig-fuckin' idea where the goods are at. That's your plan? That's what I'm going to take out to Dietz?"

Shadow was getting a little sick of listening to Gaylon. More than a little. Goddam sick. Playing the goddam financial wizard, treating them like they swept out the place, couple niggers. Couldn't keep a leash on his own wife even, probably couldn't even get it airborne anymore. "You got a better one," he said, "we're waitin' to hear. Maybe you want to come along, give us a hand. Join the prowl. Might get the old juices flowin' again, uh."

Gaylon knew when to ease off. He knew Shadow, knew the look came over him, one that was probably under the ice bag right now. He should. They'd been together a long time. It was Gaylon brought him along with him, told him he'd be vice-president in charge of quantity control, haw haw, they got a laugh out of that. Done him a favor, you think about it, got him out of the city and up here where the air was clean, clean up his complexion. But Shadow could get mean, so it was only the better part of smart to know when to back off. Which was what Gaylon did now.

"All right. I'll try and keep the sweat off Dietz. But let's see we can't turn up something quick. We all of us got a nice thing runnin' here," he said reasonably, good horse-sense talk they could both understand, the Indian too, "nice easy work, plenty of loot, and more to come. What you say we pull together, this one?"

"Gonna pull that card-countin' cocksucker apart, is what we're gonna do. Limb at a time. Feed the worms."

"Absolutely," the Indian croaked.

Gaylon couldn't see Shadow's eyes but he could bet they were burning. He'd seen that before too, like there was a low-banked fire going behind them. Fucker was for sure rowin' one oar out of the water. "Okay," he said, "okay. But let's not forget about the goods, either. Okay?"

"You've been *what?*" she mumbled incredulously, drifting up out of a sluggish bog of sleep.

"Swimming," Waverly said. "Makes you feel better. Here, have this instead."

He put a Styrofoam cup of black coffee on the nightstand and pulled up a chair beside her bed. The drape was still drawn but a little light came in around the edges. It was half past ten. He had gone fifty laps, all of them a lazy sidestroke, favoring the tender shoulder. And then he had come back and cleaned up and dressed (in the bathroom, of course, discreetly) and generally knocked about the semidark room, groping for his things. As long as he had agreed to get her started on this foolhardy mission of hers, he was anxious to get to it, get it done. Get her pointed right, and then get back to his own life. After all, this was supposed to be a holiday. Something like that. Besides, it made him jumpy just sitting around. But she never once moved, lay there face down, head under a pillow, arms extended across the bed, silky hair splayed out all over the sheet, inert as a drowning victim. He did some numbers problems in his head, three- and four-digit multiplications, and then he played some phantom blackjack hands, same place. With him there was no such thing anymore as daydreaming; either his head churned or he was unconscious, one or the other and no twilights in between. Finally he tired of waiting and went downstairs and got the coffee.

"I think we ought to get started," he said.

She merely groaned.

"It's late."

"How late?"

"Late. Drink the coffee."

She was something to see even in a dim light, rolled over now in the bed and sheet drawn up to her chin, arranging her hair with one hand and with the other touching at her raw lip, pouting. This is one, he was thinking, comes without any warts at all.

"How's the mouth?"

"Feels like somebody chewed on it. How's the shoulder?"

"You don't see any sling."

"A silent sufferer, is what I think I see. Man of secret sorrows."

Waverly looked down into the muddy pool of coffee held in his hand, as if he searched for a reply there. "Let's talk about finding your brother."

"Fine. Go ahead. Tell me. Talk."

Like every one of the handful of women he had known in his life, ex-wife Annetta in particular, she was a morning grouch.

"Help me out, will you? Give me another summary."

Irritably, she repeated what had happened in the past forty-eight hours. When she was finished he lit a cigarette, offered her one; she made a face. He puffed reflectively.

"They'll be watching your car," he said, "so if you insist on getting it, the thing to do there is simply bring it into town and stay clear of it."

"And how will that be done?"

"Very easy. Hire a couple of pump-jockey types to go after it. Have them hold it at their garage or station or whatever. Give me the keys and I'll take care of that while you get ready. Then we can get to the knottier issues."

She reached her arms above her head, stretching languidly. The muscles in her face stiffened against a yawn. "You don't want to wait? Me come along?"

"Jesus, listen to me. It's going on noon already, for one. Two is, the absolute last thing you want to do is be seen. Maybe you recall there's a couple of goons would like to speak with you. Ill-mannered ones, at that."

It was a mild enough reproof, he thought, but it made her bristle. "You're not talking to a child, you know."

"I know," he said. None better did he know. More gently, he added, "But this isn't capture the flag we're playing. I wish you'd try to keep that in mind."

"Why is it I think I'm not likely to forget?"

"I'll be back. Just stay here."

The station assistant manager (which was how the name tag stitched into his spotless green coveralls identified him: Dale, Ass Man; doubtless his little joke) was not enthusiastic. He was absorbed in a stroke magazine, savoring a Dr. Pepper, and he took his time looking up when Waverly came through the door. Eventually, and with that sure and certain faith the words were being uttered for the very first time, he said, "What can I do you for, friend?"

When the proposition was outlined for him, he whined about having no help, it being Sunday and all, who'd watch the pumps and the register. And even if he did, there was no place to keep the car except over by the air hose and that might get in somebody's way. And a Porsche, he couldn't make no guarantees it would be safe, all them crazy teenagers running loose in this town. And anyways, who'd leave a Porsche overnight in an untended lot in the first place?

It was not, Waverly thought, one of your finer "As You Travel, Ask Us" moments. "Your name's Dale?" he asked.

"That's it. Dale Moon. Didn't get yours."

"You're assistant manager. Maybe have a little piece of this place?"

"I might," said Dale Moon cannily. "Why you ask?"

"Oh, I had you tagged for a businessman." He fished out two fifty-dollar bills, laid them on the counter by the cash register. Two more like this, he told him, if you'll give me a hand here.

"How about expenses for a driver? And somebody keep an eye on your car when it gets dark."

"That, too."

"Okay, you got a deal. Be later today, though, best I can do."

"That's just fine. Appreciate your entreprenurial spirit."

"Huh?"

"Fine. Oh, by the way, there might be someone in the casino lot who'll ask you some questions, or maybe someone will come here and ask. Not to worry. The questions will be easy. All you have to say is what you know, which is nothing more than this."

Dale Moon's canny expression faded into furrows of doubt. "If this Porsche's hot, I ain't interested. I don't need no grief."

"The car is squeaky clean. You'll see ID when I come in for it, a day or so. With the rest of your money."

"How do I know you'll come through?" he asked. He had already pocketed the fifties.

"Well, you'll have the keys to some pretty solid collateral, won't you?" he said, handing them over.

When Waverly got back to the room, he found her in better humor. She was standing before the dressing room mirror, delicately applying some sort of lacquer to the lids of her eyes. The clothes she wore, silk blouse, skirt that firmly clasped her flat behind, looked to him, no expert, as though they came off no rack. She greeted him with an almost peppy, "Hi, you get the car taken care of?"; never lifting her wide open gaze from the mirror, never troubling to see for certain who was there.

He looked around the room. It was not tidy. The bags he had carried in last night after checking her out of her own room covered the dresser and part of the floor. Opened, they looked something like gaping mouths. The sheets and blankets of both beds were tumbled, and hers was strewn with assorted undergarments and a nightie. A tray of half-eaten breakfast sat on the table, bacon strips chilling in congealed grease. A forgotten cigarette smoldered in an ashtray, vanishing into a stub. Paints and powders littered the bathroom counter. Altogether, it was a scene of such casual domestic intimacy, he felt a brief, vertiginous sense of rocking backward precariously through the years to the time when he was a husband, a citizen, person for whom such scenes were part of the commonplace furniture of one's life.

"Didn't your mother teach you to pick up?" he said irritably. It just spilled out unannounced. He regretted at once he'd said it, but he had developed a singular distaste for clutter, disorder.

"My mother didn't do windows," she said, still studying her reflection. "Neither do I. You've heard of maids?"

"Confusion numbs my head, is all, and we could use some uncloudy thinking here."

He brought a chair up to the table and pushed the tray aside. In a minute she joined him.

"You're not married, are you." Flat assertion, no query implied.

"No," he said.

"Never been?"

"Once."

"Let me guess the grounds for divorce. You discovered a lipstick smudge on a glass."

Waverly stroked his chin, stared at her. "Maybe you ought to find yourself another nigger. You could try the lobby. Candidates in abundance down there."

She lit a cigarette and waved it airily. "Let's be friends," she said, and she was smiling, a genuine, tooth-display smile, no grievances in it.

"Okay. Friends it is."

The way he saw it, she needed to locate this Rusty Barker, find out what he knew. Get them together and he could bow out gracefully. That would fulfill his quota of volunteer work; he hadn't signed on for the duration. Unfortunately, there was no Rusty Barker in the directory, so he made an information call and got a number, which was different from the number Clay had given her, though it was of itself no help. Is that the Barker on . . . Garfield, he asked the operator, picking a street off the listings, making his voice desperate. No, she said, naming another street. Four-oh-eight? he asked, quivery, improvising, it's urgent I get to him, an emergency; and with that innocent heartland faith in the perfectability of human nature, she gave him the address.

"I'll go out there and see what I can turn up," he said.

"This time I'm coming along."

"That's not at all prudent."

"I'll wear shades."

"A disguise? Miss Clemmons, I expect by now you know there's no way you can ever be inconspicuous."

"Nevertheless, Mr. Waverly, I'm coming."

On the way out the door, he said, "Put up the sign for the maid, would you?"

Lloyd-Granger, seeing this rather ordinary-looking fellow in his doorway, certainly no brute or hoodlum but you never could tell, was naturally suspicious and not of a temper for any more intimidation. The girl, smashing looker except for the swollen lip, wore wraparound mirrored sunglasses, and Lloyd-Granger caught a glimpse of himself in them, a distorted fun house image of a pudgy, globular dwarf. Not in the least fierce. "I warn you," he said all the same, "any trouble or any threats and the wife summons the police."

"All we need, sir, is information. Anything you might be able to tell us about Mr. Barker's or Mr. Clemmons's whereabouts would be much appreciated. You see, it's imperative we find them. We'd be in your debt."

Lloyd-Granger produced a disdainful snort. "Debt, is it. Like your friends honor debts? Well, I say to you the same as I said to my wife: no more. This is Traverse City, after all."

"Friends?" Waverly said. "Two gentlemen, one of them on the large side? Neither very polite?" Of course it figured they would have been here, which meant they already knew everything he might learn, if indeed he was lucky enough to get anything at all from this British bulldog with the silver-jacketed teeth and the dragonslayer breath, and which also meant that even if he did, it was not likely to be very much.

"I'm sure you know them better than I," Lloyd-Granger said bitterly.

"Look, all we want from you—" Holly started to say, but Waverly cut her off with a stop-signal hand.

"You're from England aren't you, sir?"

"I am."

"Nobody knows Clay," she said, needle-edged voice. "And he's a half-brother, remember?"

The nice distinction, its point, the distancing, escaped him. He ignored it. "He gave you no idea where he is?"

"Only what I've already told you."

"And he said nothing about contacting you?"

"I've told you everything he said. Twice now."

"Then maybe it's time to tell your father. That is, if you're still unwilling to call in the police."

"You don't listen very well, do you. I can't do either of those things."

Waverly set the beer mug on the table. He lit another cigarette. Since he'd stumbled into her life, he'd given up trying to keep count of them. He took a long deep inhale. His lungs felt as if they'd been scored with ground glass.

"You know the old chestnut, the fellow with a banana in his ear? Guy comes up to him and says, 'Sir, you know you have a banana in your ear?' He says, 'Sorry, I can't hear you, I've got a banana in my ear.'" She got off half an annoyance gesture but he kept right on. "Wait a minute, there's a moral coming. I take the banana out of my ear and I don't hear anything different from when it's in. Same old dirge. Dirge is accurate, happy choice. Wait. I'll take out the banana but what you need to do is take the gauze off your eyes and squint around a little. You notice how both the people connected with your brother—okay, half—seem to have caught the early bus? You notice his landlord wasn't too keen on pitching in for improved Anglo-American relations? You notice any of that? Hold on, there's more. You remember those two truant officers last night? Felt your lip lately?" Instinctively, she laid a hand over her mouth. "What I'm saying, Miss Clemmons, is that all these things, added up, strike me, a layman at this game, as signals of serious trouble. Not for amateurs."

She said nothing for a moment, studied the expiring froth in her drink. Finally, she gave him a meager smile and said, "You have permission to call me Holly, you know."

"The message is still the same."

"You don't seem amateurish to me."

"At this, I'm an amateur." He was resolved to back-step out of this deepening swamp. On the subject of survival, at least, he was a long way from novice. There, his training had been most expert.

"I'd like you to know something about Clay," she said. "Order us another drink, will you?"

"I don't think that's very smart."

"Order anyway. I'm buying."

What he heard, predictably, was the saga of the poor little rich boy: in and out of trouble as a youth, more in than out; shuttled from one private school to the next and invited to depart from every one of them; a Northwestern flunk-out, hanging on now by a thread and a winning smile at DuPage Community College; an ongoing nagging migraine for Daddy, vast disappointment. Familiar stuff, but with one striking variation that made it more lurid. When he was five, Clay's mother (a neurotic bitch but still his mother) killed herself, and it was the five-year-old who found her in a bathtub spilling over with blood. And it was Holly who found him, hunkered down beside the tub, not weeping at all or whimpering but batting the air as though he were assailed by a swarm of unseen insects. Fifteen years of psychotherapy had covered the scar, thought Holly, but never erased it. Grown-up, Clay was a magician, used his dazzling looks and reckless charm to seize whatever he wanted, or thought he wanted at the time, later didn't want after all. It was her notion the periodic tremors that convulsed his life were his way of getting back at Daddy (whom he blamed but who was, of course, guiltless even though he had remarried eight weeks after the suicide and divorced again eight months after that), the only way he knew. She was twenty-eight, seven years older than Clay. Her own mother, another harpy, had long since vanished into other marriages, and all her disrupted life she'd stood between father and son: arbiter; peace-keeper; surrogate mother, of sorts, to one, message-bearer to the other; softener of bad tidings. It hadn't been easy; she had logged her share of shrink time, too. So maybe he could see why she had to handle this herself, as quietly as possible. And why she required his help.

It was a sorry tale, resonant with peculiar skewed echoes rising unwelcome off the horizon of his own past. But he had long ago mastered the art of silencing them, and he said, not unkindly, "That's an unfortunate story you tell, and you have my sympathies. But I don't see how it changes anything."

"Your mind, maybe? Give me another day or so?"

The wise counsel of Bennie Epstein flashed through his head. Then he looked at Holly Clemmons, a study in contrasting light and darkness framed in a wall of gold by slanted shafts of a late-afternoon sun, gazing evenly at him, and in a fingersnap it was gone.

"If your brother, by half, recommended the Park Place to you, then he must think you're there. If he calls, they'll tell him no, but he may believe you've done what he should have told you to do, registered under another name. Once he's aware of the glitch with his buddy, he might just be desperate enough—dumb enough—to come looking. You can't be seen, but I could hang out downstairs, watch for him. Hope to hell I see him before anyone else does. It isn't much. Best I can do."

"You see why I need your help?"

"Oh, yeah. Who's more clever than I."

"When will we start?"

"As soon as you pay for these drinks."

* * *

Shadow was wearing shades too, though they didn't do much to distract attention from his punished face. Gleep had on a turtleneck that covered most, not all, of the scrapes and gouges in his throat. It was still painful to swallow or speak, so he had even less to say than usual. That was all right with Shadow, who was having trouble enough keeping his mind off bloody visions of revenge. Along those lines he prided himself on his invention, and at that moment (which was middle of the afternoon, Sunday, the earliest either of them felt like getting started) he was wondering what would happen, you stick a guy's head in a microwave oven, turn it up on high, what that would do.

They were cruising aimlessly, considering how best to conduct the search, where exactly to begin. It was Shadow's idea she would naturally gravitate to the expensive hotels, rich cunt like that. Gleep didn't agree. He figured she was probably shrewd enough to hide out at some sleep-cheap. So they tried a few of both varieties, with equal unsuccess at either. Don't help none, Shadow complained bitterly, way we look, try to get any buzz out of them fuckin' nose-in-the-air desk clerks, got to say please, can't elbow nobody, use some muscle. Fuckin' Ledbetter, he ought to try it.

After awhile they simply gave up. I was right the other night, Shadow said, take from now till Moses to find her this way. He decided they should go over to Shimmers, have a beer, talk to Ladonna again. He didn't expect much but he wouldn't mind another peek at them titties, even though he wasn't too happy about her seeing him with his face busted in, didn't do nothing for his image. He was, in fact, so concerned over it, he kept his shoulders hunched and his eyes on the floor when they walked into the lobby. Had he looked up, he might have seen a pair of familiar figures, their backs to him, leaving unhurriedly by an opposite exit.

When they discovered Ladonna was no longer among the ranks of the slave girls, they were, as Shadow put it, deadfuckinended. Secretly he was relieved a little about her, but baffled where to turn next.

"We could stop in her place," Gleep suggested, trying to help out. He was having a pop, easier on the ragged pipes.

"Nah, I don't think so," Shadow deliberated, more to himself than his partner. "Could be heat over there, they found the football star with his hurt pinkies. Anyways, even if she's home, which she probably ain't these days, she probably don't know no more'n what we already got, the talking we gave her. I don't think so."

"Maybe we should see if Elmo's got something."

Shadow couldn't really believe she'd be dumb enough to go after the car even if it was a goddam Porsche, but he was out of ideas. "Might as well," he said listlessly and polished off the remainder of his beer.

His enthusiasm picked up some once they found Elmo at the casino and learned a couple dudes actually come out and got the car, about an hour back. He'd tried to call Gleep but didn't get no answer, and he'd had to go to work right after. Shadow was annoyed the numbnuts Indian hadn't stepped on them, made 'em sit still awhile. Never could count on an Indian, left their brains in the tepee; except Gleep, 'course, and he wasn't lightning-quick in the upstairs department, either. But he felt better when Elmo told them he got the name of the station they worked out of. Also, he found out it was a guy paid them to come get the car, not a broad. So Shadow could figure chances were good he was still hanging with it, Mr. Wormfood himself, going to keep on playing hero for the helpless lady awhile, and that made him happier yet. Made him feel real pumped. Real good. Heat up the old microwave and sharpen the shank—here comes Shadow. He gave Elmo a little toke for his trouble, and on the drive back into town he said, "Gleep, my man, I think maybe we're startin' to tool again."

"Absolutely."

So it was a natural letdown when the best they could get from Dale Moon was a description of the fellow hired him to send the kids out for the Porsche and not a squeezed ounce more, not his name, where he was at, nothing, even after they trotted him into the john out back (fucking filthy place too, Shadow noticed, with the paint peeling and crumpled towels all over the damp floor and the crapper going in a permanent flush, bubbling up turds and soggy cigarette butts, though that part was okay for their purposes) and treated him first to an extended chocolate swirly and then brought him up for air so Gleep could administer a little tune-up, come close to snapping an arm.

"I'm gonna leave you some instructions, Mr. Moon," Shadow said. "You payin' attention?"

Dale Moon, lying on the floor with his head supported by the stool, crumpled as one of the discarded paper towels, face streaked with a colorful blend of shit and blood, spluttered between moans something that affirmed he was.

"Okay. Now, next time this fella comes in after the car—or anybody, don't matter who it is—you're gonna say, 'Oh, gee, sorry, your car needs a little fixin', some wires under the hood, they come loose.' Or maybe you say, 'Lookit there, your tire's gone flat.' Or might be you lost the keys. Anything like that. You'll think of something. Man with a name like Moon, spade name, he's bound to have a real quick imagination.

"So anyway, while you're fiddlin' with the car, you're real friendly, way all you grease guns just naturally are, ask their names, whereabouts they're stayin', how they like Traverse City. Things like that. Oh, I forgot. Before you start gettin' your hands dirty, you remember you got to take a leak or something, and you come inside and call this number I'm gonna leave you. Ask for Mr. Little Feather, he's this gentleman here you met already. We ain't there, you leave a message. Say it's real urgent. Say your name. Then you go back to work, nice and slow, find out all that stuff I just said. You think you got all that now?"

Dale Moon blubbered that he did.

"That's real good, Mr. Moon. We 'preciate it. I know we can count on you too, because next time we stop by, something even worse'n bobbin' for turds might happen. Why, we might just have to make you clean up this hog heaven you got here, and ain't nothin' could be worse'n that."

As they pulled away from the station, Gleep said to his partner, "You sure got some way with the words." Genuine admiration.

But Shadow was not to be cheered. This *coitus interruptus* of the spirit drained all the natural zest he took in his work right out of him. Nothing to do now but try some more motels, keep Ledbetter off their backs awhile, even though he figured it was worse than useless. He felt like a lump of sour owl shit, was how he felt. "Y'know, Gleep," he said despondently, "there's some days a man's got to wonder if his whole life's just one long fart in the wind."

"Let me see, now, if I follow what it is you're telling me, Gaylon."

Dietz was sitting in a big square-sided, high-backed chair, square arms on it, looked like a goddam throne. There was an ottoman in front, but he didn't have his feet up. He sat kind of stiff, shoulders back and knees together, old-maid virgin style. One hand stroked the cow-catcher jaw, the other played with a silver ball-point pen he used as a pointer sometimes (like now) when he spoke. On the floor over in a corner, Oona was doing her nails, painting them hot pink. And Gaylon, he was in an overstuffed chair that was cushy enough but a little small, could hardly get your butt adjusted in it, and was two feet lower than the throne at least. Closer to eye level with the slant-eye twat than with Dietz.

They were in the room Dietz called the library. Two whole walls full of books on floor-to-ceiling built-in shelves, and a rolltop desk, and a globe with those bumps on it to show where the mountain ranges were. Brace of windows let in the morning sun. Some longhair music coming from someplace else in the house. Gaylon had to give the sonbitch credit: He had the real class.

"You had the lady," Dietz was trying to get out, "but you lost her. Some way or other." Gaylon was about to supply a clarification, but Dietz stayed him with the point of the pen. "Let me finish, Gaylon. I like to get things focused in my mind. Some fellow just happens along. What you might call an innocent bystander. Takes out your people. Rescues the lady. Leaves us, if I've got it correct, with a handful of . . . of . . ."

Try shit, Gaylon wanted to tell him. The word is *shit*.

". . . air. No lady. And consequently, no pilferer. And, therefore, no goods. Is that an accurate appraisal, Gaylon? Of the situation?"

Gaylon tried to tug the fold of his pants out of his crotch without it being too noticeable. "Mr. Dietz, it's like I said, last night we got a line on her car. And the last place she was at. Hawkins and Skaggs are checking all the hotels today. Matter time till we collect her. Then the kid and then the goods. How long's anybody going to stay down, town this size."

He had to give that one some deep thought, like it

was a real question Gaylon expected an answer to. "Well," he said eventually, "it's been thirty-six hours now. Thereabouts. On the lady. And the goods? How long has that been? A week?"

Gaylon was thinking, I ever get out of this with my nuts still hangin', I'm gonna get me a place in one of them retirement villages down south, Sun City, and play shuffleboard and dominoes all day and hump widows all night, that's about what I got left in me. If that. Jesus, his piles pained him. He'd like to itch 'em with a rake. "Not quite a week," he said feebly.

"Gaylon, it's Monday morning. I hoped for better news today."

Gaylon didn't know what to say to that, so he tried nothing. He studied the patterns in the carpet at his feet. Then his eyes drifted over to the Jap on the floor, buffing away like it was diamonds she polished. He thought he caught a trace of a smile on her lips, but he couldn't tell for sure.

"Gaylon?"

"Yessir."

"You remember that book I mentioned to you? The one on exceptions?"

"I remember you sayin' something about it," he said, neutral as he could. Probably a goddam quiz on it coming next.

"Well, we've got a serious exception here. Whenever they come up, what it advised—the book, I mean—was a careful review. Of the plan. Find out how to get back on course. What do you think of that idea, Gaylon?"

Idea sucks, was what he thought of it. He'd had a bellyfuckinfull of review already, but he said, "That's got to be the ticket. Get right down to business." Even to him the words sounded dumb.

Dietz just stared at him. Nibbled on the stem of the pen and let a protracted silence hang in the air. At last he said, "Good. Suppose we review. Maybe go back and see if we can't discover the root of the exception. You know where I think it is?"

Now is when it really comes, Gaylon thought. He figured you could lay odds on who it is gets to be the root. He braced himself. Turned out he was wrong, and not a bit unhappy about the error, either.

"I think it's the man who stepped in and saved the lady," Dietz said.

Way he said it, dragged it out longer even than usual, if that was possible, sounded like one of them mystery movies where when the main dude gets it finally solved and reveals who the murderer is. And it wasn't him. Gaylon's heart clubbed in his chest, he was that relieved. "That's the one, all right," he said excitedly. "He didn't go gunnin' in where he's got no business, we'd have our goods back by now. Everything runnin' smooth as the —" He was going to say skin on the head of your nozzle but he thought that might not be such a good idea and substituted glass.

Dietz nodded sagely. "That's right on the mark, Gaylon. Now, you said he's still in the picture. Is that correct?"

"That's how it looks."

"So if you find him, then, you'll find her. And our goods you lost. Didn't I hear you say your people identified him some way?"

"What they said was the guy was tagged for a counter. Up at the Indians' place."

"A counter of cards." Dietz said it like he was trying to puzzle out what the words meant. "There can't be many people can do that. So isn't it possible there might be a sheet on him? Out west, say? Or Atlantic City?"

"Jacket on him, you mean? Track him that way?" Gaylon felt the blood pounding in his temples. Rush of vigor. Renewed hope. Of course, he was kicking his own ass for not thinking of it, first place; but maybe he was going to oil out of this one yet. "That's a sensational idea, Mr. Dietz. The Indians for sure got a description on him. Picture even, maybe."

"We have associates, both places. Friends. They should be willing to help out. If I were you, I'd be making some fast phone calls."

"I'm on it right now," Gaylon said and started to haul himself up out of the chair, but Dietz was gun-sighting him with the pen, and he stopped midway, half on his feet, half in an awkward crouch.

"One other thing, Gaylon. I can't be away from Chicago too long. There's the business. And the wife, she worries. You understand how that is. So I'm going to count on you clearing this matter up. Soon. The clock's running, Gaylon."

Over the course of the weekend there was another person who wrestled with a serious exception to his plan. On Saturday Clay tried phoning Ladonna's apartment again, several times, but the results were always the same. Of course, he had to wait till night to make the calls, till all the seedy bargain hunters had cleared out and the last tacky clerk slipped on his polyester jacket and went home, for he spent the entire day hiding in the storage room. By that time he was just about ready to hang it up, get Ledbetter's goods back to him somehow, arrange some kind of truce and beat the proverbial fucking hasty retreat. Close to fourteen solid hours in that rat's den, not a window in it, gritty cement-block walls, moldy second-hand sofas and chairs that looked like if you'd touch them, they'd start oozing hair oil, spiders big as your thumb sprinting across the floor, sour stink of your own piss rising from the drain—might as well be in jail as here, half a mil in the bag beside him or not, didn't matter much.

But then after closing, the girl came around and brought a cold sixer and a box of Kentucky Fried, which normally he'd feed to the dog but which now tasted just fine. He took it out to the showroom floor where it was at least semitolerable, and after he was finished eating, he had her give him head, which along with the beer relaxed him enough he could sleep soundly through the night.

On Sunday he woke feeling a little better. The place was closed for business so he didn't have another day in the snake pit ahead, a prospect he wasn't absolutely certain he could endure. But it was early and there was time to sort things out and fit them back together again. Plenty of time. He called the apartment again and no one answered and that made him really uneasy, nobody home this hour of the day, not Ladonna even; didn't calculate at all, and it made him worse than uneasy, twitchy almost. So he paced around trying to do some tight thinking, but he soon found his eyes straying over the gaudy godawful furniture belonged in the house of a middle-class coon, and his mind sliding away from the issues at hand—plenteous enough—and into a fearsome make-believe world where he was one of those grim change-counters come to outfit a two-bedroom ranch or a rented double-wide for $849.99, three rooms complete, a knocked-up wife in tow and a squalling kid (for this was the sort of scene he had observed the day before, peeking through a crack in the storage room door), and wondering what it would be like to have to live in that world. And delighted he would never know.

The girl came by after church and left him enough food for a couple of days, said she had to go on a family picnic and might not be back till tomorrow night. She hung around for an hour or so and he was glad to have the company, even if it had to be her. To demonstrate his gratitude, he got her off by hand, didn't feel up to anything more vigorous. She had also brought along a portable cassette player with the earphones and a stack of Springsteen tapes, so after she was gone he settled onto a Naugahyde couch with foam-rubber cushions and wired up and tuned in The Boss, whom he dearly loved: "Badlands," "Cover Me," "Nebraska," "Born to Run," "Jungleland," you name it, he loved them all. Listening to "Bobbie Jean" could even moisten his eyes a little. The driving beat and mounting caterwaul voice stiffened him up again, made him feel sinewy, confident. Crystallized his extravagant dreams. He could picture himself out east, this dust-speck town well behind him, mingling in the inner circles of Rock. In this vision, Midnight was along too, worshipful and protective as always, watching admiringly as he spread the money around, every bit of it his own, not another penny doled out in microallowances from the closefisted old man, gave it up like he was laying alms on a beggar. Getting tight with the real movers and shakers of that spangly world, maybe even with The Boss himself. Why not? A guy like he was, looked and spoke and strutted the way he did, anything was possible. So long as he had the money, which he most surely did, or its readily convertible equivalent, right here in his lap. Made him wonder how he had ever entertained the notion of giving it back to that bulldog-faced sack of shit, Ledbetter.

Later in the afternoon he dragged a couch over by the stacked columns of televisions and switched one on and watched a baseball game. He dozed through the later innings but that was okay, helped pass a few of the long hours. But when he woke, it was already dark and it came back to him none of the problems had gone away. He began to fret over what the fuck to do. Had to do something, and before soon. Day like this one, he could manage, but he couldn't stay here forever, especially with the tomb of a storage room waiting just down the hall and around the corner.

TOM KAKONIS

By now it was reasonable to assume something not so good might have happened to Rusty. Which probably served him right, but that was beside the point. He had tried not to think too much about Midnight—she was always supercapable when it came to bailing him out—but he couldn't escape altogether the nagging concern that something could have happened to her, too. And if it had, that didn't make it any easier for him. In fact, it ran him right out to the end of the pier. He figured he'd better think about her, and after he did for a while, he corked up his nerve and dialed the Park Place. They had nobody by that name registered, so he described her and sure enough, the woman on the other end of the phone remembered a guest looked like the lady he said, but she had checked out a night or so back, left no messages. She remembered because there had been some other people asking after her today, couple of ex*treme*ly rude men who she didn't mind saying needed some lessons in manners, and if he was one of them or knew who they were, he could tell them that, and they could all of them just quit bothering her; this was the Park Place after all and not a missing-persons bureau, and this was a busy line.

Clay suggested she try pissing up a rope, and slammed down the phone. Where the fuck could she be, if not at the hotel? She wouldn't have gone home, abandoned him; he knew her better than that. What he didn't know was where to turn next, what to do. Without her help, how was he going to get clear of this town? Whereas before he had been concerned, maybe even a bit worried but only mildly—more irritated and impatient than worried, for his life had been one long succession of zany scrapes and doubtful crises, all of them with patented happy endings—now he felt an accelerating fear not that far from panic, the closest he had ever come to the experience of dread.

THREE

BY MONDAY NIGHT WAVERLY WAS NOT IN THE best of humors, but then neither was she. Sunday night he anchored a stool in the Park Place Lounge till closing (which was early), drinking more beer (which he decided, on reflection, he didn't much care for in the first place) and watching the lobby for any sign of the elusive brother (by half). After the bartender (same lighter-than-air kid, feet never brushed the ground, asked him how he did at the casino and he made a so-so gesture with the flat of his hand) announced last call, he took a chair in a dark and secluded corner of the lobby and watched some more, both entrances, front and side. He was doing all he could to keep down. No more surprises, those two happiness boys. A few people wandered by, none of them even faintly resembling Clay Clemmons. About 1 A.M. three drunken couples came lurching through the door, whooping ostentatiously about cards and dice and god-dam Indians, and dropping the word Vegas more than was really necessary. Once they were gone, everything fell silent. By two he'd smoked the last cigarette in the pack (second that day? third?) and he gave it up for the night.

He found the room dark, Holly sleeping, and the television on. As quietly as he could, he removed her litter and slipped into his bed and watched the screen awhile. A frenzied preacher with one of those stagy, deep-south drawls enjoined an audience burning with god lust to let Jee-Zus into their hearts and lives. They seemed eager to oblige. It was during the catalogued definition of sin (which seemed to include just about every thought and action known to humankind), Waverly fell into a beery, restless sleep.

When he woke the screen displayed a cheery morning hostess earnestly interrogating a guest on some happy problem. He got out of bed and switched off the set. He felt groggy, juiceless, and considered trying to sleep some more but knew it was out of the question. Holly was stirring, but only slightly, when he came out of the bathroom showered and dressed and feeling a little better, not much.

"Waverly?" she mumbled, her head half-buried by the pillow. "That you? Anything happening?"

He took a moment to regard the nature of women, their essential vacant carelessness, before replying. "Nothing. You may as well go back to sleep."

"Clay? You see him yet?"

"Not yet."

"What time is it?"

"Early."

She rolled over and ground at her eyes. The black hair tangled in the sheets; strands of it coiled her neck like a noose. "Umm. Where you going?"

"Where am I going? Downstairs. To watch for your brother. That's the plan, you might recall. What there is of it."

"God, you're a morning treat."

It was easier to say nothing to that, and so he did.

"You're wasting your time, you know. This hour. Clay's a night prowler."

"That may be. But trouble—the kind he's in—can shake your deepest habits." And who knows better than I, he thought, though by all appearances the notion was lost on her. "You have any other ideas, I'm open."

"You want me to take a turn? I can. If I ever come to."

Waverly shook his head slowly. "Don't you understand yet? Feel your lip again. If it could speak for itself, it would tell you to stay out of sight."

"I guess that means no. Right?"

"That's what it means."

"What am I supposed to do in this seedy room all morning? I'm awake now."

"You got me. Try the television. There's a lady on there talking about animal rights. Very instructive." He moved toward the door, but on the way out he turned and added, "Make that all *day*, by the way."

The morning passed. He spent some time in the coffee shop, at a back table with a narrow view of the lobby and a ready escape route through the kitchen. Nothing happened, no one appeared. At midday he took a break, and discovered Holly in a string bikini, sunning herself on the deck. She advised him to fuck off when he warned her once again of the risk of being seen. The room was in such god-awful disarray, he didn't stay long. Also it made him curiously uneasy, unsettled, her on the other side of the glass slider, exposed to all the State Street traffic, next to naked. He cornered a maid at the end of the hall and offered her five bucks to clean up the room right now. Maid accepted with a sly wink. Probably hoping to find a fresh trail of pecker tracks.

The afternoon passed. Same story. The lounge was open, so he sat there nursing ginger ale and wondering what had happened—what had he allowed to happen? —to this ill-conceived holiday, what he was doing here anyway, where his caution and reason had departed to.

But you could only nurse a glass so long before it was refilled, and by late in the day he felt like an overinflated balloon; take a leak and he feared he might go flying crazily across the ceiling. A hearty old boy came into the bar and took a stool near him. Tried to start up a conversation, asked where he was from. South Dakota, Waverly said, and that slowed the talk some but didn't arrest it altogether. He tried jokes next: you hear the one about . . . Waverly said he had. That took care of things.

Outside of Chop and maybe a few hard cases he remembered from Jackson and a few unredeemable psychos at Ypsi (and they didn't count), no one had more experience at looping time than he. Chop had taught him how to do hole time. Easy. Just blow on your hands. Don't eat. That always infuriates them, come and find the crusts of white bread untouched and the every-other-day slop uneaten. Never panic. So it's dark, so what? You afraid of the dark? So your world is nine by six. Your head can take you anywhere you want to go. Start with a scene from the past, any one, brief, and reconstruct it right down to the last final exact detail—it's all up there—every sense engaged; do it in color, capture every hue, shade; if there's food, taste it again, smell it; if there's flesh, feel it; hear the voices, listen for every intonation, savor even the pauses and silences. Hold it all in focus. Do that first. When that pales—and it will—do a thousand pushups, famished or not. What do you want with food? After three days the sight of it will make you retch. You say you can do chess games in your head? Play a few. Then try numbers. Pure abstraction. Start with simple ones if you have to, single digits. Work on up. Never leave a problem undone; start over if necessary. Then do a thousand situps. And then, only then, lie down on your back, not to sleep but to turn in on yourself, find the center of light in there, you'll see it, it's there, a distant speck, yellow, burnished. Fold yourself around it. Do all that and you're impenetrable, invisible. No one will ever get to you again, ever.

Nineteen years in Jackson made a mystic of Chop, and his formula was right, of course. Worked every time. But Waverly was out of practice, and for reasons he couldn't determine, even the numbers came hard today. By nine o'clock he'd had enough. He found a kid in a Park Place uniform and gave him Clay's description and his own room number and a twenty-dollar bill, and asked him to keep an eye out. The kid paid scant attention, but stuffed the money in his pocket and said he would. Holly was more right than she knew: This was indeed a waste of time, morning or night.

She was sitting on the bed, both pillows propped behind her, sipping a drink. On the nightstand were two empty glasses. The television was on but the sound was turned down, inaudible, and the actors played out some high drama in dumb show. The slider was partly open but the air was still clotted with smoke.

"Mike Hammer returns," she said.

"Empty-handed. And stiff backside."

"Seems to me I mentioned something like that. Now is when you ought to be down there."

"Yeah, well, I never was a good listener."

"I've noticed that."

She had on jeans and a halter about the width of a ribbon. Not that there was much to cover. Her stomach was flat, almost concave, and the skin was just slightly pink from the feeble northern sun. Her feet were bare, the toenails done in a shimmery aquamarine.

Waverly took a chair by the table. Both beds were made, but if the room had ever been cleaned, it had lapsed back into chaos, her things everywhere. He was past car-ing. He smoked. It was too late to do anything about the air in here anyway. "You enjoying the entertainment?" he asked.

"With television, it's the only way to go."

"There you may be right," he said. One thing they could agree on.

"Sure I am. Look at them. You want to see how acting isn't done? All that mugging, popping eyeballs. Mediterranean gestures. Makes me want to gag." She took a healthy swallow, as if to repress any such impulse.

"I didn't know you counted film criticism among your accomplishments."

"Lots you don't know. Give me one of those cigarettes, will you. I'm out. And in this lockup they're not easy to come by. When you want one."

He tossed over the pack. "Keep it. I've got plenty."

Her ritual of extracting one, getting it lit, exhaling two urgent shafts of smoke through the nostrils—all of it reminded him of a piece of stage business designed to convey testiness. Very broad, very amateurish, like the images flickering silently across the screen. Yet it seemed to loosen her some, for she said, a little less irritably, "You smoke too much. You know that?"

"Well, my thought is, it takes courage to smoke nowadays, all the evidence that's in. But you're right. I'm going to quit. Tomorrow, or by kickoff Saturday."

"You're a shithead, Waverly."

"Lovable one though."

"You think I couldn't know anything about acting. Do you know I went to Northwestern's Drama School? It's probably the best one in the country, for your information."

"You got me wrong. I think you'd be a sensational actress. In the exotic tradition. You ever see Maria Montez, the late show? That's what I mean, exotic."

"You may want to take time out and go fuck yourself."

"There's a notion. Drama school, huh. So tell me, how's the career going?"

"Career," she said, dispatching bitterness through elongated syllables. "I've got a half-brother who's a full-time career."

"Any parts?"

"A few. Little theater. Some local commercials."

"Are you married?"

She gave him a look of artful, fallen wisdom. She reached for her glass, drained it. Drew on the cigarette. Nice bit of pacing. Early Lauren Bacall. "Why do you ask? Looking to hit on me? Assault the bed?"

"You asked me."

"So I did. Well, you don't see any ring."

"What would that prove? Either way."

She picked up the phone and dialed some numbers. "I'm going to have another drink. You?" He brushed the air negatively and she shrugged. Around the recitation of her order, she said, "Answer is no, by the way. Once, like you, but not anymore. No, that's not right, not like you. Mine didn't break up over dust on the underside of a chair."

"Over what, then? Certainly not your sweet nature."

She replaced the phone and smiled at him, close-lipped. "No, it wasn't *my* nature, as you put it. It was more in the nature of an experiment. An escape, I suppose, freedom flight that never got off the ground. He was an attorney, my father's firm. Very ambitious. Very sober. Very, very dull. You understand dull? I doubt it. It's like trying to take a picture of the sour odor of a sewage plant. Impossible to get an image, even though you know it's there." At the corner of her mouth the smile curled slightly. Her eyes measured him. "Maybe you would know, dull, someone like you."

It was time to back away. He was not a skilled bickerer, didn't understand the tactics, never mind the larger strategies. Not much at conversation anymore either, except with himself. Silence opened between them. On the television a car chase (interrupted by a matronly looking woman who appeared to be singing about mayonnaise) was in progress. The camera panned in on one of the drivers, a meat-faced thug who, an instant before his car slammed into a wall, mimed the expression of terror. Both of them watched intently, as though a grand pageant unfolded. At the knock on the door, he stood up and got the drink and took it to her. She murmured thanks.

After awhile she said, "I've been in this room too long. Makes me jumpy."

As nearly as he could tell, it was intended as an apology. Her "too long" translated into something under thirty hours, but he didn't remark on that.

"We might as well talk," she said.

"No reason not."

"Why don't you tell me what you do. But don't say insurance or anything like that. I've been watching you."

Waverly got out his card and handed it over. It evoked only the customary blank look.

"Very impressive," she said finally, "but what does it mean? Are you in computers or something?"

"Only in my head."

She let the card fall. "So don't tell. I've never been much on Twenty Questions."

This was one wire-strung female. Pettish. Yet for no sound reason he could account for, he discovered he wanted to tell her. Some small part, anyway. "I play certain selected games for a living. With cards."

She clapped her hands in a counterfeit show of awe. "A gambling man! Just like in the song. How intriguing. Romantic. But where's your black coat and string tie? And green eyeshade—isn't that what they wear?"

Waverly opened his hands. "You asked."

"Why is it I get the sensation of—you'll pardon the expression—my leg being pulled?"

"Maybe you're just short on faith."

"Or long on experience. Come on, Mr. Timothy Waverly—nice melody to it, incidentally, your name, I mean; you don't talk like any professional gambler, however they're supposed to talk and if there is such a thing. Outside the movies. Your eyes aren't steely enough, either."

"Would it help if I sprinkled my conversation with the vernacular, used a lot of words like sandbagging, blind ante, seven-out, dead man's hand? Sound more authentic? Pregnant with meaning? I can if you like."

"Okay. You get to be a gambler if you want, if it keeps you happy. And I get to be an actress. What about that M.A. on your tarot card, though? Is that real?"

"Real as those framed wall hangings can ever be. Which is to say about as real and substantial as fairy gold. Add an unfinished dissertation and you'd be calling me doctor. Anglo-Saxon literature. You want to ask me something about Grendel?"

"I might if I knew who he is."

"You've already met. He's the one touched up your lip."

Waverly got to his feet. He was irked at himself, opening up this way. In all human relationships, candor is the mother of all error. Must of been Chop said that. Another lesson forgotten. "Maybe you'll excuse me now," he said.

"Where you going? Not walking away, are you? Mr. Gambling Man."

"No."

"Well, spare me the mystery. Where? Back downstairs?"

"The lobby's covered. For whatever that's worth. I'm going swimming."

"Swimming? You can't, the pool's closed."

"Want to bet I find a way? Five'll get you eight."

He swam in the dark, a smooth even crawl down the length of the pool, graceful somersaulting turns, long blissful glides: Icarus in another element. Sometimes he rolled over on his back and, still stroking, gazed at the spiderweb pattern of the dome, its perfect geometry, brushed in streaks of moonlight. His shoulder still ached, but not enough to distract him. He neglected counting laps altogether.

Had he been watching, he might have seen a lithe figure slip through the blackened entrance, tiptoe across the concrete deck, disrobe, and ease silently into the water at the shallow end of the pool. And had he been thinking, he would have known at once who it was that slid alongside him when he arrived at that end, coiled herself around him, and, in a dizzy inversion of the myth, brought him spinning out of the sea and into a boundless sky.

Later, in the room, both of them exhausted but struggling against sleep, limbs twined, but limply, as though from the aftershock of a violent collision, he said, "I didn't exactly intend—no, I suppose that's not really true."

"I was beginning to wonder about you, Waverly. Afraid you might be gay."

And while holding this body, long as his own, leaner by far, beneath the velvet flesh almost sinewy to the touch, he experienced a succession of flash images out of his not-so-distant past, unwelcome. He said nothing.

"Proves how wrong you can be." And then, sinking finally into a benevolent sleep, she murmured, "There's a few people, ones I know well, call me Midnight. You can too, if you like."

"Y'know, Gleep, it's funny how a guy's name can kind of tag him, like. Aim him the way he's gonna go."

114

"Never thought about that one," Gleep said. He wasn't sure he understood what his partner was talking about, but he figured he was going to find out soon enough.

"Take that asshole Moon, for instance. Name's Moon, right? You notice he's got a face on him about as round as the real moon? Skin on it's yellow, too, like a gook. You notice that?"

The example of the hapless Dale Moon came readily to Shadow, for they had just paid another visit to the station, a last stop on the day's desultory and profitless search. Since they'd discovered the Clemmons bitch had skipped the Park Place, the trail had chilled. None of the few motels they tried had any help to offer, so it was his idea to run another check on the car. Couldn't hurt, and at least it made him feel like he was working, maybe getting closer to that douche bag rearranged his face, which was all he really cared about at the moment. Old Moon, he about soiled his drawers, he saw them coming through the door. Started sniveling how nobody's been around yet—I'll get right to you if they do—you can count on me—no more trouble. . . . It was a howl, watching him, but it made you almost puke too, see a man be a marshmallow like that. Except as *re*inforcement, like Ledbetter would say, it was a waste of time, too. Whole fucking day was. Prolonged dejection (and this had lasted a good twenty-four hours now) had a way of turning Shadow inward, sparking gloomy ruminations on the nature of fate.

"He was just standin' under a light bulb is all," Gleep said.

"No, it's yellow all right, you get up close. Which figures, for a chickenfucker like him."

"So what do you mean? About his name?"

"What I mean is—" Shadow broke off, groping with the concept. "Look, he ain't a good case. Let me give you another one. I knew this fella in Cicero once, wop.

Name's Sal Martini. Martini, right? Now where do you 'spose he worked? Bar, where else. Time he was thirty, he was a lush, too."

Gleep looked unconvinced. "You're sayin' a dude's name makes him do things? That don't make no sense."

Even though his theory was ill-formed yet and came to him unbidden, it was his, and he had a proprietary interest in it. Snappishly, he said, "I ain't necessarily sayin' that. All I'm sayin' is there's a connection. Like the name slapped on a kid when he's born, it maybe gets him pointed a certain way. That's all I'm sayin'."

But having said it, he pondered a moment his own name, Skaggs, and as he did, a hand went involuntarily to his face, and beneath the fresh contusions, he felt the permanent craters of his acne; and he remembered as a youth gazing into a mirror in baffled awe and dismay and helpless rage at the appalling erupted reflection gazing back at him.

"Sure," Gleep said, "that's why you got your nicknames. Everybody knows that."

Shadow set his glass on the bar. He wondered why he even bothered sometimes. Talking to Gleep could be like talking to your goddam dog, if you had one.

"Nicknames come after, f'Chris' sake. You *earn* them. I'm sayin' the name you're stuck with. Y'understand the difference?"

"Yeah, I get it."

Gleep didn't really give a rat's ass, he thought about it, but he figured it didn't do no harm to jolly him along. His partner was still way down, but not half as bad as yesterday. Yesterday he was lower'n whale shit. Tonight, to help bring him around some, it was Gleep's idea they stop over here at the U and I Lounge and do in some time, have a beer or two, eyeball the young snatch. That usually trimmed him up a little. All day long they'd just been wheel-spinning anyway; nothing to take back to

Ledbetter. And they were not in any sweat to hear more of his chin dribble either. So if Shadow wanted to talk about names, he'd talk names. Whatever got him off. Fact was, in their line of work they had plenty of time for conversation, and once in a while Shadow had some real interesting ideas to tell. So he didn't mind listening, even if a lot of it sounded like it came direct mail from the puzzle house.

"I remember this dude in the joint," Gleep said, to keep things from expiring. "Beau Fly Washington Jones. That was his actual name. Spook, 'course. Biggest jail house lady you ever laid eyes on. Did half his time on his knees, other half, flat out on his belly, cheeks spread. That what you mean?"

"Sort of. But spooks, they don't really count. Any name sounds good to 'em, they'll take it, crazier the better. I'm thinkin' more like another guy I knew, he was in the can too, name of Puffer. Royal Puffer. You imagine a name like that? It's no wonder the shit came out his ears. Bragged so goddam much, I come that close to snippin' off his tongue and stuffin' it in his asshole where it belonged. Except up there it probably would of just kept waggin', just been more of the same, different end."

The spontaneous image pleased him so, he snorted in spite of himself. To Gleep that was an encouraging sign. "I thought you was gonna say he was a guy smoked a lot."

"Nah," Shadow said, abruptly sour again, "you're still missin' my point."

"I don't think so. Kid I grew up with had the name Lippert. He was like this Puffer you're tellin' me, always squirtin' off. Only he had lips on him big as two live eels. So it can work couple different ways, am I right?" Out of the corner of his eye, Gleep caught a glimpse of Shadow's fishy lips and immediately regretted saying it.

But Shadow didn't seem to notice or make any connection. "Well, kind of yes and no," he said. "See, I'm thinkin' more like it boosts him along, his name. I was growin' up, one of the families they stuck me with was from downstate. Farmers, come up to the big city. Real hillbillies, but not your worst people. Never did no beating on you, give 'em that. Well. Anyway, the old boy used to tell about a friend of his from the farm with the name Orville Spiker. Seems old Orville was a wiseass, always in the deep shit. Wild fucker, least the way they rate wild down there. Well, he gets himself a motorcycle, this Spiker, big old Harley, and one day he's chewin' up the hard road and he comes up behind a truck haulin' a load of steel rail. These rails stick out the bed of the truck, y'see. You got the picture, you know what's comin next. Real sudden, the truck stops, and old Orville, he can't brake the Harley in time. Next thing you know, it's like at a weenie roast, only Orville, he's the weenie, and there ain't no way they're gonna warm him up."

Gleep looked at him vacantly.

"You don't get it? His name's Spiker. Way he checks out, he's spiked clean through. On a rail. Spike. Spiker. Rail."

Gleep finished off his beer. Signaled for another. "That's stretchin' things," he said.

"No, it ain't," Shadow said. There was the sting of peevish irritation in his voice. "Ain't no different than a guard captain I knew in Stateville. Arlo Butcher. Now why do you 'spose a guy named Butcher would take a job like that? Tell you why. Cocksucker was so bad, he'd pound you into a hunk of raw liver in a New York minute. Spiker's the same thing, just maybe harder to see. You understand any of what I'm explainin' to you here?"

Gleep nodded at his glass. "Okay. Sure. However you want it," he said, and then he said nothing more.

Which only annoyed Shadow that much more. What was he doing, trying to explain something mysterious and deep to a beer-swilling Indian? They had cigar stores anymore, he could hire himself out. And what could you tell anybody name of Gleep, anyway? It was an interesting thought, that last one, and after a few moments' silence, he said, "Speakin' of names, which we was, what kind of name is yours? Gleep, I mean. That one of them tribe names? Got a particular meaning to you people?"

Very deliberately, Gleep turned on his stool and fixed him with a remote glare. The question caught him off balance, tumbled him back in time, and he saw again his brother, little Norbert, poor little bugger, poor little guy. Come into this sorry world with no sense at all, hardly could talk even, but always grinning, happy absent grin. Pig-in-shit happy, was what he was, Norbert. Couldn't get out the word Gilbert and when he tried, all that came was a shrill turkey squawk: Gleep, Gleep, Gleep. Pretty soon it took and everybody called him that and if ever he heard the name Gilbert, like as not he wouldn't know who was meant.

Come time for Norbert to go to school and Gleep told his mom (the old man, red half of him, was long gone, strolled into the woods one morning and never came back) forget it, let the kid be, spare him grief. Gleep knew what he was talking about; he'd been there ten years back. She wouldn't listen. No Indian school out where they lived, and being only half they probably wouldn't of took him anyway. Public school kids ragged the little guy fierce, but he didn't mind, didn't even know he was being jacked around except they were beating on him, which they were plenty. Gleep, he dropped out at eighth grade, he couldn't be there all the time. Like he should of. Kid loved his teacher, stiff old maid, cobwebs in her pussy, hated Indians, what was her name?—Bogenrude. That was her name, Bogenrude. Maybe Shadow was on to something, names.

It come Johnny Appleseed Day and Norbert brought

her a bag of apples he picked from the trees at the end of the playground. What he didn't know was that's the day they chose to bulldoze the trees, on account of the bees they attracted. Nice sense of timing, them school people. The kid saw it out his first grade window and he went plain nuts, howling and kicking, so they locked him in the boiler room and then he went hole crazy, scared, shrieking and hammering the walls and furnace. Cut his arm on a jag-edge rusted pipe, laid it right open right down to bone. Gleep sometimes wondered what went through the kid's head, all that blood. After sixth period they come to turn him loose, probably figured they'd taught the loony little breed a lesson. They had all right. He'd bled to death. Tough lesson. A sad accident they said, nobody's fault. They was sure sorry.

So Gleep waited till the day after they planted Norbert, and then he went down to the school looking for Miss Bogenrude. It was late and she wasn't around, which was lucky for her, but he found the principal, a porky shitsack kept saying, "We can discuss our differences reasonably," even while Gleep was working him out with a ragged limb from one of the apple trees. Which he figured was a nice touch. Then he dragged him out onto the grass, not quite dead but all done talking about reason, and torched the school. It seemed like the right thing to do. Fair. Nobody was killed in the fire, but it earned him fourteen years, assault with intent to do great bodily harm (which he successfully did; the principal walked with a limp, he heard, rest of his life) and malicious destruction of property. He did all fourteen, hard time, some in Marquette, some in Jackson. But he didn't regret it any. Except when he thought about Norbert (which he tried not to do very often but which he had to do now, framing an answer to Shadow's stupid fucking question), he felt a strange disturbance at the corners of his eyes, the nearest he knew to tears. Poor little bugger. Poor guy.

"It's just something they hung on me, I was a kid," he said to Shadow, and though all the ungoverned rage was there that he remembered whenever he remembered his brother, he said it mildly; no way Shadow could know. "It ain't Indian. Gilbert's my real name."

"No shit. Gilbert. You never told me that. So how'd you get Gleep, then?"

"I forget," he said. He was aware of another presence, and when he turned away he saw the dude on the next stool gaping at both of them, sporting a fraudulent smile.

"You lookin' at anything special?" Gleep said.

"I'm not quite sure. Just wondering if you boys ran into the same door."

He had on a flowery shirt, looked about the same age as Rusty and the Clemmons kid. Another wiseass college fuck.

"Door. That's real funny, you know that? Hear that, Shadow? Don't you think that's funny?" Under the stool his fists were clenching and unclenching, involuntarily.

"Hey, this young gentleman's a real comedian. He ought to be on the teevee."

"I think he needs some new lines, though," Gleep said, and he took him by the collar of his flowered shirt and brought his head down thuddingly on the bar. With what remained of his beer, he soaked his hair. The crowd milling in the aisle behind them fell away. A bartender scurried toward them. Shadow poked at his arm.

"That's good enough, Gleep. Hey, Gleep. Come on, man, we don't need no heat."

"Fuckin' comedian," Gleep growled, on their way out.

"Yeah, well, you taught him good. He's gonna have some new jokes to tell, next time out."

"College fuck."

Gleep wished he was better with words, like his partner was.

"Ahh, don't think about it no more. Let's go see what wall Ledbetter's up now. What do you say?"

While not literally on any wall, Gaylon was nonetheless agitated enough to attempt scaling one if he thought it would help. Trailing a blue vapor from his gnawed cigar, he paced like a man beset by demons, which to his thinking was precisely the case. Certainly he was too twitchy to sit, even if his flaming piles would have allowed. He couldn't remember the last time he'd had a healthy dump, something more than a meager collection of mouse turds to show for a quarter hour's violent, teeth-gnashing, skin-popping effort. Have to detonate his bowels next, make them move. Already he had been through a pint of Jim Beam and his head felt as though it were clamped in a vise. Under the saggy chest fat, his heart thumped dangerously.

Where were those two dog-fuckers anyway, gone all day and not a word? While he spent the better share of his day on the horn to Atlantic City, Vegas, Reno, even out to Tahoe, trying to get *something* rolling. Dietz's name got him through to the right people, but it didn't carry the heft it was supposed to. Nobody stood at attention, they heard it played. Said sure, we'll look into it for you but it will take some time, couple days on the inside, working off just a description, no photo. It's time is what I'm short on, Gaylon pleaded, for all the shit that cut. We'll get back to you, was what they told him, hang loose. The "hang" part they got right, he didn't have something for Dietz soon. Didn't take no twenty-twenty to see that coming down. Fucking Indians was to blame, too goddam thick to get a picture of the counter. Description was the best they could do, had no experience with real pros at it, they said. We'll look out for him, though; anything shakes down, we'll get to you. Sure they would. Send a postcard. Or a smoke signal. Which he supposed was the reason God made Indians: to fuck up the steady people in this world.

Along about eleven, Shadow and—speaking of Indians—Chief Crazy Horse come breezing in like they'd been out taking the night air, doing a turn on the deck of a cruise ship. They had nothing, of course, nothing except beer breath and a ragged story how they put in a day covering motels, come up zip. It was all a wash. You couldn't count on nobody no more, not even the ones you done right by. Whole world was going to shit.

Gaylon sat them down for a locker room talk. He started out calm, heated up as he got into it. First he explained the famous patented Dietz plan, the only one going. He instructed them to keep after the motels, keep a watch on the car, and keep in touch, for Chris' sake, phone in four, five times a day. Once he got the counter's name, a day or so, they could run him down easy. They better run him down and they better get to the goods quick or they were all of them into it up to the ears. Hawkins, he could dig out his wet boots again and get in line at the car wash where Shadow first found him (Gaylon wanted to say head on back to the reservation, peddle beads and belts, but looking at him, stony as a monument in the park, he decided against it). And Shadow, he could brush up on rolling drunks. That's what he sat them down and told them, tried to jam through their cinder-block skulls this was getting *serious*. The Indian just stared at him, blank-eyed, and Shadow just smirked, said to Gaylon, you got to learn to wind down, you're gonna get one of them coronary arrests and that's a long term bust, y'know, haw haw. That's what he needed, a stand-up comic.

He hustled them out but after they were gone he still felt tight, too charged for sleep, so he called the Korean spa in town and had them send out a girl. They had some decent slash there and usually they came dressed in the billowy harem-girl outfits he liked to see. This one looked like she just got off the boat, which it turned out she had, been in this country only three days, she told him in her lockjaw English, liked America real okay. She was squat and dumpy too, no Oona by a couple country miles. And even though she did a lot of squealing, Gaylon still couldn't get it up; and with her still squirming away all over him, earning her pay, he fell into a dazed sleep, the end of a malignant day.

For someone arrived at manhood squarely in the heat of the sexual revolution, Timothy Waverly had a remarkable innocence of women. The reason for this poverty of experience could be easily traced (which was what he was doing, at her kittenish prodding, come up for air twenty-four hours into that submersed marathon: "Why is it women are such a mystery to you, Waverly? Tell."). Born into a religious family, the muscular Christian variety, locked on diligence and achievement and charity and wholesome good fellowship, all the old verities, he did everything right, not out of conscious choice—this is a good, this is not—but simply because that was what you did. His father, a professor of biblical history and minor scholar, had flown a jet in the Korean War. For a hobby he restored old cars, and every morning at sunup he ran five miles, long before it was fashionable. When he spoke, it was in measured phrases, editing thoughtfully as he developed his ideas, as though he were delivering a centennial anniversary address even if you were merely inquiring the time of day. Waverly's mother was assistant director of the Calvin College Library, and one of his sharpest memories of her (for she died when he was nine, victim of a most virulent form of leukemia, one day there, a week later vanished) was when the family gathered on

Sunday evenings, he and his sister settled on the living room floor, his father in an easy chair sucking the obligatory professorial pipe, the three of them listening dutifully as this gaunt, intense woman with the flyaway hair and the narrow-margined face and sorrowful eyes read aloud from the metaphysical poets (now and again swiping at a tear after a particularly poignant line) or the *Religio Medici* or some other edifying text. Later in life he sometimes wished there had been the opportunity to know her, though other times he was content with the handful of images that came to him on occasion.

Since it was tacitly assumed in this widower's household that everyone would excel, quite naturally that is what he did. In high school he was an honor student with an unsurprising affinity for the humanities disciplines. He was also captain of the swim team and a tournament-level chess player who, for diversion or escape from tedious lectures or conversations, played out masters' games in his head, analyzing the moves. He was never class president but it was invariably his advice and help the principal solicited whenever any monumental school crisis seemed to be brewing. He had dates, all he needed, but no girl friends.

At seventeen he was smitten with the daughter of another Calvin professor, a plain, sweet-tempered, timid girl with no hips or bust whatsoever and a libido as quiescent as his own. That was all right. That was the sort of undisturbing arrangement he wanted, or thought he wanted, all along (though sometimes as they clung together at school dances while the slow sad music wove a sorcerer's spell about them, magic spell of serene harmonic love, over her shoulder he caught glimpses of other couples grinding pelvises in the darker corners of the gymnasium floor). But later on, as the earnest romance blossomed, sometimes in the front seat of a car their chaste kisses veered abruptly into a flurry of hot groping and, her fingers brushing the inside of his thigh, she administered what he assumed was a handjob, or the nearest thing to it.

It was not, however, until he reached the advanced age of twenty that he was officially initiated into the adventure of sex. By then he was a junior at Calvin, a promising student of literature and languages, and a swimmer successful enough to occasionally find his name in the sports section (back pages) of *The Grand Rapids Press*. But to his astonishment, the professor's daughter threw him over for a druggie with sleepy sensual eyes and Brillo-pad hair; and one night shortly after this incomprehensible debacle, in an anguish of bitterness and blighted trust, he joined his teammates on a South Division Street spree. The next morning he woke in a vile motel room with a bursting head and a black prostitute beside him in the clammy-sheeted bed, snoring through a gaping pink cavity of a mouth. Furtively, he dressed and fled. For weeks after, he examined his genitalia for telltale signs of some dread malady, and for a good many years that was his only encounter of that kind.

After he graduated he won a fellowship at the University of Michigan. His sister, three years older, was already there, married to a student of accounting and, a gentle disciple herself of the "All Creatures Great and Small" philosophy, training to be a veterinarian. Within a year he had a masters degree in English literature and a stormy fling with a buxom poetess from Staten Island, a tireless inventor of opaque free verse and erotic games. It was that affair, he saw in retrospect, that led indirectly though quite inevitably to the calamity waiting for him just around the corner and down the street, for it persuaded him of his worldliness and impregnable luck (the poetess was, by the way, nominal wife to a senior professor in his department, a peevish scholar known for his encyclopedic learning and relentless, unforgiving inquisitions of degree candidates; miraculously, he remained perhaps the only person in Ann Arbor ignorant of his mate's unusual avenues of creativity).

The following year, to shore up his lagging finances, he taught two sections of freshman composition, and it was in one of them he met the girl who would become his wife. Her name was Annetta Trumbill and she came from a small town in Iowa called What Cheer, which should have told him something, alerted him right away, but didn't. She was at the university on an athletic scholarship, basketball. In high school she had won all manner of awards for her physical prowess (which did not, however, extend to the bedroom; there she was third string at best, performing like someone going through a listless isometric drill, but he would not discover that until much later, too late). A picture of her returned to him now. She was a big girl, big shouldered, round and muscular, with a round open face, tanned skin, cartoon button eyes, and short brown hair thick as moss. The papers she wrote dealt with such topics as the comparison of Nautilus machines with free weights and the pros and cons of steroid use among athletes. She was not an accomplished writer. She began seeking out his help, turning up regularly at the closet-sized cubicle assigned him as an office. To retain the scholarship it was necessary to keep her grades up, and she sat rigidly alongside his desk, brows knit in sober attention as he explained the mysteries of the semicolon or the nuances of the phantom antecedent. Sometimes during those sessions she pulled her chair in close and occasionally, leaning over to study a particularly baffling emendation on one of her essays, a breast would brush his arm, almost casually. Just enough to make him think about it.

One night she came to his study carrel in the library, deeply distressed, assailed by nagging problems with an uncompleted research paper due the next morning. (Her topic: the causes and treatment of tennis elbow.) In his patient commiseration, the breast brushing turned to urgent pressing, and soon enough they found a dark secluded aisle in the lower regions of the stacks and there, under the long rectilinear shelves filled with the books of the wise, the research paper deadline was extended indefinitely. More such tutorials followed, many more. At least one too many, it seemed, for ten weeks later she announced she was pregnant. Because it was still in his nature to do the right thing, they were hastily married, and seven months after that he was father of a son, an inept, bewildered, twenty-four-year-old head of a household, all his soaring dreams and ambitions rudely brought to earth.

Apart from the child, the boy, there was nothing, well, felicitous about this union, he said to Midnight, winding down the confessional she had teased out of him during their first extended break from each other. It began because Midnight had been wonderstruck at his fumbling eagerness, a man his age; she wanted to ask him where he'd been but put it more kindly instead. It was faintly amusing to watch him uncover appetites and an endurance he never conceived he possessed, almost like initiating an adolescent, though there was nothing adolescent about his hard tight body. For a man I care something about, she told him, I'm a Dr. Pepper girl: ten, two, and four, and that's both halves of the clock, Mr. Gambling Man, that's the way it works.

Betweentimes they ate ravenously from room-service trays, drank a little, not much, hooted at the television, slept fitfully. Clay was not utterly forgotten. She placed a call home, managed to sort out of Drucilla's squawking replies the fact that he had not turned up there. And at her insistence, Waverly pulled on shirt and trousers and went down to the lobby to reengage the lookout. But that was the extent of their search. After hearing the first installment of his sorry tale, she felt toward him something peculiar, novel, difficult to identify because it was entirely foreign to her; and for the next twenty-four hours, she performed with no less intensity and zeal but with something curiously close to—what could she call it but tenderness?

"You're a student of the drama," Waverly said, "you can appreciate some of the Sophoclean elements in the fall of cards. Conflict's built right in. Unities are there, of course. You've got your inflexible rules, rewards, punishments, certainly the tangle of character and fate. Catharsis when it's over, regardless of the way it went. Only thing lacking, I suppose, is a theme. If there's a point to any of it, it escapes me."

"Why did you get into it then?" Midnight said.

Waverly considered his answer carefully before he said, "Variety of reasons, none of them very interesting."

"You could try me. My dance card looks empty. For the next half hour or so."

Beyond the window the sun was slipping under the horizon, departing with a fanfare of gorgeous lavenders and pinks and yellows and violets streaking the pale sky. The room was fading into darkness. Their chairs were pulled together and they each held a drink, she her gin concoction, he another beer. The heady fragrances of sex rose from the crumpled bed behind them. It was in just that bed he had spent the better part of a staggering two days, and the only thing in his experience remotely comparable was his calling. Which was partly why he addressed it now, partly in answer to another of her peremptory questions: "How is it a mild-mannered student of literature becomes a gambler, Waverly? Explain that, will you."

An invitation to try her. He hesitated. There was something special going on here, unique. To him, at least, and if he had any judgment at all (and in recent years his well-being turned on an ability to make sound judgments), to her as well. For the first time in longer than he cared to remember, he feared there was something to lose, more than merely the measure of a game. He calculated the risks. Finally he said, "Okay. I did time in prison. Seven years. Learned a number of things there, among them how to focus. Which is really all the cards require. That, and a little luck now and again."

A gulf of silence.

"I killed a man. My wife's attorney. If there is such a thing as an accident, I expect that's what it was."

"How did it happen?" she said. Her voice was flat. He could detect nothing stiff or wary in it, not an altogether bad sign.

"Maybe you remember that in a divorce it's not uncommon for the husband to get stuck with the injured woman's attorney fees. This lawyer was a nasty battler. Mean-spirited by nature, the kind of guy who'd run over stray dogs for sport. Took a real delight in his work. And he was no fool. He sniffed out a weakness I never knew I had, an absolute, implacable hatred of authority. Well. I owed him four hundred dollars, court order, and I decided to pay him off in pennies. At the time it seemed like a sensational idea, though of course it came to me through a fog of booze and other assorted nostrums."

A telescoped image of that long, monstrous day flashed through his head: bursting into Annetta's apartment unannounced, a raging, cursing, drunken angel of vengeance, all the fury unshackled, turned loose, upending furniture, ripping phones from the wall, pummeling the treacherous cowering Arthur, terrorizing—till a rising wail came to him from somewhere and he whirled about and discovered his son crouched in a corner, tiny arms cuffing the air, screaming. What have I done? Stooping over the child, stroking his hair gently, tenderly, his own words: "I want you to remember this day. All your life I want you to remember it. What that woman brought me to." Words spoken to a shivering two-year-old. Or to himself. Flight. A refocusing of the rage. The quizzical look on the bank teller's face when he demanded the pennies. The attorney's triumphant scorn when he presented them.

"Pennies?" Midnight said, restoring him to the now. She did a quick lateral toss of her head, the way women with abundant long hair will flutter it out of their eyes or off their shoulders, dimly conscious of the current of sensuality in the motion. "Four hundred dollars in pennies?" It came on a giggly ripple, wrapped in genuine mirth, gift-wrapped, and Waverly felt a surge of relief.

"You should try lugging them around sometime. Forty thousand of them, eight bags, fifty worth in each. Not so easy. And after all that work it seemed unfair when he came storming out of his office, lots of shouts and bluster, said he didn't have to accept them, they weren't, in his words, legal tender. I showed him tender. There was some noisy arguing, mostly in the 'your mother wears army boots' vein, then some pushing and shoving. Now, my colossal mistake was I had a gun along—god knows why. It wasn't loaded, I'd never fired one in my life; it never even made it out of my jacket pocket. But it was there, and it didn't do my cause any good. Because in the scuffle, you see, he got his head banged on the corner of a desk. Next thing he knew he was warbling tenor in That Choir Invisible. And bars were clanging shut behind me."

"Pennies," she said, "a murder over pennies. You are a crazy son of a bitch, Waverly. I wonder if you know that."

He couldn't see her face in the dark, but it sounded as though she was still smiling. About crazy, she was probably right. Hearing the story told aloud, it seemed halfcomical even to him. "That's what the judge said, but not enough to make NGRI."

"What's NGRI?"

"Not guilty by reason of insanity. That's what my lawyer was after. And if ever there was a legitimate plea, mine was it. You said it yourself. But he couldn't quite convince His Honor. In this state they've got something they call guilty but mentally ill. In theory it's supposed to be humane: an asylum lockup till you're rational enough to understand the punishment. Then the punishment. In practice it works rather differently. It's directly to Jackson, no passing Go."

"Jackson's the prison?"

"It's the prison."

"How did you manage? Someone like you?"

"What you have to picture here is a middle-class white boy, twenty-six, comes from the kind of sheltered life I described to you, never's seen the inside of any institution more threatening than one of higher learning, never had to ball a fist in self-defense. Inmates in Michigan have got a saying: In Ionia you learn how to fight, in Marquette how to do time, in Jackson how to die. Problem was, I'd missed two grades. The rest of them hadn't. Couple of months in population and they broke me. By then I was certifiable."

"What does that mean, population?"

Either she wanted to know or she wanted to keep him talking. One or the other. This part of the story was not so funny now; and though he tried to scrub it from his tone, inflections, some traces of the dark appalling secrets these revelations evoked came creeping in all the same. Population? He could tell her what it meant but how could he explain what it was. Even to try was to run the risk of a convoluted sanctimony. Chop had once called prison a sanctified place, and it took him years to grasp what that meant. So how could he explain? Population? Call it jungleland, house of mirrors, kingdom of the sociopaths, country of rage, where betrayal is the norm, payback the canon, and mercy never understood or long forgotten. Or call it a pipe laid across the small of your back, a broom handle up your ass, a shank in your ribs. "It means you were utterly alone," he said, "no one to protect you."

She reached out a hand and laid it across one of his. "You're not there anymore," she said gently.

"No."

"You're here. You survived."

It was not a word he had much use for—*survived, survivor*. Too pat, too easy, too much in vogue: Oh, I managed somehow to survive the horrid company, the overdue check, the gruesome cocktail party. Emerged, is what he would have said. After he had absorbed the last beating, had the last train pulled on him by a pack of savage blacks, he lay on a cot in Protection, trussed in a straitjacket, waiting to be shipped to Ypsi. Decompensation, they called it. And as in a dreadful vision, a figure loomed over him, face zippered with scars, villainous ridge of brow, gelid eyes that regarded him distantly, a specimen under glass. No more, he whimpered, no more. You know Anglo-Saxon? The voice came on a subdued rumble. He said he did. Old Norse? Some. Latin? Yes. You get back here—and you will—come and see me. Help me with them and I'll maybe show you how to get along in here. Ask for Chop.

"With some help," Waverly said. "I came back from the state's puzzle factory eighteen months later. Stamped sane. There was a fellow in Jackson helped me get by. A lifer. Most singular man. His name was Wesley, but they called him Chop. For the way he got there. Murdered his wife and her lover with an ax. Dismembered their bodies. Then he discarded the ax and sat there in a puddle of blood waiting for them to fall on him, and they did. He'd been there since he was twenty, nineteen years. I think he was the finest man I've ever known. A kind of tarnished saint."

He could feel her fingers tightening. For a time she said nothing. Then, "You and he weren't . . . ?"

"No, not what you're thinking. Not at all. In a place where sex is a punishment, a payback, he was celibate by choice and tough enough to make it stick. No, it was a trade we had. I taught him what I remembered of a couple dead languages, he showed me how to save my life."

"Your wife—what did she do to you? To bring you to that?"

"Another man. What else?"

"Don't you think your reaction was a little . . . extreme? For infidelity? Especially these days."

"It seems that way now, it didn't then. Maybe because he was my brother-in-law. The accountant. I liked him. We were friends. It wasn't a question of trust. I couldn't conceive anything like that. To me it was very near incest."

Midnight removed her hand, fumbled with a cigarette. Once lit, its glowing tip pierced a tiny hole in the dark. "That's not how you define incest, you know," she said evenly.

"I understand that. But you see, even though it wasn't your happiest or most prosperous marriage, they were taking everything. Everything that mattered. And as a matter of course. Brazenly. Unrepentant. My son, they took him. My old man, indirectly they got him. He died a couple of years after, overdose of shame, I imagine. I had the normal affection for my sister. Growing up, we had been close. They may as well have done her in, too. She did about a year of in-house therapy, lives somewhere in South Dakota now, a hermitess. Grows herbs and runs a kennel, last I heard."

"So you killed her lawyer. Why him?"

It was Chop guided him down the snarled path of self-forgiveness. Who knew that scorched terrain any better? Cancer is the supreme mystery, he liked to say, ultimate necessity. And we are cancers; without us the world would be engulfed in pride, the arrogance of its own counterfeit order. Our purpose is to ambush that pride, make mockery of their fraudulent notions of order. Our function is holy. The lawyer's death a ritual sacrifice, cautionary lesson in humility, the restoration of a truly moral order. "When payback time arrived," Waverly said, "he was handiest. He was there."

"All this happened in Michigan," she said carefully. "You live in Florida. Let me take a guess. Your ex and family live here, this town."

"Right on the money."

"Is that what brings you here? Another payback?"

"I don't know exactly. Wish I did. Wish I could explain it to myself, what I'm doing here. Some vague notion of seeing my son again, speaking with him, maybe even persuading him to come live with me. Crazy as that must sound. Or maybe an even blurrier one of the payback you mention, even though I know it's impossible. In the person of the boy, they hold the ultimate hostage. So what could I do to them? Even if I wanted to and—" he hesitated, uncertain how to say it, or if it should be said at all —"I'm not sure I do anymore. Since I stumbled into you."

In the granite silence that once again hung between them, all he could hear was her exhaling sigh and the disjointed messages of ghosts whispering in his ear. And all he could feel was the distancing, the backsinking scramble up a steep mound of loose sand.

At last she said, "You remember what I said to you the other night? About dull? I was wrong, I apologize. This is a melancholy tale you bring, Waverly."

So it was, and needing no underscore from him.

"I've known a lot of men in my life. You can probably tell. With all of them I was, oh, negligent. Careless, I suppose. Maybe I was too . . . secure."

"But not now."

"No, that's the curious part. I've never felt more secure than right now. There's never been anyone treated me quite the way you do."

He couldn't tell for certain what that meant and he might have asked, but for the tapping at the door. He would remember those words later, wondering where he miscalculated, where he went wrong. But the knock, though neither sharp nor insistent, startled him, and he said, "Did you order another drink?"

"I forget. Must have. You want to get it?"

"Ledbetter? Monte. New Jersey. You remember we talked, couple days ago? Said Dietz had a little problem out there?"

"Yeah, right. That's right. You got anything for me?"

"Think maybe I can help you out. Fella you was telling about, I think it's the same one we walked here. About three years back."

"You got a name?"

"It's the same fella, his name is Waverly. Tim-o-thy Wav-er-ly," he said, lengthening the syllables. "You get that down?"

Gaylon was scribbling on the back of an envelope on the counter by the phone. Chapped ass notwithstanding, he was planted on a stool, slabs of rump drooping over the sides. The news was so electrifying he had to get off his feet or he might have swooned. "Yeah. Yeah," he said, "but whyn't you spell it out anyway."

It was spelled for him.

"Anything else? Any stats?"

"Nothing much. I ran a cross-survey for you but he didn't turn up anywhere else. No address that checks. Nothing cute, partners, disguises. Not a high roller, slow and steady. See, sheet on him was done before my time, but he must not of been your average numbers freak. Took 'em nearly six weeks to get on to him."

"But you're sure this is the one?"

"Got to be your man. Everything you gave us squares."

"Listen—Monte, is it? I got to thank you. Mr. Dietz thanks you."

"Consider it a comp. No problem. And you give Dietz our best. Tell him don't be a stranger."

"I'll tell him that."

"Hey, you have yourself a nice day now."

Gaylon replaced the phone and looked at his watch. It was well past five. Once today, at noon, Shadow had bothered to check in. Once. Close to six hours ago. Nobody listened anymore. And if they did, they acted like we were playing a game of wet towels here. Probably figured he had it easy. Try a turn with Dietz sometime, find out easy.

He called a few likely spots but it got him exactly zip; nobody had seen them. An anxious, sour bile churned in the lower regions of his belly. His asshole felt like a dart board, tournament time. Even his legs ached, all the rug running. He wondered what it would be like to be healthy, flat in the stomach, firm butt, thighs that didn't wiggle like oatmeal porridge when you walked. Jowls without marbles in them, shooter size at that. Have your hair again. He wondered what that would be like. Step right out on a beach somewhere with a jockstrap bathing suit on, cooze hanging on you because they wanted to, not because your wallet's fatter than your ass. Shit, never mind any of that even. Strike it. How about shoveling in a meal without it backing up, dick that flew higher than half-mast, dump that didn't blow your eyeballs? How about any of that?

It's good health that counts, Gaylon had concluded when, an hour later, the phone jangled him out of his reverie.

"Hey, Gaylon. Shadow. What do you hear?"

"What do I *hear*?" he bawled. "Hear? One thing for

sure it ain't been is this fuckin' telephone ringing. Where the fuck you been? I said call in."

"Gay-lon. Sweetheart. What I tell you about slowin' down. You forget already?"

Wait till this is over, Gaylon said to himself. Just wait. We'll see slowing down. Aloud and a little more modulated, he said, "I think I got what we need." He told Shadow what he had learned, read the name from the back of the envelope.

"You want to spell that."

He spelled it.

"That's terrific news, Gaylon. Next time we see you, we'll maybe have a couple guests along."

"I hope that next time's going to be real soon. I'm tellin' you, Dietz has got more than just a case of the red ass. He's all done two-stepping."

"Come to that, huh?" Shadow said, same wise-fuck tone of voice.

Gaylon's breath came out a little whistle. Through his mouth, around the soggy tail of the cigar, he took another. And then he said, "Shadow, you and me, we go back a ways, right? So I was blowin' any smoke up your ass, you'd know it. What I'm tellin' you here is how it is." He despised the piping weakness in his own voice, but what could you do? For now, what could you do?

"Okay. I got the name. You go pour yourself a shot of Maalox. Stretch out. Take an eye rest. Me and Gleep will go to work. I'm bettin' you'll have company out there before you wake up."

"You think so?"

"Guaranfuckintee you."

Clay had been in the storage room so long he feared he might be hallucinating. His head felt inflated, and extraordinary images trailed through it: some sexual, some hilarious, violent, a few in color, placid and dreamy, many others fantastic, peopled with grinning demons. His body, on the other hand, seemed to be contracting, all the proud musculature shrinking, melting away. No wonder. All day Monday, Tuesday, and now they were having their goddam Moonlight Madness Sale: DOORS OPEN TILL MIDNIGHT!(Midnight . . . where was she . . . send help)—PRICES SLASHED!—EASY TERMS!—CASH AND CARRY!—MAKE YOUR BEST DEAL!

He was wedged in behind some packing crates, for they were even back here, rubbing greasy palms over greasy sofas, haggling over nickels and dimes. And he sat on top of five jumbos, with dust in his mouth and spiders inching up his leg, couldn't move, couldn't see, barely breathe. Madness—they had that right. No more of this, he told himself. Made a vow. Tomorrow he was out of there. Fuck the risk, the cost. Better dead than buried alive.

They stood side by side at the phone carrels in a corridor off the lobby of the Holiday Inn. Shadow took the glitter spots, Gleep the fleabags. It required maybe ten minutes for Shadow to put down his phone and tap his partner on the shoulder and say, "Bingo." And in fewer than that he was leaning over the Park Place desk, treating the freckled, flame-haired girl behind it to a crooked grin, dancing with her over the room number. She said she was new at the job and they told her not to give out that information, but she'd be happy to ring up there, let him talk to Mr. Waverly first, that was how they did it at the Park Place.

"See, this is a surprise thing," Shadow said. "Like a little joke we want to do. Mr. Waverly, he'll get a real kick out of it."

Gleep made an appreciative grunt. It was good to have an audience. Especially on this one coming up.

"Sorry. That's hotel policy."

"Just doin' your new job, huh."

"That's what they pay me for," she said brightly.

Shadow let the grin shut down. It was okay to fuck around a little, have some fun, but he didn't need no warmups, leave the game in the locker room. Five days he had waited for this, had it all rehearsed in his mind. And here stood a fire engine cunt in his way.

"Look, coppertop. I told you how it was. I'm not makin' myself clear? You got a problem with hotel policy, I got the answer. You don't have to tell us nothing. Just slide that register book over some. I promise not to peek. So does this gentleman with me. Right?"

"Absolutely," Gleep said. "You got our word." He was feeling good too, catching the spirit.

"I've told you I can't do that. Now if you don't want—"

"Don't want what," Shadow said, and he reached across the desk and took the register. She gave him one of those astonished, "This can't happen in Traverse City" looks and grabbed for it, but he caught her at the wrist and nailed her hand down hard. After he found what he needed, he relaxed his grip but did not release it, and when he looked up, her mouth was quivering and her eyes filling with tears. Shadow allowed his expression to crack open again, this time in an amiable solicitous smile.

"Y'know, that hair you got, it makes me think of Orphan Annie. You remember her? Funny papers? Remember how she was always gettin' herself into the darndest scrapes? Took that big raghead, bail her out, one who wore the bloomers—what was his name? Punjab? Big Stoop? —something like that. Anyway, he worked for her Daddy Warbucks and he'd come by and yank her out of the soup. See, I'm thinkin' you're sort of like little Annie, I bet, get yourself in all kinds of hot water. Am I right?"

"No. Yes."

"Well, which one is it?"

"Yes."

"That's what I figured. Okay. Now look at it like this. Suppose you was tied down out in the middle of a road someplace, and here comes this big truck at you, smokin', gonna flatten you. Let's say it's a sixteen-wheeler, one of them big mothers, go choo choo. What you got to picture in your mind is this gentleman behind me, he don't get what he's after, he's that truck. But I gets here just in time to cut you loose, save you, like that raghead I was tellin' you about saves Annie. 'Course I ain't wearin' bloomers, just your normal American clothes, but it's the same thing. You see that?"

"Yes. Please, I—"

"Wait. I ain't quite finished. Way I see it, you owe me a little thanks. But that's okay. I don't want nothing. Except that you don't get yourself back out on that road again, so to speak. By doin' something dumb. Like callin' up the room and spoilin' our surprise. Or callin' security. See, what if next time I ain't around to grab you out of the way? That'd be a heck of a shame. Hope this is plain, this little story I'm tellin' you."

As they hurried up the flight of stairs and down the corridor, Shadow said, "We better move smart here, Gleep. I got a feelin' little Annie didn't take my story to heart. She's thinkin' security anyway, could see it in her eyes. I got a instinct about them things."

"That part about the rig goes choo choo, that was real good."

Shadow had heard it from the coloreds in the can, but that was years ago and he didn't feel obliged to credit his sources. Besides, he really was in a hurry. Anxious, almost. He didn't want some rent-a-cop fucking things up, now they were this close. "Oh, there's more comin'," he said. "Lot's more."

At the door, he turned to Gleep and said, "You got your piece?"

Gleep patted his chest. The .38 Colt Special made scarcely

a ripple in the loose fitting jacket he wore for work like this.

Shadow knocked softly.

A voice behind the door said, "Yes, who's there?"

For Gleep's benefit, he mimicked the words silently: yes, who's there? Did it wide-eyed and sissy-looking. What he said was, "Room service, sir. Got a bottle of wine for you, compliments of the Park Place. It's for the Labor Day holiday coming up, for all our guests." It was an inspired idea of his; who'd turn down a free drink?

"No thanks."

"I'm supposed to leave it, sir."

The door opened the tiny width the latch chain allowed, and Shadow moved aside while Gleep planted his foot squarely in the middle and shoved. The chain went flying and the door caught the man behind it full face, sent him reeling. Shadow stepped inside and flipped on the light. Gleep got the door behind them. The man was slumped against a wall and he had both hands over his whacked face, but it was the counter all right. Shadow knew. He wasn't likely to forget. The counter, Mr. Timothy Waverly, the worms' dinner, main course. And over there, scrambling out of a chair and trying to pull a sheet over her twat, was the dessert. They had sure enough pulled the lever on a hot slot this time.

Shadow wagged his head slowly, pursed his lips, doing a naughty-naughty face. He laid a finger alongside his nose, way Johnny Carson does just before he says something real funny. Taking his time. Then he rubbed his chin and felt the raw abrasions still there. And then he said, "Maybe you remember us, Mr. Waverly. The other night, out at the casino? We remember you. And 'course this lady without no clothes on. Real handsome squeeze she is, too, bareass like that. Anyway, we didn't think we got introduced proper that time, so I just said to myself, we ought to stop by, say hi. Get acquainted. Folks call me Shadow, and my friend here, one holdin' that Colt in his hand—husky fella, ain't he?—he goes by Gleep. Now we all know each other, we'd be real honored if you'd both slip on some clothes and come meet another friend of ours. He's a real funny guy, regular circus clown, you'll like him. It ain't dress-up; don't wear nothing fancy. Oh yeah, before I forget, some other friends of yours, Mr. Waverly—you sure got the friends!—from out in Atlantic City, they asked would we say hi for them, too."

FOUR

FIRST THEY TOOK HIM INSIDE THROUGH A
garage entrance and down a flight of stairs and through
a dark space and past a door into a furnace room illuminated by a single overhead bulb. Then they had him
stand with his forehead pressed against the concrete wall
and his legs extended while they patted him down and
emptied his pockets. And then they told him to turn
around.

"Welcome to the gym," said the runt who had identified himself as Shadow. "We call this the gym because
we like to get our exercise here. Keep in shape. Fella that
owns the place—friend I was tellin' you about?—he's
real generous about lettin' us use it. He'll be down to say
hello soon as he gets done talkin' to your girl friend
upstairs."

The room was long, twenty-five feet or so, and narrow,
no more than nine. The squat furnace more or less cut
it in half: on one side, stacks of packing boxes and an old
dresser and kitchen table and chairs covered with a filigree
of basement dust; on the other, nothing at all, just the
three of them standing there. The floor was bare and
three walls were concrete, the fourth some unevenly tacked
blond paneling. There were no windows and only the

one door, and the Big Foot called Gleep blocked that. Shadow stood directly under the bulb, his scabby features framed in a nimbus of yellow light. His shoulders were high and tight, and he was breathing through his mouth, quick audible breaths, like an eager hound. There was a luster in his eyes. Waverly knew the look: couldn't wait to get to it.

And it was coming any minute now and there was nothing he could do or say could delay or forestall it. No reasoning, no pleading, certainly not the simple truth he was merely a cypher in this contest, a spectator who wore innocence like a souvenir of his stainless, lost youth. And it was going to hurt, that much he had learned. All that remained for him now was to get deep inside himself, cushion that hurt. If he could remember how. He tried to reconstruct the steps in the drill: maintain eye contact but say not a word, utter no sounds; get in some deep breaths if you can but not exaggerated ones, noticeable; loosen all the joints and muscles, start at the toes and work on up, make them gelatinous; and then—hardest part of all—turn inward, take yourself out of there, find that center of light.

He was out of practice. It had been a few years.

Already he had violated the first principle on the drive from the hotel. Sitting in the back with the Colt nudged against his ribs, he asked to smoke and received a permissive grunt. He shredded a couple of matchbooks, display of fear, and managed to get bits of them between his teeth and lips, which might help some, not much. Where they were headed, he couldn't tell: out of town, around the bay, off the highway and into some thick woods where the houses were set well back from the dirt road and wide apart. In the streaks of headlight, he saw small animals darting through the trees. At a right-angle curve, a raccoon poised motionless in the ditch, eyes like signal beacons in the black night. They hadn't bothered with blindfolds, which meant it was a one-way trip. Small surprise. Up front, Midnight sat rigid as a piece of metal sculpture, while Shadow, nonstop monologist, remarked on weather, road conditions, points of local interest, the general state of things, in the easy conversational tones of a genial tour guide. When they arrived he went around to Midnight's door and ushered her out with an elaborate bow and flourish. Some porch lights went on and a pear-shaped silhouette appeared at the front entrance, whisked her inside. Returning to the car, Shadow had said, "She's gonna be occupied a while, Miss Clemmons. What do you say we go in and have a little private chat of our own."

And now, faced off in the furnace room gym, the chat was about to get underway.

"You sure ain't been very talkative tonight, Mr. Waverly. Something botherin' you? Your face sore, where that door caught you?"

Waverly stared at him and said nothing.

Shadow's eyes held the steady gaze a moment, then shifted to the floor. "Bet that's it, the door. What do you think, Gleep?"

"Got to hurt some."

Nothing like it's going to, Waverly thought. He kept quiet.

"I got to apologize for my friend here," Shadow said. "Sometimes he just don't understand he's bigger'n your average, stronger. Can be meaner, too. Why, back in his school days, teachers wanted to lay the lumber to some pupil had it coming, they'd call on Gleep. Teachers, they'd ask the questions and old Gleep here, he'd be right behind, do the hosin'. And that's when the answers was right, too."

He liked that enough to pause for a little nostalgic chuckle. "Them was the days, huh Gleep?"

"Absolutely."

"Reason that comes to mind is because we want to ask you a question, sort of like school days. It's a real easy one. Smart fella like you, you ain't gonna have no trouble with this one. Ready?"

Waverly made no response.

"Okay. Miss Clemmons's brother, he's got some goods don't belong to him. Belong to my friend upstairs, and he wants 'em back. That's natural, you can understand that. These are top-shelf commodities we're talkin' about, and besides, stealin' goes against the law of our land. Now, you and her been playin' grabass last few days. Probably longer'n that, maybe you two put the boy up to it, got him off the straight and narrow. We don't know, and 'course that really ain't none of our business. Either way, we figured you could help us out, tell us where he's at. That's the question. Told you it was easy."

"Here's the answer," Waverly said. "You're going to do what you want, I understand that. But for the record, I didn't nick your goods. I don't know where they are or where the brother is. Neither does the lady upstairs."

Shadow made a negative gesture with a waggly finger. "That ain't the right answer, Mr. Waverly. Disappointin', smart fella like you. I think you better try again."

Waverly went silent. He heard the voice, of course, but paid no attention to the words. Rather, he concentrated on the looseness and he had it elevated, but only as far as his lower torso, and so when Shadow gave a flick of the chin signal and Gleep came slamming into him, he raised his arms instinctively, covering his head against the first blow. It took him on his crossed wrists and was not immediately painful, but its force drove him back into the wall. The next one went to his rib cage, whacked the wind out of him and sent his arms dangling to his sides. Those that followed alternately snapped him up and back, braced by the wall, or bent him in two. The last one before he slumped to his knees came down like a rocket on the back of his neck. Then, like the shell of a building toppled by a wrecking ball, a backswung forearm sent him sprawling face first onto the cool cement floor. A boot slammed into his kidneys, dispatching a series of explosions up the length of his spine to the base of his skull. A cough came bubbling up his throat. He tried to suppress it, but it broke on a sluggish current of blood and green bile and tooth chips and shreds of matchbook. From some altitudinous distance he could hear Shadow saying, "Hey, Mr. Waverly, it's okay. It causin' you any discomfort, you can say ouch. Out loud even. Won't bother nobody. Neighbors out here are way far down the road."

It's not like the movies, he had told Midnight. Get up and start trading punches. Do some flashy karate kicks. If he knew any. Say something cryptic, ironic. He had taken some clubbings before, but he couldn't recall anything like this. This was a serious workout. With more to come.

A hand grabbed a swatch of hair and yanked his head from the floor. It was Shadow, stooped down on one knee, face thrust in close, so close Waverly could make out a thumb-sized pustule on his needle chin, ripe yellow cone, badly in need of squeezing.

"Smarts a little, don't it. Remember? That's what you said yourself, other night."

Waverly brought his left elbow up vertically and drove it into Shadow's jaw. It felt very much like he was moving against the resistance of water, slow motion. Consequently, he was surprised and modestly gratified to hear the astonished, outraged squawk, and his last thought before fading out under the furious pummeling was to wonder whether he had succeeded in popping the unsightly zit.

* * *

As nearly as a portly man could stomp, Gaylon came stomping into the kitchen. His baggy face was gray with anxiety. "What the fuck you doing up here?" he said.

Shadow and Gleep sat at the table with two Buds and a plate of cold chicken between them. Shadow's tongue, maddeningly and with a will of its own, was busy playing over the spiked edge of a fractured molar. He gave a shrug.

"What's that mean?" Gaylon demanded. "I asked what you're doing here."

Shadow made the tongue hold still long enough to say, "We're takin' a recess break, Gaylon. School starts in again, few minutes. Soon as he wakes up."

"Well? Anything?"

He shook his head negatively.

"How do you read it?"

"Too early to tell."

"What's too early? He knows or he don't. How long's it take you guys anymore?"

Shadow's tongue was reengaged, so Gleep, stifling a burp, volunteered, "This one takes a nice touchup. He ain't no rookie."

Gaylon glared at him and got out a cigar and clamped it between his teeth. Then he turned to Shadow and said, "I need a play-by-play, I ain't going to consult no Indian. I want to know how things stand."

Gleep's mouth tightened but he didn't speak. It was Shadow said, "Gaylon, for Christ's fuckin' sake, keep your head on. If he knows anything, we'll get it for you. Set your ass down here and get outside one of them drumsticks."

"Sweet Jesus fuck," Gaylon said. "I called Dietz tonight, told him we'd have it wrapped by tomorrow. You hearing me? That's tomorrow like in twenty-four hours tomorrow. And you're talking eats." Nevertheless, he sank onto a chair, glanced at the plate, removed the cigar and picked up a thigh, and began gnawing at it.

Shadow waited till Gaylon's mouth was bulging and then he said, "You ain't told us how you're doin'."

Gaylon did a time-out wiggle with his fingers.

"You get 'er wet yet?" Shadow said, winking broadly at Gleep, who sat there with a Texas-size scowl on his face. "Maybe you ought to try jammin' a coke bottle up her snatch. That always makes 'em squeal. Tell you about anything you want to hear, just so's you'll do it again."

Gaylon either missed the mockery or overlooked it. He swallowed noisily and said, "So far I got no better luck than you. Nothing."

"Well, you whackin' her around some, ain't you?"

" 'Course I am. What'd you think. Sure."

But the truth was Gaylon wasn't any good at this anymore, and he knew it. He had tried to talk to her, good common-sense talk, reasonable, make it sound like maybe they could strike a deal. Like he didn't want no trouble, just information. Shadow gone, she wasn't scared anymore, just stood there hands on her hips, lip curled, sneering at him. Even had the stones to say heavy trouble is what you got, you don't let me and my friend go. Jesus, she was fucking threatening *him!* Everything was turned inside out, this world.

So he tried to pretend in his mind it was Mardella he had there, runaway bitch, and he gave her a couple openhanders. What does she do? Comes at him with her fingernails, looked like bear claws, and he got covered just in time or they'd be playing tic-tac-toe on his face right now and wouldn't that be something, try to explain to Shadow. Or Dietz—think about that.

He was too old for this, tired. He didn't take no pleasure from it anymore, like when he was a young piss-and-vinegar buck. Man his age ought to have some calm in his life. *Dignity*, that was the word. Like Dietz had it. Man his age, this business, he ought to be upstairs in his BarcaLounger, sipping a Wild Turkey straight up, listening to the goddam opera or whatever, while the grunt work went on down below or someplace else. Fat fucking chance, way things always turned out for him. Nope, no pleasure in it anymore. Which was why he'd been hoping to shit Shadow and Tonto over there, belching like a foghorn, would have something by now. Which if they didn't get tonight, he might as well get measured for a long box, book a ticket on a hearse.

Gaylon ground off the last sliver of meat. Wearily he said, "Let's go see what the counter's got to say. See can he add up to twenty-one yet."

" 'There is no fate that cannot be surmounted by scorn,' " Chop had once instructed him, quoting Camus. But then there's all kinds of scorn, too. Dumb kind is defiance. Dumb because that's what smokes them up, that's what they got to see. They need something out of you, and it's a desperate need. Calamity, anguish, passion, violence, grief, mischance—they're all a collaboration, require a connection. You want to juke fate, don't deliver. Disconnect.

It was instruction Waverly remembered too late, floating like an ether-borne angel, dreamily, returning from some landscape of the night and peeling open one swollen eye and then discovering where he was, discovering three of them now, looming over him, a new one, worried-looking blimp, porcine featured, wore his pants riding high over the terraced sausage rolls of fat, clown fashion, must have a zipper in them a yard long, chewed a nervous cigar. It hurt to speak, but before he thought to restrain himself, he said in a raspy croak, "Going to rain tonight. Here comes a hog with a turd in its mouth."

The blimp-clown looked crestfallen. He shook his head

sadly. Gleep stepped in and, punching downward, rammed a fist into Waverly's sternum. It was only then, after the impact, he realized he was propped in a straight-backed chair, arms and legs bound. He spit out a little blood. When he breathed, it felt as though something was scraping his lungs.

"That any way to say hello," Shadow said, "man takes time out his busy schedule, come down and get acquainted? They sure didn't learn you no manners at card school. Learned you a big mouth is what they did. Wonder just how big."

He straddled Waverly and placed his thumbs inside the corners of his mouth, fitting them carefully, clear of the teeth. And then he began to tug laterally.

As the pain widened across his head, Waverly smothered a rising shriek by forming the words *Risus Sardonicus*, seeing them, focusing on them, and picturing the distended smile being shaped on him now, smile of death, smile that says Look, the joke's on you, monstrous joke and somehow you missed it, biggest laugh of them all. And though he was not successful in containing the thrashing of his body, he fixed on the image and fixed his eyes on Shadow, methodically pulling his face apart.

"That's good enough," Gaylon said finally. Made him seasick, watching this shit happen. Why couldn't things go easy?

Shadow released his thumbs and came whirling at him. "Enough? What's enough? You gonna take a turn, show us how it's done? Somebody give you back your nuts?"

His whole spindly frame shook with rage. Face looked boiled, scalded. Eyes a pair of ice picks. Fucker was close to losing it again, and so it astonished Gaylon to hear himself say firmly, "Enough is when I say it is. And when it ain't, I say that too. Either way, I'm the one says it. Get out of here now, go turn on the teevee. Watch the ball game awhile."

And he was even more astounded to see him actually do it, took the Indian too, banging the door behind him. Maybe I still got a little of the old rumble juice left in me, Gaylon thought; little balance still in the bank.

Waverly's mouth sagged shut slowly, flaccid as a rubber band with all the elasticity gone out of it. There was a distant clamor in his ears. His gaze was blurry but he held it on the figure who stood regarding him quizzically, one hand stroking the fleshy furrows drooping from his chin, the other plucking delicately at his rump, as though to extract from it inspired harmonic chords. It was a comical sight, as much as he could make of it, but his lips were too numb to move, no danger of collaborating in any further grief.

Gaylon came around behind him and undid the ropes. "There," he grunted, "show you we ain't all animals and scalp hunters here." He went to the other side of the furnace and returned with a chair. He planted himself in it, feet flat on the floor, hands clasped under the substantial arc of belly. He waited a minute, nice dramatic effect. Then he said, "My name's Ledbetter. I'm the one you want to deal with. Guess you can see that, huh?"

Waverly sagged forward in his own chair. For a moment he feared he might slide right on out of it, onto the floor. Best as he could, he braced himself. He made no reply.

"You and me," Gaylon went ahead, "we got no quarrel. I can see you're an intelligent man, probably got an education. Figure your own point spreads, so to speak, make your own plans. I'm betting you're sharp enough to spot when you got to make an exception, your plan. Y'know, back away, circle around a little, come at it another angle. Get the right return on your money. You understand what I'm explaining to you here?"

Gaylon wasn't absolutely certain he understood any of

it himself, but he liked the soothing rhythm of his words, the melody.

Waverly stared at him.

"I ain't going to try and shit you because I figure you're already way ahead of me, guy like you, way down the pike. See, here's the whole thing. This boy, Miss Clemmons's brother, he's walked away with a stash of our goods. You can guess what I'm sayin' when I say goods, but you don't have to 'cause I'm going to tell you so we're startin' out straight up, no games. Extra fine blow is what it is. Half a mil worth. Up to me to get it back."

Gaylon made his expression grave. He tried the pause again, see if it would dent the blank-faced fuck. When he got no reaction, he resumed.

"Now, I'm in business. Businessman. In business there's no room for grudges, you know that better'n me, your business. And I don't hold none—him, his sister, you. I was sittin' in your chair there, I might find that hard to swallow too, so let me tell you my proposition. You, me, Miss Clemmons, we'll leave together, just the three of us. Them two monkeys, they stay here. Right here. You take me where the boy's at and you go in and talk some sense into him, tell him how it is. The lady stays with me in the car. Once you get my goods back, I cut her loose, we shake hands and go our own ways. Fair business trade."

Gaylon had been extemporizing, but as he heard the arrangement unfolding, it sounded even to him the very essence of sweet reason. He was particularly taken by the business theme. Nice solid ring to it, nice touch. Like Dietz would do it. He put one chubby knee over the other and said, "So. What do you think? We got ourselves a deal? What do you say?"

What did he think? Say? What Waverly was thinking about was his Wham-o slingshot and the slaughter of rats. Once, doing ten days hole time, he had reconstructed the memory the way Chop said, in its entirety, down to the last fragment of detail; and now, unaccountably, bits of it came to him again.

He was fifteen—no, sixteen at least, he was driving —when he bought it ("Wham-o: hits like a twenty-two"), secretly, surreptitiously, a departure from the norm, from everything done right (for who in the Waverly household would be aberrant enough to hunt rats by night). On those nights he slipped it under his jacket and left the house and drove to a dump outside of town, circumvented the bolted gate and eased the car (his father's, of course, borrowed for some fabricated lofty purpose: youth fellowship, swim practice, serious study), lights out, navigating by moonlight through the ragged hillocks of muck and trash. And then, crouched motionless on the hood, heavy-duty flashlight balanced between his feet, Wham-o poised, a bag of steel pellets at his side, he waited, listening for the first puzzled twittery chirps (clear as birdcalls, he remembered) to come rising from the mounds of offal surrounding the car. Listening for the first sounds of a scuttling movement toward it, beneath it; and then the bolder sounds, the nipping, poking, hissing, scratching, clawing; the sounds of brutal urgent appetites everywhere. Abruptly he flicked on the light and without exception always caught one startled, frozen in its beam, frozen in the last instant of its life before the pellet exploded dead-on between its glittery eyes. And if he was quick enough and lucky enough, he caught a few more out of the pack retreating in every direction, trailing a farewell chorus of savage frenzied squeals. And if he doused the light and waited silently in the dark on the hood of his father's car, displayed some patience, he could repeat the scene as often as he liked, for the rats were not quick studies and they came in an inexhaustible supply.

Curiously, that was what he thought about, gazing into

the pouchy disconsolate eyes of this buffoon opposite him, this harlequin of menace, greed, appetite. That, and all he had ever despised without quite knowing why, both sides of his cleanly shaved life, the God-loving side, with its fraudulence come cloaked in purling agreeable tones, and the other side, God-hating, where extortionate authority came on naked as a rivet-gun fist. And it required first a murder of his own and then the twisted vision of an ax murderer to make him see it. And now this, to put it in focus again. Chop was right all along. Disconnect. He was ready. He lifted his gaze to the yellow bulb, and what he had to say to Gaylon was nothing at all, for he was slipping away, out of there, gone, got down into the passageways and corridors reaching without end behind his very own eyes.

Gaylon gave it a minute more. Made him uneasy, fucker gawking at him that way, face all smashed and caked with blood. He stood up and moved around out of his line of vision.

"Maybe you ain't payin' close attention, what I'm offerin' here. Flip side is I walk out that door and in comes a psycho and a redskin, and neither of 'em exactly got a crush on you."

He made it come on hard and tough. Like jerk-off time was over, shit or get off the fucking throne. He got nothing.

"Look," he pleaded, "you got one foot on the banana peel and the other one in the air. I'm tryin' to help you out here."

Nothing.

Heavily, he stooped down and secured the ropes again, yanking and tugging at them. Upstairs he said to Shadow, "I can't do no good down there. Cocksucker's on a Jesus Christ trip. Go try again. Just the muscle, save the cute stuff. And don't wax him yet, y'understand. I'll say when."

* * *

They went at him with boots and fists and the blades of their hands, as instructed, and when he slipped under they brought him around with a bucket of water and then they went at it again. Finally it was Gleep who said, turning away, "Shit, he don't know. If he does he ain't tellin' us."

Shadow kept at it but his arms were leaden and his breath came in hawking gasps, and most of what he threw was feeble cuffing. Eventually, run out of gas, he quit too, and then there was nowhere to aim his lonely fury but at his partner.

"You goin' pussy on me?"

Gleep gave him a look just shy of contempt.

"Pussy?" Shadow repeated. His fishy lips, stunted jaw, were trembling. Like a sissy kid just before the waterworks turn on.

"Hey," Gleep said, "don't mix me up with somebody else. I ain't that lardass up top. Wasn't me made this dude a hard case."

"You think I give a fuck what he knows or don't know. What he did out the casino, I *owe* him. So do you."

"That's dog shit," Gleep said, "owe. You ain't never had nobody dust the floor with your ass? C'mon."

Shadow didn't say anything for a minute. His tongue had found the cracked tooth and was lubricating it again. He looked back at Waverly, hunk of stubborn meat strapped to the chair. He looked at his watch. Late. He was tired. Then he said, "Get the bucket."

"Why? He's awake."

"Get the goddam bucket."

Gleep took it over.

"Give him a cold shower."

"You can see he's fucking awake."

Shadow jerked the bucket out of his hands and emptied

it over Waverly's head. He didn't move. His eyes were open.

"He better be awake," Shadow said, and then to Waverly he said it again: "You better be awake. Better hear this. We're leavin' now, go wash up, have a beer, cop some z's. Sounds good about now, don't it, beer? Too bad we can't bring you one, but ain't that the way life goes—sometimes you get to fuck the bear, most times the old grizzly, he fucks you."

It made him feel a little better, talking around it, making it up as you go. Quieted him down, always did. Fucking Ledbetter and Gleep, what did they know about a man's feelings? What he did, who he was? Turdball and a breed—and *they* were telling *him*? See who'd do the telling.

"Anyway, you rest up awhile. Couple hours, we'll be back. But I want you to think about something while we're gone. Here's what it is. Did you know if you take a shank—thin blade, razor edge, sort of like the one I'm packin'—and if you're real careful with it, you can slit the skin right over the eyelids and just kind of slide the eyeballs out enough they're still attached, hangin' down loose on the cheekbones. You know that? It's a fact; I seen it done once. Was done to a walleye spade had the bad habit staring at folks. Way you do. Well, you get a whole different look at the world that way, old eyeballs danglin' out there in the breeze, starin' down for a change 'stead of straight on. Yessir, see things a lot different, I bet. You think about that, you're takin' your rest. Give it some heavy thought. We'll be down, talk to you again. Meantime, take a good look at things right side up."

You can start with the notion of an aperture, a gap, a hole, which implies two sides, inside, out. A mouth, say. With split lips, thin stream of air coming through. From the outside in. Then you can advance to the sensation of something cool on those lips; cool swirling around a tongue too thick for the mouth, hanging victim's tongue; and cool going down. And then, like forms taking shape, outline, dimension moment by moment under an ascending light, the viscous blur erasing all distinction between subject and object, inside and out, will begin to give way, dissolve. And you're on your way back.

He could make out a ham-size hand, a Dixie cup, a figure of some amplitude, bulk, the basement room. He could feel a metronomic thumping, head to toe, the beat of pain. He tasted water. Heard a low rumbling voice, very near a growl: "How you doin'?" He was coming back.

It was the one called Gleep, pulled up close in the same chair the fat one, one with all the syrup, had occupied. He put the empty cup on the floor. He was relaxed, smoking thoughtfully. "Want a puff?" he said.

Light as it was, the cigarette stung his prickly lips. Stung on the inhale too, a strange welcome singeing in the throat and lungs. A trickle of smoke escaped him. From inside to out. He was certainly back. Irrevocably back.

" 'nother?"

Waverly tried to shake his head but it went downward rather than sideways.

Gleep ground the butt under his heel. He studied him a moment. Appraised him. Then he said, "You been in the joint." It was an assertion of shared experience, not a question.

Waverly didn't try to speak yet.

"Where was you?"

"Jacktown," he said, and the sound of his own voice, sandpaper wheeze, stunned him. Voice of an ancient rummy.

"Figured. When was that?"

"Seventy-six to eighty-three. One time-out. Ypsi."

"Ypsi. Then I bet you was Five Block."

"Five. Right."

The curious turns of chance, of which there had been a few in his life, never failed to astound Gleep. "I come down from Marquette, seventy-eight," he said. "Did six, Jacktown, last two of 'em on Five. Don't place you though."

"Zoo was full, those days."

Gleep snorted. "Huh, zoo. That one you got correct. What level you on?"

"Top."

"I was down on two. Remember how you'd catch the green blazers on the catwalks?"

"Shit shower."

"And the asswipe fireballs?"

"Spud juice? Crack your skull?"

"Them classes they had, gonna reha*bili*tate you. Meat on the seat."

"The birds on the ceiling. Remember them?"

"Yeah, them fuckin' birds." Gleep scratched his stiff hair, chuckled to himself. He was swamped with memories. "How'd you come out, the eight-one trashin'?"

"What I did," Waverly said, "I kept my head down." Even shaving the syllables, slurring, it was painful to get the words out, but coming a little easier. Surprised him, he still had some of the words. What he couldn't figure was what was going on here.

"You was smart. I did three months in the pound afterward. Got in some nice paybacks though. Was worth it." A scowl passed over his face at this memory. He lit another cigarette, dragged on it and held it up, an offer.

"Don't mind," Waverly said.

The smoke burned yet, but the ache in his chest was almost pleasurable, dampened the throbbing there. Coming off of Gleep as he leaned in close to balance the cigarette was a heavy odor of beer.

"You remember a dude, never knew his name, went by Dog? Colored boy? On three?"

"Dog," Waverly said, trying to picture him.

"Doper. Psycho clean through."

"That takes in about everybody, Five."

"Yeah, but Dog, he was wacko. Said he controlled things through the teevee."

The murky picture came into dim focus. "Claimed he could send fuck signals through it? Knock women up? Think I heard."

"That's the one. Dog. I mean, we was crazy but he was tunes, Captain Tunes. You know he'd kista-stash a Butterfinger bar, no wrapper, and then he'd eat it back in his cell?"

"Didn't hear that."

"True fact. Also he was a snitch. Fuckin' dingleberry snitch. We got him though, eighty-one. Got him a room in the crippled-coons home permanent."

Both of them were silent awhile. Waverly watched the scowl fade, displaced by a glazed, faraway look. He was mystified. A couple of crusty veterans, chewing over the old days, exercising the earned right of selective recall. What was going on?

After a time Gleep said, "You take a Jacktown scrubbin' real good, y'know that."

"Thanks."

" 'bout as good as I seen."

Waverly nodded. It was gratifying to see he could make his head move the direction he wanted now.

"Only guy I seen done it better was a inmate name of Chop. You know him?"

"I knew him," Waverly said.

"Sort of figured that. Old Chopper, nobody like him." Gleep looked down at his bruised knuckles. "You come close."

"He was something," was all Waverly could think to say.

"Hope to shit, he was something. Saw him get burned once out in the yard. Gang of your blacks again, Young Boys Ink, out of Detroit. Real mean. They put a wall around him, nobody could get to him. You never seen a poundin' like that one. Broke both his legs. Fingers too, one at a time. They'd of waxed him for sure, the blazers didn't step in. Put him in hospital six months, heard."

"When was this?"

"Oh, eighty-three, four. Right before I was walked. After your time, prob'ly."

"How'd he do?"

"Did just fine. Them spooks, they didn't get nothin' out of him. Not a howl. Sound one. Stared 'em down and then got off someplace like he wasn't there. Like you done tonight. Which is what put me in mind of Chop."

"You know him well?"

"Yeah, pretty good. Well, good as he'd let you. He was, y'know, on his own planet. That's how he got by, 'spose, doin' life. Thing about old Chopper, for a hard case he was a human being."

The memory of Chop rose like a phantom breeze off the landscapes of their past, touched each of them.

"Y'know," Gleep said, looking away, "this"—specifying *this* with a sweep of one enormous hand—"ain't nothin' personal. It's just . . ." He searched for the proper word. "Employment."

"I understand."

"I was you, I'd tell 'em. What the fuck."

"What the fuck," Waverly said.

"If I knew."

"If."

Gleep said no more. He sat gazing at the floor awhile and then he was gone, and after a time Waverly slid into a twilight, numb but still conscious of the electric storms pulsating through him and awake enough to recognize he was wondering: wondering if he had dreamed the whole thing, the presence, talk (for it had the vivid sentient power of a waking dream); and wondering if he had dreamed the other one's dark warning tale of slashed eyelids and if he hadn't, how he would do when the time came, how Chop would do it. Strapped to the chair, tracking down the labyrinths of chilly dreams.

It was something resembling a squawk or a screech brought him around, high-pitched, muffled, spaced in measured intervals, like a phone jangling in a distant attic room. He didn't want to know what it was, wasn't interested, but it persisted and eventually he opened his eyes. A few feet away Midnight was sprawled on the floor, legs extended and bound at the ankles. Her wrists, also bound, were crossed in front of her and her mouth was taped. Except for a purplish splotch on one cheek, she looked uninjured. But her head was bobbing frantically and her eyes alternately locked on his and dropped downward, as though directing him to something. The urgent squawks kept on coming.

It took him a moment to understand. To grasp the fact that his arms were dangling limply at his sides and his feet free to move. If they would. Steadying himself with both hands on the seat of the chair, he shifted his weight onto his legs, started to rise and pitched forward onto the floor. He got to his knees and made it over to her on all fours.

"Waverly, Jesus, what have they done to you?" was the first she said once the tape was off.

He was tugging feebly at the rope on her wrists. Get that and she could do the rest. "Called a touchup," he said.

She had her ankles drawn up and was working on the

last knot. Then she leaned over and cradled his chin in one hand and with the other brushed the matted hair, sticky with dried blood, off his forehead. "What have they done?"

"How'd you get here?"

"The ape man. King Kong. Can you move?"

"He cut me loose?"

"I'm not sure. The light was out. Can you move? Walk?"

"Run would be better."

"Can you?"

"I can try."

Yanking, heaving, her arms locked around his chest and her fingers laced tightly, she got him to his feet, more or less upright, supported by her thin shoulders. It occurred to him she had remarkable strength for someone so delicately fashioned. "You do good work, lady. Put you in, the Mother Teresa award."

"Can you walk?"

"Easy. One foot front of the other."

But his first step was little more than a halting lurch, and the second not much better.

"I don't know," she said.

"I can," he said hoarsely. He was thinking less about his splashy legs and more of his eyelids, remembering the warning, knowing it was no dream. And knowing equally he would not handle it well, not that one. Not enough Chop in him for that one. "*Can*," he said again.

She put a cautionary finger to her lips. "Still, now. I don't know who's upstairs."

"Stairs might be tougher." He had forgotten the stairs.

"No stairs. We're ground-level. There's a door down here. If they're not both locked."

"Let's find out."

Miraculously, the door to the furnace room fell open and they groped through the dark space to another and that one gave way, too. And then they were out in the night, putting the house behind them, staggering through some scraggly brush and into the trees, Waverly moving his legs with the deliberate mechanical precision of a windup doll, Midnight stumbling some, sometimes buckling under his weight but then recovering, urging him on with sharp hissing sounds, unintelligible.

"You should play the lottery," Waverly said to her. "You've got the touch."

Clay didn't know where he was headed but that was okay, anywhere would do as long as it was away from here. Waking this morning (Thursday, he had calculated, had to be Thursday; almost lost count of the days), he'd had some second thoughts about making a run for it. Till he took one look around squalor city. That was enough, that made up his mind. He squeezed through an upstairs window, early, before anyone arrived to open, and set out up the road. For the moment all that mattered was the movement, the outdoors air, sun again, warmer than usual today, good solid feel of his muscles limbering up again, of himself. Something was bound to come to him, some scheme. Matter of fact, when he thought about it, there were some pencil-neck rubes from the gym over on Garfield where he worked out sometimes, always hanging around asking advice on how to build pecs and lats like his. One of them ought to be honored to help out a little. It was a notion anyway, a place to begin.

Cars whizzed by. The lunch-bucket brigade, nine to five time-servers. None of that for Matthew Clay Clemmons, not as long as he held this bag of grade-A nose candy. Good as money in the bank. Roll it over into hard currency, coin of the realm, and he was on his way.

A sheriff's department black-and-white rolled up from behind, slowing as it passed. The officer treated him to an envious, disagreeable stare. Clay was used to that. But it occurred to him it was not too prudent to be tooling around with a satchelful of controlled substance slung over his shoulder, and he hadn't the slightest idea where to stash it. Safely, that is. He didn't go through all this grief only to have the goods disappear on him. At the same time, it would be hard to convince some slack-bellied cop, nothing better to do than roust a guy for the hideous crime of having a decent body, that he had rais-inettes in there.

Very shortly the dilemma was resolved for him. A couple of girls in a pickup pulled over and offered him a lift into town. He piled in. They made some broad hints about partying down after they got off shift, the Big Boy. Pair of tragic dogs, but they did have the wheels. And he was considering junking the gym plan and greasing them instead, right up to the second intersection stoplight where he discovered, parked in a self-serve station just across the street, the most inspiring sight he had laid eyes on in better than a week.

"Fortune smiles on her favorite fucking son," he said, and he leaped out the door of the idling truck. " 'Bye, girls. Have a nice day."

There it sat, the sleek, satin-black Porsche. Midnight's ultimate pride, and there it sat. Which meant she was still here, hadn't abandoned him. Mingled with his elation was a feeling close to remorse for ever entertaining the notion she might. Of course the car had to be locked, naturally, God bugger it. He leaned against the door, lost in thought, figuring his best moves. When he looked up it was into a pimple-plagued face topped by a ratty, spiked do. The cash register jockey, asking how come he was here, hanging around this car.

There was a variety of responses he could make, but it struck him the most appropriate was, astonishingly, the truth. "This belongs to a lady I know. Friend. Well, she's my sister actually. She asked me to pick it up for her. You want to get the keys."

"Huh, you think I just got in off the back forty? Forget that shit."

"Look, her name's Clemmons. If I wasn't being straight with you, how would I know that? Hers is Clemmons, so's mine. Show you ID. Five in it for you."

"No wh-ay hoe-zay. Moon said don't let nobody fuck with this auto-mo-*beel*. Like in nobody. You dig?"

Jesus. This close. And square in the path an asshole bumpkin kid who'd seen too much television and too many drive-in movies. "Who's Moon?" Clay asked.

"Dale Moon," the kid said, inflecting upward, as though amazed anyone could be untouched by the fame of Dale Moon. "Manages the place."

"Okay. Lady leaves a Porsche, she leaves an address. A number. Let's call and get her permission." Clay spoke clearly and reasonably, though what he felt like doing was kicking the little turd in the balls and simply taking the keys. But he didn't need any more trouble than he already had.

"Don't know nothin' about that. Moon just said watch out for it. Don't let nobody near it. So you better scoot."

"How long has it been here?"

"Why should I tell you. You ain't even suppose to be by it."

Clay took out his wallet and gave him a five, served it with a disarming grin. "About how long?"

The blotched forehead knotted, agonized effort of concentration. "Shit, I dunno exactly. Four, five days. Was here when I come in Monday. But I wasn't here when —"

"When the lady brought it in. I know, I know. Okay. But she must have left a number. Just give me that and there's another of those bills for you."

"No address," he said firmly and with a ring of conviction, "no phone. Besides, you gotta be shittin' me. Moon said it was a guy left it. Said to call him, this guy come after it. Not to let him have the keys till he got here. Moon, I mean."

"A man left it?" A man? What the bloody fuck could *that* mean? She wouldn't have brought some overnight along, not on this jaunt. Maybe she'd hired a detective after they failed to connect. Or maybe—and this sent a rush of anxiety through him—they'd got to her, Ledbetter's goons. There was no way he could know for certain, and for now not a goddam thing he could do. Anyway, there was the more immediate concern of the goods, their temporary disposition. Very serious concern.

And then it came to him with all the intense sudden clarity of a divine insight, divinely ordered. The whole concept, clear as polished glass, the way out. Leave the goods in the car and stop waltzing with this featherhead hick. Get on over to the gym and scam some loot off his fans, enough to persuade the jerk-off manager to cough up the keys (hundred ought to do it and he had almost forty left on him), get back here, slide under the wheel and put some dust between him and Michigan's wonderland. He didn't dare think about Midnight yet. Later, maybe, if he could keep covered till after dark, maybe he'd swing by the Park Place, see what he could turn up. Or try phoning there again. Something, anyway. It would come to him.

Cost him a full twenty to get pimples to open the hatch and to reveal when the fabled Moon would be in. "Shows up in the afternoon. Different times. By three though." A little over seven hours to do it in. Baby food. He went striding off in the direction of Garfield, staying with the residential streets. Keeping down. No sense pushing his luck now.

The young man with the pimples and the hair went back to his cash register. He considered calling Moon and telling him what happened, but he had the nagging suspicion if he did, somehow he'd lose out on the twenty-five. Why should he? Nothing had really *happened,* if you thought about it. City boy with all the muscles comes by and leaves a bag in the car. So what? Car was still there, wasn't it? Nothing changed. No skin off his ass. Moon's, either.

It worried him a little but not for long, and after making change a few times, he soon forgot all about it. What he also forgot was that Thursday was Moon's day off.

"You know, Gaylon, I find myself at something of a loss. For words, I mean."

The voice of Gunter Dietz, disembodied though it was, came direct from the deep freeze, freighted with a distant menace. Time's up was the message in the spaces between the words. Gaylon's hand, the one that held the phone, shook. The other one, clutching a water glass full of Old Crow, did, too. The knuckles on both of them were yellow as buttermilk. Into the speaker he said, "Mr. Dietz, all I'm asking is one more day."

"It's not a question of time anymore, Gaylon. I think you're missing the point. It's more a crisis of, well, confidence."

Gaylon pictured him sitting at his rolltop desk in his gentleman's library, sipping a lemonade, got up in his fucking sissy-boy shorts, probably pink today, gripping *his* phone nice and relaxed and talking mildly into it, softer than ever if it was possible to do that without finally just lip-synching his thoughts. But the wheels turning steady all the while, computing, judging, reckoning; measuring dependable old Gaylon for a fucking shroud.

"They got to be right out here in the woods," he said. "Guy was in no shape to get far. I saw to that. And one of the boys I got tracking them," he added hopefully, "he's an Indian."

"The fish again."

"Huh?" What the fuck was he talking, fish? "Don't follow you, Mr. Dietz."

"You said there were Indians who guaranteed a catch. Of fish. I believe you said that, the other day. Remember?"

Gaylon made a little bark intended as a laugh. "Oh yeah, that. But anyway—"

"The reason I recalled that," Dietz broke in, "the fish. The reason was, it seems to me, that's about the sum of what I've been getting since I've been here. Guarantees. But no fish."

"Mr. Dietz, I—"

"Let me finish, Gaylon. Our organization stands to take a substantial loss if those goods aren't recovered. One way or another. I have people to report to, same as you. Shareholders, you might think of them."

There was an interval of silence. Gaylon couldn't tell whether he was expected to put something into it or not. He tried not.

"I've got to leave today," Dietz went on. "Get back home. Holiday and all. The wife's having some people in. For dinner. Neighbors, and some friends."

Yeah yeah yeah yeah—wife, neighbors, friends, dinner—what's next? Goddam menu? Guest list? Spit it the fuck out, Gaylon said, thought, wished he said, wished he had the scrotum weight to say, wished he was someplace else listening to something, someone, else, wished it wasn't such a slippery splintered world he inhabited, everything infected, gone wrong. The water glass was half down. If it had been a bowl of soup in front of him, he'd have drowned by now, nodded off and drowned waiting for Dietz to get to the bad news.

Eventually he did, and in the hardest, wintriest tone Gaylon had ever in his life heard. "You've got till Saturday. Noon Saturday. I expect to hear some good news by then. If not, I'll be sending in a replacement, clear this problem up."

This pause was long enough Gaylon knew it was his turn to speak. Say something. But what was left to say? More reassurances? Guarantees? Pleas? He was fresh out of all of them. His eyes roamed about the house that had, at one time, meant so much to him, represented so much. The late-morning sun slanted through the bay window and warmed his fleshy neck. Nevertheless, he felt cold.

"Gaylon?"

"I hear what you're tellin' me, Mr. Dietz."

"Saturday noon," he repeated, the last he said.

Gaylon put down the phone and stared numbly into his glass. Saturday noon. Forty-eight hours. This time he wasn't going to make it. He got out a cigar and lit up. Might as well. Condemned man's always entitled to a last smoke. And so he sat there, lost in mournful rumination and gripped in the paralysis of ruin and despair.

Dietz, at that same moment, was also engaged in somber reflection, pondering darkly the subjects of incompetence and ingratitude, the bane of visionary entrepreneurs everywhere. He felt a powerful urge to beat on something, someone, and his hands were balled into tight fists, and shaking. After he calmed down some, he picked up the phone again and dialed a Chicago number.

"Yeah?" came a rude voice over the line.

"Eugene? This is Gunter Dietz speaking."

"Oh, Mr. Dietz. How's she goin'?"

"Fine, Eugene. Just fine."

"That's real fine. Somethin' I can do for you?"

"There might be, Eugene."

"You name it, Mr. Dietz, it's done."

"Well, the thing is, I've got a messy little personnel problem. With some people in Michigan. I thought maybe you could locate someone, help me clean it up."

"Like a popper, huh?"

"Something like that. Yes."

"That hadn't ought to be no trouble, Mr. Dietz. Always glad to pitch in."

"That's what I like to hear, Eugene. Now let me explain what I have in mind."

Shadow came out of the woods about two miles from Gaylon's house. He was sweaty and beat. He squatted down in some scrub grass by the dirt road and waited for Gleep. Enough of this open-air shit, it felt good to rest. His pants were ripped at the knee, caught on a branch, and his right forearm was bleeding from when he stumbled over a mossy rock and went sprawling into some brambles. Probably poison fucking ivy, his luck. What was he doing anyway, battling a goddam forest. Gleep, okay, that was different. Playing at Cochise, that come natural. But he was from the city, for Christ's sake, Chicago; closest to woods he ever seen till he got up here was Lincoln Park. Which was as close as any normal guy, stand-up, had his head buckled on correct, would ever want to be. For all he knew there was bears in there, or snakes, and he wasn't too partial toward either.

Shadow was sweaty and tired and bleeding a little, but mostly he was consumed by a fury elemental and without flourishes. And all the more potent for being internalized, nothing to ventilate on. Yet. The bellowing and yapping, howling, the stuck-pig shows, they were for the likes of a Ledbetter. Not his style. No. They'd had him and lost him, Mr. Cocksuck. No way could it happen, yet there it was. Okay. Okay. But they were going to connect again, and soon; Shadow could feel it right down to the marrow of his bones. There had been a few times in his life, not many, he'd had that feeling, that utter certainty. It was like holding a pair of fireworks dice and knowing—just *knowing*—your arm was oiled and you got a money roll coming out. Good feeling, and he had it again now, but packaged in contained rage and telescoped onto one man, one ceremonial act. For reasons he didn't fully understand, it was the Timothy Waverlys he hated and feared more than anything else in this world. It was their stares, their remote glacial stares, seemed to penetrate right down to the core of his malignant, fragile heart, expose him, diminish him, vanish him finally. Lay the eyeballs out on the cheeks and let them stare from a different angle, see who did the vanishing then. The broad, kid, goods, anymore they were sideline action, Gaylon's problem. Shadow, he had an errand to run, delivery to make, special, personal: Mr. Timothy Waverly? Express mail, sign here. Oh, they were going to connect again. And when they did there'd be no more bashing parties, next time. Next time was the blade.

Except that next time ought to be *this* time, way he felt, this moment, right now. And here he was, farting into trees, Gaylon's idea naturally, and coming up dribble shit. Naturally. They weren't going to find them in any woods and Shadow knew it. Or rather sensed it, and trusted his instincts. Should have trusted them all along. Instead of listening to that crybaby.

Earlier Gaylon had come storming into the back room where Shadow was crashed, catching his little snooze, earned one at that, the work he'd put in. Come shaking him and squalling like some dust-mop-head grandma got her coin purse lifted. Gone, they're fuckin' gone! We got zip now! What am I gonna do? Tell Dietz? What the sweet holy fuck am I gonna do? Slapping at his forehead with the flat of his hand. Tearing down the stairs, back up, all over the house. Moaning, It's history now, history. Might as well been bawling, he was that close. Bad as a baby fish, first time in the hole. Make a man almost sick to see it.

Shadow had found Gleep asleep on a couch in the

sun parlor. They went down below and checked things out: chair empty, ropes and tape on the floor, lower-level door wide open. Scumsuckers were sure enough gone, both of 'em. How'd this happen? he said, and Gleep merely shrugged. He tried to run it by in his head, puzzle it through. Gaylon's slick idea was to give it an hour or so till wormfood come around enough to watch real good. Then bring the cunt down, whack her around some in front of the boyfriend, see what that might do for his fogged-over memory. That part was okay, made a kind of sense. But somewhere in that hour in there, three of them zonked out, the circuits blew. How? Shadow believed he was honing in on something when just then Gaylon come busting through the door, pounding them on the shoulders like some goddam coach got a new game plan. In the trees! They got to be right out there in the trees! Shadow cut him off cold. Gaylon, he said, while you was in here chattin' with our boy alone, you didn't maybe fuck with his ropes any, did you? For a minute there Gaylon looked like he got his bell rung, then he come on swinging: What if I did? It was just to loosen him up some, oil him. When I seen it wouldn't help, I got him strapped back up tighter'n a fresh punk's bunghole. Shadow looked at him hard. You sure about that last part? Gaylon squawked out, Sure I'm sure. Christ, you oughta know, you was the last ones down here. Anyway, what counts ain't *how* they got sprung. They *are* sprung. You boys got to go find 'em. Flush 'em out. How far could they get?

So they fanned out in two wide arcs from the house and swept in zigzag patterns through the thick woods. And now here he was, balked, bone-weary, couple of good hours blown right out the ass.

Gleep came ambling up the road, moving like he was out for a morning's bird watching. Shadow hauled himself onto his feet. He swiped at his torn, stained, filthy slacks and sport shirt: new outfit, too, picked up just the other day, Sears, ready for the rag heap now. "You see anything?" he said.

"Unh unh."

"Nothing? No sign?"

"Nothin' that direction. You?"

"I did, would I be on my ass in the grass? Thought stalking woods was what you people did."

Gleep looked at him and didn't answer right away. What he finally said was, "Woods is scarce, Jacktown."

"Okay, man, I hear you. Let's head back."

They set out for Gaylon's place, Shadow in the lead, sticking with the road. Neither of them spoke for a time. The sun was directly overhead, but a cool easy wind sifted through the trees, turned up the leaves. A flock of white-bellied birds traced looping circles against a mild blue sky. Fifty feet ahead a small animal raced across their path.

"Ought to have me a squirrel rifle," Shadow said.

"That's a rabbit."

"Rabbit rifle, then. Whatever."

They walked on.

Shadow's mind was occupied. Busy thinking ahead, crafting a plan, but gliding backward too, poking at the riddle.

"Don't it seem peculiar to you," he said, "them getting away like that? Gleep. Don't it seem, y'know, queer?"

" 'spose so. Didn't think about it much."

"Think about it. Along with me. We had him all trussed up, right? Nice and snug?"

"Absolutely."

"The Clemmons bitch, she was tied, too."

"That's what Ledbetter said."

"Okay. She's up, he's down. Three of us, we're taking our little break. Little snooze. So how do they get loose, first place, and how do they get together, second place?

He's got to have help, shape we put him in. To get out of there, third. Answer me that one."

"Beats shit out of me. Maybe Ledbetter ain't so handy with the ropes as he says. Maybe he needs to go to knot-tyin' school. Learn something more'n a granny."

Shadow kept walking, but he slowed down so he was even with Gleep. "That could be," he said, "but you'd figure he'd take better care, all he stands to lose. Think about some other way."

"What other?"

"That's what I'm askin'," Shadow said, and he stopped and turned to face his partner. "All that leaves is you and me. And I guess you know where I'm at, that counter."

Gleep looked at him narrowly. "Maybe you got something you want to tell me."

They watched each other a moment. Then Shadow said, "Got nothin' to tell you, Gleep. I'm just, what you might say, speculatin' here."

"You got some problem, you better say."

"No problem. But this speculatin' I'm doing, goes both ways, frontwards and back. What happened, what's going to happen. I'll find him, Gleep. You know that."

"Never thought no different. Tell you this, though. He don't know nothin'. He did, we'd have it by now."

"Don't mean shit!" Shadow said fiercely, underscoring his words with three squared-off chopping motions of his hands. Then, more calmly, "He knows, he don't. That ain't what this is about no more. You see that?"

"I see it. So we find him."

"Oh, I will find him. But all this speculatin', it's making me wonder where you're going to be when I do."

"Where you figure I'd be? Speculatin'."

"That's what I'm askin'."

"Where the fuck I been," Gleep said, "ever since we teamed up? Since you come and got me off that car wash, got me fixed up, this turn? Be right where I always been, is where I'll be. You don't buy that, we better hang it up right here."

The words came spilling out. A furious glint flared in his eyes. Shadow held up the palm of one hand.

"All right. Okay. You understand what I'm gettin' at. Man's got to cover his back, line of work we're in."

"You asked, that's the answer."

Shadow gave him a slow motion punch on the arm. Comrades again. "Good enough for me," he said. "Any day of the week. Let's go see what dumb idea pissbrain's hatchin' now."

But when they arrived at the house what they discovered was not a cunning hatcher of schemes but a dejected, beaten man. Gaylon was slumped in an overstuffed chair, gazing at the floor. Everything about him—jowls, chins, belly folds, hams—sagged. Desolation's gravity. He didn't look up when they came through the door. "You didn't find them," he said heavily.

"Face it, Gaylon. They ain't going to hide out in no woods. Not them two. They're maybe into town by now, no further'n that."

"We got to refigure," Gaylon said, but there was no force in his voice. It had a dull, towel-throwing quality to it, the resonance of defeat.

It was mildly disturbing to Shadow because in all the years they had been together he had never seen him quite like this. He decided he liked the old shit-snorting Gaylon better, the twitchy blustering whale. Of the two. "Dietz give you an extension, huh," he said. Rag him a little. Bring him around.

"I got till Saturday. That's the end."

"Saturday, you'll be home free."

"Yeah. Home free. You want to call stiff city that."

Shadow drew up a chair and sat down opposite him. "You got to be cool," he said. "Loose. Nothing's going to happen. Except good." This was unfamiliar country for him: solace, comfort, pity. He was out of place there, a stranger fumbling with an alien tongue. He glanced over his shoulder at Gleep standing in the hallway, an absent look on his face. No help there. "We're going to find them," he said and, almost in afterthought, "get the goods back, too." What he wanted to convey was some of the sure sense of inevitability he felt back on the road. Trouble was, he didn't have the words.

"I'm history," Gaylon mumbled. "This is the end."

"Hey, Gaylon. Come on. We got to see things positive here. Look at me. I look worried?"

To Shadow's considerable surprise, Gaylon, as though responding to a directive, did just that, looked at him. Lifted eyes filmy with tears. The meaty lips quivered. "You been a friend, Shadow. Hawkins there, too. But me, Saturday's the end."

Shadow's store of sympathy, in short supply anyway, was all but exhausted. What he felt like doing was laughing out loud. What he did was rise awkwardly and say, "I think maybe you better let me and Gleep take care of things. We got some ideas. Tell you what. You stay right here and we'll get back to you. Okay? Gaylon?"

Gaylon nodded dismally.

"I'm tellin' you. When you hear from us, it's going to be Christmas time news. Champagne time. Fartin' through silk again."

In the car on the drive into town, Gleep said, "Makes you 'bout heave up, don't it."

Shadow responded with a grunt. He was looking out the window, smoking and thinking. Sorting it out. The woods faded into grassland, brown fields.

"You do good work, hand holdin'," Gleep said. "But what's them ideas we got?"

"Fucked if I know," Shadow said, and truthfully, for he had none. Only the serene knowledge that this tangled little episode in his life was moving rapidly and as if by magic toward a happy ending. "But that don't matter. I wasn't just shittin' that jelly ball, y'know. We're gonna find them."

They passed through the village of Acme and the fields gave way to gas stations, bait shops, canoe liveries, motels, antique barns, fried-food cafes. At the city-limits sign, Gleep said, "Where to?"

"My place. Going to get myself spiffed up, boy." Shadow looked over at his partner. "You ought to do the same. There's good times ahead, Gleep, my man."

"We're the Leaches," Midnight said brightly, voice of sick-room cheer. "Mr. and Mrs. Archie Leach. You know who that is?"

Waverly was rubbing at his rheumy eyes. But lightly, ever so lightly. He tried to edge himself up against the headboard, failed. Apart from his fingers—and they were playing out—nothing seemed to want to work. He felt nailed to the bed. There was a coarse blanket over him, pulled to the chin. Underneath, he could feel he was naked. The room, what he could see of it, was foreign, shabby, tiny, barely big enough to change your mind in.

"First I think I'm supposed to say, 'Where am I?' "

"Sugar Beach Resort and Motel. Nice snug harbor. Maybe a little inelegant, but safe. Don't you want to know who you are, Mr. Leach?"

"Bet I'm going to find out."

"Cary Grant. That's how we're registered. Archibald Leach, Cary Grant. And you thought my drama training was so much fluff."

"Shows how wrong a man can be."

She sat in a chair at the foot of the bed, and by sighting down the length of his body, not moving his head, he could make out her blurry image. Her hair was wet and clung to her neck and bare shoulders like streaks of black paint. She was wrapped in a large towel. She seemed to be smiling. "Can you eat?" she asked, holding up a Styrofoam cup. "I got you some soup."

"Try a cigarette first."

She lit a Carlton and came over and fit it gently in his mouth. Lit another for herself and sat beside him on the bed. She brought with her a fragrance of bath oils and dusting powders.

"Do you have much pain?" she asked. "Don't say only when I laugh."

What he had was not pain so much as a decentralized pulsating throb. Like someone encased in ice and precipitantly thawed, all the nerve ends ticking. "I've felt better in my life," he said. He touched at his face gingerly, the way a blind man constructs an inner vision from the contours under his fingertips. It felt raw, lumpy. "Looked a little better too, I expect."

She leaned over and brushed his forehead with her lips. "You look just fine," she said.

"What time is it?"

"Must be around nine." The curtains were drawn and the room dark, but for a single dim lamp on the dresser. "At night."

"What day?"

"Day?" An eyebrow arched steeply. "It's Thursday. The day after."

"You going to tell me how we got here? Wherever here is."

"Here is still Traverse City. Or close by. We were in the woods and you couldn't go any farther. You don't remember that?"

Waverly shook his head no. That he could make it move was an encouraging sign.

"I left you hidden in some brush and went on ahead. There was a house, cottage. I pounded on the door—it was still dark, you understand—and a man opened up.

180

Sweet elderly gentleman, in his underwear. Lived alone, a widower, he said. He's the one carried the day, really. But then I do a terrific lady in distress, too." She smiled faintly. "I guess you already know that."

"What did you tell him?"

"Improvised. A party down the road, too much liquor, some bullies, drunk, a fight, help help—that sort of thing. I can be very inventive, when I have to."

"He got us in here?"

"In his mighty Sno Commander. What he really wanted to do was take us in, call the police. I cut that off. We couldn't have been more than a couple of miles from . . . them."

"How?"

"How what?"

"You said you cut that off. How?"

"Why all the questions? We're out of there aren't we?"

"I want to know where things stand this time. What's in the wings."

"All right. I talked him out of it. He was sweet but sort of senile. I've learned some cunning too, Waverly. Since you. You'd have been proud, I think."

"I am," he said, remembering, all of it coming back, or most of it. Some of it. He was wonderstruck to be here, alive, his eyeballs still in their sockets. Damaged goods, but still intact. "I owe you."

"How does that joke go? The harelip lady, after a certain kind of lovemaking, says, 'You don't owe me nothin', honey, just give me a kiss.' "

There are any number of ways to deal with it, Waverly thought, the miracle of apparent deliverance balanced against realities too bizarre, a widening dread. Hers was playfulness. Better that than hysteria. Better by far. And he meant what he said: She had come through, one way or another, though the details seemed somehow ajar, didn't quite lock in place; and he owed her more than she would ever understand. He turned slightly and stubbed out the cigarette in the ashtray she held. A thin shaft of pain plowed through his chest, and he winced.

"You okay? You going to be all right?"

He put his hands under the blanket and touched at his ribs. It was somewhat reassuring, parts of him working again at his bidding, pain or not. He flexed his legs at the knees, jiggled his hips. "About thirty percent right now," he said. "Feels like nothing's broken. I'm coming around."

"Afraid I don't do the angel of mercy very well. Cleaned you up, tried to make you comfortable. I thought about getting a doctor."

"Smart move, you didn't. Where's my clothes?"

"Why?"

"Why? Because we've got to get moving, out of here. And now. They found us once, they will again."

He braced his hands on the mattress and pushed himself half-upright. Slowly and with all the purposeful caution of a brittle-boned octogenarian, he slid his legs over the side of the bed. Midnight watched him.

"A little hand here wouldn't do any harm."

"You may as well accept it, Waverly. You're not going anywhere tonight. Tomorrow's soon enough. Things to do tomorrow."

"By tomorrow I could have a very skewed vision of the world. Not a metaphor. Come on."

She kept on watching.

Under his own power he got to his feet and stood there a moment, wobbling. He gave her a shapeless grin. "There. See. Told him it couldn't be done, so he tackled it with a smile. . . ." But a fog descended over the room and the earth began to sway beneath him.

She rose up quickly and eased him back onto the bed. Propped a pillow under his head and tucked the blanket around him again. ". . . And he couldn't do it," she finished for him. "Not tonight anyway."

The towel had fallen away and her tight small breasts moved like roving gunsights, moved as she moved, a fluid grace.

"Nurse Clemmons, you're out of uniform."

She produced the Styrofoam cup and a plastic spoon. "Eat soup, you nasty naked man."

Soup was cold but he didn't say so. Before long he felt drowsy, and gestured enough. Flashing through his head were the things to attend to, many things, crucial. He tried to fix them, impose an order, but sleep was crowding in. "Don't go out," he said. "Whatever you do, don't go near that hotel, Park Place. And stay clear of your car. They'll be watching. Tomorrow we'll get one, rent one, something. Get out of this town. Find a way."

She nodded at him tolerantly, wisely. "Tomorrow," she said, and then she set the cup aside and put out the light and slid in under the blanket, settling the length of herself against him gently.

"Don't think I can do you much good tonight," he mumbled.

"Wrong again, Waverly. You don't have any idea how much good you do me."

And she spoke no lie, there in the dark. What defines *good*? There was the chaste feel of him, the leanness, the hard battered toughness. And there was the mystery of him, and the innocence. The fragile cynicism. Artless tenderness. All that was good, for it was outside the range of her experience. Till now. She had never, when she thought about it, actually cared for anyone—Clay, well, that was different, accidental, an accommodation, now become an obligation, from which she would probably never be unshackled. The word *love* had never been part of her lexicon, wasn't yet, and she doubted it ever could be. But some peculiar law of compensation seemed to be operating here, and it impelled her to wonder if finally she were being called to account. The balance sheet of the heart. No, she had not lied to this sleeping man beside her, this stranger. Not about the extraordinary unexplored territories they had journeyed together, and in under a week, the blinking of an eye. If there was a definition for love, maybe that was it. That much was the truth.

But she had not told him all of it, either. How the sweet and senile old man was neither all that sweet nor all that senile, and how it required some small share of her talented stroking to get them as far as town. How she had already been, while he slept, to the Park Place, not once but twice. How the Porsche was already recovered and was right now nestled out of sight between two Winnebagos in the Sugar Beach lot. And how tomorrow she was going to need his help one more time: spring Clay free of all this and put the whole sordid fugitive episode behind them. And then they could complete the journey. Wherever it might lead.

It was shortly after two when Shadow heard a knock on the door of his second-floor efficiency. Had to be Gleep, so he called out a greeting and went right ahead patting talcum over his freshly shaven face. Bring the shine down a little. He rubbed some oil into his sparse hair, parted it meticulously, sprayed his pits. Then he put on the chartreuse shirt with the vertical stripes, lengthened him out some, and scrutinized himself in the full-length mirror on the back of the bathroom door. He was not entirely dissatisfied with what he saw: sporty-looking dude, a study in green, the pale shirt against forest-green double-knit slacks, a thin lime-colored belt, all of it set off by polished burgundy loafers. Dressed to—haw haw—kill.

He felt good. No accounting for it, way things seemed

to be shaking down, but there it was. Good. Better than he could remember feeling in a long time. How could he explain it to a lump like Gleep out there: *seemed* ain't always *is*. An inner vision of certitude had taken hold, and he sensed he stood on the edge of something mysterious, predestinated. And though he was eager to get on with it, watch it unfold, he was also curiously relaxed too, as though nothing he might do or not do could alter in the slightest any of it. Under the layers of talcum, his blotched face glowed, and the reflection in the mirror gave him back a beatific smile.

"My thought is," he said to Gleep a moment later, "they got to make a run for the car."

"Which one? He was drivin', too."

Gleep was sprawled all over Shadow's favorite chair, a black bean bag he kept in a corner of the tiny living room. The weight of him splayed it out, damn near collapsed it, and Shadow frowned, seeing him there. He considered saying something about it but then rejected the notion. Why tarnish the good feeling over a chair, even if he was proud of it. Happy thoughts only, today.

"Porsche," he said. "Look at it this way. His car's got to be back at the hotel, and they're not going there. Ain't that stupid. Not to the heat either, what they're into. They got no money, clothes. They got nothing. And both of 'em are draggin' ass. Where they going?"

"Leaves the Porsche," Gleep said with a shrug.

"You got it. And we got a real cooperative Mr. Moon sittin' on top that vehicle. We wanted, we could just hang out here, wait for the phone to ring. Guarantee you, it'd be him."

"So that's what we do? Wait here?"

Shadow deliberated awhile. His impulse was to do just that, wait, for he was convinced his scenario was right on the money. On the other hand, man had to be practical too, least make a show of earning his keep. Couldn't hurt to drop in on Moon, cheer him up a little. Keep him honest. Didn't matter either way; either way he was golden. "No," he said finally. "Nice pretty day like this one, we're going out and get some air. Maybe have a chat with the Moondog, or maybe feed our faces first. Plenty of time."

At about that same time, Clay came through the doors of the downtown Big Boy and plopped himself in a booth near the cash register up front. He ordered coffee and a Farmers omelette and told the waitress to bring him a tall glass of ice water. He was thirsty and hungry and just about done in, all the walking, halfway into town, all the way across it and all the way back. Flyspeck burg or not, that was a lot of stepping, more than he was used to, especially after this past week. And all of it for nothing too, a clean wash. Couldn't cadge a dime off any of those dickheads at the gym. Lots of sorrys, no cash. Which left only the cunts from the pickup this morning, and that meant a burned bridge to mend. It was a fallback position, at best, and he was already perilously close to the wall.

Nevertheless, Clay had confidence in his powers, his magnetism; he wasn't all that worried. He spotted one of them cleaning a table over by the garbage heap they called a salad bar, and he cranked up the old boyish grin, sent it flashing telepathically her way. Soon the message got through and she came breezing past his booth, pretending to ignore him. He reached out and caught her by the wrist.

"Hey, pumpkin. I'm back."

"Big deal," she said, unwinding his fingers one at a time, elaborate show of disdain. She looked at him without smiling. But she didn't move away either, and he knew it was simply a matter of time and some patient wheedling. He knew women, girls, even the unblessed kind like Darla here (as the name tag on the uniform,

MICHIGAN ROLL

earth-brown and food-stained, identified her), with her knobby nose and tombstone teeth and semaphore ears. Mole on her cheek that qualified, in her case, as an ugly mark. Frizzy ginger hair. Jesus, it was wondrous what you had to bring yourself to do sometimes, to get by.

"Party still on?" he said.

"Huh! Some party boy you are, way you went bustin' out of my truck."

There was a coy grievance in her tone. Demand for penance. "Aw, Darla," Clay said, "come on. There was this guy across the street I had to get to. He had something of mine. The light was changing, traffic. What could I do? You got my apologies. Come on."

"I don't know. We got feelings too, y'know."

"I'm back, aren't I?"

"Yeah, how long for this time?"

Bitch wanted some groveling. What she really deserved was the plate of eggs smeared on her grocery-sack getup, add a little color to it, set off the ketchup splotches. Not a fucking thing he could do though; for right now, Miss Hash Browns was the only game in town. He tried another tack, thrust his arms overhead in a languid stretch, give her a shot of his torso sweep. "Long as it takes," he said.

Darla gazed at him appraisingly. She shifted her weight from one leg to the other, touched at her wiry hair. "We don't get off till four. That's over an hour."

"We?"

"Marlene and me."

"Who needs a Marlene. It's your truck, right?"

"My stepdad's."

"Whoever. Two of us, we can have a real sugar party." He paused, turned the all-purpose grin into a sly conspiratorial smirk. "You like to maybe go on manuevers, do some tooting? You ever do it under the influence? We're talking rockets, Darla. Star wars."

187

Darla's unlovely face opened up. Her lower lip drooped greedily. "You got stuff?"

"Fellow I had to see this morning? He's holding it. We'll need some change, though. Not much."

"I get paid today. And I got a Christmas Club account, at the bank."

"That's my girl," Clay said, and then he wagged a cautionary finger at her. "Not a word now. Get me some more of this mud, will you? I'll be right here."

One door closes, another opens up. When you're born worthy. Get all the gear. He put his legs out on the worn vinyl seat and watched her scurry off for the coffeepot. Settled in for the wait. Home free, or as good as. What he had neglected to notice, however, so intent his creamy conversation with poor ugly Darla had been, was the two figures he feared most in this world passing directly behind her in the aisle and sitting down not four booths away.

Clay ran. He had been glancing idly about, thinking, This is probably the last time in my life I'll ever be in one of these fried-air palaces, when his eyes met Shadow's, locked with them, and he bolted and ran, the hostess bawling after him something about a bill. He threaded in and out among the tourist throng on Front Street, but within a block the crowd thinned and whatever cover it offered was gone. He swung left on Park, heading for the beach, or somewhere, couldn't think where—get clear, make a dash for it? Get back in the crowd, get lost in it? Where? One voice in his head kept cheering him on: Run, run, you can make it, you're better than they are, faster, younger, smarter, run; another shrieked where where where Jesus where? On impulse, he turned into the alley behind the store buildings and doubled back in the direction he had come, weaving through trash bins, dumpsters, parked cars, loading vans, irritated clerks sneaking a smoke. Shrewd move, throw them off. Maybe. Over his shoulder he heard, or didn't hear, the pounding of heavy feet. He was too terrified to look back.

Coming out of the alley on Cass, he spotted two schoolmarmish ladies herding a gaggle of squealing kids toward the pedestrian tunnel under Grandview, passage to the zoo. He sprinted across the street and eased in among them, flashing a twisted grin at the astonished harrumphing ladies. Inside the tunnel the children's delighted screeches echoed shrilly off the damp walls. A hand grasped at his, and he jerked away.

"It's okay, mister. There aren't any snakes in here. Mrs. Dunkel said."

It was a child, a girl, came up about as high as his knees. She gave him a solicitous smile. "I'll hold your hand if you're scared."

"Thanks," Clay said, "but I'll make it."

Ten feet more and it was true. Out of the tunnel, mingle with the zoo mob, parents and their brats, slip off down the beach and back into town or someplace, phone Darla—it could all work yet.

"You going to ride the train?" the child asked him, and he was about to make some reply when it was done for him.

Shadow, leaning against an interior wall at the tunnel exit, sucking a toothpick nonchalantly, said, "No, sweetie, the nice man ain't going to ride today. He didn't pay for his ticket."

Clay spun around. And there stood Gleep.

"Y'know, Gleep, somebody walk on by, they might get the idea you and me was makin' a jail house san'wich, this nice chunk of white meat here."

Shadow was alluding to the way they sat, the three of them squeezed into the back of the Caprice, Clay in the middle. They were parked on a side street, away from the downtown bustle. Occasionally a car went by, but not often. Down the block an old man in his undershirt mowed grass. In the next yard some children tormented a chained dog. The sky was full of pulsing blue heat, unseasonable, not a wisp of a cloud; and the air inside the car, windows up, was close and dry. It was necessarily cramped, given Gleep's bulk and Clay's shoulders, and Shadow had to sit with one cheek on the seat and the other halfway up the door. That was okay. Didn't mind a bit. Not with this kind of luck, exceeded even his most fantastic imaginings.

A baffled fly crawled across the windshield. Shadow watched it awhile, fascinated. He said, "See that dumb fuckin' fly, Clay? See him?"

Clay's eyes, blank as knotholes, didn't move. Moment by moment his deeply tanned face was turning the color of sun-bleached grain, a miracle of pigmentation, only in reverse. The flat of the knife Shadow held caressed the line of his jaw.

"I'm suggestin' you take a look at that fly there."

"Yes, yes, I see it. Fly."

"Poor little fucker. Whole big world out there, go buzzin' around in, and he can't figure what's keepin' him out of it. Got to be able to see it, right?"

Clay didn't answer till the knife began turning slightly. Then he said quickly, stammering some, "Right, right, he can see, that's right."

Shadow glanced over at Gleep, who moved his head slowly, seemed to be suppressing a smile. And ordinarily that would have been enough, an amused, satisfied audience; but Shadow sensed he was on to something, this fly thing. Couldn't pinpoint what exactly, something. He decided to follow it further, see where it took him.

"But he can't get past," he said mournfully. "Got to make him crazy, is my thinkin'. Got to say to himself: Lookit out there, lady flies to jump, picnics, world full of dog shit. And he can't get at none of it. And it's glass is all it is. Nothing but a piece of glass. Ain't that remarkable, and kind of sad? Clay?"

"I never thought about it," Clay said, no hesitation. The knife was stroking his neck.

"I know you never did. That's your problem, part anyway. But I'm askin' you to now. Think. Along with me. Y'see, maybe you and me, Gleep here, everybody, we're same as that stupid fuckin' fly, crawlin' some piece of glass we can't get by, either. Can see through it but we can't *see* it. Know what's on the other side, or oughta be, but can't figure no way to get to it. You understand any of what I'm sayin' to you?"

"Yes. I mean, I think so. Yes. I'm not sure."

Neither was Shadow sure, though he was certain the image had something to do with what had been happening to him since he came out of the woods this morning, the gradual unveiling of his occult vision. He had been right to believe in it, for here was the incontestable proof sitting beside him, cringing like a whipped hound under his blade. And the goods, the other two, card counter in particular—a full reckoning was inevitable, a matter of course and time only, and not much of that. Maybe it all meant that finally, after half a muddled lifetime, he had seen his pane of glass and, recognizing it, had found a way out. And if that was true (so his logic led him), then it meant also he was invested with powers, some peculiar magic, a wisdom, set him apart from other men. Broad new vistas seemed to open up before him, limitless and vast.

Quite unexpectedly, and for no good reason he could think of, he leaned over the front seat, cupped a hand, and in a single darting motion plucked the fly from the windshield. He made a tight fist, held up his arm triumphantly. "Well, this one ain't ever going to know no better. Not like us."

Gleep's face, he noticed, wore the dull placid expression of a cow just dropped a steaming turd. For one melancholy moment Shadow wondered what would become of him, now his own life was so mystically changed and nothing would ever be the same again, ever. But then he saw Gleep stifling a yawn, and with a puzzled irritation he said, "You ain't interested, Gleep, none of this?"

"It's pretty good, what you're sayin'. But how about we get on with it. Hot in here."

Shadow fit himself back into the abbreviated space on the seat. He held the knife in front of his eyes, gazed at it as though he was offering up a prayer. "On with it," he intoned, and then he turned and thrust his face close up to Clay's. "You remember your buddy, Rusty?"

"Rusty? Sure, yes, Rusty."

"You seen him lately?"

"No."

"I knew you was going to say that—no. Know why?"

"I don't know," Clay whimpered. A nerve under his eye began to tick violently. "Please, I don't know."

"Hey, hey, hold up. Don't start blubberin' yet. I ain't askin' nothing big and important here. Just you know how I know. That's all. Give you the answer even. I know—Gleep does, too—because we know Rusty had a little accident. Well, more'n a little one, actual'. Hurt his hand real bad. About the only work he can get now is stompin' grapes, one of them wine factories."

Gleep gave a short chugging laugh.

"You don't want nothing like that to happen to you," Shadow went on, "all them puff muscles you got on you. Spoil your pussy hustlin'. Am I right?"

"Yes. I—"

Shadow laid the knife on Clay's trembling lips. "That's good. That's an answer. You're doin' real fine. Now, I got just one other question. Only going to ask it one time. Ready?"

Clay moved his head up and down.

"Where's the goods?"

"Looks to me," Shadow said as, five minutes later, they pulled into Moon's station, "like we got ourselves a little snag here."

Clay was leaning over the front seat, stabbing a finger at the vacant space where the Porsche had stood. His eyes were steep with terror. "I swear," he said frantically. "I put it in the car. This morning. My sister's car. A Porsche. I swear."

Gleep yanked him back. "We know the car, asshole."

"Oh yeah," Shadow said, "forgot to mention. We already got acquainted with your sister. And her boyfriend. She looks like real sweet nookey, your sister. Little skinny maybe."

He was just producing words, to fill in while he gave it some judicious thought. Up to him now, make all the right decisions. He was put off by this complication, but only mildly. Everything was going to fall in place. Matter of fact, it was kind of entertaining, watching it all unroll; sort of like it must be driving a mountain road all spirals and dead man's curves, squealing them, hitting full bore, reckless of caution. Didn't matter none: Destination was the same, that wasn't going nowhere.

"Do some dustin'?" Gleep said to Shadow. He held Clay by a hank of hair at the back of the neck. He had never liked this punk, even the few times he had seen him. Made him think of the weight slingers in the Jacktown yard: all oiled beef outside, dry pussy in. And he liked him even less now, wet-eyed and snively.

"No, not quite yet," Shadow said. He switched off the ignition and tapped on the wheel. From where they were parked, he could see inside the station. No Moon. He thought about it a moment more, all of it, and then he said, "I got a instinct here, Gleep. Let's go see. Bring the boy along."

The pimply youth barely looked up from the cash register as they came in. A portable radio at his elbow blared a country tune, and he was snapping his fingers to the beat.

"Hi there," Shadow said. "We're lookin' for Mr. Dale Moon. He around?"

"Nope."

Shadow tilted his head. Rubbed the side of his nose patiently. "Can you tell us maybe more'n 'nope'? He been around? Comin' around?"

"Moon's day off today. He ain't been in."

Shadow reached across the counter and hit the Off button on the radio.

"Hey, that's Loretta Lynn."

"Yeah, I know. Real good singer, Loretta. But she'll be back on again. Meantime, we got a little problem here, maybe you can help us. Got to do with that Porsche car was sittin' out by your air hose. One that ain't there now. You know where it went to?"

That Porsche sure was everybody's favorite auto-mo-*beel* today, the young man was thinking; his own too, seeing it had made him more jack than he earned take-home in three days. And he wasn't about to give it up either, not a fat nickel, not to Moon and not to this scrub got the tomato-paste face and not to the muscles boy from this morning, standing over in the corner with the jumbo Indian. No wh-ay! That money was his. "Lady come and got it," he said, skipping the part about the fifty he took off her before handing over the keys. "Said it was hers."

"When was this?"

"Two, three hours back. I dunno."

"Mr. Moon, he didn't say make some calls, anybody come for that car?"

"Unh unh. Just said don't let—" He broke off, saw what he had gotten into.

"Yeah? Don't let what?"

"I don't remember."

"Sure you do," Shadow said, and he came around the counter and backed him against the candy shelf on the far wall. "He said don't let nobody fuck with that car, didn't he. Take it. That's what he said." Shadow was dead-on in the kid's splotchy face. They were about the same size; if anything, he was the larger of the two (which was a welcome switch), looking into the crafty eyes from a slight downward angle.

"He might of said call him. I was gonna try but the lady said it was hers. Like I told you."

"So you just hand over the keys, huh? Just 'cuz she said?"

The young man's mouth twisted grotesquely, as though he'd swallowed a bite of spoiled food. "She had ID, too. That insurance proof paper, got the vehicle number or whatever it is. She said she'd call the cops if I didn't give 'em to her. What the fuck am I suppose to do?" It was all a lie, of course, but he was boxed-in, desperate.

"Lady slip you a bill or two, did she?"

"No, unh unh. No."

"Why is it I get the idea you ain't being totally straight with me? Why is that?"

"Tellin' you what happened. All's I do is work here."

Shadow looked at him steadily. He was trying to fit things together in his head, but there was something about this little swamp toad, the defiant squirmy ugliness maybe, that disturbed his concentration. "Let's try something else," he said. "See that boy over there, young one with the build?"

"I see 'im."

"You ever seen him before?"

"Yeah, sure. Today. Said it was his car too, something like that. I didn't let him take it, though."

"That's it? That's the whole thing?"

"He put something in the hatch. Bag."

"Give you a little pocket change, too?" Shadow said, pressing the point, bringing it full circle, God knows why. Had nothing to do with anything, kid hustled some coins or he didn't; just he was curious and anymore that was reason enough. Also, up close this way, Shadow was struck by a vague feeling he had seen this woeful face before, or something resembling it, seen its look of a furtive animal cornered in its lair, hunkered down and snarling over a hard-to-come-by carcass, slab of bloody meat. He watched the eyes skid about desperately, seek the floor. And then, astonishingly, as though through a window of time, he recognized who it was he saw: himself, none other, twenty years back, a sidewalks hustler, raw urchin learning to make his own way in a predatory world, cut adrift from it by the nasty joke of a body he inhabited and a face that every morning announced in blossomy festering sores the wicked luck of his birth.

"Been a good day for you," he said, "ain't it. Moneywise."

The head moved in a slow, hopeless nod, and a hand extracted the bills, offering them.

Shadow patted the mottled cheek gently, almost affectionately. "What's your name, boy?" he asked, and waited for the miraculous reply he somehow knew was coming.

"Willard."

For just a sliver of a moment he was disappointed, but he said, "Well, maybe it ain't Willis but it's close. Willard. That's a good name, too. You watch out for yourself, Willard. Stay ahead of the curve."

In the car Gleep said, "What's goin' on, Shadow?"

Shadow didn't answer. He was headed for the Park Place, and when they arrived he pulled up at the entrance and let the car idle. He found a scrap of paper and pen in the glove compartment and thrust them at Clay. "Write what I tell you," he said. Then he took the note inside and, very deferentially, asked the woman at the desk to pass the message along either to Mr. Waverly or Miss Clemmons, in person or over the phone, either way. He gave her a ten for her trouble, and a warm thank you.

On the way out to Gaylon's, Gleep asked again: "What's goin' on?"

"You still don't get it, do you, partner? Ain't nothin' going on. Well, maybe I'm mellowin' out some, my sunset years. Nothing to sweat. Y'see, I figured them two was in this right from the start. Scam was way too big for this poor fuckhead"—specifying Clay with a thumb—"to think up alone."

"You think they're comin' back to the hotel? Hadn't we better wait?"

"No need. We did, we'd just be sittin' there pissin' in the wind anyway. How I see it, they ain't so stupid they're gonna poke their heads up outta whatever hole they got down into. Not after last night's scrubbin'. But they ain't smart enough to split town either, while they got a chance."

Gleep was still mystified. "How come you figure that?"

"How come? You think on it, Gleep. You got a brother-sister team here, right? Blood relation, loyalty, that kind of shit? Dumb, maybe, but that's how it looks to be. The cunt, she ain't goin' to leave without him. We already seen that. There's our ace."

"How about the counter, though?"

"Now, it was up to that one, we could kiss the goods goodbye. He'd know better. Except she's leadin' him around by a pussy leash. We seen that, too. So he ain't so bright, either."

Gleep was not yet satisfied. "Okay. Supposin' all your

figurin' is correct. They stay down, how they gonna get his note?"

A thin smile, suprisingly tolerant, worked its way across Shadow's face. This part, the certainty, the inevitability of things, would be impossible for someone like Gleep to grasp. Maybe for anyone. No good even to try, there. He chose a simpler route. "They'll call first, don't y'see. Park Place was where they was intendin' to meet all along. They call, get the message, see we're holdin' a real heavy bargain chip. Collateral, y'might say. No, we don't got to do diddly. They're gonna come to us. We got 'em gift-wrapped now, all three of 'em, goods, too. It's Christmas in August, Gleep, anytime, you learned to live right."

"They'll kill you," Waverly said. "Simple as that. You meet them—anyplace, time, doesn't matter—and they'll kill you."

He had listened, quietly and without interrupting though with a gathering impatience, as she offered a second, edited account of the previous day. But when she got to the nub of it, this simplistic scheme to rescue the wayward brother and ring down the curtain on a magical jubilant ending for all concerned, not least the two of them, then the absolute best he could think to say was just what he did: They'll kill you. Distancing himself by the choice of pronouns.

It had seemed much too effortless, neat. The night before was when he should have caught the inconsistencies, dangling threads of narrative. Blame it on the serious cuffing and the pain and the wonder of being alive. But early this morning, lying awake in bed, the first doubts and questions began to burrow into his head. How was it, again, they were here? And what happened to the other team? Good sports, read the score and conceded? Sure.

She was asleep beside him, facedown, one arm across his chest, the other over the side and brushing the floor.

Her drowning-victim posture. Gently he disengaged the arm and tested himself, first by sitting, next standing, then moving. The pulsating throb was gone, replaced by a bone-deep ache. He went into the bathroom and examined his face in the mirror. A half-resemblance, features tuberous, discolored, askew, gave him back a crooked smile. Smile said, You did it again, boy, fleeced them again. He stepped into the shower and turned the water on hot as he could stand, which was about lukewarm. He wasn't ready to look at his body yet. Enough it was working, reluctantly doing what it was told.

When he came out of the shower, he noticed his toothbrush and shaving gear laid out carefully by the sink. He thought about that awhile. He tried to use them both but without much success. Some back teeth were cracked and his gums bled at the touch of the bristles. And even a whisper of the blade set little currents of blood flowing down his raw cheeks and into his neck.

Back in the room, navigating by the light from the bath, he discovered a bag, one of hers, crammed full of clothes. Some were his. Hanging in the closet were his jacket, tie, slacks. He dressed. Then he sat awhile longer in the dark, his eyes focused on his thoughts. And then he pulled open the drape and let the morning sun come flooding in.

Midnight made some vague noises of discontent. Groaned a little. Eventually she rolled over. "Waverly," she said dreamily and, seeing him on his feet, clothed, moving under his own steam, "Recovered. Look like warmed-over hell. But recovered."

"Yeah, well, that's life in the big city. Now, suppose you tell me what's really going on."

Her emended version of the sequence of events the day before: "Listen, it was a circus. He was trying to hit on me, Mr. Golden Age, out in the woods. Ugh. Tells you something about our kindly seniors, like making a case for involuntary euthanasia. Anyway, the best I could get out of him was a lift into town. And that grudgingly. He dropped us here, far as he'd go, and drove off pouting.

"I thought we were clear but I was wrong. Let me tell you, Samaritans are scarce in Traverse City. It's the no shoes, no shirt, no service ethic. No bags, money, credit card—no room. The shape you were in didn't do much to quiet their doubts, either. I suppose we did look like a couple of refugees from a street brawl but, honestly, I was getting rattled. I thought about the police but that didn't seem prudent, not after everything that had happened. And what you'd told me about your past, here in Michigan."

Listening to her, Waverly thought, was rather like watching a skilled broken field runner: shift, dodge, find the creases, weave, but when they brought you down, blame it on the botched block. Evidently, the way it was unfolding, he got to be the errant blocker.

"Didn't leave much," she was saying, "not if I was going to get you out of here. So I talked to this man, clerk, reminded him of his Christian duty and guaranteed him I'd be back. Also helped that I left my earrings as collateral; Christ, either one of them would buy a year's stay in this dump. Even this trainable could see that. They wouldn't let you stay in their office, so we put you in a hammock out back. In the shade. You remember any of that?"

Waverly signified silently he did not.

"I hiked into the hotel. Not your casual morning stroll, by the way, from here. Don't give me that look. I understood the risks. They had me along too, remember, those choirboys, you called them. What else could I do?

"I got them at the hotel to open up the room. You know I can be persuasive, when I want. Talked my way through worse tangles than that, Lord knows. Okay, maybe not worse. Knottier. Never mind.

"I always keep a spare hundred in my bag. Emergencies. You know, the kind a girl sometimes encounters. My thinking was we needed a place for you. Safe place, for the night at least. And we needed a car, to put some distance between us and them, once you were ready.

"I took the money and got out of there. I had no idea where the keys to your car were, so I walked to the station where you'd left mine. Some repulsive little worm there wasn't going to give it up. Fifty changed his mind. Which left fifty. That and one earring got us in here. By then it was noon."

During most of this part of the monologue, she had been glancing about the room, evading his stare. Now she fixed her gaze on him. More than a trace of bruised defiance came into her voice: "Look, Waverly, I hope you realize none of this was easy. By that time I wasn't exactly a candidate for Miss Northern Michigan myself."

To display sympathy, he turned up his hands. She proceeded.

"I got you settled and then I just collapsed in a chair. I couldn't think anymore or do anymore. I must have been out three hours, probably longer. When I woke, you were moaning in your sleep. None of our problems had gone away. We had a car but no money, not a dime. We had a place but good for one night only. And yes, I knew, I understood, they were going to find us. If I didn't do something. It was making me dizzy, all of it. I'm not like you, Waverly; I don't do puzzles well, and I've never been in this sort of thing before."

Like you have, he might have finished for her, though he didn't. It was mesmerizing, watching her work. Whole story was so shot full of holes, so fantastic, it was probably true. And it was leading somewhere. That he knew.

"Then I remembered. What I'd forgotten to remember, actually. In my cosmetics case I keep a credit card. Small account, but it would do. But of course it was back at the hotel. I drove there, and this time I got the manager and a security type to come along with me to the room, invented some tale of belligerent drunks down the hall. I got the card and, as long as I was there anyway, packed a quick bag, some things for both of us. There was no indication anybody had been there. Not till I got to the lobby and was about to leave. Woman at the desk called me over, said a man left a message. Said I couldn't have missed him by more than a quarter of an hour. Shame, she said.

"It's there on the table. I think you ought to read it."

Waverly went over and got the note. There was a package of cigarettes there too, so he smoked as he read.

Dear Sis,
I'm staying with the gentlemen you met last night. They invited me. Also they asked me to ask you to bring their personal belongings. Then we can get together and go sailing or something. You can call them at the number below. I hope you'll call soon. No later than tomorrow. Friday. Everything here is real fine. So far. Have a nice day.

love,
Clay

p.s. be sure and bring your friend along too

When he looked up, she said, "Yes, it's his handwriting. Not the words, of course, but he's the one who wrote them."

"And they still believe we have what they like to call their goods."

"Well," she said, brushing the inky hair that fell across

her shoulders, an easy caressing motion, "that's the thing of it. Now we do."

Her scheme was simplicity itself: phone the number; arrange a meeting at some neutral spot, a public place, say, this afternoon; accomplish the exchange—the bag in the back of the Porsche for Clay, even trade, everybody happy; back away cautiously; run like hell. And then, she implied, with this mean episode well behind them, then the two of them could pick up where they had left off that night (*That* night? It was less than thirty-six hours ago!) in the Park Place, explore how far it might take them. And that is when he said, flatly, "They'll kill you."

"Waverly, I'm asking you to understand. He's my brother."

"Half, you told me. And brother or not, he's heavier than you want to carry."

"Who else is there for him? I can't go to the police. As deep as he's in this, he'd end up in prison, and how long would someone like Clay last there."

"In population, about three minutes. An outside estimate."

"That's why I've got to help him. I don't care what he's done."

"Why? You enjoy playing the martyr? Can't you see you're being used? You're less even than a pawn in this."

"Used? Tell me about used. All my life he's used me. Traded off my weakness, counted on it."

"Weakness? How?"

She looked down at her hands, seemed to study them a moment before she spoke. "It doesn't matter. There's a commitment there. A bond I can't break. I haven't any choice."

"Yes you do. You can get behind the wheel of that car out there and drive."

"No," she said simply, "I'm not leaving him now. Who

should know better than you what they'll do to him if we don't get their damnable goods back to them."

Who indeed, Waverly thought, feeling the dull ache that suffused his body and remembering the miracle of his own eyes, still intact. One miracle per conflict, though, and theirs was expended. "People like your brother," he said, "wear calamity like a second skin. Go near them and you go up in smoke yourself. I've got to tell you this: I'm not so sure, from everything I've seen, he hasn't got it coming. But that's no matter. It's got nothing to do with it, finally. Hand over the goods, don't, it'll all come to the same. That's the rules. That's payback."

"But I thought if we gave it back—"

"Your thinking is wrong," he said bluntly, marveling at the childlike innocence that rode just beneath the haughty brittle surface she displayed to the world. But then there were all kinds of worlds, too, and there was no way she could have any experience of the one she was tampering with now, and at her peril. More gently, he said, "The goods are only half of it. They aren't going to be satisfied till your brother's taken out. You too, if you get into it."

"Then what can I do? I need your help," she pleaded, and she was weeping now, what appeared to be genuine tears. "There's more to it than you know."

"How much more?"

She told him.

She and Clay shared the same father, yes, but they had been more than brother and sister. More. How it began, she couldn't recall exactly, or her censors had erased. Why? That she knew. When? A few years ago, coming out of a psycho ward, pumped full of Haldol, his eyes all glassy and his body shrunken and trembling, speech slurred—and no one to care. Who cared? Daddy, off with his high-priced women? Leave it to the shrinks, was Daddy's way. So she was elected. Who else was there?

She comforted him. He liked to talk with her. Sometimes he made perfect sense, the old confident Clay, full of arrogant bounce. Just as often he rambled, spilling out incoherent stuff, his mother, the bathtub of blood, what he must have done, guilt, that sort of thing. Talk got him through the day. But what about the night, taunting visions, monstrous dreams, what about them? First she held him in chaste embrace while he brushed back her hair—he admired her hair, its texture, color, length—and whispered eagerly, disjointedly the riddles of a fevered suicidal thirst. You say you understand insanity, Waverly; he was insane. Then. And it's like a virus, contagion. How do you escape it?

Inevitably, in time, the embrace was no longer innocent. She had since learned, maybe to rationalize, maybe simply to rescue herself, to place no blame, accept none. Blame him? His nature? Her own? Their blood was mingled; what she did, she did freely. She had saved him, that time. And it was years ago. She apologized to no one.

All through this bleak recital, Waverly had kept silent, following selected motes that rose in the bands of sunlight and vanished in the air. Listening to her story, he could see, through time's heavy mists, himself again: frenzied, betrayed, bankrupt of all reason and perishing—seeming to perish—in the terminal disaster of violence misplaced and utter despair.

She said finally, defensively, "I've told you my nasty little secret. You've told me yours. Now tell me—which is worse?"

Fair question. Murder, incest, treacheries, madness—it was a solid lineup, a sorry catalog. Lots of blurry echoes here. Irrelevantly, he remembered a line from *Alice*: " 'Tut, tut, child,' said the Duchess. 'Everything's got a moral if only you can find it.' " Because he had once been a literary man, such thoughts still came to him on occasion, mostly unbidden, though he never spoke them and didn't now.

He recognized he was arrived at last at the crossing waiting for him in Traverse City, as he had sensed—guessed? anticipated? known?—it would have to be, though in his most fantastic imaginings he could never have foreseen it taking this peculiar form.

"Say something, Waverly."

"What would you like to hear?"

"That you'll help me today. This one last time. Then you can judge me at your leisure, if you're still interested."

"Of course I will," he said, and he was smiling. Life was full of riddles, some more comic than others.

She seemed to misinterpret the smile, but favorably. "I don't know how to talk about love, Waverly. What it means, even. After all I've done, it would be blasphemy for me to say it. But there's something between us, whatever the word. You know that."

"I know. We'll have a chat about it again sometime."

There could be no such thing as an edge, not with them, but going into it this time, he wanted something to shrink the staggering odds. Apart from the lunacy with the lawyer (a decade back, delirium, it didn't count), he had never packed in his life, was innocent of all weaponry except the jail house variety, and no length of radiator pipe was going to shield him now. No shank either, no store-bought Arkansas Toothpick. Not against the likes of a Shadow. He had seen too many Shadows, knew their moves. Lightning in a bottle, scrawl a signature across your face before you could blink. Best of circumstances, he was outclassed; a colossal mismatch, the shape he was in now. So he had to think of something, and there was no luxury of time.

Midnight was in the bath, getting herself showered and primped and powdered, presumably. Probably applying makeup. Tonight's prom date. Unless he was mistaken, she was singing softly. Give him a thousand lives and he would never figure them, women. He returned to what he did understand, and its urgency. Came up nothing. And since there was nowhere left to turn, he turned where he had always, over recent years, turned. He got a long-distance line and dialed Mr. Bennie Epstein, Palm Beach Gardens, Florida, collect, Timothy Waverly calling. Mr. Epstein agreed to accept the charges.

"Hey, Timothy," came the hearty rumble over the distance that severed him from his other, ordered life, almost forgotten. "You find that shade?"

"Lots of shade, Bennie."

"Should have stayed on, boy. Cooled way down, day after you left."

About that, staying, he was surely right. Too late, but right again.

"Also them contractors. They got to play the flabbiest hands in town. Sent out Angelo and even he administered a little whuppin'. You imagine? Angelo?"

"What did I say?"

"Score for you. But you'd of done real good, you'd been playin'. Like in famous. There was money to change hands here, other night."

It wasn't a whine exactly, his tone, but it had its trace of grievance. Waverly ignored it. "Next time," he said. Next time? He had to pause to wonder at his own arrant pride, unwillingness to believe in the possibility, the near certainty, of his own death.

"So," Bennie said quickly, for the greeter in him was discomfited by the smallest silence, "you called me. Always good to chin with you, Timothy, but I'm suspectin' you got a reason. Besides tradin' weather reports."

"Reason. Yes. I thought you might be able to help me out."

"You need cash?"

"No. Connections. You still have some here, Michigan?"

"Michigan, yeah. Real Michigan. Detroit, places like that. But you're in Traverse City, I remember correct."

"So that's what I'm asking. You know anybody here? Traverse City?"

"Might not hurt, you tell me why."

He knew at the outset this question would be coming, yet uncharacteristically he had prepared no reply. "Why?" he said.

"We got an echo, this line?"

"Okay. I need to put my hands on a piece." Into the ponderous sigh that came rolling across the miles, he added hastily, "It's not what you think."

"You seen the ex, right?"

"Wrong. I've not been near her." Or thought about her, it occurred to him, or the once brother-in-law, their treacheries, or even the lost son. Not directly, till now, and now they seemed to him little more than phantom images from a melancholy dream. The measure of the weight of the passions and griefs of the past. "For all I know they may not even be here," he said. "Anymore."

"What I'm hearin', I think, is a lot of foo poo. Shittin' a shitter, Timothy. Don't ever succeed."

"Put it this way, Bennie, speaking of foo poo. I'm in over my ears. You going to help me or not?"

"What you're askin', I want to say not."

"One syllable."

There was a silence, brief by anyone's standards, protracted by Bennie's. Then he said, "I know a fella—*of* a fella—maybe connected. I just heard of him, y'understand. Never met. Name's Ledbetter. Gaylon Ledbetter. More'n likely he could fix you up."

Waverly laughed till his eyes grew wet, and then he laughed some more, couldn't restrain himself, laughing at all the mad gods of chance roamed the spheres, gaming with everything, everyone beneath them. You want an aspirin? Try this cyanide. Here you dishwasher, garbage hauler, shoe clerk, here's the lotto ticket, numbers filled in for you, winner. You getting old, creaky, about to expire? Have some monkey glands, express mail, Switzerland, help yourself. Got a body like a fortress, young, sculptured, impregnable as the Maginot Line? Here come the doctors through the Argonne Forest, end run, turned the corner on you, lugging X rays, mournful-faced, no cure for that one yet, condolences.

He laughed and laughed. Gaylon Ledbetter, Bennie's connection. Picturing him there, in the basement gym, Waverly was struck by the more than faint resemblance to Bennie himself, might as easily, in another place, time, circumstance, been Bennie. His sides shook with laughter.

"Hey, I know I got a jacket for a stand-up comedian, but you could share the gag maybe."

Waverly, still catching at his breath, said, "I'll tell you when I see you."

"You want to say when that's going to be?"

"Soon, Bennie. Soon."

"This help you out any? Besides the belly laugh, I'm askin'."

"It was fine, Bennie. You did good."

"Okay. Talk again. And hey, Timothy, keep your eye on the deck, huh. I worry about you, boy."

They were parked in front of a sporting goods store Waverly had selected by running a finger down the Yellow Pages.

"I can't go in there," he said, "face I'm wearing. But you can. This is what I want you to do. Say you want to buy a shotgun. Play it fluttery—oh, I'm just a helpless female in this rough macho world of yours, I need your manly advice—what am I doing, coaching you?"

"Why am I buying a shotgun?" Midnight asked.

"Jesus, lady needs a motivation for her character? Come

on, use that inventiveness you were telling me about. Tell them it's a gift, your nephew, uncle, cousin—I don't know. You'll think of something."

"I'm not asking for in there," she said, nodding toward the store. "That I can handle. It's you I'm asking."

"You still don't know why?"

"I'm asking."

"Okay. Call it insurance. Term life. Short-term. Say it again: They're going to try and kill us, all of us, you, me, your"—mumbling the word—"brother. These are the kind of people want it all."

A look he couldn't interpret—skepticism? fear?—crossed her face. "Guns," she said. "Shotguns. What do I know?"

"See how good you are. Take that act inside and you'll do just fine."

"Huh, some act."

"Listen, on shotguns you know about as much as I do. Just get something with heft to it, no BB guns. Not a single shot. And not one of those pump jobs either."

"What else?"

"That's it. My fund's exhausted. We're in their beneficent hands. Do your best."

She put a hand over his. It felt very cold. "I'll try, Waverly."

It was, he supposed, a show of tenderness or, more likely, need, but his emotions were too disordered, cluttered, for him to respond. "I know you will," was the best he could muster. "And don't forget a box of shells," he called after her.

Half an hour later she emerged carrying a long elegant zippered case and a small bag. She dumped both of them in his lap. "They speak a foreign tongue in there," she said.

Waverly opened the case and examined the weapon.

"What you have there, before I forget, is a Browning side-by-side, twelve-gauge, thirty-inch barrel, gold-plated trigger. I can't remember the rest. Box of shells is in the bag. Oh yes, they assured me it would stop a buffalo."

He removed two shells and fit them into their chambers. Cautiously, keeping both hands clear of the trigger, he tested the feel of the gun, its weight.

"Looks good to me," he said, "my untutored eye." He extracted the shells and zipped up the case.

"They were trying to sell me something called an S.O.B. They got a terrific hoot, saying that. It looked cheap."

"Pays to shop around."

"I didn't buy the cleaning kit. Assumed you weren't into memento gathering."

"That's a good guess."

"So. Will this one do?"

"Long as it fires, it'll do."

She looked at him warily. "You're not really intending to use that?"

"It would be nice not to. Who ever knows."

He put the gun and the shell box in the back, and then he drove till he came to a hardware store. He pulled over at the curb.

"Next errand," he said. "I want you to go in there and get me a file. Heavy-duty one. Heaviest they've got."

This time there were no questions. When she returned he put the file beside the gun and swung the car around and pointed it in the direction of State Street. He went past the Park Place as slowly as the traffic would allow. Half a block away was a place called D. J. Kelly's. He remembered it from the morning he had strolled through town, peering in: dining room one side, bar the other. "That, I believe, is our spot," he said.

"Spot?"

"Tonight."

At the next intersection he turned right, into the residential streets. He was looking for something secluded and quiet yet close, something ideal he doubted he was going to find. Strike the first one, Washington Street, directly behind the Park Place: an old court house building, historic preservation, hard up against a law-enforcement complex, long rectilinear structure all concrete and glass, followed by a church. Definitely wouldn't do. He went over a couple of blocks, driving slowly, taking his time, searching for the right combination of streetlights, trees, shrubbery, alley. Finally he pulled up by a rickety garage set well back from a crumbling stucco house two doors from a corner. The lot was large, plenty of space, though too much of it was open, a parched lawn full of quack grass and assorted weeds. The garage fronted on a paved alleyway. There was an elm tree beside it, pitted with disease, and more trees up by the house and in the adjoining yards. That was good. There were no bushes or shrubs, but three large trash barrels, lidless and overflowing, stood near the door. At the end of the alley and across the road, down maybe fifteen feet, was a streetlight. Two more, either end of the block. Not so good. But it was the best he was going to do.

"And this," he said, "is our other spot."

"For what?"

"Don't ask."

They were back in the room at the Sugar Beach. It was past two o'clock and he was weary already, wanted to lie down and blot it all out for the handful of hours remaining. Not quite yet. First he went to work on the serial number of the shotgun, filed it away. And then there was one thing more to do, most important of all, and trickiest. He dialed the number at the bottom of Clay's note and glanced up at Midnight sitting on the bed, her ankles tucked under her, features taut and anxious. A voice on the other end, remarkably cheery, said, "Mmmyello." He recognized it as Shadow's.

"Waverly," he said.

"Mr. Waverly. Been hopin' you'd call. Seein' you left so sudden, other night."

"Then you're not disappointed."

"Oh no. Hey, how you feelin' today?"

"About half. No serious complaints."

"Nobody listens anyhow."

"It's a mean world."

"Boy, ain't that the truth. Say, speakin' of world, you seein' it okay? Gettin' some nice good looks at it straight up?"

"It's looking reasonable, from here. You want to talk about anything else, now we've covered my health?"

"What would that be?"

Waverly didn't say anything for a moment. Then, "Maybe I've got the wrong number. I could hang up, dial again. Start over."

"You sound kind of grouchy, Mr. Waverly. We're just chattin' here, passin' the time of day. What can we do for you?"

"We could think about a meet."

"Gee, that'd be swell. Always good to get together. Whyn't you come on out."

"Yeah, this is the wrong number."

"You got some place else in mind?"

"Say Kelly's. Tonight. Ten o'clock."

"Gosh, I don't know. That's pretty late."

"That's when we're free."

There was a little giggle came down the line. "Free. That's a good one, Mr. Waverly. Well, I expect we can work things out, this end. Now, you do got them commodities. And you are plannin' to bring them along."

"Same as you're planning to bring the kid."

"Why sure. He's lookin' forward to seein' his sis again. Least that's what he told us, once we got him to quit bawlin'. He ain't no hero, like you. He's right here, you want to talk to him."

"That's okay. I trust you."

"Trust is what makes business work. Made this country great."

"Ain't that the truth," Waverly said.

"See you tonight, Kelly's. Y'know, they serve up a real tasty burger there. Side a slaw. You're going to enjoy it."

As soon as he put up the phone, Midnight said, "Is Clay all right?"

"They aren't going to hurt him yet. Probably made him soil his pants, though."

"Why did you say at night? Why not now? Wouldn't daylight be better? Safer?"

"Wouldn't mean a thing."

She lit a cigarette. He noticed her hands were not at all steady. "But if we have to leave? In the dark?"

"That's our best chance."

She got up and walked to one end of the small room, back to the other, back again, trailing smoke. She planted herself by the door. A stance just short of belligerent. Petulantly, she said, "What are we supposed to do till ten? That's eight hours."

He stood up and went over to her, put a hand on her shoulder, gently. "I could say relax. Or watch the teevee. Or sleep. Meager jokes, all. Tell you what I'm going to do. I'm going to lie down on that bed over there and try and picture the scene, clear as I can. Once. And then I'm going to empty my head, and wait. You can join me if you like."

"This time it would be me, couldn't do you any good."

"You're not hearing what I'm saying."

Her face was chalky, and she chewed at her lip. She stabbed out the cigarette in an ashtray on the dresser, and then she put her arms around him, held herself very close. Her whole body shook. "I'm scared, Waverly. I mean terrified."

A little later, lying beside him, she said quietly, voice of a child, "Do you have it yet?"

He was gazing at the ceiling. It took him a moment to answer. "Have what?"

"The scene."

"Yes."

"How does it end?"

"Satisfactorily."

She said nothing for awhile. And then, almost timidly, she asked, "What are you thinking, Waverly?"

"About the Zapotec Indians, in Mexico. Did you know they have a word in their language, means 'a captive when they ate him'?"

FIVE

THE MAN LOADING THE TRUCK OF THE THUN-
derbird was square-framed and lumpy, solid yet, but running a little toward fat. He had a beefy, brick-colored
face, skin coarse as sandpaper, flattened nose webbed with
purple spider veins, twilighting hairline and—his most
prominent feature—watery, bulging eyes. His eyes had
the quality associated with certain saurian species, empty
of everything but an instinctive predatory spite, sweeping
and indiscriminate. Guessing his age, most people would
have put him near fifty, though in fact he was ten years
younger, and for all his bulk moved rather nimbly. In
the trunk were two bags he had packed directly after the
call came through. One contained the usual accessories
of a short trip: clean shirts, socks, underwear, toiletries;
the other, his working gear: one Colt Python .357 Mag-
num; one .25-caliber semiautomatic pistol and silencer;
four shell boxes, two for each weapon; two pair of gloves,
one plastic, one leather; and his Statue of Liberty knife,
for luck.

It was three o'clock. He had calculated the drive should
take a little over five hours, but the holiday exodus was
already underway and the Detroit traffic moved at a glacial pace. Eventually he got onto the Lodge and followed

it till he picked up 96. Once clear of the city, he began to make time. By seven he was in Grand Rapids and he hung north on 131. A few miles up the expressway, he spotted some golden arches and pulled in and ordered a Big Mac, large fries, and black coffee to go. He would have preferred to take a break from the road, but he wanted to be there early enough to do some prowling, maybe get started tonight, maybe even, with some luck, get things wrapped up. So he ate while he drove and when he was finished, flung the residue out the window and got out a box of Milk Duds, savoring them, one after another.

When he arrived on the outskirts of Traverse City, he swung into the first station to present itself. He strode inside. Behind the counter was an elderly man whose sunken features were set in a benign smirk.

"Phone book," the man demanded. The years in his line of work had honed his speaking style to a flat, telegraphic delivery.

One was produced for him.

He ran a stubby thumb down the L's till he came on Ledbetter, Gaylon-Mardella, and then he thrust the directory in the grinning face and said, "Whereabouts is this address?"

The old man brought it in close and squinted over the top of the glasses riding low on his nose. "Well, lemme think now."

"Think quick, willya. It's late."

"Only half past nine."

"Up here, that's gotta be late."

"Ah, you young folks, always in a rush. You get to be my age you—"

He cut him off with a hand wiggle. "Look, no grief, huh. Just the directions."

The old man's vision was too dim to distinguish the frozen stare leveled on him at that moment, and he said cheerily, "Okay, hold your water. You got a few miles to go yet. Place you're lookin' for is up past Acme. Out in the woods. Good fishin' out there. Better let me draw you a map."

After Waverly was graduated from the Forensic Center, magna cum sane, and returned to Jackson for the remainder of his sentence, Chop sought him out and advised him: "Nobody can give you your nuts and nobody can take them away. Where you been, Ypsi, that's nothing, that's a country club. I been there. Here is different. Here you got to be mean, dog-ass mean. They'll open you up for a smoke or a butt fuck—you know about that already—or just for a laugh. Watch you bleed. They turn you out once and you'll be anybody's punk, which is the same as everybody's. Which is a hard way to go. Stand up and you'll be okay, even if it's over something senseless, and it will be, even if you get your ass whipped, and you will sometimes. But that's another lesson, how to lose. First I got to see you win a few."

Chop gave him a two-foot length of pipe from his personal arsenal, and a day or so later he had to use it on a red-bearded biker tried to jump him in the dressing area outside the gang showers. The biker had a lockjaw Slavic name, so he went by the straightforward, unequivocal Polack. His arms were adorned with tattoos, serpents coiled around the words *ASS* and *WAR,* representing the twin poles of his interests and the limits of his experience. Also around his bull neck he wore a silver cross on a chain dangling to the peak of a swelling solid belly he used as a battering ram in conflicts such as this. It was sudden, explosive, deadly and brief, over in two long minutes or less and ending with Polack on the floor, the ASS arm clutching the belly and the WAR, a shattered collarbone. Chop watched appraisingly from a steaming shower stall. Later, assisting him with his own multiple contusions, many of which were inflicted by the efficient use of the all-purpose cross, Chop remarked, "You handled that moderately well, except emotionally. Too much personal involvement, rage in you. None of this is personal, you got to understand. Raging against Polack, that's like cursing a sun that's scorching you, or a freezing wind. Polack, he's an imbecile but he's all right. He won't bother you anymore. You may become friends."

"But am I going to make it?"

"You got some potential. Have to see. Incidentally, you've got too much backswing on your pipe."

It required two more encounters, similar ones, for Chop to be persuaded. The first of them, with a scrawny smackhead, was a clear victory though both combatants did a ten-day in the hole (when he came out, his eyes dark and vacant as abandoned caves, Chop said, "You're going to need instruction, that end of things, different kind of test entirely"). The second, a pair of blacks, was by the kindest construction a standoff, and for a month he nursed separated ribs. But the day after, Chop invited him into his cell and put on his state-issue wire-frame glasses and got out two texts and said, "Now what do you think, we begin with the Middle English and go back or the Old English and work up? You're the expert; which is best?"

All this is what Waverly was thinking, lying on the bed thirty minutes before the appointed hour, smiling inwardly at the memory and taking solace from it, and courage. Midnight was already up and dressed and pacing, unlimbering her anxiety. It was time. He went into the bathroom and scrubbed his hands thoroughly and stung his scored face with a splash or two of cool water. He rinsed his dry mouth. Slipped on his jacket and knotted and adjusted his tie. He was trying to liken the ritual to the routine preparation for just another round of play, the recreational blackjack the other night, say, though he recognized these dealers were all mechanics and the house advantage powerfully stacked. A dozen or more times he had run the scene by in his head, till it was fixed, the way it was supposed to unfold in a cinematic world of happy endings. But now, rehearsing it one final time under the harsh light, he was struck by the myopia of his fantastic hopes. Nevertheless, when he came back into the room, his voice was steady as he said to Midnight, waiting at the door, "Ready? Let's get it done."

But for the sun's violet benediction on the horizon, it was almost dark; and the moon, rising, laid a shimmery blessing on the calm waters of the bay. The lingering warmth of the day and the cool of the approaching night met and fused in delicate balance.

He drove with exaggerated caution, mindful of his speed and all the signals, a substantial citizen deferring to the urgent Friday traffic. A few blocks from downtown, he turned off onto the back streets and found his way to the alley and the garage. There were no lights on up at the house, which was a piece of luck, but he cut the Porsche's lights all the same and eased it alongside the garage till its rear end was dead even with the trash barrels. Then he got out and opened the hatch. He shoved the goods bag as far up against the back of the seat as it would go, and then he took the shotgun out of the case and put two shells in its chambers.

As best he could in the darkness, he examined one of the trash cans, running his hands through moist loose garbage, orange rinds, coffee grounds, chicken bones, assorted muck. Wouldn't do. The next one, however, with its refuse crammed into unsealed plastic bags, would. He juggled the bags so the shotgun would fit between them, slide in and out easily; and then he placed it inside, barrel down, and very gently took it off safety. If you looked closely, the tip of the stock was visible and was unmistakably that, a gun stock, but there was nothing he could do about it. He fit a few more shells around the plastic bags and then took the gun case and the shell box and put them on the floor of the car up front, dropped the hatch, and came around to Midnight's side. All this time she had been silent, gazing at the windshield. She asked him nothing now.

"We'd better start," he said. "It's a few blocks. Want to be punctual."

For a moment she didn't move. Then she turned and looked at him and gave a barely perceptible nod.

They walked over to State and down to Park. Both streets were clogged with cars and they had to wait to get across. Some horns blared. Exhaust hung in the still air. Waverly tapped his heel on the curb. He checked his watch: ten minutes past ten. "What is this traffic," he said irritably, and she replied, her first words of the evening, "It's Labor Day. The weekend. Remember?"

"Slipped my mind."

A gap opened in the line of cars and they set off, sprinting. Kelly's lot was full and there was a knot of people milling about the entrance. He took Midnight by the hand and threaded through them and past the door. Inside was mobbed. He poked his head into the dining room, saw nothing. His face, he noticed, evoked a number of queasy stares. "Try the bar," he said. The current of the crowd carried them a few feet into the racketing room. Whoops, shouts, yawps, tinny laughter, babble—the music of sanctioned bedlam. They were fastened in the crush, growing desperate till he picked out a thin arm flailing the air, beckoning. It was Shadow, seated at a table along the partition wall. Beside him was Gaylon Ledbetter, looking dazed. The conversationalist, Gleep, was nowhere in evidence, and neither was Clay Clemmons. "Here it comes," he said to Midnight and shouldered a narrow passage through to the table.

Ledbetter had a cigar stuck in his mouth, but his eyes

were downcast and his face glum. Shadow, in contrast, beamed. "Holy shit, Mr. Waverly. Look like the truck you hit got the better of you, facewise." And then, acknowledging Midnight with a touch at the brim of a phantom fedora, he said, "You got to pardon my French, Miss Clemmons. Here, sit, sit. We was gettin' worried about you two. Thought you might of got lost." He was all teeth, all squinty smile.

"Yet here we are," Waverly said. He held a chair for Midnight and took the one opposite Shadow.

"Yeah, you sure are. Listen, holdin' on to them spots for you, it was murder, all these good-timers out tonight. Plain murder."

"Very thoughtful. I guess that means we owe you."

Shadow made a ha-ha sound. "That's real amusin', way you put that." A twittery waitress hurried past and he caught her by the arm. She treated him to a scowl, but he held her firmly. "Drinks around. We're celebratin' here. What'll it be, folks?"

Ledbetter pointed to the empty glass in front of him. "Same," he mumbled. Midnight looked to Waverly for direction. He nodded affirmatively, and in a voice very small she asked for white wine. Waverly's ginger ale order lifted an eyebrow on Shadow.

"Okay," he said, summarizing expansively, playing mein host, "you got your wine, your Shirley Temple there, two sames." He released his grip and the girl huffed away.

For a long moment no one had anything to say. Midnight and Ledbetter studied the tabletop. Waverly and Shadow continued to watch each other. Shadow's smile never faltered. There was something in it almost genuine, nontheatrical, though something spectral, too. Finally, Waverly said, "Well, we've gotten through the amenities. You care to discuss anything else?"

"Oh yeah, we got lots to talk about." He reached into a back pocket and pulled out a wallet and handed it to

Waverly. "First though, before I forget, this here's yours. You left it out to Gaylon's the other night."

"Thanks."

"All the money's there. You can check, you want."

"Remember I said I trust you?"

Shadow did a recollective fingersnap. "That's right. You did say that."

"I did. But you know, looking around here, I'm beginning to get a very bad feeling."

"That so. Why is that?"

"Well, maybe I'm overlooking him, but I don't seem to see Miss Clemmons's brother. Anyplace in the room. You see him?" he said to Midnight.

Without looking up she said, "He's not here."

Shadow leaned back in his chair and made a steeple with his fingers, a shrewd banker now, pondering the wisdom of a risky loan. "Ain't that peculiar," he said. "What you call a, y'know, coincidence. See, I was gettin' that same feeling you was sayin', I seen you come in tonight. And didn't see no bag."

"Why am I reminded of our phone conversation today. You want us to go back, come in the door again? Start over?"

"I was hopin' that wouldn't be necessary," Shadow said, and he was about to say more when the waitress appeared and set out the drinks, squaring them like chessmen on a board. Waverly gave her a bill from his wallet and she made change. Shadow waited for her to leave and then he resumed.

"Okay, maybe we could quit jivin' each other, you think?"

"Fine here. Let's have a look at the kid. Then we can talk about the goods."

Ledbetter snorted contemptuously. "Bein' up here don't mean we're off the farm," he said. To all appearances he addressed his glass. His head was sunk in neck, face awash in chins. The stump of a cigar, still in place, had gone out.

Shadow pushed at air with the flat of a hand. "No, hold up, Gaylon. Man's got a point. It ain't unreasonable, want to see what you're tradin' for." He paused and looked at the ceiling, a moment of self-communion. "Tell you what, Mr. Waverly. We bring the boy in, let you see he ain't damaged—which he ain't, by the way, little blubbery maybe but good as new—and then you and Miss Clemmons can show us where the goods is at. Sound fair?"

"It's a start."

"Got to start someplace," Shadow said amiably, "do any business." He raised an arm in summons and two ample figures materialized in the aisle beside the table.

Midnight looked up, startled, and said, "Clay. Are you all right?"

Clay gave a quick glance at Shadow and then moved his head up and down weakly. The muscles swelled under a tight polo shirt, but there was a look of supplication on his face, dread in his eyes. Standing alongside Gleep, he appeared almost shrunken.

"There's your goods," Shadow said. "Where's ours?"

"First he walks."

A gust of confounded air escaped Ledbetter's lips, sounded curiously like a woof. Shadow's smile diminished. "Walks?" he said. "What makes you think he's gonna walk?"

"Because those are the terms. How it is."

"Give you this, Mr. Waverly, you got a set a brassplate balls on you. For now, anyhow. Next we'll be hearin' you two want to hike right along with him."

"That would be good, too."

"You was sayin' about trust, minute ago. This what it means, huh?" There was a note of injury in his voice, very near to hurt.

"Your goods are just up the street. Couple of blocks. Let him walk and I'll see that you get them."

One of Shadow's hands dropped below the table. "You're a real white trader, Mr. Waverly. Supposin' I was to tell you I was holdin' a piece down here, about level with your nuts."

"Have to say that would be awfully dumb, with all these revelers. If you were to tell me that."

He brought the hand up, empty, and laid it on the table. Simultaneously did he tighten the corners of his mouth, resurrecting the smile. "Yeah, white trader," he said again, clearly taken by the phrase. "Nobody get up on you, bet." He turned to Clay. "Boy, you like to step over to the Holiday Inn awhile? Wait there till we got our business settled up here?"

"Shadow, what the fuck—" It was Ledbetter, a panic croak.

Shadow cut him off. "Stay cool, Gaylon. Drink your drink." He looked hard at Clay, but his voice was mild. "You'll be sure to wait there, won't you? For your sis and her boyfriend?"

"Yes," Clay said, "I'll wait. Yes."

"You promise?"

"Yes."

"Say you promise."

He said it.

"I think you may be shittin' me, boy. Don't matter none. You take it in your head to run, we'll find you. Found these two, didn't we? You just keep lookin' over your shoulder."

Clay mumbled something.

Shadow cupped one ear. "Didn't hear you."

"I'll wait there."

"Okay. You can move along now."

Clay looked back and forth between Shadow and Gleep. He glanced once at Midnight, his features knotting in a peculiar blend of sorrow and terror and remorse. He hesitated, but only for an instant, and then without a word scurried through the crowd toward the door. Gleep stood there shaking his head wondrously. Ledbetter said, "For Christ's sake, Shadow, you're givin' away the store. He's goin' to run."

Shadow's expression didn't change, but he issued a heavy sigh. "Gaylon, you had your shot. Blew it. Now I'm recommendin' you shut the fuck up. You heard these people. We got trust here. Ain't that right, Mr. Waverly?"

"Trust," Waverly echoed, and Ledbetter's head sunk lower, as though the supporting bones in his neck were crumbling.

" 'Course that trust, it's got to go both ways. So Gaylon, whyn't you just tag along, see the boy holds up his end of the bargain."

Ledbetter looked up sharply. "You sayin' I should follow him? Me?"

"That's right, Gaylon, that's what I'm sayin'. Little fieldwork do you some good. Whip you back into shape maybe. We'll catch up to you out at your place. Won't be long."

Obediently, Ledbetter got to his feet and went charging into the crowd.

"Wait a minute." Waverly said, "That's no clean walk."

Shadow leaned back in his chair and opened his hands in a gesture of mock entreaty. "Aw, c'mon, Mr. Waverly, it's just a little insurance for Gaylon. You can understand that, stake he's got in this transaction. Anyway, it ain't what you'd call an even footrace, that boy against Gaylon here. C'mon, fair is fair."

Waverly tallied his options. There weren't many. He could stonewall on the goods, of course, but if the kid was going to run, he'd show the likes of a Ledbetter his heels. If he was fool enough not to (and unhinged as he'd looked, that was a distinct possibility), well, there was nothing more could be done for him anyway. And it didn't escape Waverly that with Ledbetter out of the picture, there was one fewer side of his own to cover. He did a helpless shrug.

"I was hopin' you'd see things right," Shadow said. He patted the empty chair and motioned Gleep to sit. "Okay," he said to Waverly. "Now we got that all squared away, everybody feelin' good again, we can maybe talk some real business."

Waverly reached into his pocket and took out the keys to the Porsche. "Sure," he said. "It's like I told you. Bag's a couple blocks from here. In a car. I'll point you there and you boys can go help yourselves."

Shadow laid his chin in a hand, rolled his eyes. "Hey, Mr. Waverly. We was born at night, Gleep and me, but not last night."

"Never hurts to ask."

"Yeah, I was sittin' that toaster seat you're on, I'd maybe ask, too. Oh, I will take them keys, though. Seem to remember you like to use 'em for knuckle-dusters. You remember that, Gleep?"

Gleep gave Waverly a long enigmatic stare. He acknowledged the question with a grunt.

For a fraction of a moment, Waverly said nothing, calculated. Then, very deliberately, he placed the keys on the table between them. "Okay. But we've both still got a problem here. Let me lay it out, see if you follow. I'm a little unclear yet how we're supposed to walk out of here, Miss Clemmons and me. Of course, that's our part of the problem. But then you don't know where the car is, either. For sure. That's your part."

Shadow picked up the keys, leisurely fashion, dangled them from his fingertips, studied them. "Boy, that does sound like a spic standoff," he said finally, "that problem you're sayin'. Maybe the lady's got some ideas on it." He shifted his gaze to Midnight. "What do you think, Miss

Clemmons? We ain't heard much out of you tonight. Feelin' okay? Sick or something?"

Once again Midnight looked to Waverly for direction, and catching it, Shadow said, "You sure got this one packaged, Mr. Waverly. Case of pure dick-whippin', looks to me." His eyes swayed between them. He grinned widely. "I got to think he ain't been doin' much for you though, last couple nights. Shape he looks in. Maybe that's it, why you're quiet, I mean. No nookey, right?"

"No, that's not it," Waverly answered for her. "What she's thinking is what it must be like, woman have to hump a pusball like you. Shock rendered her speechless."

Shadow chuckled a little. Easy, tolerant chuckle. "Funny you mention that. I was thinkin' along them same lines. Man can't help it, special-lookin' lady like this." He did a half-bow at her, and watched her shudder. " 'Course I know you got firsts here," he went on, speaking directly at Waverly, "so I was figurin' how to help out, seein' as how you probably ain't been gettin' it up regular lately. Was thinkin' what we might do—after we get our business all accounted—what we might do is snip off your knob and let her get a taste of it. Unattached, you might say. See, that way you could watch too, dependin' on how your eyeballs is hangin', 'course." Now he turned to Midnight and asked solicitously, "How's that sound to you, Miss Clemmons? Whole new kick, huh, and if it don't work out, there's always me and Gleep."

"God, I've got to get out of here," she said. Her voice quaked, borderline hysteria. She started to rise.

"Sit down," Waverly said, and after she did, he looked at her steadily and said, "Hold on."

Shadow seconded him. "Yeah, hang on there, won't be long now. Just keep 'er wet."

A rousing cheer came from behind them and two old villains, stout and boiled-faced and blessedly free from wives for a night, staggered toward the table.

"It's the little lady from the Parlor," one of them announced, loud enough as though it was intended for the assembly in the room. "You remember us?" he bawled directly at Midnight. "Ernie and me?"

"I, uh, yes, I remember," she said uncertainly, desperately, not remembering.

"Park Place bar," the spokesman said by way of further explanation, "other night. Remember, we were talking gambling?"

Shadow's mouth went ajar. Waverly said nothing but his hands gripped the table. Midnight's fingers played nervously over the stem of her glass. "Yes, I do remember," she said.

"So. You wipe out the Indians? Up to the casino? Take some scalps?" He rocked backward slightly, holding a tenuous balance. Friend Ernie sported a genial narcotized smile. Gleep's face darkened, but he didn't move.

"I couldn't find it," Midnight said and then, quickly, "But I'd like to go now. Will you take me right now?"

"Hey, hold up—" Shadow started to protest, but Ernie laid his bulk across the table and stuck his face in Midnight's. "Be honored," he slurred.

"Your friends don't object," the other one said, startled and not quite believing in this marvelous good fortune.

"They don't," she said, and before anyone could move or speak, she was on her feet and squeezing behind Waverly's chair and grasping the arm of the one more or less standing.

"You fellas mind, we steal your lady couple hours?" he asked, still unconvinced of his astounding luck.

Ernie hauled himself upright and explained, stiffly formal, "We're genemum."

Shadow and Waverly exchanged stupefied stares. Then Waverly turned in his seat and looked at Midnight. She avoided his eyes. Shadow saw it all, and his wicked smile fell back in place. "Naw, that's okay," he said. "You run along, have yourselves a good time. We'll catch up to her later."

"Super," the one whose name was not Ernie said. Then, magnanimous in victory, "You boys want to come along? Casino? Roll some dice? Laughs."

"No!" It was Midnight's exclamation. "No, they can't come now."

"Lady's right," Shadow said. "Not quite yet. We'll be along." He was leering at Waverly, and snickering.

"Shame."

The two aging rakes slipped proprietary arms around Midnight's waist, and standing there, weaving a bit, the three of them resembled a doubtful dancing trio about to undertake a snappy number.

" 'preciate your . . ." Ernie searched for the elusive word that would describe their gratitude. "Time," he said. His eyes did a bleary circuit of the table, settled on Waverly. "What happen' your face?"

"An unlucky accident," Waverly said.

"You take care of it, hear? See a doctor."

He led the threesome in an uncoordinated step backward and began to maneuver them away. Midnight brought them to a stop and turned just enough to look at Waverly. "I'm sorry," she said. "I can't—I'm sorry."

A desolate, nameless ache rose in his throat. He had the wistful sense of the traveler, been down this road before. He shook his head slowly. "Have a good life," he said and watched as they disappeared, lurching merrily into the crowd.

Shadow said, "Looks like all your friends gone and left you twistin' in the wind, Mr. Waverly."

Gaylon turned his Caddie at the corner and went inching down Front Street, yellow-knuckling the wheel and swiveling his head side to side frantically. Nothing. Walks was empty. There was nothing. Rotten thieving fuck was ducked down for sure, gone. Just like he'd said. God-damit, he'd *told* Shadow, warned him. Nobody listened to old Gaylon no more. A car came roaring up behind, tacked onto his ass end, then squealed around him, honking. The driver, another punk kid, flipped him a furious bird.

Gaylon got to the Grandview intersection just in time for the light to go red on him, and he sat there helplessly, temples thumping, sweat puddles forming in every crease and fold of his body. He felt headachy, all the booze, worry, doubt, roller coaster of hope-despair. Too much stress, man his age, too long a time. And then, to his utter astonishment, utter disbelief, he caught sight of a wedge-shaped figure shuffling across the road, looked to be heading for the Holiday Inn. Gaylon had to bat his eyes a couple times, but sure as shit, it was the cockfucker himself, doing just like he was told. A fucking miracle.

On the green, he eased ahead and swung left into the lot. Place was crammed full, Friday night Shimmers crowd, not a goddammed spot to park anywhere. Got to think clear now, steady. He pulled up under the canopy, like he was going to check in, and let the car idle. He reached over and retrieved the piece he'd stashed in the glove compartment. Waited. In a moment Clay came down the walk in front of the building. About ten feet from the entrance he paused, glanced about as though he was confused, dazed, not exactly certain where he was. Now's the time to collect him, thought Gaylon, before he starts getting jackrabbit ideas. He poked his head and an arm out the window, snapped his fingers in summons.

"Hey, asswipe. Over here. Now."

Shitscarfer looked like he just caught his thumb in a hot socket. For one heart-stopping moment Gaylon feared he might try a run, which if he did would be nothing but double bad news. No way could Gaylon use the piece here, and no way either could he snare him, kid go stutter-stepping through the rows of cars. But instead, what Clay did was come slouching meekly around the front of the car, stoop in close, and say, "Mr. Ledbetter"—like he barely could remember who he was talkin' to—"I'm doing what he said."

Jesus, Shadow, he must of done a world-class persuadin' number on this one. Good old Shadow. Never again would he doubt him. Never. "That's good, you're doin' that," Gaylon said toughly. "Only now you do what *I* tell you. Get in the car."

"But he said to wait. Please."

"Plans got changed. Get in."

Gaylon gave him a good look at the piece. One was all it took.

Back at the house he pulled in the garage and brought the door down with the genie switch. He felt a little groggy yet, almost light in the head. His hands, he noticed, were trembling violently. He remembered the open bottle on the kitchen table. Go pour a tall one. One, get steady, get well. He motioned Clay out and ahead of him. They went inside, down the hall to the kitchen. Gaylon flipped on the light over the sink.

"Get a couple glasses and that bottle," he said to Clay. Might as well give the spooked turd a drink, be his last one anyway.

Clay did as directed.

"Out there," Gaylon said, indicating the dark living room. "You on the couch."

He was about to settle into his own favorite chair when he made out a pair of feet resting on the ottoman. "Shadow? That you?"

" 'Fraid not, Mr. Ledbetter."

"Who is it?"

As his eyes adjusted to the dark, Gaylon could distinguish a large and unfamiliar figure sprawled in the chair. Hands in tight black gloves and a pistol in one of them, leveled on his chest. The attached silencer gave it the ominous appearance of a cleanly shaved-off rifle barrel.

"You *are* Gaylon Ledbetter." It was a tone of voice halfway between a statement and a question.

"Yeah, but—"

"You want to set that piece on the stool there. Butt end first."

Gaylon bent over stiffly and laid the gun alongside the feet, which hadn't moved. For a moment he was too stricken to utter a word.

"Put that stuff on the floor and come on over here." This was addressed at Clay, who came across the room and stood beside Gaylon. "Your name wouldn't be Clemmons?"

"Yes sir."

"Huh. Pair to draw to."

"Look," Gaylon said, "we're gonna have the goods back tonight. Dietz said I had till tomorrow noon. You can call him." He was conscious of his voice, a soprano squeal. His knees felt buttery.

"Sure. Meantime, let's take us a little stroll. Woods out there."

He rose up out of the chair and with the weapon gestured them toward the door. Clay began to turn compliantly, but Gaylon remained rooted to the spot. "Give it an hour," he pleaded. "You'll see. Forty-five minutes."

"C'mon. You're just pitchin' pennies at the moon here."

Gaylon's mouth was working wildly but nothing intelligible seemed to want to come out. His hands fanned the air. He looked at Clay, and finally he was able to sputter, "You got any idea what's happenin' here?"

Clay gave him a sober empty smile, and Gaylon was about to say more when the man holding the gun stepped over and brought a knee jarringly into his groin, and whatever words Gaylon intended to speak terminated abruptly in a stifled shriek.

"You got to read my lips?" the man said. "I'm askin' you to move. Oh, yeah. Stop by the garage first. Seen you got a shovel in there."

When he saw he was being led off State Street, Shadow stopped abruptly and put a restraining hand on Waverly's elbow. "Whereabouts you say this vehicle's located?"

"Another block or so."

The block they were facing was illuminated well enough, but the next one was darker and the one after that darker still. Shadow looked dubious. "You wouldn't be thinkin' anything cute?"

Waverly shrugged. "Maybe you'd have preferred downtown. Some spectators." He was wedged between the two of them, Shadow and Gleep, another trio, not quite so merry.

Shadow thought it over a minute. "Okay," he said. "Keep walkin'."

Midway into the second block, he stopped them again. "You better give him another feel," he said to Gleep. "Case he's got some big-league moves on his mind."

Gleep pointed to a tree in a yard back from the sidewalk and Waverly dutifully went to it and put his hands on the trunk, extending his arms and legs.

"Y'know, that's your whole problem," Shadow said, "playin' out of your league. Three of you. You was all minors."

"Am I going to get to do this to you?" Waverly said, alluding to the patdown. "Fair is fair. Remember?"

"Fair?" Shadow said with a short, unmirthful laugh. "We already been too fair, Mr. Waverly, lettin' your friends—guess they're your friends—hike, way we did. Pretty generous, is my thinkin'. Anyway, how you going to get fair? There's two of us. You notice that?"

"I noticed."

"Clean," Gleep said.

"That's good. You noticed, I mean. Also that you ain't packin' no foreign objects. You better turn around now."

Waverly turned and Shadow came in close and brought the back of a hand across his face. In a voice cold as a mountain lake, he said, "All the fuck-around games is over, Mr. Waverly. Where's the goods?"

He could taste the blood leaking over his lips from the fresh rupture in his skin. Thin salty taste. He was getting mightily sick of being the one did all the bleeding. "Around the corner," he said. "In an alley. In the Porsche. Think you can follow that?"

Shadow punched him once, the level of the belt line. It was not a heavy blow and he stayed on his feet, but wobbling some. In a remote province of his head, a whirlwind gathered.

"Case of wise fuck, that can be terminal too," Shadow said and got behind him and shoved. "Move."

Against the garage, the Porsche took dim shape in a silvery streak of moonlight. Once he saw it, Shadow stepped out in front and made for the car. Gleep fell in beside him, peering curiously into the hatch. "Goods in there?" he asked.

"Let me take care of this, f'Chris' sake," Shadow said irritably. "You just watch him. Careful."

But by then Waverly had edged over alongside the trash can. Gleep was a yard or two away. Perilous margin.

Shadow fumbled with the lock. Half in the dark, half backlit by the moon, his face bore the expression of an ill-made gargoyle. "Put a little hair around it," he mumbled to himself, words that were to be the last he would ever speak. He lifted the hatch and gave an abundant sigh, and then he stooped down and leaned in to retrieve the bag of goods.

Now Waverly could feel the trash can pressing against his thighs. His fingers groped for the stock, and when they found it he yanked out the shotgun and swung it first on Gleep, backing him away with a silent, universally understood jabbing motion. Then he spun to his right and, from the calm eye of the whirlwind storming through his head, pronounced Shadow's name, and when Shadow turned and looked quizzically into the parallel barrels aimed at his throat, Waverly said, "Your turn for a new vision of the world." Shadow opened his mouth, tried to get something out, but Waverly squeezed the trigger and behind the blast came a fierce howl, like the trumpeting of a maddened rogue elephant; and Shadow's head went sailing off its mooring, trailing streamers of blood and gristle and chips of bone, porcelain white; and what Shadow saw, if he could see at all from those astonished offended eyes, was the rocketeer's vision of a world spinning away, receding at an alarming pace.

Waverly leveled the gun on Gleep.

"You killed him," Gleep said, flat, empty of emotion, reconciled. "You got one more round, that cannon. You goin' to use it, better do it now, all the good it'll do you. There'll be somebody else right behind me. Jacktown slugger like you ought to know that."

"I know." Lights were winking on up and down the street. "So better we both get out of here."

Gleep stared at the shattered body. He didn't move. "This one, he was my partner. Bughouse maybe, but not so dumb. He said you was in this all along."

"You believe that?"

"Lookin' that way."

A siren wail spiraled in the distant air. Waverly would have liked to think it through, weigh the odds, but it occurred to him there was no pattern to impose anymore, or order, or meaning. And no time. And, finally, no matter. "All right," he said, gesturing with the gun barrel. "Over there."

He followed Gleep part way across the alley, and then he swung about suddenly and pointed the gun at the

Porsche's gas tank and fired. An explosion rocked the night. The raised hatch looked curiously like a wide-open mouth, dragon mouth, feeding on what remained of Shadow's flapping sputtering popping body. A tongue of flame shot from it, ignited the garage. Waverly approached close as he dared and heaved the shotgun into the blaze and ducked away. "Now what do you believe?" he said to Gleep.

"Dunno no more. Run, I guess."

In opposite directions, they ran.

SIX

IT WAS A STAGY THROAT CLEARING WAK-
ened him, followed by the amused, somewhat patronizing
question: "You always sleep in a tie?"

First he had to get his eyes pried open and his bearings
partly gathered; then he could think about composing a
reply. He was—where again?—the Park Place room. Why
here? Well, why not? It had been a place to go. A half-
drained Seagrams bottle stood on the nightstand, and an
ashtray spilling over, and a glass full of disintegrating
butts floating in an amber pool. A rank sour odor steamed
the bed, and he was the only visible source. His skull
levied an urgent fine and the rest of him, a long-term
one; and, yes, he had slept—passed out, more accurately,
unseasoned drunk—in his clothes, all of them, including
the tie. And now a stranger occupied the leather chair by
the window, at once placid and magisterial, as though
he had reserved and paid for the room, rightfully belonged here. And the stranger said, insistent but not un-
pleasant, "Well, do you?"

"Got to be ready for early-morning guests," Waverly
said. "Look your best." In the way of reply, that was his
best this morning.

"Check your watch, you'll see it's not exactly early. Also

a mirror. No way you're going to look pretty today, my friend, that face. Tie or not."

No need to ask, he was heat. All the giveaway signals were in place: thrifty-acres sport jacket and shiny pants, tailored in Taiwan; face a relief map of cynicism and melancholy dismay, always contiguous countries; voice, even in its counterfeit display of concern, a sandpaper swipe at the ear. And the baggy look they all seemed to get, in time. This one had probably started out skinny, years ago, and lingered too long over pie and coffee in all-night cafes. The bone structure of his face was narrow, but the jowls were dragging and a series of terraced wattles depended from a primary chin. Shoulders were meager and chest flat, almost sunken, with a gross paunch swelling beneath it.

"Name's Slate," he said, "Max Slate. Grand Traverse Sheriff's Department. Some people like to call me Clean, make a little joke. Clean Slate."

It sounded very near an invitation to count himself among those humorists: Go ahead, boy, you call me Clean. Waverly knew the drill: first the stroke, then, if needed, the gloves, then bare knuckles and a knee in the balls. It was the rhythms you had to listen for; transitions could be sudden. He decided to say nothing just yet.

"So. You want to tell me how it happened?"

Waverly gave him his best vacant stare.

"It's your face I'm referring to."

"Oh, that. Shaving. I've got one of those sensitive skins you hear about. On the television."

"Yeah, just looking, I can tell you're the sensitive type. Giving you any discomfort, is it? Your shaving scrapes, I mean."

"No, it's nothing. Builds character."

"Character," Slate repeated, enunciating deliberately, as though he was trying to extract the very essence of the meaning of the word.

Waverly pushed himself up in the bed. He got a cigarette from a near-empty pack among the nightstand litter. The initial puff elevated a dizzying nausea from the bottom-most zones of his viscera through belly and chest. With an effort, he forestalled it at the gullet, nick of time.

Slate, who evidently missed nothing, asked, "You feeling okay? Not going to puke are you?"

"I could maybe take a leak."

He made a sweeping gesture toward the bathroom. "Don't have to ask permission. It's your room."

Waverly got to his feet and steadied himself with the elaborate, dignified caution of the gravely ill. He could feel Slate's amused eyes on him all the way. He ran the water in the sink hard as it would go, cover for the gurgly retching noises he made, fooling, of course, no one. The mirror confirmed Slate's assessment of his face, but he could have guessed at that. No surprises there. The time—well into the afternoon—was another matter. Last night he had come back here—where else left to go?— and ordered a bottle ("You pick the brand," he recalled telling them at room service) and tried to think clearly about things, what had just happened, what he had done. About Midnight. Instead he had drunk himself stuporous. Now, in a fraction of a moment, he had to try again, prepare for what was ahead. No success. All coherence seemed to have departed from his life.

"Now how you doing?" Slate asked him as he settled into the facing chair. Mock solicitude.

"Doing just fine, Mr. Slate. But it's always good to know someone cares."

"Little too much holiday whoopee?" he said, still in stroking gear.

Waverly worked up one of those tearoom smiles. There wasn't anything he could do about this, none better did he know. But he didn't have to make it easy for him, either.

"You mentioned something about character, minute

ago. I was thinking on that while you were in the john freshening up. Character." Slate spoke quietly, a man of theories and contemplation, but some of the natural spite was creeping into his voice. "Take your jacket, for instance, you want to talk character. Timothy Waverly, it says, educated man but a real heavy menace, particularly it comes to threatening women, wives. Real bad. Lawyer-waxer too, and graduate of the twitch factory and our own Michigan walled-off Astoria, Five-Blocker at that. Makes for good reading, all your exploits."

Preliminaries were abruptly over. Main event on the way. "You got to the bottom," Waverly said, "you also saw duly released, March 26, 1983."

"Yeah, I read that part, too."

They took a pause to study each other. It was Slate who resumed. "Timothy, that's a cute name. Bet you had a lot of boyfriends, down SPSM."

"Mostly it was fighting off the green blazers. Put a man in uniform, does weird things to his libido. Mixes it up. But I expect you know all about that."

Slate grinned wickedly, exposing a mouthful of tarnished silver. He did a nice practiced cool, except for his breathing, which was audible, almost a subdued pant.

"Well," Waverly put into the otherwise silence, "we've chatted about my health and my history and my sex life. Anything else you'd like to cover?"

"Seems like there was one more thing." He tapped a temple with his knuckles, shaking loose the memory. "Oh yeah, I. got it now. Was going to ask if you might of heard something last night."

"Something? Can you help me out a little?"

"Why sure. That's what we're here for, your law-enforcement agencies. Help out. What I got in mind is like an explosion. You know, boom in the night."

Waverly did the tapping number on his own temple. "No . . . no. I must have missed that one."

"That's a real shame, you missed it. Peculiar, too. Could hear it all over this end of town."

"I'm a deep sleeper."

"Bet you are."

Next pause. For Waverly this one was welcome. He had held on to the adjustable smile, but all the ends of his nerves were galvanized. Slate looked relaxed enough to doze off himself, as if the mere topic of sleep could turn him drowsy. "You want to know what it was," he said, "that boom?"

"I was thinking if I was patient, maybe you'd tell me."

Slate leaned forward in his chair. The paunch did an accordion crumple. The voice went low and confidential. "It was a Porsche car that blew up, Timothy. Couple blocks from where we're sitting right now."

"Lesson there. Buy American."

"Yeah, well, there's more than that even. See, somebody was in that car. Deep-fried now. All we got's a pile of cranberry jelly, looks like what's left of a head. So we don't know who he is. Yet."

Waverly shook his head dolefully. "Accidents," he said. "Glad you came by to alert me. Safety is everybody's business."

Slate chuckled an appreciation. "Problem is, Timothy, there's been a whole rash of accidents lately." He started enumerating them on the fingers of a hand: "First you got your mysteriously exploding vehicle. With a poor unfortunate soul in it, that's two. Then about a week ago, we had a boy got his hand all chewed up." He flapped his own tally hand violently, a kind of visual aid. "Ordinarily, that'd qualify as one of your accidents, except that this boy can't explain how it happened. Matter of fact, he can't talk at all. They got him in a rubber room—you remember them—anybody comes in, shrink, nurse, anybody, he starts howling. Sad case. Few days before that we find ourselves a colored gentleman, ditch out by the airport. He's got a new mouth carved for him, spare, little lower down from the original. Neither is doing much smiling. How many's that make?"

"Mouths or accidents?"

"How many?" he demanded, not so sportive.

"I count four. Unless you figure the guy and the car as one. Then it's three."

"Four," Slate said, more evenly. "Inside of two weeks. Which is a good-size number for us, Traverse City. Your mom-and-pop murder, that's about the heaviest we ever get up here."

"Bad news comes in bunches."

"Don't it. Oh, we got one more to count, Timothy, For five."

"What's that one?"

"That one's you," Slate said, and there was an ill-concealed distaste ran the edge of his voice. He watched Waverly carefully.

"You here to charge me with something, Mr. Slate?"

"Why, you want to call a lawyer? What's a cocksuck like you tell a lawyer: Defend me or I'll kill you?"

"Maybe I'd start out softer. Friendly. Way you do."

"You want to tell me your whereabouts last night?"

"When you tell me what I'm charged with."

"How about coincidence, book you on coincidence. Things running good this quiet little town, business good, tourists having fun, spending their money, merchants happy. Then the accidents start up. Roll over a rock or two and there you are, bigger'n shit."

"Which statute is that again, coincidence?"

"Same one gives me the authority to ring your bell a time or two, I take it in my head to do that. Make them zippers in your face permanent."

Waverly turned over passive hands. "Been done before," he said.

"Can see that," Slate said fiercely. Then, with a sure

sense of timing, he sagged back in his chair, reached in his pocket and got out a package of gum. He unwrapped a stick for himself and offered Waverly one.

"No thanks."

"Sugarless."

"Thanks, no."

Slate shrugged his narrow shoulders and thrust the gum in his mouth. He was an intense chewer, jaws grinding furiously, yet his next question was affably couched, interested. "Where is it you're living now'days, Timothy?"

"South."

"South. And what is it brings you north, visit our community?"

"It's the air."

"Yeah, we got the good air up here, don't we?"

" 's truth."

"Some of your best on God's green earth. Wouldn't also be your ex living in town, brings you here, I mean. You wouldn't be thinking to cause her and her family more grief?"

"You do your homework, Mr. Slate." It came out a compliment, which was as he intended. Overnight and they had the full sheet on him. He was genuinely impressed.

"We try and keep up. Give you another for instance. That south you're saying, that's state of Florida, Palm Beach Gardens. Am I right?"

"Right again."

"Now there's another of them coincidences I was speaking about. See, Timothy, I got a place down in Juno Beach. Mobile home, double-wide. Juno Beach, that's just north where you're at, I remember my geography."

"Practically neighbors."

"That's it, neighbors. Which is why I got a neighborly interest in you. Come July one, next, I'm hanging it up. Put in thirty-four years, Timothy, eleven of 'em Pontiac containing the coloreds till they outnumbered us. Come out here for the peace and quiet, but even that's getting scarce now'days. No rest, your wicked. Least not till one July, eighty-seven. Then it's golden-years time for me."

"Good for you."

"Yeah, but maybe not so good for you, to finish the point I was making. See, I vacation down there every winter. Been doing that for years now. Don't take long, my line of work, you get to know people. West Palm Chief, for an example for you, he's a good friend of mine. Next time I see him—which will be January—I'll tell him you and me got acquainted. Might be he'd like to drop in on you now and then, make sure everything's running smooth."

"Appreciate your concern. I'll watch for him."

"Don't mention it," Slate said. He removed the gum and examined it with all the fascination of a lapidary stumbled quite by chance on a precious stone. "Sweet taste's all gone," he said, and fixed the wad to the underside of the chair. Then he hauled himself up and stood directly over Waverly. "Well, got to scoot now. Sure been a pleasure talking to you." For a moment it appeared as though he might extend a parting hand, but instead he said, "Oh, I'm going to operate off the assumption once I leave, you'll be packing your bags and heading back south. As in today, this afternoon. Hope I can plan on that assumption. See, Timothy, what we don't need, Michigan general and Traverse City particular, is any more like you. You follow what I'm recommending to you here?"

Waverly took as deep a breath as his achy chest would allow. Wondrously, the danger point seemed to be past. "I think I've got it now."

Slate put a hand on his shoulder and squeezed. "Good boy," he said.

He watched Slate move heavily, paunch in a lateral sway, toward the door. Before he got beyond it, Waverly said his name: "Slate?"

"Sir?"

"Indulge me. Why is it I'm walking, all those coincidences?"

"You don't know?"

"I'm asking."

"You really don't know," he said. The matter-of-fact tone didn't conceal his surprise. "Okay, no harm telling. Looks of you, you got it coming. The nigger at the airport, he's a five-and-dime hustler out of Saginaw. Whoever opened him up was doing his part to keep Michigan beautiful. Kid with the fresh stump was dealing at the funny-cigarette level, our sources say. Probably got in over his dumb-shit head. I got a notion, strictly an instinct, you understand, that the crispy fry in the Porsche is going to turn out to be another of your undesirables. Porsche brings us to you. This morning we talked to the lady owns it and——" Slate paused, read his expression. "Surprised? Maybe not your big city up here, but we do our stuff. I was guessing you already knew what she had to say."

"Why don't you tell me anyway. Round off the story."

"She said the vehicle must of been stolen. She wouldn't know though because she was busy last night. Real busy. Seems you slept over, Sugar Beach Motel."

Waverly lowered his head and began to laugh softly.

"You're not telling me it was any different?"

"No," Waverly said, his laughter turning to a spasmed cough. "No, it's the way she said."

Slate glared at him. "Makes the boy giggle, huh, that little story. You know, Timothy, all the years I been in this business, it's the broads I could never figure. I checked this one out. Here's a young lady, comes from a good family, home. Respectable people. Money, influence. Class. World by the balls. And she's running with a piece of puzzle-house dog shit like you. So how you going to figure?"

"It's a mystery," was all he could get out.

"Mystery, yeah. Well, don't matter. Once you're out of town, that beautification project I was speaking of, that's complete anyway." Slate stood there a moment longer. "So you have yourself a nice trip now."

When he passed the Ishpeming city-limits sign, his own trip concluded, Gleep drove directly to the site of the elementary school where Norbert had bled to death in the basement boiler room, long ago. An entirely different building stood there now, another school, and where the apple trees had once been was now a paved-over parking lot. Gleep tried to reconstruct an image of his brother but memory, apart from the chirped sounds of his garbled name—Gleep! Gleep! Gleep!—failed him. Nor could he call up clearly the day he assaulted the cowering principal and sent the school up in flames and changed his own life forever. Still was worth it, he thought, though the blurred recollection of flames reminded him of last night and Shadow and the Jacktown card counter and the fingersnap choice he had made and the ones he might have made. A flood of curious emotions washed over him, utterly alien to his experience and too tangled to examine or confront.

He got back into Shadow's Caprice and drove through town. He turned onto the street where the house of his boyhood once stood, and of course it was no longer there, leveled and grown over with weeds. He took a dirt road into the woods, followed it several miles till he arrived at the lake where, dead of winter, he would sit hunched over a hole in the ice, savage winds assailing his ears. He sat there now, warmed by a dog-days sun, wrapped and folded in time, wondering at the riddles of choice and time, listening to the phantom whispered voices rising off the green water on the winds of the past.

Gunter Dietz, at that same moment, was also deeply concerned with choices and time. He sat in the masculine study of his North Shore Chicago home, watching a phone that resolutely refused to ring. For over forty-eight hours he had heard not a word, nothing, and waiting did little for his temper, even though he prided himself on being a calm and patient man.

The rest of the house was in a tumult of feverish activity, his wife's last-minute party preparations. Only cultivated, interesting people had been invited, so she said. Three of them, weekend guests, were roaming about now, and if they were representative, then he might better have stayed in Michigan, seen to business himself. One, a fag owned an art gallery downtown, spent most of the day in a silk robe, and came weighted down with neon jewelry including pearl studs, both ears. The other two, a couple, were Jews: he a bearded U. of C. professor, physics or some goddam thing, and she, as far as Dietz could tell, employed full-time in the capacity of taunting bitch.

Last night the three of them were shooting pool in the game room, Dietz and the wife looking on, and the professor kept talking about the "elegant geometry of the game." Couldn't handle a cue worth a shit. Dietz felt like getting in there, run a rack or two, show them how it's done, but he knew that would only annoy his wife. Then the Jew girl, fast disappearing a bottle of brandy, came up to him and asked, very sweetly, if he suffered from aphasia, and he said I, ah, hope not, and she gave him a villainous smile. Later he tried to look it up but couldn't find it anywhere in the dictionary.

So today he kept to himself in his study. He considered

making a follow-up call but soon rejected that notion: Anxiety equals weakness, and the man in charge could never afford the luxury of such displays. At two his wife stuck a louring face around the door and hissed, "Guests." He joined them, three couples who kept apologizing for being *so early!* and who declared, a little too loudly, they were already drunk as lords. Dietz mixed more drinks, did his best to make conversation. Around three the Jap houseboy (who was Oona's uncle or cousin or some relation) tapped him on the elbow and said there was a call on his private line. He excused himself and went into the study.

"Yes," he said into the phone, not at all displeased with the way it came out, soft and modulated, controlled.

"Yeah, who's this?"

"Dietz here. Eugene?"

"Oh, Mr. Dietz. Didn't sound like you."

"It's me, Eugene. I've been waiting for you to call."

"Yeah, sorry about that. Ran into a little snag with my first contact. His old lady's expectin', so he figured he hadn't ought to take no work would maybe keep him away from home too long."

Dietz took a shallow breath before he spoke. "I need this cleared up, Eugene. Now. Thought I made that plain."

"Don't matter none, Mr. Dietz. I got us another fella. Out of Detroit. Lots of experience, good references. He got up there last night."

"Then you've got news for me."

"Well, kind of yes and no."

"What might that mean?"

"Guess it shakes down half good, other half not so good."

"You're going to have to do better than that. This phone's all right."

"It's washed, for sure?"

"Trust me, Eugene."

"Okay. Well, this Detroit boy, he just called in. Said your personnel problem up there, that got taken care of last night."

"The merchandise?"

There was a hesitation. Then, "I'm thinkin' that's the bad part, Mr. Dietz. He ain't been able to turn that up yet."

Dietz had been standing. Now he sank heavily into a chair. "What's the problem?" he asked, holding his voice as steady as he could.

"Kinda hard to say. Sound of it, there was a whole lot of people playin' with the pads on last night. Heat's been diggin' around in it, too. You want, I can give you the play-by-play."

"No details, Eugene. What I want is that merchandise back. What's the line on that?"

"Well, our man, he's been keepin' his ear to the ground, picked up a little. That card shuffler, one you was sayin' might be staked in it? Heat must of figured same way. Looks like they got nothin' to nail him on though, so they're showin' him the road outta town."

Under his breath Dietz muttered an uncharacteristic obscenity. The card counter again! Dietz could feel the threads of control unraveling at flash speed. His impulse was to bring a fist down hard on the desk. Instead he said, "Has he got it? The merchandise?"

"Ain't no way to tell for sure. Least that's what Detroit says. He wants to know should he keep trackin'."

"You tell him to get that merchandise, Eugene. Make it a hat trick. And tell him this last one's a punishment. I want him to lay on some heavy hurts. You tell him that."

"He's, uh, gonna ask is the bonus money we talked about, is that still on."

"Yes, the goddam bonus money stands."

"I'll tell 'im, Mr. Dietz."

"And fast. I want it done fast."

"Don't you worry none. This Detroit boy's a quick starter. He'll put a stamp on his ass. Special delivery. You got my guarantee."

Another guarantee. Dietz, whose whole body seemed to be quaking, head to foot, as though from the sudden onset of a chill, had to think about that a minute.

"You still there, Mr. Dietz?"

"Still here, Eugene."

"Anything else?"

"No. Soon as you hear anything, you call me. You got that?"

"You'll be the first. Now you have a real good weekend, Mr. Dietz."

The Jew girl had been trailing him all afternoon, and finally she cornered him by the magnificent stone fireplace in the library.

"You must read a great deal, Mr. Dietz. All these books."

"When I can," he said coldly. "Business keeps me occupied."

"Business," she said. There was slush in her voice and she weaved a little, keeping on her feet, but there was a diabolic glitter in her sodden eyes as she asked innocently, "Is it true what they say, you're a mobster? A *gang*land overlord?"

Dietz made an arctic smile and didn't reply, but what he was thinking was how this cunt would melt down into a nice supply of soap.

He set down his bag and laid the room key on the counter. The woman behind it glanced up from a ledger, did a perfect cinematic double take at the sight of his face. She worked her mouth into one of those sickly charitable grins people will reserve for wickedly disfigured cripples, asked how she could help him.

"I'll be checking out now," Waverly said.

The smile turned puzzled. "But it's"—she looked at the clock on the wall—"after four o'clock, sir."

"Is that a problem?"

"Well, not exactly. But you see, ordinarily checkout is noon. Or one even. This time of day, I'd have to charge you for another night."

"So be it," he said.

She got the bill tallied and stapled and was about to hand it over when a thought seemed to come to her. "You're Mr. Waverly."

"That very man."

"I almost forgot. There's a lady, left a message. She wanted you to meet her in the lounge."

"A lady."

"Yes. I think she's still in there. Would you like me to see?"

"Thanks, I'll manage."

He stood in the entrance a moment. She was sitting at the bar, identical spot where he'd first seen her, a week and a day ago. Like then, the room was otherwise empty. Idly, she stirred the drink in front of her, and fixed him with a distant gaze. He walked over and took the seat beside her. He watched her, saying nothing. He was not of a humor to make it easy on anyone today.

At last she said, twitch of a smile, "So. And how was your day?" Her voice was wispy, reedy, thin, the accents of a troubled child. Under the expertly applied makeup, her face looked weary.

"Been worse ones," he said, "though maybe not in recent memory. You?"

"Oh, about half."

"Half," he repeated, pensive and unsullied by any irony.

"Buy you a drink? There's a bartender around here somewhere."

"Another time. I've been invited to get moving."

"Waverly, I need to—"

He put up a deterrent palm. "No. No you don't. There's no need. What you told the police today, that was enough."

She looked at him hopefully. "It felt good to say it. To be able to say it. Like an atonement. Of sorts."

Interesting choice of words, atonement. He suspected she was innocent of its roots: *in harmony, at one.* "Now we're square," he said, "you and I. Even."

The flickery smile went bleak. "You don't want to hear any of it? What happened? How I got here?"

To rescue you, was the substance left unspoken, carry the day. She was one of a kind, this woman. "It doesn't matter," he said.

"To me it does."

"Then I expect you're going to tell me," he said. From where he sat he could see a uniformed cop sprawled in a lobby chair, feigning an interest in a newspaper. Let him wait.

"Yes, I am. That's right. I am."

She delivered her story in a voice shaded by a curious mix of desolation and belligerence, using her hands expressively, shaping nimble gestures. Last night, after she left Kelly's with the two ancient nasties, she talked them into stopping at the Holiday Inn. That was not so difficult since both of them misread the request, particularly bottle-courage Ernie, who kept squeezing her thigh with a bony, liver-spotted hand. Clay was nowhere in sight. She got them to drive her around, searching, but not for long. Soon the dawning recognition of their diminishing chances for getting a little action turned them ugly. Not runnin' a taxi, Ernie sneered, and they dumped her unceremoniously on a back street.

There was nowhere to turn for help. Only herself. She tried to think the way he would think. If he was there. But she couldn't make sense of it anymore, any of it. What had happened, what she had done. She remembered the Sugar Beach, and set out walking. Along the way she heard an explosion, sirens, but she was too numb to put any of it together.

The room, the bolt, the chain lock—that was as far as she could take it. Safe once, safe again. The day—the whole long week—had been surreal, tapped too many foreign emotions. She fell onto the bed and slept. Fantastic dreams invaded her sleep.

The next morning—this morning—she woke to an insistent hammering at the door. Wakefulness more terrifying than any dream. And still no help anywhere. She peered around the edge of the drape. Police, two in uniform, one not. The immensity of relief, a kind of reprieve, left her drained, sagging.

"That would be Slate and company," Waverly said. "And that brings us up-to-date."

"There's a little more," she said, and the story went on unfolding.

She let Slate into the room. He was affable and courteous, seemed to know a great deal about her. All the same, his eyes kept straying from her to the battle-zone bed and around the shabby room. It promised to be a high-wire act, this conversation.

He told her about the Porsche and she registered appropriate dismay. A theft story came to her effortlessly. But then he told her about the body in the back of the car, watching her reaction, and the shock she displayed was this time genuine, unstaged. Had to be you, Waverly. Who else? An emptiness overtook her, the more wrenching because it was so alien and so vast.

No, she heard herself replying to Slate, no idea who it could be. Car was in the lot last night.

He asked if she happened to know a man name of Timothy Waverly. Trolling, from the sound of it.

She did. Why?

No special reason, Slate said. Except this Waverly character was a bad number and they knew he was in town.

Part of the job, keeping track of your undesirables. They were watching him right now, figuring to have a little chat with him later in the day. Which is why it would help, anything she could tell him. How good they were, uh, acquainted.

Those were the words he used: "Waverly character," "bad number," "undesirables," "acquainted." For a chip of a moment she had the peculiar sensation of time rolled back, a forties film, herself a lesser player but with a crucial plot twist turning on the delivery of her next lines. With eyes carefully averted, and in those resigned tones becoming a fallen woman, the kind that ought to play with a fossil like Slate, she said; I'm afraid he's not a likely suspect for you. You see, the fact is he spent last night with me. All of it.

Slate seemed rattled, confused. And not a bit cheered. You're sure about that, he said.

I always know who it is I spend the night with, Mr. Slate.

He had a few more questions but they were nothing to handle, factual, routine. Through her responses she let him know there was money here, influence, and the quirkiness of the rich, explains everything. She could do that particularly well. He volunteered transportation, help, but she waved the offer away airily. Her father, the attorney, would engage someone to attend to things, insurance claims, details, such things. She gave him an Illinois address and a number to call. If he had to. He said he hoped none of this had soured her on their little community. She assured him she was rather taken by the place. Quaint.

And then he was gone. She got the clerk to arrange for a rental car, and a little later so was she.

"And here you are," Waverly summed up for her, "come to salvage the ruin of the day."

"Well, here anyway."

"Your brother? What about him?"

"I don't know," she said listlessly. "I called home, no one had seen or heard from him. Once he got out of that bar, he probably took off like a rocket. God only knows where he is now. After all this I'm not sure I care anymore."

"Let me give you a piece of unsolicited advice. If . . . when you find him, tell him not to forget what they said last night. About looking over his shoulder. Tell him he'd better act on it. This isn't finished yet."

"I'll remind him. Next time I see him. But right now I'm here. With you."

"So you are."

"Look, Waverly, there's no way I can ever make you understand. Last night. I know that. But I want you to know, what we had, what was *there*—well, I've got no precedent for it in my life."

It was somehow disconcerting, hearing this. His gaze shifted to the back bar, the floor. "If you want my thanks, you have it."

"What I wanted was for you to know."

It was the sort of empty conversation did nothing more than ripple the widening distance between them. "Now I do," he said, putting a note of finality in it.

Her earnest features seemed to crumple some. "Will I ever see you again?"

It was phrased around a tremor, but by now he was alert to those vocal talents of hers. Yet this was unfamiliar, carried a ring of supplication in it, almost genuine. He recognized just how much was at hazard, his reply. "Doesn't seem likely, does it. But then who ever knows."

"Well, I've still got your card," she said, extracting it from her purse in a show of proof. "But there's no number on it. Are you going to give me a number?"

Waverly had to think about that a moment. "Why would you want one now? After all that's happened."

"Oh, I don't know. I might need advice sometime. Or just a friendly voice on the other end of a line. I don't want it ending quite like this, Waverly."

Against every instinct he knew to be rational, he gave her the number of Bennie Epstein's Key Line Services.

She wrote it carefully on the face of the card, and then, smiling at him, a wise, secret smile, said, "Florida. Winter's coming on. Maybe we'll run into each other again one day."

"Maybe."

"Goodbye, Waverly."

She fluttered out of her chair and turned and walked toward the door with an amplified precision, as though the soles of her feet had lost all sensation. He was on the slender edge of calling something after her but was unable to summon any words, not even her name. And then she was gone, leaving him to speculate on how many human connections one is allotted, per lifetime, and to wonder if his quota was used up.

He steered the Mazda down a pleasant, tree-banked Traverse City street. It was the street on which would be located the Foss residence, Arthur and Annetta. A last errand before departing, on order, and for good. He drove slowly, squinting to read the house numbers. A Sheriff's Department black-and-white idled at a corner two blocks back.

It was no trouble whatsoever, finding the place, for a sign with their names carved in wood and nailed above the garage door announced it. He went on by, turned in a driveway a few houses down, came back and pulled over at the curb across the street. He left the engine running but didn't move from behind the wheel. Just looking, folks, nothing to get nervous about. Exercise in morbid curiosity, perverse nostalgia.

But there wasn't all that much to see: bilevel ranch,

attached two-car garage complete with obligatory basketball hoop and child's bike leaning against the far sidewall, well-tended lawn with strategically spotted shrubs and Blue Spruce trees, some beds of flowers here and there. Little slice of Americana, heartland. About what he expected. There was no one out front, but he could hear a lawn mower racketing in the back. He slid the car in gear and edged forward for a better look. Though he couldn't be absolutely certain—ten years, after all—the figure piloting the mower, moving in and out of his line of vision, had to be Arthur. And if it was, he looked remarkably fit, almost youthful. Trim figure, erect carriage, purposeful gait. He wore denims and a T-shirt, sneakers it looked like. A pipe projected from his mouth like a stiff dark weapon. From this distance his hairline appeared to have held rather well, not a trace of recession.

So not everything turned out the way it should. None of it, in fact, for at that moment a youthful figure appeared in the yard, a delicately-built boy, bearing a glass of something or other. Lemonade, perhaps. He came up alongside Arthur and tapped him playfully on the hip, signaling him to stop. Arthur took the glass in one hand and tousled the boy's hair with the other. In return, he got a look of pure worshipful devotion.

There was no opportunity to see more, even if he'd wanted. The black-and-white eased up by him and the officer, looked about twenty-one and still crafting an attitude of menace, poked his head through the window and drawled, "This ain't exactly the road out of town, friend."

"Maybe I'm lost."

"Whyn't you just follow me, then. I'll get you aimed the right way."

Ten miles south of Traverse City, the black-and-white turned onto a side road and parked. Waverly kept going, and the officer gave him a mock salute as he passed.

MICHIGAN ROLL

He drove with the window open wide, and between cigarettes, drew in deeply the aseptic, forgiving Michigan air. But he also attended closely to the rearview mirror. His alert to Midnight held equally for himself, more so: The paybacks were far from over yet. It was only prudent to assume they had already got to Clay, and with the goods still missing, they'd be tracking him next. Somewhere out there, behind him, or maybe up ahead, around the next turn, was another figure, even as Gleep had warned. Nameless, this one would be, faceless, rising like some dusky funnel-shaped cloud in the near distance and bearing down fast. There were strategies to design, urgent details to sort out and order. He had to bring them into focus, and without delay.

But the counterfeit security of the moving car and the serene, wide-flung landscape lulled him into something curiously approaching reverie. The highway shimmered under a dwindling sun. Clusters of trees swayed in a mild breeze. Already some of their leaves were flecked with yellow, beginning to turn. The fields were mostly yellow too, or dull brown. Two months, three, they'd be buried in snow, brilliant as polished silver by day, pale blue at night. He remembered it, but only dimly. The way he remembered a son, pastel shades, scarcely at all. For a while he considered the riddle of fatherhood, a child victimized into life by a random act of lust and now lost forever, another man's son. Which led to thoughts of Annetta, her luckless lawyer, the years in prison and the ones that followed, the inception of this ill-starred journey and the lurking madness that inspired it. And from there to Midnight escaping on the arms of a pair of drunks, tossing over her shoulder an offhand apology (pity they're going to kill you, sorry); and her errant brother, a dead man, if not now, then surely very soon; and the incinerating body of Shadow; and the enigma of Gleep. And inevitably to the terrible mysteries of chance.

A curious wistful hollowness came over him, the hollowness of the present. What he needed to find was a release from these broken shards of the past, scattered but not gone. What he needed to uncover was a strategy formulizing life, wresting free its secrets and restoring order.

None occurred to him.

But Chop occurred to him. Chop the consummate strategist, the ultimate maze runner; he would have thoughts on all these matters. That was the thing to do, talk with Chop.

He felt better at once. He stepped up the speed and a little after seven was in Grand Rapids. At the airport he made some calls, people with a pipeline inside the walls. No, Chop was not at Jackson anymore. Been at Ypsi since, oh, about May. Gonna see changes, you go visit. Ain't the old Chopper. Line is, they broke him.

Gloomy intelligence. He listened, but he didn't believe it for a minute.

He explained to the lady at the car-rental booth what he wanted to do: keep the Mazda another day or so, drop it off at Detroit Metro. She said that would be fine, additional charge of course, otherwise just fine, regarding him doubtfully, trying without success to keep her eyes off his battered face. Finally she asked, "You have a, uh, accident?"

"Should see the other guy," he said. The thought generated a small smile.

"But the car is . . . ?"

"Intact. Undamaged. Out in the lot, you want to look." She didn't, and he was on his way.

Two hours later he turned off at an exchange linking Ypsilanti and Ann Arbor. It was a broad, busy thoroughfare with a number of motels, a few with vacancy signs still illuminated, most with a stark red NO. He drove slowly, checking them out. Time now to attend to those details. Neglect them at your peril.

He spotted a saggy, fading relic of a hostelry with a marquee announcing hopefully: WELCOME BOWLERS! SPECIAL RATES! This could be what he was after. Its lot was full and a flock of people milled about the lobby, but it appeared to be still soliciting guests. He pulled over, parked under a light, got his bag, and went inside. For a while he mingled in the crowd, taking a close look around. There were four wings to the place: three with two levels of rooms, the fourth, a single level featuring bar, dining room, gift shop, and desk. They enclosed a grassy courtyard dominated by a large, glass-walled indoor pool. It was long, rectangular, and accessed only by the lobby wing or by a door at its far end opening onto a postage stamp sundeck cluttered with lounge chairs and potted plants. But for a couple of dim safety bulbs, it was dark now and evidently closed for the night, doubtless as a measure of protection for the rowdy company. Up and down the corridors there was a riot of partying, doors wide open, throbbing music, booze-sloshed couples in silky emblemed shirts reeling from room to room. Exactly what he was looking for. He went back to the desk, paid for a room with cash, and signed in under the name Chad O. Glip. It was a little joke he was making.

"What happened to you?" the eyebrow-arching clerk asked him. "Somebody make a strike in your face?"

"Closer to a spare," Waverly said.

"Well, you got lucky tonight anyway. This is the last room we got. You with the bowlers?"

"Only in spirit," he said, and then at the blank look, added a negative toss of his head.

"Can't give you the rates then. Sorry."

"Perfectly all right. What do you have here? Convention?"

"Sorta like that. Some city leagues come out for a get-together. Every Labor Day. Warmup for the season, you might say. Hope a little commotion don't bother you."

"Not a bit. Bowlers, they're my kind of people."

"Okay," the clerk said, handing over a key, "you're on the south wing, second floor."

Waverly climbed a flight of stairs and threaded through a press of bodies in the hall till he came on his room. Nothing much to it, standard hotbed decor. It overlooked a secondary lot filled with rows of unevenly parked cars. He scanned them from the window. The T-bird he had first picked up on—or thought he had—somewhere around Lansing was not out there. Not yet anyway.

He set down his bag and examined the room service menu by the phone. Among the many offerings was something called a Tail-Gater Special: four kinds of cheese, tube of salami, chips, bean dip. Feeds six easy, was the claim. He dialed the number and ordered five of them. "Beer too," he said, putting some slur in it, "let's have some beer, party goin' on here, and half-dozen bottles of sauce, variety, bourbon, gin, a scotch maybe, you pick 'em, and—oh yeah—don't forget a knife for the salami, good sharp one." As soon as it was delivered, he swung open the door and stepped into the hall and called, "Party in here. Drinks and eats on me."

The Thunderbird was parked out of sight in a dark alley directly across the street from the motel, and the man slouched behind the wheel was surprised and more than a little puzzled. This was not your slickest way to get into the wind. Or was it. From the looks of all the cars in the lot, the place had to be full. The lobby was jammed with staggering boozers. Rackety music thumped through the walls of the bar. Saturday night, holiday, summer's end, a gathering of bowlers, damp-mattress get-down like this one—it more or less figured. But it wasn't making his life any easier.

He did some thinking on the matter. As he saw it, the problem was two-pronged. On the one hand, there was the merchandise to recover if he wanted to collect on that bonus; on the other, were the instructions to make this one sting a little. In his experience that could get messy. Noisy, too. Somehow, these two charges had to be reconciled.

He concluded finally there was too much action in there to touch on him tonight. Maybe this mark had some quick-step moves in mind, maybe not. No percentage, running any amateur risks. Tomorrow was Sunday. Sunday was always a good day.

The next morning Waverly went down to the dining room and took a booth along the back wall with an unobstructed view of the entrance. He ordered coffee and sat there watching, marking time. The thick condiment air churned his stomach, and the veins in his temples seemed to pulsate. He was stiff and aching right down to the bone, but nowhere near as weary as he should be. The electricity of danger charged through him. Maybe it was fear. Or maybe it was this voyage of memory coming up, just ahead. Or some combination of the three.

At this early hour the room was silent and nearly deserted. Not good. But before long some of the good-time keglers, glum and flogged-looking, came shambling in. That was better. A few of them, dimly recalling the night before, hailed him without much enthusiasm. He waved back, same level of vigor. By eleven the place was packed. Spirits and swollen heads were beginning to revive, and he overheard some plan-making for tonight's frolics. In spite of a morning's wandering deliberations, he had arrived at no coherent plan of his own. If in fact there was someone on to him already, there might be temporary safety in numbers. That was as far as he got. And heavy on that *temporary*.

He gave it another hour and then walked out to the desk and booked the room for another night, once again paying in cash. A generous toke got the Mazda delivered to the door. "Yes sir, Mr. Glip, have it brought right up." The Thunderbird was nowhere in evidence, which established nothing, of course, but which prompted him to wonder if the phantoms existed only in his head. Nevertheless, he locked the doors and got out of his jacket pocket the knife he had filched from the Tail-Gater feast. It was the standard kitchen variety: wooden handle, four-inch blade, reasonably sharp. Not much of a weapon. Better than nothing. He laid it alongside the seat and put the car in gear and sped away.

Eight miles south, the Ypsilanti State Hospital sat out in the middle of flat brown farmland, an enormous sprawling complex of streets and grounds and buildings, three-story, brick, dull and grainy with age, many of them interconnected, fortress-fashion. It was bigger than he remembered, much bigger, but then his experience was limited to one secluded corner, and that from the inside and years ago. And the Forensic Center was itself set apart from the rest of the hospital by a high metal fence topped with razor wire. Serious buildings, on remote, serious ground.

Visits commenced at one. He joined the mass of people, most of them surly-looking blacks, lined up at the gate. It was a sweltering, sun-flooded day, the sort of day that prompts strangers to trade casual remarks about weather. No one in this company chose to speak, though when one o'clock came and passed and the gate remained secured, a gigantic woman with stiff jelled hair planted her hands on mountain-ledge hips and declared, "*Boo*-sheet! This ain't nothin' but plain ol' ga-dam *boo*-sheet!" Another, male, muttered, "Mothafucks like to see you sweat."

About fifteen minutes after the hour, a guard—attendant, they were called here—in jeans and cowboy boots and faded flannel shirt appeared at the entrance and came

down the walkway and without a word, opened up. He
led the column back into the waiting room and took a
seat behind a scarred wooden desk. On it was a stack of
forms, and the other visitors snatched them up and began
scribbling. Waverly had no experience, this end of things,
so he followed their lead, completed a form and fell in
at the end of a new line reaching back from the desk.
Slowly it inched forward. When his turn came he handed
over the form.

"ID," the attendant said. He had a narrow triangular
face, hard small jaw. His eyes were expressionless, neither
bored nor engaged.

"What?"

"I gotta see ID. Pitchered."

Waverly opened his wallet and displayed a driver's license. The attendant examined it, squinting back and
forth between likeness and man. "Don't look much like
you," he said.

"I don't photograph well."

"Something happen, your face?"

"It's the picture. This is how I always look."

"Hey, man, that's real funny," he said, scowling. "What
ward's he on?"

"No idea."

"For comin' all the way from Florida, you don't know
much, do you." He got out a patient roster and ran a
finger down it, lips moving as he read silently. He picked
up a phone, dialed, and said Chop's name into it. Then
he took a cycle magazine out of the desk drawer and
began flipping pages absently.

Waverly stood there, waiting for direction. He remembered this type well: indiscriminate spite, terminal mean-
ness. Okay. He gave it a minute, then he said, "You want
to tell me the rest of the drill?"

The attendant indicated the congested room with a
sweep of a hand. He didn't bother to look up. "Sure.

You just find yourself a chair. Somebody'll be down to get you. Before too long."

Of course by now all the seats—two vinyl couches and some burn-stained plastic chairs—were taken. Waverly stood along one wall. The chill conditioned air was stale and blue as lingering smog. A discolored carpet covered part of the floor, and the walls and ceiling were pitted, like splotches of blasted armor. He ran a hand over the back of a couch beside him and his palm came up greasy and vile. Everything about the place was ragged and malodorous and soiled, announcing a kind of prideful neglect, authority's prerogative. It was coming back to him, how much he despised authority, always had, but never fully understood.

Another attendant came through the locked door behind the desk and called out several names. Waverly's was not among them. Some visitors got to their feet and formed a shuffling line outside the closet of an anteroom leading to the wards. In turn, they climbed onto a platform and stared numbly ahead while the attendant searched them with a hand-held electronic scanner, sweeping it like a magic wand over limbs and torso and head.

More time passed. A little before two, his name was called. He took his place on the platform, lifting his arms to accommodate the search. The attendant took him through the door and up a flight of stairs. More locked doors sprang open at some unseen signals. It was distantly familiar, no substantial changes since his stay almost a decade ago. He followed down a ravaged corridor into a large room with two long tables set back to back, each with a wire screen running its length, patients on one side, visitors on the other. At the far end of one table, a figure lost in clownish, outsize state-issue clothes slouched stork-shouldered in a chair. The attendant pointed at him. "There's your man," he said, smirking some. "Lotsa luck, talkin' to him."

Waverly turned in his pass at the desk and was reminded, "Visits is an hour, remember."

"I think I've got it mastered now."

The screen brambled Chop's features, gave them the loose appearance of a face reflected in a pool of stagnant water. And it was a mummified face Waverly gazed at, yellow and spotted, a blue tinge of beard along the blade of jaw, eyes dark as caverns and nested in spidery wrinkles. All the old scars seemed to have faded, but a new one, raw and livid, rose in a quizzical arc above a shaggy brow. The nose was bent at a tortuous angle, nostrils moist, seemed to be dripping. The hair, once the color of ink, was matted and mostly white. And the hands—they were the hands of a cripple, an arthritic, gnarled and bent as the branches of a diseased and dying tree.

"Chop," he said, "what happened?"

No reply. Instead he brought a twisted claw to his forehead and massaged it slowly, as though he was wrestling with a particularly knotty question.

"It's me, Waverly. You remember."

"Waverly?"

"Anglo-Saxon Waverly. Latin Waverly. Remember?"

A thin wolfish smile cracked the sunken face. "Course I remember. You think they got to me yet?"

"Never crossed my mind, Chop. Never believed it."

"Timothy, right?"

"That's it."

"Don't," he said irritably.

"Don't what?"

"Believe it. What they tell you. Nobody knows what's inside my head. I'm just ticking time here. Be gone soon."

"Where to, Chop?"

He gave a sly superior chuckle and tapped a temple. "Where, that's up here." Then he glanced around warily and leaned into the screen and shielded his mouth with the back of a hand. "Northville."

Northville. Waverly remembered all he had heard about Northville. Last stop for the hopelessly insane. "You sure that's where you want to go?"

He drew back, registering astonishment, offense. "Sure? Course I'm sure. Northville's quality time. Waltz time." Then, softening a little, "You'd like it there. Got a swimming pool, they say. Olympic-size. You swim, didn't you say?"

"I probably told you that."

Chop snapped a finger. "There you are."

Waverly got a cigarette. The tapping, firing, inhaling, following the trail of smoke drifting toward the ceiling, he turned it all into a protracted ritual, the ceremonial rite of an infinite sorrow. Or stalling for time. A silence unaccountably close to hostile unrolled between them. It was a mistake to have come here.

There was no air conditioning above the first floor, and the room was packed full, a rodent's den of pungent human odors magnified by heat. At the opposite table a black woman held a wriggling shrieking infant. She squawked to make herself heard. Other strident voices ricocheted off the walls. One—deep, guttural, laced with scorn—rose above the din: "Aws-hole. Kawksucker." It was the patient sitting directly to Chop's left, a youth with a shaved head and the build of a sumo wrestler. He addressed a fiftyish man with a heavy Slavic face and weather-coarsened skin. "Kawksucker," the patient repeated, "I don't do nothin' you say to. Just send me my clothes and a thousand dollars a month. I don't talk to you." He rumbled out of his chair and two attendants materialized at his side, laid restraining hands on him.

"I don't talk this fucker no more."

"Okay, okay. Relax. We'll take you back."

The visitor looked bewildered. He stood up and said something in the staccato of a Balkan tongue. In a moment both were gone.

"That's Kotkowski," Chop said. "Call him Krakow here. Rapist. He's got no use for his old man."

"So it seems."

Chop suddenly grinned. "I was a kid, my old man used to get in behind me and deal me a solid one, back of the head. Whap! About took it off. I'd say what's that for? and he'd say, 'That's for the one you did I *didn't* catch you at.'" The grin shut off, and Chop looked at him thoughtfully. "What do you think about that?"

"I think your old man was the kind of teacher we need, this world."

"Yours do that?"

"No, he never did."

Chop wiped his damp nose with a forearm already glazed with dried snot. "Waverly, right? Iced a lawyer? Been to college?"

"Still here, Chop." He glanced at the clock on the wall. Of the hour he had anticipated, coveted, ten minutes had elapsed.

"You knew dead languages."

"So did you."

"No more."

"Why not anymore?" Unless it had changed, the Center that Waverly remembered had no lockstep routines, no work, little in the way of recreation, activities; nothing really, nothing but time.

Chop's eyes shifted about cunningly. He lowered his voice to a whisper. "No time to study, like we did on Five Block. Polish this act. Northville. Anyway, they fry my brains here. Twice a week. Hard to memorize anymore. You forget things."

Which is one way, Waverly thought. He had come looking for answers and that was maybe the best he was going to get.

As though eavesdropping on his thoughts, Chop said, "You got trouble, right?"

"Yes."

"Trouble," he said, shrugging. "Everywhere's trouble. You know what they say I got, Waverly?"

He could guess but he asked anyway.

"Schizophrenia. The voices you hear—remember them, down the hole?—they're delusions, fantasies, hallucinations. That's their words. That's schizophrenia, they say. Incurable. Either that or"—the face went crafty—"I'm faking."

"What do you say?"

"Me? I say one man's hallucination is another one's vision." He paused, and a fierce light came into his eyes. "Outside of that—and talking to you here—I say nothing. You know why?"

"Why?"

"It's the words give you away. And the silence, that's what takes you where you need to go, you want to be well. You ought to know that. Part way, you been there. But that's just the start of the journey, Timothy, where we were."

"What journey, Chop?"

"Nothing you want to get cured of. It's all those words coming out the holes in their faces, that's what needs curing. Think about it, Timothy, the trail of words left behind you, lifetime's worth. Try and count them. Staggering! Fill a public library, one man's words. Why, Jesus, the number of times you say 'in my opinion' or 'to be perfectly honest with you,' that'd take a fat volume. Consider your 'fuck yous.' Whole shelf. And the thing of it is, Timothy, it's spirit breath they're riding, all those words. It's your spirit leaking out the hole in your face, that's the sickness, and the only way to heal—" He stopped, as though he were aware suddenly the words spilling from his own mouth and the disease they sought to describe were one and the same. But then, not quite finished, he said more. "Northville's a tomb, they keep telling me here.

Buried alive. Like it's a threat. Once I told you these places are holy. Something like that, I said. You remember?"

Remember, remember, remember, this place, that one, those words, some others—he had come to assay forgetfulness, not memory. Yet out of deference to this man who had been his friend, out of that memory, Waverly said, "I remember."

"I was right!" Chop said exultantly. He lifted his eyes to the ceiling and then the moment of jubilance seemed to pass. He studied his twisted hands dourly. "Ah, it's all a scam. You know how that goes. Tell a hundred lies a day, half of 'em to yourself. But you got trouble, remember the things you learned in here. Some of 'em were good things, useful. How to get by. Live behind your own eyes. Scrimmage on your own turf, nobody else's. Price of courage, Timothy, you learned it don't come cheap. Trouble comes, you think on them things."

The catalog of lessons once mastered but maybe forgotten or lost or maybe only mislaid somewhere. He would have to do that, think about them again. And soon. But just now he couldn't look at him anymore. The screen that separated them was anchored in a strip of mildewed wood, and a battalion of tiny red ants scurried about its base. He couldn't stay here any longer. He rose and signaled for an attendant.

"I've got to leave now, Chop. Is there anything I can do for you? Books? Money? Anything?"

"You got money?"

"Some. Enough."

"You're on the streets now?"

"Three years, Chop."

"What do you do?"

"For a living?"

"For money."

"I play cards."

"Cards. How do you do?"

"Pretty well. When I pay attention. And the luck is right."

"Luck," he said, and his caved-in features made the shape of a rueful smile. "Luck, chance. Chance is the toy of God. Somebody's words."

"Goodbye, Chop."

The attendant appeared and guided him toward the door. He hesitated a moment, recalling one last question, turned. "Chop, do you remember anyone on Five Block named Gleep? Big dude? Indian?"

"Gleep? No . . . no. Can't place that one."

Waverly passed through the waiting room and out into the dazzling, sun-scorched afternoon. He looked around cautiously. There were plenty of citizen types strolling around the grounds, so he walked down the block to a picnic bench set in the shade of a tree outside another wing of the hospital. It was not part of the Center, no high fence circled it and patients appeared to come and go freely. A few of them lay sleeping on the grass, mumbling snippets of their mysterious dreams. Over by the chapel another patient stood rigid as a pillar, a soiled sheet draped over his head. In an alley a grizzled old warrior picked through a dumpster with all the fixed concentration of a scavenging bird, occasionally stuffing something or other into a pocket or into his mouth.

The Mazda was parked directly across the street. Beyond it, between hospital and highway, lay a broad, incongruous golf course. A foursome of attendants practiced their strokes earnestly, preparing to tee off. In the city of madness, the solemn pursuit of tiny white balls across an expanse of velvety grass seemed no more aberrant or bizarre than sanity's pursuit.

He watched them awhile. And as he did, Chop's elusive words swam through his head. What he needed was an interpreter, someone to translate all those indecipherable messages into direction, order, plan. The imponderable questions he had brought here, they would have to go unanswered. Chop, drifting in and out of his own delirium, was a mentor for another life, another time. Just now what he needed was a blueprint for survival. None seemed forthcoming.

At three o'clock, the gate clanged shut behind the last visitors departing from the Center. They hurried to the parking lot at the end of the block. And as the last of their cars rolled out of the drive and down the street, Waverly could see, still remaining, one vehicle that had neither started up nor moved, a Thunderbird, a lone man waiting impassively at the wheel. Waverly got to his feet and with a quickened pace, not quite running, crossed over to the Mazda. He recovered the knife and slipped it into a pocket, and as he drove past the Hospital entrance and onto the busy highway he could see the Thunderbird easing unhurriedly into the line of traffic behind him. And as he considered his dwindling options, a fragment of Chop's cryptic advice returned to him: Scrimmage on your own turf.

Six hours later Waverly sat with a company of bowlers in the motel bar, swept into their camaraderie by a readiness to pop for rounds of drinks, the always welcome Mr. Glip, big spender, heavy wallet compensating for disagreeable mashed-in features. By now they were at the anecdote-trading juncture, reprising contest glories past. Waverly made a show of listening attentively, smiling a lot, but he was occupied with his own thoughts. A final rehearsal, of sorts.

As far as he could determine, everything was in place. Or as near as he was ever going to get it. Stashed under a lounge chair in the darkened pool was the leather bowling bag he'd nicked from a party room earlier in the evening. The inside door to the pool was securely locked but the other one, opening onto the sun deck and court-yard, now had a matchbook wedged in its jamb. He had managed all this by distracting the kid charged with herd-ing out the last poolside drunks and locking up for the night: some noisy banter and the offer of beer. A Coors for an outside chance at his life. Bargain transaction.

The man coming for him would be after the goods first, the payback a close second. What he couldn't know was that the goods were nonexistent, a handful of ashes; and what he would discover, in this scenario, was a swim-mer floating easily in the deep water. He would be wary, of course, professional, and doubly alert now to any sort of snare. Gun leveled, he would take a position well back from the pool's edge. Maybe he would be like Shadow and there would be some initial verbal sparring. "Like them water sports, huh?" he might say.

And Waverly, buying an instant of time, would say whatever came into his head: "Can't beat 'em. You ought to come in. Water's fine. Little chilly at first."

An instant is all it would be, no more, and then he would get to the matter of the goods, and Waverly would tell him they were at the bottom.

"You better get 'em up here," he would say. "Yourself, too."

Waverly would do a surface dive, recover the weighted bag—first removing the knife that would be in it by then—and swim to the side of the pool. He would swing the heavy bag out of the water, barely clearing the deck. And then the other one, gun still trained, would step in just close enough to lean over and grasp the handles; and Waverly would thrust himself up and bring the knife across the hand on the bag, and there would be a scream but it would be muffled by the ventilator fan, and the gun would fall onto the cement, and Waverly would snag him by the coat and they would both go tumbling back-ward into the pool and . . .

Running it by in his head this one last time, he was struck by the feebleness of the plan, turning as it did on the precise orchestration of moves by himself and his antagonist, a synchronized, deadly pas de deux. But it was all he had. No alternatives. And though his nerves were tight as drawn wire, he felt curiously empty of indignation at a fate that had brought him here. If Chop was right, if he was merely another of God's toys, perhaps the game would be played in his own element, on his own turf.

At nine-thirty he shoved his chair away from the table and rose unsteadily, pleading an urgent need for sleep. Apart from some good-humored joshing, nobody paid much attention as he tottered toward the door. He hesitated there a moment, tapped at his head as though something of monumental significance had just occurred to him, and then went back to the bar and asked for a couple of sixers, bottles. The sinkers for the bag.

In the rooms and hallways, the parties were beginning to heat up, and he waved away the invitations to join in. He had been to several already through the late afternoon and evening, keeping in crowds and nursing ginger ale. At the end of the first corridor, he slipped past the interior door leading to the courtyard. Night was settling in, and a sky full of rushing clouds brushed the face of a pale moon. He crossed the sun deck and set down the six-packs and tested the door.

It wouldn't budge. Somehow he had miscalculated. The matchbook wasn't enough to hold it ajar. He drew away trembling hands. On the other side of that door was his turf; out here he was snookered, dead meat. He was conscious of the remorseless beat of time ticking silently behind his back, running out. He remembered the knife. Maybe, just maybe, he could fit it into the narrow aperture between door and jamb, and with some gentle tugging spring the lock. There was a sharp, metallic snap, and when he examined the weapon on which his whole plan turned, what he discovered was a wooden handle with a tiny stump of fractured blade. No weapon at all. And nowhere left to hide.

By now his eyes were accustomed to the dark. He looked around feverishly. The lounge chairs were set one on top of another in a wobbly vertical stack along the pool wall. A hose lay on the damp deck. Evidently tonight had been cleaning night, which probably accounted for the unyielding door, for all the good that intelligence did him now. An unstable, top-heavy stack of chairs, a hose and a dozen bottles of beer: the sum of his resources. It wasn't much.

He looped the hose around the back legs of the supporting chair and drew the two ends over by a large potted corn plant at the side of the deck, a distance of no more than ten feet. Quietly as he could, he shattered one of the bottles, leaving only a neck to grasp and a jagged edge. And then he ducked down behind the plant and with a metronomic precision shifted his gaze back and forth between the two interior entrances to the courtyard. They were located at either end of the wing opposite the sun deck and they were the only other way in. The man stalking him would be coming through one of them and very soon now. And as he waited there in the dark stung by a wintry breath of fear, another token of Chop's counsel came back to him, on courage, its substantial cost. . . .

"Wanta make yourself a fifty?"

"Hey, I'm not into that stuff," the cocktail waitress said pertly. "And if I was, fifty wouldn't buy you nothin' much at all."

The man asking the question sat alone in a back corner of the crowded bar. He had waited a moment or two after Waverly's stagy exit and then summoned her to his table. "You ain't heard the offer yet," he said. "See that fella just left?"

"Oh yeah," she said, staring pointedly at the change on the table. "He tips real good."

"Get me his room number, you got the fifty."

The waitress was a thirtyish woman, a little too old for the perkiness she affected. She had abundant ringlets of slicked blond hair and a shrewd painted face. She looked at him narrowly. "Whyn't you ask up at the desk?"

"I'm askin' you."

"We're not suppose to give out guests' room numbers."

He got out a roll of bills, peeled off a fifty, and laid it on the table by the coins. "Maybe you make an exception. This time."

In all her experience, and it was plenty wide, she had never seen eyes like the ones on this dude. Once, on a trip out west, she'd stopped at a roadside attraction, reptile gardens, and she'd gazed with a kind of stricken awe at the collection of snakes and lizards in their glassed-in cages. It was feeding time, and one of the snakes had a live mouse clamped in its sprung jaws. The mouse's head and trunk were out of sight, but the tail was still wiggling. There was a ripply motion under the snake's skin and its eyes seemed to glitter wetly, not so much from any malice as from some raw, brutal appetite. She'd never seen anything like it and never wanted to again. But now, meeting this dude's cold, depthless stare, she felt as if she was. Five minutes later she was back with the number of Mr. Glip's room. She was not unhappy with the money, but she was happier yet to see him gone.

He was in no special hurry. He had him boxed in now. Getting to the merchandise and getting him out of there quietly, that could be delicate. But he'd had enough of dancing around. There were bowlers still gathered in the lobby and spilling out of rooms, but it was a thinner crowd than the night before. He'd worked under tighter conditions than these.

He climbed a flight of stairs and walked to the south wing. Fewer people were hanging out on the second floor, but as he approached the specified room, a stubby little runt with a broad open face, flushed with drink, came down the hall.

"Yo, big fella. Come on join the party."

"Get lost."

"Ah, come on. Beer and tail, plenty of both."

"Said get lost, bug-fucker."

There was something in that remote growly voice that sparked a warning signal in the runt's bleary head, and he backed away and vanished, mumbling, "Fuck you, Charlie," but under his breath, softly. As soon as the corridor was clear, the man slipped on a pair of skintight leather gloves, got out a piece and attached a silencer. He held the gun inside his jacket and tried the door. To his considerable surprise, he found it was not locked. With the gun leveled now, he pushed it open slowly. He stepped inside and looked around warily. All the lights were on, but it was obvious there was no one anywhere in the room. Every dresser was open, as though for inspection, and the bag on the bed was wide open, too. In the bath he discovered a message scrawled in soap on the mirror: Catch you poolside.

Cute. Very cute.

He took one more quick look around, knowing the merchandise wasn't going to be there. He removed the gloves, detached the silencer from the piece, and put them all back in their designated pockets. An orderly man. Then he left the room and walked to the stairwell at the end of the hall. A window there offered a clear view of the courtyard. The grounds and the sun deck appeared to be empty, the pool dark. No visible movement anywhere.

Down on the first floor, he turned the knob on the lobby door to the pool. Very lightly, very quietly. Locked. He went all the way to the end of another wing and tested the door to the courtyard. This one opened. Across the grass and behind the sun deck was the only other entrance to the pool. He figured it was a pretty fair bet that one would swing open, too. For anyone dumb enough to try it. Which he was not.

He stood there a moment, peering into the dark, giving it some thought. Okay, he said to himself finally, games you want, games you get. He walked back to the bar and got the cocktail waitress off in a corner. "That fifty," he said, "one other thing I want you to do. Thinkin' maybe I'll take a little swim. But the door out there's locked."

Waverly never saw him coming. In his scenario the only possible approach was through the courtyard, and so he missed altogether the figure that came along the inside of the pool, moving deliberately, keeping in the shadows, keeping down. Waverly was kneeling behind the corn plant, his eyes sweeping the yard, his back to the pool door. He heard a barely audible hinge creak, and when he looked over his shoulder, what he saw was the shape of a heavy figure framed in that door. The features were indistinguishable, but there was no mistaking the outline of a gun in one hand, its barrel elongated by a silencer. A corrosive, rumbly voice, full of baleful news, announced, "Know you're out here, dog stool. Better just pack it in now. Game's over. You lose."

Waverly flattened on the ground and yanked the two ends of the hose, and the stack of chairs went clattering onto the deck. The figure leaped through the door and jerked to the left, facing the toppling chairs in the classic gunman's crouch, feet planted wide, both hands on the weapon. There was a short, crisp report and a bullet ricocheted off the brick wall of the motel and went whining through the air. Waverly lunged across the slender distance between them and speared into him, blindside, raking the bottle across the face. Blood squirted over his hand and a confounded screech echoed through the night.

The gun clanked onto the cement, but a backswung elbow caught Waverly squarely in the chest and he dropped the bottle and fell away, doubled over, all the wind thumped out of him. He heard the unmistakable ping of a switchblade, and he looked up in time to see the figure lurching toward him, one hand clutching the lacerated face and the other, the knife hand, lashing blindly.

Waverly snatched up one of the chairs and like a lion tamer gone suddenly, recklessly mad, drove it into him, blunting the charge and springing loose the knife. But in a flicker of an instant, the chair was yanked away and flung across the lawn, and before he could dodge or run, he was seized in a bone-splintering embrace, lifted bodily into the air, arms pinned at his sides, legs thrashing helplessly. A lethal hug, forcing out his last gagging breath. Over the siren wail going off in his head, he could hear a furious guttural snarl, not quite animal but something very nearly less than human, too. It was carried on the incongruous perfume of garlic softened a little by Sen Sen, and the contorted face behind it was washed with blood. Waverly squeezed his eyes shut, clenched his jaws, thrust his head back and then brought it down thuddingly into that blood-streaked face, which seemed to splatter under the impact like a lump of moist clay. The snarl went gurgly and the circling arms momentarily slack, and they stood there, still on their feet both of them, but only barely.

Waverly took a stuttery step backward and braced himself against the glass wall of the pool. Just in time for the shower of wild punches that fell on him, connecting often enough and heavy enough to drop him finally to his knees. He caught a foggy glimpse of a small wooden crate in the tall grass along the wall, overlooked before somehow, and almost within reach. He scrambled for it, the fists hammering him now with the speed and weight of accelerated pistons.

He groped in the crate for a weapon, any weapon, and came up with a plastic bottle, chemicals maybe or maybe some lye-based cleaning solution, no way to tell and no matter, nothing left to lose. Abruptly the pummeling stopped, and as he struggled with the lid, a coil of hose looped around his neck and snapped his head back. A knee dug into his shoulder blades. Lightning scrawled a signature behind his eyes. The world went spinning. A muffled voice riding a spluttery liquid wheeze declared, "Kill you, sonbitch, kill . . ." Operating from somewhere below the level of thought, Waverly sprung the lid and brought the bottle up and around in a wide arc, splashing in the general direction of the voice.

The hose loosened and fell, and from some enormous distance he heard a high thin squeal. He turned and through a widening blur made out a figure breaking into a frantic dervish dance. Gasping, quaking, he hauled himself up and grasped another of the toppled chairs and, swinging it like a clumsy bat, slammed it into the dancer, who staggered a moment, then stumbled into him, bringing them both down in a theatrical buckling fall.

Waverly tried to crawl away, but hands gripped him securely at the ankles. He couldn't move. With whatever was left in him, he tugged one foot free and drove it back onto the top of the skull, and then both feet were free. Still on all fours, he came around and lifted the inert head by a hank of hair. The head swiveled in his hand. "Kill you yet," came the fierce, defiant pronouncement. And he was still struggling to boost himself up onto his elbows when Waverly smashed his head into the concrete. "Down, goddam you! Stay *down!*" Waverly did it again. And again.

This time he stayed down.

And Waverly, on his hands and knees beside him, chanted over and over: "Now who you gonna kill? Now who you gonna kill?" as though it were some elemental mantra invoking the storm of all his rage.

Slowly, the fury drained out of him. He got to his feet and stood there trembling, trying to recover some wisp of sanity, control. He glanced about him. No one had appeared in the courtyard. Not yet. If the sounds of struggle had been heard, there was a chance they might have passed for just more party howls. A perverse curiosity overtook him. Maybe he had some time. Not much. The plastic bottle lay in the grass along the deck, and he picked it up, fumbled in his pocket for a match, struck it, and read the label by the tiny flickering light: Muriatic acid, handle with extreme caution.

Waverly stooped down for a look at his nameless, fallen antagonist. Rolled him onto his back cautiously. Blood leaked across the slashed face. The mouth was agape, exposing an impish, outthrust tongue. Spittle bubbled over the torn lips. The breath came in strangulated heaves. And one eye was cleanly punctured. He was far from dead, but there was nothing to be gained by killing him now, more likely a great deal to lose with another stiff left in his wake. He would revive soon, this one, but it would be a good long time before he resumed business as usual. If ever. Waverly leaned in close. "Game's still on," he croaked in an ear partly severed and dangling dangerously. "But you're benched."

SEVEN

TWO HOURS LATER WAVERLY WAS ON A plane winging for West Palm and home. Home. Or the furnishings thereof. There would be others behind this last one—and if not, if they couldn't track him, then one day soon the colleagues and friends of Max Clean Slate would come swooping in and scoop it all up for him and set him on the road again looking over his shoulder, bound for another place masquerading as home.

Throughout the flight the woman in the next seat spoke volubly, reflecting on an Erma Bombeck life of happy zany problems. Listening to her, he felt like a man in shock, nodding affirmations and occasionally even interjecting a polite query to move the rambling chronicle along, but all he could really make of her was the gaping hole in her face and the tempest of words and air proceeding from it.

He had phoned from Metro and Bennie was waiting in the crowd at the gate, impossible to overlook in his tangerine sport shirt and plaid Bermudas, an immense pudding of a man, with dollops of freckled fat drooping from elbow and knee joints. When he spotted Waverly his eyes went buggy and his dewlaps shook.

The Bennie Epstein greeting: "Jesus Q. Christus, somebody did the dumping number on you, Timothy. Face looks like a psychedelic doodoo."

"Nice to see you, too."

"C'mon, let's get you out of here, post f-word haste. Before they send in an EMS unit. Or the stiff limo. Go hide in a corner someplace, I'll get your gear. Gimmie the tags. Jeezus."

He waited on the walk outside the terminal. The night air was steamy and damp, same as the morning he left, and already his shirt was clinging wetly to his back. So not everything was changed.

Half an hour later they were headed up 95. Bennie drove his pink Seville, one of the several cars he owned. Pimpmobile, he called it. He maneuvered in and out of the traffic nimbly. For a good share of the drive he was uncharacteristically silent. But finally he got to it.

"Y'know, I got a whole line of special painkillers, you ain't feelin' so hot."

"I'm doing all right, Bennie."

"You gonna let me in on what happened?"

It was only fair to tell him. All the plans—the going partners, expanding, scooping in more loot—they were all annulled now, along with any semblance of order. He would have to tell him, but not now, not tonight. "Tomorrow," he said, "tomorrow we'll talk about it, okay?"

"A cooze involved is the odds-on bet, right?"

Waverly displayed the palms of his hands.

"But not your ex, huh? Or her hub?"

"No."

"There's a switch. Somebody different this time."

"Right."

"Wouldn't be the same lady put in a call for you today, my number?"

For the first time in longer than he cared to remember, Waverly had begun to unwind. Now he felt suddenly very alert again. In as neutral a voice as he could produce, he said, "What was the message?"

"Said she needed to talk to you. I got a number, back at my place."

"You get any more than that? Who it was? What it's about?"

"Answering service took it, not me. Just said to call midnight, was all. That a name or a time?"

Waverly was barely conscious of his long, weary, ambiguous sigh. What now—more advice, more trouble? Another urgent claim on his services, levied out of the certain knowledge he would always be there, half a continent away or not? Distances were no measure of whatever it was between them. Maybe he would be there, permanently on call; at that precise moment he didn't know for sure. Nor could he tell if it was dismay he was feeling just then, or a peculiar sort of relief. It was something else to be sorted out tomorrow, but now, partly in answer to Bennie's question and partly in response to his own tangle of emotions, he said, "Both, I guess."

"This call," Bennie said, glancing at him shrewdly, "it's more Michigan, right?"

"'fraid so."

"You ever gonna get your head on straight, Timothy?"

"Ah, well, you had to be there."

Bennie snorted at that. "Be there! You forgettin' SPSM? Every place you been, boy, I been there day before yesterday."

"So you have. I've not forgotten."

"You know what your problem is, Timothy?"

"I had a premonition you were going to tell me."

"What's that, premonition?"

"Just tell me."

"It's the numbers," he said, slicing air with a meaty hand for emphasis. "Cards, numbers, them you can do. Always could."

"Cards have no memory, isn't that what they say?"

"Dunno what *they* say," he said impatiently. "Do know you kept us in smokes with 'em, Jacktown. You remember that?"

"All you could inhale."

"And then some. But you get away from them cards, numbers, step up from that table, you was dog food. Never get straight. You was worse'n Chop."

"Not anymore."

"What, you see him?"

"This very afternoon."

"No kiddin'. Old Chopper. How's he holdin' up?"

Waverly had no clear answer for that question, so that's what he said. "I don't know."

"Where's he at now?"

"Forensic Center."

"Good on him. Beats Five Block. Them shrinks get him rehabilitated yet?" he asked, guffawing at his excellent joke.

"Not yet, I think."

"Get him a scholarship to acting school, maybe. Yeah, well, them was the days," he said, dismissing them. He had the natural-born optimist's healthy-minded disinterest in the past. The North Lake Boulevard exit was next up, and he slid into the right lane behind a truck puffing soot into the sticky air. "But these is the better ones. What you want to do? Drink? Get laid? Eat? Something to eat, I bet. They feed you that Kennel Ration on the plane, you got to be hungry. We'll stop at Iggy's."

He turned onto the exit ramp and swung into the lot by Iggy's Sub Shop. He cut the engine and looked at Waverly appraisingly. "You better wait here, don't want to scare 'em inside. I'll bring out the eats. What's your pleasure?"

"Whatever you have. Surprise me."

"Can't do that. You know me: Swiss cheese and tongue, on black. Comin' right at you."

Waverly watched him bounce through the door of the deli. Through the window he could see him at the counter, gesturing expansively, mouth going tirelessly while he tugged at the shorts bunched in his crotch and arranged the few limp strands of hair over his globe of skull. Bouncy Bennie Epstein, the Maimonides of fortune, chance.

And sitting there, he thought about Chop, about all he had heard today: the words and voices and screeches and groans. He thought about other things as well. Promises, deadly paybacks, measureless griefs, the treachery of hope. He thought about them. He wondered if Chop, spirit coiled, retreating into an oceanic silence, could be wrong. He didn't know. It was as if life came to him now reflected off a slightly warped mirror, its images slightly askew, slippery. Nothing was what it seemed. But he was struck with the melancholy knowledge that, unlike Chop, wherever he himself might travel, whatever adventures lay ahead in whatever remained of his life, he would carry with him always and forever the unalterable, impenetrable baggage of himself.

In a moment Bennie was back. He handed Waverly a sub and began tearing at his own. And then, sensing something of his friend's mood, he said around a mouthful of black bread, "Listen up, boy, your old uncle Bennie here. Snatch is the easiest thing in this world to come by. Also your biggest poison headache, guy like you. It ain't like money. Which is why we're gonna get you back in the steady action, soon as that face gets so you can't sell sideshow tickets to it. Chippers City again."

There was nothing Waverly could do but shake his head and smile. He stared out at the lights of the traffic fleeting down North Lake. He felt very strange. Like a time traveler returned for a brief sojourn, other voyages ahead.

About the Author

TOM KAKONIS was born in California, squarely at the onset of the Depression, the offspring of a nomadic Greek immigrant and a South Dakota farm girl of Anglo-Saxon descent gone west on the single great adventure of her life. He has traveled widely and worked variously as a railroad section laborer, pool hall and beach idler, army officer, technical writer, and professor at several colleges in the Midwest. He makes his home in Grand Rapids, Michigan, where he is completing his second novel.

THE MEASURE OF A MAN
IS HOW WELL HE SURVIVES LIFE'S

BOLD NEW CRIME NOVELS BY
TODAY'S HOTTEST TALENTS

BAD GUYS (July 1989)
Eugene Izzi
_____ 91493-8 $3.95 U.S.   _____ 91494-6 $4.95 Can.

CAJUN NIGHTS (August 1989)
D.J. Donaldson
_____ 91610-8 $3.95 U.S.   _____ 91611-6 $4.95 Can.

MICHIGAN ROLL (September 1989)
Tom Kakonis
_____ 91684-1 $3.95 U.S.   _____ 91686-8 $4.95 Can.

SUDDEN ICE (October 1989)
Jim Leeke
_____ 91620-5 $3.95 U.S.   _____ 91621-3 $4.95 Can.

DROP-OFF (November 1989)
Ken Grissom
_____ 91616-7 $3.95 U.S.   _____ 91617-5 $4.95 Can.

A CALL FROM L.A. (December 1989)
Arthur Hansl
_____ 91618-3 $3.95 U.S.   _____ 91619-1 $4.95 Can.

Publishers Book and Audio Mailing Service
P.O. Box 120159, Staten Island, NY 10312-0004

Please send me the book(s) I have checked above. I am enclosing
$_____ (please add $1.25 for the first book, and $.25 for each
additional book to cover postage and handling. Send check or
money order only—no CODs.)

Name _____

Address _____

City _____ State/Zip _____

Please allow six weeks for delivery. Prices subject to change
without notice.   MS 9/89

WANTED

True Crime From St. Martin's Press.

ULTERIOR MOTIVES
by Suzanne Finstad
When Flamboyant tycoon Henry Kyle was found
murdered in 1983, it was only the beginning...
_____ 91185-8 $4.50 U.S.   _____ 91186-6 $5.50 Can.

DEADLY BLESSING
by Steve Salerno
The tragic consequences of a marriage between a
wealthy young power broker and a local waitress.
_____ 91215-3 $3.95 U.S.   _____ 91216-1 $4.95 Can

THE SERPENT'S TOOTH
by Christopher P. Anderson
The story of an extremely rich family destroyed by
greed...and murder.
_____ 90541-6 $3.95 U.S.   _____ 90542-4 $4.95 Can

CELLAR OF HORROR
by Ken Englade
What police found in Gary Heidnik's basement went
beyond mere horror...
_____ 90959-4 $4.50 U.S.   _____ 90960-8 $5.50 Can

Publishers Book and Audio Mailing Service
P.O. Box 120159, Staten Island, NY 10312-0004

Please send me the book(s) I have checked above. I am enclosing
$ _____ (please add $1.25 for the first book, and $.25 for each
additional book to cover postage and handling. Send check or
money order only—no CODs.)

Name _____

Address _____

City _____ State/Zip _____

Please allow six weeks for delivery. Prices subject to change
without notice.

2TC 1/